MARY LYNN BAXTER

is a master at creating spellbinding tales of
passion and desire. From Silhouette Books,
here are three smoldering stories set in Texas,
where the only thing that burns brighter than the
sun is the love between the heroes and heroines of

TEXAS HEAT

SLOW BURN
He thought she was after the family fortune—
but all she wanted was his heart.

AND BABY MAKES PERFECT
Was their love strong enough to overcome a
family feud...and make a family of their own?

EVERYTHING BUT TIME
Fate handed them a second chance
to reclaim their love....

"Ms. Baxter is a power to be reckoned with
in women's fiction."
—*Affaire de Coeur*

MARY LYNN BAXTER

Author of more than thirty-five novels, with some 12 million copies of her books in print around the world, Mary Lynn Baxter is an acknowledged master of the romantic genre.

Mary Lynn majored in Library Science at the University of North Texas and became a school librarian. Eight years later, she felt the need for change. This book lover became a bookstore owner. Now she could sell the romance novels she'd loved as a girl. "I can't begin to explain how I felt the first time I opened a box of new books in my own bookstore and sold them. But after fifteen years, I wanted a new challenge," says Mary Lynn.

She then prepared herself for the ultimate challenge— fulfilling her lifelong aspiration to place the vivid plots and characters in her imagination on paper. "Writing is my ultimate love, and nothing compares with the satisfaction of creating new characters and devising a new plot." Mary Lynn's first book, *All Our Tomorrows,* was published by Silhouette Books in 1982. With the publication of *Saddle Up,* in April 1996, she received the distinction of a listing on the *USA Today* bestseller list.

She's also dedicated to her volunteer work at a local hospice and to helping the elderly. And somehow, Mary Lynn fits in a lot of quality time with her husband, who is, of course, the prototype for all her best heroes.

MARY LYNN BAXTER

TEXAS HEAT

Silhouette Books

Published by Silhouette Books

America's Publisher of Contemporary Romance

SILHOUETTE BOOKS

ISBN 0-373-20168-0

by Request

TEXAS HEAT

Copyright © 1999 by Harlequin Books S.A.

The publisher acknowledges the copyright holder
of the individual works as follows:

SLOW BURN
Copyright © 1990 by Mary Lynn Baxter

AND BABY MAKES PERFECT
Copyright © 1992 by Mary Lynn Baxter

EVERYTHING BUT TIME
Copyright © 1984 by Mary Lynn Baxter

Visit us at www.romance.net

Printed in U.S.A.

CONTENTS

Dear Reader,

I've always been proud of my Texas heritage, so it's a special thrill for me to have three of my novels that are set in my home state presented together. These books—*Slow Burn, And Baby Makes Perfect* and *Everything But Time*—all share the lush East Texas backdrop of stately pine and oak trees I love so much, as well as the blooming dogwoods and lovely azaleas.

An added bonus to an anthology like this is the opportunity to share my earlier works with newer readers while allowing my loyal fans to reminisce.

Many of the other things I love most about Texas are captured within these pages. I hope *Texas Heat* will give you a taste of the enjoyment I have known living and writing about my beloved piney woods of the Lone Star State.

Mary Lynn Baxter

SLOW BURN

One

Marnie Lee heard the commotion behind her and turned her head around.

Although Spencer's Place, an exclusive restaurant in west Houston, was crowded, she had no trouble figuring out why. A woman commanded the center of attention. Several persons were gathered around her. Then they seemed to back away, leaving the woman standing alone center stage.

Marnie gasped. Directly in her line of vision was Joan Collins, the superstar of the television show *Dynasty*.

Marnie's companion, Lance O'Brien, chuckled, effectively drawing her gaze back to him.

"I take it you're impressed," he said, laughter still in his voice.

Marnie knew he was making fun of her, but she didn't care. After all, how often did one get to see Joan Collins?

"Of course, I'm impressed," she said, smiling, "and so are you, only you won't admit it."

"Well," he drawled, easing back in his chair, his green eyes twinkling, "now that you mention it, she is a looker."

Following her acclaimed entry, the celebrity, a dazzling smile on her face, began moving toward Marnie and Lance's table. For a moment they watched her in action, spellbound. It was only after she was seated at a table by the window and batting her eyes at both her escort and the maitre d' that they turned away.

"I'm in shock," Marnie said. "I had no idea stars ate here."

"I take it you like the places I choose?"

Marnie's eyes sparkled. "That goes without saying."

Exclusive, classy restaurants, however, were just one of the amenities that Marnie had enjoyed since she'd been dating her boss, Lance.

From under the thick screen of her lashes, Marnie studied him, wondering again why she couldn't fall in love with him. She had concluded some time ago that the fault lay with her, because there was certainly nothing wrong with Lance, at least not as far as his appearance was concerned.

Not only was he good-looking and charming, he was the only son and heir of Tate O'Brien, who controlled Tate Enterprises and who seemingly had the power to turn sawdust into money.

So what if Lance's mouth and chin showed a definite weakness? Those flaws had been overlooked by a number of women; Lance had a reputation for being a heartbreaker.

Suddenly Lance chuckled, breaking her train of thought. "Wishing, huh?"

"Of course," Marnie said. "What woman doesn't wish she looked like her?"

"As far as I'm concerned, you look better."

At age thirty, Marnie could pass for twenty. She was tall and slender and moved with the grace of a dancer. Short, naturally curly light brown hair surrounded a heart-shaped face. Eyes like enormous black velvet pansies looked from under long lashes. When one first saw her, the words *remote* and *glorious* came to mind.

Marnie smiled. "We both know you're exaggerating, but it's nice to hear anyway."

Before Lance could comment further, the waiter seemed to appear from out of nowhere. Smiling politely at Lance, he asked, "Are you ready to order, sir?"

Lance turned to Marnie and raised his eyebrows inquiringly. "Same thing?"

"Same thing."

Having been to Spencer's Place with Lance on two other occasions, Marnie always ordered the house specialty—the Crabmeat Lorenzo. It was delicious, but then so was everything else on the menu.

While Lance discussed an appropriate wine with the waiter, Marnie's gaze wandered around the room. The mood in the front dining room, where they were sitting amidst a subtle decor and gleaming crystal, contrasted sharply with the middle room and colorful bar that sported bawdy paintings of nude ladies.

"What are you thinking about now?"

Once again swinging her attention back to Lance, Marnie smiled. "Actually, I was thinking how nice it is here and how much I'm enjoying myself."

"Yeah, it is kinda nice to relax after this week. God, it was a bitch."

A tiny frown blemished Marnie's forehead. "I couldn't

agree more. It's been a long time since I've worked that hard.''

But she didn't mind. In fact, hard work was her bailiwick, having recently been promoted to the engineering department where she was now an assistant on a special project.

Lance pushed a loose strand of brown hair from his forehead, then grinned. "Me, too. If this project won't make the old man happy, I don't know what will.''

"I presume you're referring to your father.''

Lance's grin was no longer in evidence. "One in the same, though I'm sure he wouldn't appreciate being called an old man." He suddenly grinned again, as if picturing Tate's reaction to his statement.

"I'm sure you're right," Marnie said, though she had never met the widowed Tate O'Brien. Rumors regularly floated around the office, hailing the big boss as more of a womanizer than his son.

Lance sighed. "I know I'm right. My dad doesn't tolerate imperfections in himself or anyone else, especially me.''

"Well, as you say, he's bound to be pleased with the work you're doing on this project." Marnie's tone was light. "After all, you took his idea and made it work. Now we've got a government contract.''

Though Lance's features brightened, his tone was cautious. "Yeah, who'd have thought Texas Systems would be asked to experiment with another type of plastic explosive?" He shook his head. "It's amazing.''

"But exciting." Marnie shifted in her chair, oblivious to the clanking of silverware and glasses around her. "I've never worked on anything that's top secret before.''

"Neither have I. Just hope we can give Uncle Sam what he wants."

"We will," Marnie said with confidence. "This project is going to put us on the map. You just wait and see."

"All I'm hoping for at the moment is to simply pull it off so that dad will get off my back."

It was a known fact that Tate was eager for his only son to eventually take over his entire business conglomerate, so that Tate could retire to his ranch and raise quarter horses. In order for Lance to learn the business from the ground up, he was being shifted from one company to the other, one department to the next.

"Don't worry, you'll do fine," Marnie said softly.

Instead of responding, Lance looked on as the waiter poured the wine. After sampling it, he murmured, "Mmm, perfect."

Once the waiter had disappeared again, Marnie reached for her glass and raised it to her lips. "You're right. It is delicious."

"Could you get used to this?" Lance asked, taking a slender hand in his.

Marnie slowly lowered her glass back to the table. "What do you mean?" Her tone was hesitant.

"You know what I mean."

Marnie shook her head as she carefully withdrew her hand. "No, I'm afraid I don't."

"Gonna make me spell it out, huh?"

"Guess you'll have to," Marnie said lightly.

Lance leaned back and stared at her with serious eyes. "What I'm saying is that you…we could dine like this every night—"

Marnie laughed, interrupting him. "You might could, but not me. Remember, I have to work for a living."

"You wouldn't if you married me."

Marnie's jaw went slack. "Excuse me."

"You heard what I said."

"You're...you can't be serious."

"Oh, I'm serious, all right. I've never been more serious."

Marnie blurted the first thing that came to mind. "But...but you're younger than I am."

Lance laughed. "Three years. Big deal. So, will you marry me?"

Marnie's heart sank. She shouldn't have been shocked by his impulsiveness, but she was. And flattered. No doubt about it, Lance O'Brien would be considered quite a catch. He had it all—looks, money, prestige and charm. However, Marnie had no intention of falling victim to that charm, especially now that her life held such promise.

But things had not always been this satisfying for Marnie, far from it, in fact. After having worked her way through college because her widowed father made very little money at his job in a small East Texas town, Marnie had been certain she was destined for great things, only to suddenly learn that her father had Alzheimer's disease.

Immediately Marnie had scrapped her own plans, making Silas Lee's well-being top priority. Though the following years had been riddled with hardship and pain, she didn't regret them. What she did regret was having to finally put her father in a special home.

While she missed him terribly, her highly challenging and rewarding work had been her salvation. It had taken the edge off her grief and had bolstered her confidence and given her financial security.

It was her new-found independence she treasured the

most and guarded fiercely, refusing to take to heart any man's advances, especially those of Lance O'Brien.

"Well?"

Just as Marnie groped for something to say, the waiter arrived with their dinner. A sense of relief surged through her.

Once the waiter had departed, the silence continued as each concentrated on the entrées. However, the crabmeat tasted like a mouthful of paste in Marnie's mouth. It was useless; she couldn't pretend Lance's unorthodox proposal hadn't unnerved her.

The more she ate, the worse the food tasted. Finally, after eating at least half of it, she gave up and laid her fork down, then reached for her wineglass. Over the rim, she noticed Lance watching her. He, too, seemed uninterested in his food, though he'd managed to eat more than she had.

"Perhaps you'd care for a dessert," the waiter asked, suddenly appearing out of nowhere.

Marnie shook her head. "No thank you."

"Me neither," Lance said.

It was only after the tantalizing aroma of coffee drifted from the fine china cups that Lance spoke again.

"Well?" he repeated.

In spite of the seriousness of the situation, Marnie smiled. "Well, what?"

He again reached for her hand and squeezed it. "This is no game, Marnie."

"Do you make a habit of proposing to all the women you date?" she asked, forcing a lightness into her tone that she was far from feeling.

Lance's mouth formed a petulant slant. "I'm serious, Marnie. I'm in love with you and want to marry you."

Although Marnie did not take his proposal seriously,

she nevertheless felt a trifle uncomfortable. Determination glinted in his eyes.

"You don't mean that, Lance."

"Yes, I do," he said stubbornly.

"You know I'm honored—"

"Dammit, Marnie, I don't want you to feel honored. I want you to say you'll marry me."

Marnie lifted her eyebrows. "I do believe you're serious."

"You're right, I am."

"Oh, Lance," she said, holding his gaze, "you know I've enjoyed seeing you these past months. But you also know that I've never pretended to be anything other than your friend."

"That can't change?"

"No, I'm sorry, but it can't. While I enjoy your company, I don't want to commit to anyone." Marnie's tone was gentle. "For the first time ever, I'm satisfied with my life. I want to enjoy my work and my freedom." She meant that, too. But even if it weren't the case, she was not in love with Lance O'Brien, nor could she ever be.

Lance leaned forward, that determined glint still in his eyes. "You're not going to get off the hook so easily. I'm warning you here and now, I'm not giving up."

"And I'm warning you that you're wasting your time."

Lance grinned, then stood. "Are you ready to party?"

"To party?" Marnie repeated, staring at him blankly.

"Yeah, my dad's throwing a shindig. We're gonna crash it, so I can introduce you."

TWO

Marnie remained silent as Lance wheeled his Seville onto the blacktop road that led to the O'Brien ranch. She was loath to admit it, but her heart was pounding louder than usual.

While Lance had denied a second time that there was anything wrong with crashing his father's party, Marnie's doubts persisted. Even if Tate did not object, she did. Fraternizing with the rich and famous held no interest for her. Still, she was curious about the T Bar Ranch.

Not only had there been gossip pertaining to the man himself, but his private domain, as well. Supposedly it was a showplace, as on more than one occasion visiting heads of states had stayed there.

During the fifteen-mile trip, very little conversation had taken place between Lance and her. Several times she had looked at him, noticing each time that his jaw was set at a stubborn angle. Since they had left the restaurant, he hadn't said any more about the proposal.

But she feared he didn't intend to give up even though she felt certain he wasn't serious, despite what he said. As with the sundry other women in his life, she was just a passing fancy. When he realized she had no intention of sleeping with him, he'd cut her loose. Lance wanted a playmate; she wanted a soul mate.

She'd miss him; she couldn't deny that. Though spoiled and selfish on the one hand, on the other he was fun loving and eager to please. Still, as she'd told him, she didn't love him and knew she never would.

Now, seeing the lights from the house twinkling like stars through the thick foliage, she turned toward him.

"It's not too late to change your mind, you know."

Taking his eyes off the road, he returned her stare, a grin plastered across his handsome face. "Hey, come on, where's your sense of adventure? Anyway, Dad's not that bad. It's only when I'm around that he seems to take on a different personality."

"So what's the purpose of our coming here, then?"

Lance sighed with exasperation. "I told you I wanted you to meet him."

This time it was Marnie who sighed. "All right. Whatever you think best." Why argue with him, she thought. Actually, she was making far too big a deal of it. Tate O'Brien was no god.

Lance braked the car on the circular drive in front of the sprawling, brick house. Huge oak and pecan trees hovered over the structure, and Marnie had the feeling she had entered an enchanted forest. How lovely, she thought, entranced, watching as the moon spotlighted the poised elegance of the entryway.

"We won't stay long, I promise," Lance said.

Marnie's smile was skeptical. "Why is it that I don't trust you?"

"Because you're a distrusting female, that's why," Lance said, tweaking her on the nose.

Marnie rolled her eyes. "Let's go."

The instant she stepped into the fresh night air, the smell of honeysuckle caressed her senses. She paused and breathed deeply, reveling in the sweet scent. Close by, crickets chirped, while the wind whispered through the trees. The spring evening was perfect. If it was left up to her, she would sit in the swing on the porch and never take a step inside.

"Come on," Lance urged. "I want a drink."

When they reached the massive front door, Lance didn't bother to knock. Instead he thrust it open and with an innocent smile, indicated that Marnie should precede him. The instant she crossed the threshold into a large foyer, she came face-to-face with an overweight, stern-faced woman.

However, when she saw Lance, her lips spread into a wide grin.

"Lord a mercy, I was beginning to think you'd crawled off somewhere and died."

"And leave you," Lance responded heartily, "the best cook in the entire state of Texas? No way," he added, leaning over and giving her a kiss on the cheek.

"Then why haven't we seen more of you?" she demanded, blushing.

"Because I've been working, that's why."

The woman snorted.

Lance laughed, then turned to Marnie and reached for her hand. "Annie Bullock, meet Marnie Lee."

Marnie extended her hand and smiled warmly. "Hello, Annie."

"Hello ma'am."

"Annie's all things to all people in this household. In fact, without her, this place couldn't function."

"He likes to exaggerate," Annie said, leveling gray eyes on Marnie. "But it's nice to hear anyway."

"Where is everybody?" Lance asked, changing the subject. "On the deck?"

Marnie was wondering the same thing. Although she could hear soft music, clinking glass and muted laughter, she hadn't as yet seen anyone.

Annie cast her gaze sideways. "There and in the den."

"Grandmom, too?"

Annie's face lost some of its animation. "No. She called saying she didn't feel well."

"Mmm, hope it's nothing serious."

"I'm sure it isn't or your dad would've called off the party."

"Speaking of Dad," Lance said, cupping Marnie's elbow, "it's time we made our presence known."

Annie smiled. "Hope you'll come again, Marnie."

"Oh, she will," Lance said, urging her forward.

After giving Lance a dark look for answering for her, Marnie scanned her surroundings. The interior was breathtaking. To her right was a formal living room, its walls lined with what Marnie guessed were highly prized paintings. Beyond she could see a hallway that led to the bedrooms. On her left were the kitchen and formal dining room.

It was obvious that when this home was constructed and furnished, money was no object. It reeked with opulence.

"Well, what d'you think?" Lance asked, still holding her elbow.

"Need you ask?"

Lance chuckled. "Dad had it built a couple of years ago, right after he started grooming me to take over the business. Grandmom decorated it for him."

"Is she your dad's mother?"

"Yep. She's some lady, too. I'm sorry you won't get to meet her tonight."

"Me, too," Marnie said, just as she and Lance paused on the threshold of a magnificent room that spanned the back of the house.

"Want a glass of wine?" Lance asked, drawing her attention back to him.

She smiled. "Please."

"Don't move." Lance squeezed her elbow. "I'll be right back. Then we'll circulate."

A number of guests thronged the large deck, wandering in and out of the double doors thrown open to the warm spring night. There were clusters of people standing on the lawn, sharing drinks and animated conversation.

Marnie couldn't help but breathe a sigh of relief that she was appropriately dressed. Her long-sleeved turquoise silk jumpsuit and silver looped earrings blended in with the cocktail dresses, both long and short.

Focusing once again on the room itself, she perused the premises. But instead of taking in the rustic beams overhead or the huge fireplace, her gaze fell on a tall, broad-shouldered man with a mustache standing a few feet away.

A sudden and unexpected tingle climbed Marnie's spine. Even if he hadn't resembled his son, instinct would have told her that the man was Tate O'Brien. It wasn't so much the way he was dressed that set him apart, though his casual navy jacket, gray slacks and yellow shirt were certainly in contrast to his guests' formal attire.

No, it was the man himself. Cool arrogance seemed to radiate from him. Here, she thought, was a man who was used to giving orders and having them obeyed.

Marnie tried to remove her gaze but found she could not. Blue eyes that burned like coals continued to hold her captive. There was something magnetic about him, as well, something larger than life that made her want to reach out to him. Such a thought was so ridiculous, it was terrifying. She felt herself turn pale.

Then, suddenly, he bent and said something to the stately blond woman at his side.

It was only after Tate straightened and began moving in her direction that Marnie panicked. Surely he wasn't going to seek her out? Of course, he was, she told herself. After all, she was a stranger. Logic told her that seeking her out was *exactly* what he would do.

Where was Lance? Frantic, she searched the crowded room.

"Missed me, huh?"

Lance's voice grazed her ear, and she went limp with relief. "Yes, as a matter of fact I did," she said, "only not for the reason you're thinking."

As if unaffected by her dry tone, Lance grinned and handed her a glass of wine. "What's up?"

"Your father. That's what's up. If I'm not mistaken, he's heading our way."

"So you didn't want to face dear ole dad alone." Lance leaned closer to her ear. "All you have to remember is that his bark's much worse than his bite."

Marnie gave him a dark look before Tate O'Brien once again consumed her vision. He had stopped within touching distance. Unconsciously, Marnie stepped back as the full impact of his rugged good looks struck her like a blow.

Like his son, Tate had the same wide forehead and high cheekbones. But there the resemblance ended. His hair was thick and dark with a spattering of white above each ear. His sensitive lower lip balanced by a resolute chin would have gone a long way toward making his face perfect had his expression not looked so grim.

"Hello, son."

"Hello, Dad," Lance said, placing an arm around Marnie's shoulders and pulling her against his side. "I'd like you to meet Marnie Lee."

As if it were foreign to his nature, Tate smiled, then nodded. "Ms. Lee. It's a pleasure."

But it wasn't, Marnie thought. He wasn't pleased; he wasn't pleased in the least. To her dismay she felt a flush stain her cheeks, his quick appraisal making her uncomfortable as well as contributing to the strained atmosphere. "Same here, Mr. O'Brien," she replied in her coolest tone.

"Have we met before?" he asked, a frown altering his brow.

Lance cut in. "Marnie works for Systems." He paused and winked at Marnie. "Actually, she's our new project assistant and works directly with me."

"I see," Tate said, giving Marnie another long look, a look that had an even more unsettling effect on her. It bore the stamp of cold hostility and wary distrust. For heaven's sake, who did he think she was—a gold digger out to trap his son?

Refusing to let him intimidate her, Marnie squared her shoulders and smiled.

"Surprised to see me…us, Dad?" Lance asked, changing the subject.

Focusing his attention back on his son, Tate said, "As a matter of fact, I am. So tell me, what do you want?"

Marnie almost gasped aloud at his rudeness.

Lance flushed. "What makes you think I want something?"

"That's the only time you ever come home, isn't it?"

"Well, this time you're right," Lance said flatly. "I wanted you to meet Marnie."

For the moment no one spoke. Forgotten were the laughter and cocktail conversations behind them. It was almost as if the three of them were alone in the room.

Tate was the first to break the heavy silence. "Ms. Lee, will you excuse us for a minute? I'd like to talk to Lance alone."

"Of course." Marnie couldn't think of anything she'd like more than to be rid of Tate's charismatic presence.

Lance turned to her. "Will you be all right?" he asked, his tone conveying concern.

Marnie nodded. "I'll be fine. You go ahead."

Tate's eyes sought hers, and she felt herself blush.

"Make yourself at home," he said. "Join in the party."

Disconcerted, she smiled lamely. "Thank you."

Although his deep, rich voice was polite and unemotional, Marnie was not fooled. Tate O'Brien did not like her. On the heels of that certainty came another: he would make a very formidable enemy.

Standing like a statue, she watched Lance and Tate disappear through a door adjacent to the bar. As if feeling her gaze on him, Tate turned. For the briefest of moments, their eyes met again and held. Then, turning, he closed the door behind him.

Marnie shuddered.

Tate's office had its own distinct personality. Here he could relax and, for a blessed moment, forget his work and the huge responsibilities that often mastered him.

The room, with its light walnut paneling, thick tan carpet, bookshelves lined with books, paintings of prized quarter horses and massive walnut desk, seemed to hold him. At this point in time, however, the room failed to render its soothing effect.

This evening he couldn't kid himself. He knew why. Nevertheless, the thought made him fiercely angry. Marnie Lee. She was the culprit; she was responsible for a fire burning in his gut.

Since Stephanie's death there had been many women. They had moved in and out of his life like a revolving door. Yet few had made an impression, certainly not a lasting one. And he had never said the word *love* to another woman, nor did he intend to.

So why had his reaction to Marnie been so quick, so intense? Granted, she was lovely.

Her hair, shining like spun gold, had framed her face; her generous breasts had filled the outfit she was wearing.

Still he'd had other women equally as beautiful, if not more so. But there was an innocent allure about her. She probably wasn't aware of it, but she was the kind of woman a man would throw a few punches to get to.

His son proved to be no exception.

Sighing deeply, Tate switched his attention to the muted sounds of laughter and clinking glass. If he were to turn his head a tad, the deck would be in full view. He knew it would be cluttered with guests taking advantage of the perfect weather.

The party was in full swing; his guests were having a good time. But right now he wasn't concerned about the success or failure of his party. He was concerned about Lance and his relationship to Marnie Lee.

From behind him the sound of a sigh, deeper than his own, forced him around.

"Don't you think you've stalled long enough?" Lance seemed to be hanging on to his patience by a thread. "Just say what's on your mind and be done with it. Marnie'll be wondering what's happened to me."

Lance was sitting in one of the leather chairs, arms folded across his chest, legs sprawled straight out in front of him. His features were pinched, effectively depicting his surly attitude.

"Let her wonder," Tate said, his tone acid.

"What's that supposed to mean?"

Tate cleared his throat and returned his son's hostile stare. The conversation was off to a bad start; he had told himself he would use patience in dealing with Lance, but lately, whenever they got together, patience flew out the window.

Lance again shattered the silence. "What the hell's going on?"

"Calm down." Tate's order was withering.

Lance flushed. "I wish you'd stop treating me like a kid, like I don't have enough sense to get in out of a good hard rain. For chrissake, Dad, I'm twenty-seven years old."

"Then bygod act like it."

Lance lunged to his full height, his face blood-red. "Look, if all you brought me in here for is to argue, then forget it. I'm leaving."

"Sit down." Tate's tone was cold and brooked no argument.

Lance's fury seemed almost palpable, but he sat down, albeit ungraciously.

"That's better," Tate said. Again, he knew he was

going about this all wrong. He vowed to contain his anger.

"Okay, so what have I done wrong this time?" Lance demanded. When Tate opened his mouth to answer, he went on, "I've been busting my ass on this special project, and up till now I thought everything was going okay."

"It's not your work," Tate replied soberly. "At least not directly."

Lance arched an eyebrow. "Ah, ha, I get it; you're steamed because I borrowed some money from Gran and haven't paid it back."

"While that doesn't make me any too happy, that's not the reason I wanted to talk to you." Tate rocked forward for emphasis. "But now that you mentioned it, you sure as hell better pay her back."

"So, if it's not Gran and it's not work..." Lance's voice played out.

"Marnie Lee. It's Marnie Lee." Tate watched his son carefully, half expecting him to explode. Instead he looked dumbfounded and confused.

"Marnie? I don't get it."

"Oh, I think you get it, all right," Tate sneered. "In fact, I think you get the *complete* picture."

Lance's mouth tightened, but he didn't say anything.

"For god's sake, I'm not blind. I saw the way you looked at her."

"And *I* saw the way *you* looked at her!"

Tate's eyes narrowed dangerously. "Dammit, boy, watch your mouth."

"Sorry," Lance muttered, averting his eyes, as though he realized he had gone too far.

For another long moment neither spoke. They simply

stared at each other, their harsh breathing the only sound in the room.

As if finally conceding defeat, Lance flopped back down into the chair. "So what about her?" he demanded. His tone was testy at best.

Tate hesitated and chose his words carefully. "I don't want you to see her anymore, that's what."

For a second time blood rushed into Lance's face. "Just why the hell not?"

"Because I don't want a replay of the last fling you had."

"Marnie's different."

Tate laughed without humor. "If I recall, that's what you said about Melissa."

"Well, we proved the baby wasn't mine, didn't we?" Lance wiped his brow. His discomfort was obvious.

"It could've been, though. Right?"

"You know the answer to that," Lance said petulantly.

"You damn right I do. That's the reason for this conversation right now. When are you going to learn you can't fall in love with every girl you meet and promise her the moon?"

"I told you, Marnie's different."

"I beg to differ with you." Tate's tone dripped with sarcasm. "True, she's better-looking than the others and seems to have a little more breeding, but that doesn't mean a damn in the scheme of things. I still don't want you involved with her."

"Is it because she works for the company?" Lance sounded a tad desperate.

"You haven't heard a word I've said, have you?" Tate asked, clearly frustrated.

Lance stood again and shoved his hands down into his

pants pockets. ''Yes, I have, but I told you, Marnie's different.''

''Spare me. She's probably after your money, just like Melissa was and the others before her.''

''No, she's not!''

''How do you know?''

''I just know.''

''Do you know anything about her family, her friends?''

''I know enough.''

Tate muttered a stream of epithets.

''Well, since you opened this can of worms,'' Lance said, ''you might as well hear it all.''

Tate tugged at his mustache. ''Hear what?''

''I've asked Marnie to marry me.''

''You what!''

Lance's chin jutted defiantly. ''You heard me.''

''Oh, for heaven's—'' Tate began with suppressed violence, only to suddenly break off. With great effort he fought to control himself. He knew if he said anything else, he'd regret it.

''She's a warm, wonderful person, and I love her,'' Lance was saying.

''Love! You don't know the meaning of the word. When are you going to learn *lust* is not love.''

''I'm sorry you feel that way, Dad,'' Lance said without emotion, ''but I've made up my mind and there's nothing you can say or do to stop me.''

With that Lance turned and walked out of the room, slamming the door behind him.

Tate had no idea how long he stood there in the middle of the room, his heart pounding like an out-of-shape runner climbing a steep hill. It was all he could do to keep from charging out the door and hauling his son back into the room.

And do what? he asked himself. Argue some more? Pound some sense into him? Hardly. He couldn't afford to add more fuel to fanned flames. Another expletive singed the air, but it didn't make him feel better. When had he and his son become adversaries instead of friends? he wondered. He could remember the time they used to be buddies, used to enjoy each other's company.

God knows, he loved him. Was Tate's mother right? Was he too overprotective? But then he had a good reason for doing so, only Lance didn't see it that way. Again Tate paused in his thoughts to rub the back of his neck, hoping to relieve some of the tension lodged there. It hadn't worked a little while ago, and it wasn't working now. His insides remained tightly knotted.

No way was he going to stand by and watch Lance ruin his life. He would find a way to stop his son from marrying Marnie Lee.

Suddenly he snapped his fingers, then reached for the phone. After punching out the numbers, he waited.

"Neal, O'Brien. I want you to run a second security check on someone. Pronto."

Three

"Well?"

"Well what?"

In the soft semidarkness Marnie searched Lance's features. "That innocent act won't work with me and you know it," Marnie retorted. She'd wanted to question him earlier, but common sense warned her to hold her tongue.

They were in the driveway of her condominium now, and she knew Lance hadn't gotten over his anger. Perhaps fury was a more appropriate word, Marnie thought, her gaze still on him. But instead of returning her scrutiny or answering her question, he continued to stare ahead in brooding silence.

In that moment he looked exactly as his father had looked after he'd walked out of his study, a thundercloud ready to erupt.

During the time they had been behind closed doors, Marnie had meandered around the room, sipping on her

wine, only to eventually find herself out on the deck.
Several couples she didn't know had spoken to her, while
two men had approached her and asked if they could get
her another drink. She had politely declined, her mind
occupied with what was taking place behind closed
doors.

It had been only moments after she'd wandered back
inside the house that they had appeared. The instant
Lance had spotted her, his face had lost its sullenness and
he'd winked. Tate's, however, had remained granite hard.
He hadn't even bothered to look her way.

Arrogant bastard, she'd thought then, and still did.

Finally breaking into the heavy silence, Marnie said,
"I take it your conversation with your dad was not a
pleasant one."

Lance's laugh was harsh. "That's putting it mildly."

"It was about me, wasn't it? Your disagreement, I
mean."

Lance twisted slightly to face her. His lips were drawn
into a fine line. "How'd you know?"

Marnie shrugged her slender shoulders. "Intuition, I
guess."

"Well, you're right," Lance said flatly.

For some unexplainable reason, Marnie felt an instant's anxiousness in the pit of her stomach. Was it possible that her job might be in jeopardy?

Marnie's tone was hesitant. "Why was I discussed?"

"I told him I was going to marry you."

There was an instant of absolute silence.

Marnie's heart sank. "Oh, God, you didn't. Please tell
me you didn't."

Lance's lips formed a pout. "I sure as hell did."

"You know, Lance," Marnie said with saccharine
sweetness, "if I weren't afraid of being cooped up in a

little room all day long and forced to sew, which I detest, I'd gladly strangle you."

An uncertain smile replaced the pout.

"It's not funny," Marnie snapped.

Lance scratched his ear and sighed. "No, I guess it isn't, but damn…" His voice faded.

A fiery glint lit Marnie's eyes. "You had your nerve, especially after I had made it quite plain that I had no intention of marrying you—or anyone else, for that matter."

"And I warned you I wasn't taking no for an answer."

"So what did he say?" Marnie asked, despising herself because she was curious. When Lance didn't respond, she continued. "He doesn't think I'm good enough for you, does he?" Even to herself, her voice sounded choked.

Lance shifted uneasily. "Don't take offense. He doesn't think anyone's good enough for me. He looks at me as one of his prized quarter horses."

"Maybe that's his way of showing you he cares," Marnie said.

"Yeah."

"I don't suppose you bothered to put his mind at rest by telling him that I'd declined your offer of marriage?"

Even though the darkness hampered her vision, she knew Lance's face turned red.

She turned away. "No, no I guess you didn't."

Suddenly feeling drained, and realizing this conversation was going nowhere, Marnie added, "Look, it's getting late. I should be in bed. Tomorrow, as you well know, is going to be another busy day."

Lance reached for her hand. "You aren't still mad at me, are you, honey?" His tone was cajoling.

"No, Lance, I'm not mad at you. I'm just furious."

He gave her a blank look, then laughed. "Good, that means I still have a chance to change your mind."

She opened her mouth to say something, only to snap it shut. Nothing she could say, she realized, would dent his thick skull. Shaking her head, she merely opened the door and stepped out. It was only after she'd let herself inside the condo and flipped on the entry-hall light that she heard him crank the car and drive off.

Closing her eyes, she sank against the door.

Marnie took a sip of the hot decaffeinated coffee and wiggled deeper into the plush cushions on the sofa. She was too keyed up to sleep, so she hadn't even bothered to go to bed.

Her shapely legs, covered by her flimsy robe, were resting on the glass-topped table in front of her. Feeling the hot liquid steal through her like a soothing balm, she smiled and closed her eyes.

But her feeling of contentment didn't last long. The events of the evening rose again to haunt her.

"Don't think about him," she hissed aloud. "Forget you ever met him."

That was a joke, she thought, curling her lip scornfully. How did one go about forgetting a specimen like Tate O'Brien? She certainly could not. While she had disliked him on sight, she had found him fascinating, as well. Maybe it was his rugged good looks that had commanded her interest. She'd often heard the statement that a man looked better as he grew older, while a woman looked worse. Where Tate was concerned, that was true. Office gossip had him at forty-five, fifteen years her senior. Yet, she'd bet he'd never looked better.

Furious with the mind games she was playing, Marnie

took another gulp of the coffee only to suddenly cough, nearly choking on it.

"Damn," she muttered, slamming her cup down on the table beside her. Then, determined to get hold of her scattered emotions, she curled her feet under her and looked around.

No matter how low she was feeling, the sight of her lovely home almost always cheered her up.

The condo had six rooms: a living area with two skylights and a fireplace, a kitchen with an adorable breakfast nook, two bedrooms and two baths. With its traditional furnishings, it exuded warm, cozy comfort.

She had worked damn hard to get it, too. But then she'd had to work hard for everything she'd ever had. Lance hadn't, she reminded herself. That, along with the fact that she didn't love him, was exactly why marriage between them could never work.

Their life-styles differed, as well. Yet, she had nothing to be ashamed of. Though she was reared with no amenities, she was proud of her family and her upbringing. Most of all, she was proud of her accomplishments. And nothing or no one, she vowed, was going to undermine her success or her newfound contentment, least of all Tate O'Brien.

Suddenly feeling the need to cling to something familiar, her eyes strayed to the collection of pictures adorning her mantel. One stood out: a picture of her father dressed in overalls. A huge grin lit his face. Unwinding her legs, she got up and walked to it and with her index finger, traced the frame lovingly. Though she tried to blink them back, tears burned her eyes like fire.

Silas didn't even recognize her now, and that broke her heart. Still she would never forsake him. That was why this job meant so much to her. In addition to providing her with this condo, it allowed her to keep her father in that very expensive home.

Thoughts of Tate O'Brien once again flared in her mind, and her blood turned to ice water in her veins. Damn Lance and his proposal. If he caused her to lose her job...

A sob caught in her throat at the same time the doorbell rang. Startled, Marnie peered down at her watch. Eleven-thirty. Frowning, she crossed to the door and stared out the peep hole.

Then wide-eyed, she flung the heavy door open. "Why, Katie, what on earth brings you out this time of night?"

"Saw your light and thought you might offer this poor, tired soul a cup of decaf coffee."

Marnie grinned as her next-door neighbor and friend, Kate McCall, crossed the threshold. Dressed in a conservative blue flight attendant's uniform, she could have passed for a strict teacher in a private school if she hadn't smiled and shown her dimple.

"Don't tell me you just got home," Marnie exclaimed.

"From New York, no less."

Marnie laughed again. "Well have a seat and I'll take pity on you and pour you a cup of coffee."

Following her divorce a year ago, Kate had left her job at a computer company and gone to work for American Airlines. Like Marnie, she had been looking for a way to escape her grief. They had become firm friends.

Marnie saw the tired lines around Kate's eyes, and her heart went out to her.

"God, what a day," Kate said, collapsing on the couch.

"You look it, too." Even though Kate was just a year older than she, tonight she looked ten.

Kate feigned anger. "Thanks a heap, friend."

Smiling, Marnie disappeared into the kitchen. Moments later she returned with her cup refilled and another one brimming full for Kate.

"Well, let's hear about your day," Marnie said, sitting down on the opposite end of the couch, then handing Kate her cup.

Kate latched onto it with a sigh. "There's nothing to tell, really. Supervisors were on board, and everyone was chasing tail trying to please." She paused and blew on her coffee. "After we landed, several of us went out to dinner to celebrate their departure."

Marnie sighed. "I can sympathize. My day wasn't a whole lot better."

Kate raised her dark eyebrows. "Your day or your evening?"

"What made you ask that?"

Kate shrugged. "I don't know. There's just something not quite right about your eyes. You're worried about something, right?"

"You're much too nosey for your own good, Kate McCall." Marnie's smile took the sting out of her words.

Kate batted the air with her free hand. "Friends are supposed to be nosey," she countered, unperturbed. "It isn't your father, is it?" Now there was an anxiousness to her tone.

"No...no, he's the same."

"Does it have anything to do with Lance?"

An affirmative nod was all Marnie was able to get in before Kate went on. "So, what happened?"

Without answering, Marnie leaned forward and adjusted the pillows behind her back.

Kate's blue eyes never wavered from her.

"How 'bout something to eat?" Marnie said suddenly,

desperately, realizing how close she was to tears. And the last thing she wanted to do was cry in front of Kate. God, but Tate O'Brien had certainly done a number on her. Damn that man.

"Hey, you are upset. Didn't you just hear me tell you that I came straight here from the restaurant?" Kate frowned. "But in answer to your question, no I don't want anything to eat. What I do want is for you to confess. Furthermore, I'm not budging until you do."

"It's…Lance."

"He didn't dump you did he?"

"No, quite the contrary."

"Ah, ha." A slow, knowing grin spread across Kate's lips. "He asked you to marry him, I'll bet."

"Yes, he did," Marnie said quietly.

"Praise the Lord. I certainly hope you had the good sense to say yes."

Marnie blinked, then stared at her friend, her eyes enormous in her pale face. "Surely you aren't serious."

"Of course, I'm serious." Kate wrinkled her forehead and edged forward on the couch. "Why, Lance O'Brien is every woman's dream. Not only is he good-looking, but he has money to burn."

"But I don't love him, Katie," Marnie wailed.

"Pooh, that's not important."

Marnie struggled to hold on to her patience, knowing it was too late and she was too tired to be having this conversation. But short of telling Kate to mind her own business and go home, she had no choice but to hear her out.

"Well, it's important to me," Marnie said, her tone sober.

Kate bounded off the couch, then immediately peered

down into Marnie's face, an incredulous expression on hers. "Why? I bet you can't answer that."

"Oh, come on, Kate, how can you ask a question like that? You know yourself that even with love, it's difficult to make a marriage work." Marnie paused and spread her hands, trying to get her point across to her friend. "Sometimes impossible, right?"

For a moment Kate averted her eyes, as if unable to meet Marnie's intent gaze. Then she faced her squarely and said, "Wrong. I didn't love Grant the way I should have going in, but that wasn't all that broke up our marriage. It was money," she added bluntly. "The lack of it."

Marnie sighed deeply and didn't say anything.

"Look, sweetie," Kate said, following the short silence, "you can tell me to go take a flying leap if you want to for interfering in your business—" she grinned lopsidedly "—but you know I care what happens to you."

"I know."

"I see how hard it is for you to keep your father in that special home, how hard you have to work."

"Oh, Katie, I know you care. And you're right, it is tough. But that doesn't mean that I should marry the first rich man who comes along. I couldn't be happy living that way."

"So I can only assume then that you're waiting for a hunk to walk up to you and sweep you off your feet?"

Suddenly Tate O'Brien's face again rose to the forefront of her mind. Mortified, Marnie turned away from Kate's probing stare, but not soon enough, she knew, to hide the color that surged into her face.

"So, I'm right," Kate said, chuckling. "That's exactly what you're waiting for."

Both relieved and thankful that Kate had misunderstood her discomfort, Marnie smiled. "Maybe...I don't know. But what I do know is that I could never fall in love with Lance O'Brien, even though he is a lot of fun."

"Well, I can understand that, especially after being closeted with your father for so long and never having time to play. And from what you've told me, Lance certainly knows how to show a woman a good time." Kate smiled without envy.

"Unfortunately it might not be *me* he shows a good time any longer."

Kate sat back down on the couch. "Because you turned down his proposal? He's upset, huh?"

"To tell you the truth, I'm not sure Lance has taken no for an answer."

Kate shook her head. "I don't get it. If that's the case, why won't you be seeing him anymore?"

Ignoring her, Marnie latched onto an errant strand of hair that grazed her cheekbone and toyed with it for a minute. Then, thrusting it behind her ear, she said, "It really doesn't matter about Lance because his father, Tate O'Brien, doesn't like me."

"So?"

"So if Lance wants to continue the life-style to which he's accustomed, he'll have no choice but to give in to his father's demands."

Kate was clearly puzzled. "He works, doesn't he?"

"Of course, he works. At the moment he's actually my boss. *However*—" Marnie stressed the word "—the salary he makes isn't enough. It's as simple as that."

"So dear ole dad doles it out for the right to control his life."

"That's it in a nutshell."

"So how do you know Daddy doesn't approve of you?" Kate pressed.

Marnie couldn't help but smile at the way Kate said "Daddy" as if it was some kind of contagious disease that should be avoided at all cost. "He thinks I'm a gold digger."

Kate slapped her neck and laughed out loud. "You've got to be kidding?"

"No, I'm not kidding," Marnie said, her lips now set in a taut line.

"Did he actually call you that to your face?"

"No, but I could read it in his eyes." Suddenly seeing the lack of understanding on Kate's face, Marnie told her all about the party. What she didn't tell her friend was her volatile reaction to Tate.

"Wow," Kate said when Marnie finished.

"So you think your job could really be in danger?"

Marnie suppressed a sigh. "I hope not, but you never know."

"So are you going to humor 'Daddy' and stop seeing Lance?"

For the first time in a long while, Marnie's eyes lit up. "Probably not."

Kate grinned. "Atta girl. And if 'Daddy' pulls anything underhanded, you can slap him with a harassment suit."

"Sure thing," Marnie said drolly.

Still grinning, Kate stood. "Well, I gotta go. As it is, I've overstayed my welcome. In the morning I wouldn't blame you if you came looking for me with a shotgun."

"When that alarm goes off at five o'clock, I may very well do that."

Kate leaned over and gave Marnie a quick bear hug.

"Good night, and thanks for the coffee. Talk to you later."

Marnie returned the hug. "I'll keep you posted on what happens."

"That goes without saying," Kate called over her shoulder, letting herself out the door.

Marnie heard him before she saw him.

She had only minutes before entered Lance's office, having brought with her important paperwork on the project that had to be completed before noon. She'd needed absolute quiet, and since Lance was out of town, she'd opted to use his office.

Now clutching the papers tightly in her right hand, she hoped her ears had played a trick on her. Her heart sank. They hadn't.

Once again Tate's deep, rich voice assaulted her senses.

"I'm not asking, Ms. Purcell. I'm telling you that I have to see Ms. Lee. Now suppose you tell me where she is."

An assistant was minding Marnie's desk, and Marnie could imagine how intimidated she must be with Tate looming over her, his blue eyes as cold as the Arctic.

So desperate was she to calm her own hammering pulse that she missed the assistant's reply. It didn't matter, however, as the door to Lance's office suddenly flew open.

Marnie stood motionless in some fragile balance between anticipation and fear as Tate O'Brien cleared the threshold and crossed into the room, Stetson in hand.

Startled beyond words, she stared at an altogether different man from the formally dressed stranger of the party. Gone were the slacks and sports coat. In their place were a chambray shirt and Levi's pressed to a sharp crease.

Against his smooth-shaven face, his mustache seemed more prominent than when she'd first met him, and his dark salt-and-pepper hair longer and more mussed. But neither of those imperfections dampened the blatant sexual charisma he exuded. In fact, she wondered what it would be like to kiss a man with a mustache. She wondered what it would be like to kiss Tate O'Brien... *You're losing it, Marnie!*

His eyes were on her; everywhere they touched, her skin felt hot. Refusing to let him see the effect he was having on her, Marnie stepped from behind the massive desk, which was strewn with papers, and walked straight to him.

"Good morning, Mr. O'Brien," she said, trying to keep her voice steady. Dismayed, she realized she sounded out of breath.

Although he lifted an eyebrow slightly at her smooth approach, his harsh features did not relent.

"What can I do for you?" she asked when it became apparent he wasn't going to answer her greeting.

"What do you say we cut the pleasantries and get to the heart of the matter?"

"Oh, and what would that be?" she asked, hugging her icy hands to her sides.

If possible, Tate's features hardened even more. Yet his eyes continued to roam over her, searing her skin. "Oh," he said, mimicking her, "I think you know."

Marnie felt herself panic, but not because of his threatening presence. Her apprehension stemmed solely from the way he was scrutinizing her; it was the same way he'd scrutinized her at the party—with something on his mind other than his son's welfare.

"Look, Mr. O'Brien," Marnie said, gathering her shredded nerves together and trying to ignore the way her nipples had tightened, "I won't be dictated to. I—"

"Somehow I don't think you're in a position to threaten me, Ms. Lee."

Marnie opened her mouth to speak, only to swallow an angry retort. Then spinning around, she made her way to the window on the other side of the room and looked outside, her thoughts racing. She wouldn't let him do this to her. True, she loved her job; she *needed* her job. But there were other jobs in the marketplace, and with her experience she could get another one. *But not one that could offer the same challenge and the money,* she cried silently.

She didn't have to turn around to know that he was behind her. She felt his warm breath on the back of her neck. She shivered as a chill darted through her.

"I want you to leave my son alone."

"Please," she said faintly, "you're blowing this all out of proportion."

"I won't have you marrying him for his money."

She swung around; spots of red in each cheek had replaced the pallor. "How dare you say that? You don't know a thing about me!"

"The hell I don't! I know everything there is to know about you. Remember, you're working on a high-security project, and don't forget I own this place."

"You mean you—you…deliberately pulled my file…." The thought of him prying into her life nauseated her.

"That's right, Ms. Lee," he said in the same accusing tone.

"All this because your son took me out a few times?"

She had a sudden and overwhelming desire to laugh, to be hysterical about the whole thing. It was so ludicrous.

"We both know it's more than that." His voice cracked like a whip.

Trying hard not to choke, Marnie moved suddenly and quickly away from the window. And him.

Her ploy didn't work. Either he was too furious to pick up on the rebuff or he didn't care. He simply shifted with her.

"How much, Ms. Lee?"

"How much what?"

"Don't play games with me," he said, lowering his voice. It literally vibrated with fury as he went on. "How much money will it take to make you leave my son alone?"

"How dare you!" Marnie cried, raising her hand with every intention of slapping his face.

Tate was too quick; he caught her wrist in midair. They glared at each other in silent rage.

The clock on the wall chimed the hour. Sunlight flooded the room, danced across the furniture. Nearby, someone pounded on a typewriter. In the distance a door slammed shut.

Neither was aware of the sights and sounds around them—only each other. Their chests heaved. Their breaths mingled. Their eyes sparred.

"Oh, why the hell not," Tate muttered, then reached out, jerked her roughly against him and ground his lips onto hers.

Instantly Marnie's heart pounded against her rib cage. Simultaneous sensations of hot and cold gripped her. It was only when she felt his tongue invade her mouth that she came to her senses and began to struggle.

"No!" she whimpered, pushing against his chest.

Gulping for breath, Tate let her go.

For another sizzling moment they stared at each other, their breathing ragged, both unable to cope with what had happened.

"Damn," Tate said, rubbing the back of his neck.

Marnie wrapped her arms around her body and bit down on her lip to steady it.

Finally, after what seemed an eternity, Tate spun around and stamped toward the door. He had his hand on the knob before a word was spoken.

"Don't think for one second this changes anything," he said, his voice harsh with bitterness, "because it doesn't."

The moment the door closed behind him, Marnie managed to stumble to the desk and sink into the chair, fearing she might at any moment lose the contents of her stomach.

Thirty minutes later she was still sitting there.

Four

The wind rattled the windows of the barn like an unwanted visitor.

Tate, however, paid the outside elements scant attention. He was too busy venting his frustrations on the bale of hay in front of him. His heart pounded; sweat popped out on his forehead and upper lip.

His shoulders burned like pokers. Still he jabbed the hay with the pitchfork and heaved it up and forward, sending it sailing from the loft to the floor below. He had stable hands to do this back-breaking chore, but he'd opted to do it himself, thinking it was just the tonic he needed to settle down.

His face, etched in a deep frown as he stripped a glove from one hand and mopped his brow, continued to mirror his frustration.

It was past time he did some soul-searching, something he hadn't been able to do since he'd grabbed Marnie Lee in a fit of anger and kissed her. Instead he'd concentrated on keeping the dull ache inside him from turning into despair. So far he'd failed miserably.

Over and over in his mind that kiss repeated itself. He remembered every detail of that moment. He remembered the feel of her lips against his, their trembling softness. He remembered the feel of her hard nipples as they were pressed against his chest.

Nothing short of a miracle, he guessed, could wipe that memory from his mind. And now, as before, his body responded, which only added to his confusion; it was something he couldn't recall ever happening.

So what would it be like to make love to her?

No! Never. Not her. Everything that was decent inside him rebelled. He wouldn't compete with his son!

His face grim, Tate shoved the glove back on and stuck another bale of hay, tossing it below. Although he'd asked himself umpteen times why he'd kissed her to start with, he hadn't yet come up with an answer. Nor could he figure out why she triggered both his anger and his libido at the same time.

Hell, he wasn't interested in getting involved with a woman. Affairs only complicated things. For the first time in his life, he was in a position to do exactly as he pleased. His dream of raising and training quarter horses was finally becoming reality.

Yet Marnie Lee had touched something inside him, something heretofore untapped. She made him ache, which was all the more reason to fire her, he told himself, if she failed to heed his warning.

"Hey, watch where you're throwing that stuff, will ya?"

Tate peered over the edge of the loft into the upturned

face of his foreman, J. D. Rowe, a big, burly man with a beer belly.

"Sorry," Tate muttered, "didn't hear you come in."

J.D.'s grin was guileless. "Naw, I guess you didn't at that. You were too busy giving that hay bloody hell."

"Is there something you want?" Tate asked pointedly, glaring at him.

J.D.'s grin didn't so much as waver. He merely removed his hat and scratched his head as if he had all the time in the world.

Tate wasn't surprised by his foreman's lack of intimidation. Not only was J.D. the best foreman in these parts, but he was a good friend, as well.

In spite of himself, Tate smiled back and merely waited for his slow-talking foreman to say what he had come to say. He didn't have to wait long.

"Just thought I'd check to see if you wanted me to ride with you over to the Kelly place to look at that mare. If not, I'm going to mend those broken fences in the south pasture."

Tate slammed a palm against the handle of the pitchfork. "Dammit, I forgot about that appointment."

"Well, do you want me to tag along or not?"

"No, you go ahead and take care of the fences. They're more important."

"All right, see you later," J.D. said, turning and shuffling off.

A short time later Tate walked out of the barn, only to stop abruptly and curse.

Fran Hunt, the woman he'd been seeing a lot of lately was strutting toward him. Her face, framed by thick blond hair that fell to her shoulders, was unremarkable, but her body more than compensated for that flaw. Long legs, tiny waist and exquisitely-shaped breasts rounded out the package.

However, she was the last person Tate wanted to see right now.

"Hi, honey," Fran said in a sugary tone, stopping only a hairbreadth away from him.

"Hello, Fran," he answered on a sigh.

Her lower lip protruded. "Is that the best you can do? How about a little kiss."

Unconsciously, Tate stepped back, the thought of kissing her suddenly abhorrent. "Not now, Fran. I'm too dirty." He forced a smile, hoping to take a little of the edge off his rejection.

"Why, honey," she cajoled, sliding her hands up and down the front of his damp shirt, "you never let that stop you before."

With supreme effort, Tate hung on to his temper, trapping her hands, then removing them. "Not now, I said."

Her features hardened. "I don't know why I put up with you. When you want to, you can be a real bastard."

"No one's twisting your arm to stick around."

As if fearing she might have pushed him too far, Fran softened her tone and smiled. "Will I see you tonight?"

"Maybe."

"Well, when you make up your mind, let me know, you hear."

With that she turned and walked to her car. Tate watched while she cranked it and jerked it into gear.

Then blistering the air with another expletive, he stamped toward the house.

"Daddy, I'll see you tomorrow, okay?"

Silas Lee sat statue still in the leather wing chair and continued to stare out the window.

Marnie knew he wasn't seeing the beautiful landscaped grounds that surrounded this special-care facility, just as he hadn't seen her when she'd walked into his room a little while ago. Yet she went through the motions, pretending the disease hadn't robbed him of his mind as well as his dignity, pretending that he understood everything she told him.

Vigorously Marnie blinked back the tears that blurred her vision and gave his frail shoulders another quick hug.

"When I come back tomorrow, I'll bring you some more of your favorite candy." She almost choked on the lump in her throat. "I—I see…you're just about out."

Again, no response. He merely looked at her through vacant eyes. After looking at him another long moment, Marnie lifted dejected shoulders and crossed to the door. Once there, she paused and turned around, scanning the room with tear-filled eyes, as if to reassure herself that her beloved had the best that money could buy.

The large, airy room bore all the comforts of home; she had seen to that. Pictures that were special to him adorned the walls and littered the top of the chest of drawers. A braided rug, resting on top of the carpet, added another cheery dimension. Plants on one windowsill added still another.

If she'd had her way, though, he'd be at home with her. Such a move was out of the question; she could no longer handle him. Brushing the painful thought aside, she twisted the knob and whispered, "Goodbye, Daddy."

By the time she made it to the office, Marnie was once again in control of herself. But then, she'd had no choice. She had to bury her problems behind the church-house door, the way her father used to tell her. *Cry, sure, but get past it. Life goes on.*

She had just reached her desk and was staring with

remorse at the mound of paperwork on it when Lance entered the room.

"Hi," he said, and perched on one corner of her desk, a wide grin on his handsome face.

"Good morning," Marnie responded.

His grin collapsed. "Is that all you have to say?"

"What did you want me to say?"

"Something other than a grumpy good morning, that's for sure."

Marnie slipped her arms out of the jacket of her peach linen suit and draped it over the back of her chair. "Sorry, but grumpy's the way I feel. I've just come from seeing Silas."

"Any change?" Lance asked, shifting his gaze as if he was uncomfortable.

"No, but thanks for asking anyway."

Lance smiled lamely, then changed the subject. "I have some good news."

Marnie's face brightened. "Oh?"

"Albert and the two other engineers have finally narrowed the design plans for the explosive down to two."

"Oh, Lance, that's wonderful."

"Yeah, but it's about time."

For weeks a core of engineers had been working on various designs that would not only perfect the plastic explosive but perfect it to such a degree that the government would be satisfied. That in itself had proved to be a major sticking point as each design had its pluses as well as minuses.

During this critical period Marnie had been responsible for gathering together the massive amount of paperwork and getting it on to the computer. The information included details describing how each design functioned, how each was maintained and the conditions under which each was to be used.

"Well, don't keep me in suspense," she said at last, when Lance was not forthcoming with any more details.

"They decided to go with the timing device. From now on, it'll be referred to as 'one-off chip.'" He paused and tossed a folder down in front of her. "It's all there. Read it for yourself."

"Do you think Uncle Sam will be pleased?"

Lance stood. "We'll just have to wait and see, won't we?" He grinned his little-boy grin. "But I'm pleased. And I hope to hell Dad will be, too." His face lost its animation. "But then, one never knows about him."

Marnie could testify to that but, of course, she didn't. She never told Lance about the incident in his office, nor did she intend to.

She wished she could wipe it from her own mind. But no matter what she did, she could still feel the imprint of those hard, taut lips grinding against hers. She had seen him only a few times, but already she felt something, some emotion she couldn't identify. And the fact that he was Lance's father and so much older than she didn't come into it.

Suddenly Marnie swallowed against the lump in the back of her throat and turned her head away so that Lance wouldn't see the confusion mirrored in her eyes.

"Marnie?"

She spun her head around. "Sorry," she said, flashing him a bright, apologetic smile for woolgathering.

"I'll pick you up at eight."

Marnie's smile slipped. "Do you think that's a good idea?"

"Sure, why not?"

For some reason his cocky, flippant attitude irritated her. "You know why not," she snapped.

He chuckled, then leaned over and kissed her on the cheek. "If I promise not to mention the word *marriage*, will you let me take you to dinner?"

"Lance—"

"We'll call it a celebration dinner." He angled his head. "Come on, what d'you say?"

Suddenly she thought of Tate's warning. "All right," she said recklessly. "I'll go."

Even for a Friday night the restaurant Lance chose was crowded. The Back Porch was another favorite of Marnie's. She had been here several times with Kate. In addition to the relaxed atmosphere, it had the best salad bar in Houston, along with the best pizza.

Tonight the band in another room was playing a Kenny Rogers oldie. While the waiter filled their wineglasses, Marnie tapped her foot to the music.

They had already ordered. Marnie chose pizza on whole-wheat bread with lots of tangy tomato sauce and good, gooey mozzarella cheese, while Lance decided on the lasagna.

Once the waiter had gone, Lance asked, "Glad you came?"

Marnie smiled. "You know I am."

"Then let's toast to the success of the project, shall we?"

Marnie reached for her glass, only to suddenly stop. The color drained slowly from her face.

Standing in the doorway and staring straight at her was Tate O'Brien.

"Marnie, what's wrong?" Lance demanded. "Are you sick or something? You look like you've seen a ghost."

For another long moment Marnie remained as though caught in a freeze-frame, unable to take her eyes off Tate. It was only after he turned his attention to the woman at his side, the one who'd been with him at the ranch, that Marnie dragged her gaze away from his commanding figure.

Even so, when she faced Lance again, it was Tate's image she saw. Maybe it was the lighting, but Tate's face had appeared a deeper tan than usual, as had his bare arms. His hair, while a trifle unruly, complemented the blue shirt that was unbuttoned far enough to allow a smidgen of chest hair to show. Thighs, muscular and trim, filled his jeans.

"You're not going to faint on me, are you?" Lance was asking.

Marnie smiled bravely, though her stomach was heaving. "It's...your father."

"Here?"

"Yes, here." Marnie's voice quivered slightly.

Lance's snort of disgust could not be ignored. Then beginning to mutter under his breath, he swung around.

Tate and his companion were threading their way through the tables toward what Marnie prayed was the veranda. But in order to reach that section of the restaurant, they had to pass beside her table. Her pulse rate climbed.

"I can't imagine what he's doing here," Lance said, his features grim.

Marnie pushed her lips together. "It's simple. He's spying."

Lance opened his mouth to reply, only to suddenly close it as a shadow appeared over the table.

Marnie's mouth went dry. Lance stared at his drink. Neither said a word.

Then Lance raised his head and said, "Hello, Dad."

A thick artery pulsed in Tate's throat. "Son. Ms. Lee."

"What brings you and Fran here?" Lance's tone bordered on hostility. "I never knew you liked pizza."

"There's a lot you don't know about me."

Lance clamped his lips together.

Marnie had purposefully kept her eyes off Tate, opting instead to concentrate on the woman Lance had called Fran. Obviously bored with what was going on at the table, Fran had turned her attention to another one nearby and was chatting with its occupants.

Not bad, Marnie mused to herself cattily, taking in Fran's voluptuous figure.

"Well, you two have a nice evening," Tate was saying, his tone smooth and unaffected.

Marnie jerked her head up, knowing Tate meant for her and Lance to have anything but a nice evening.

"Yeah," Lance said, sarcastically voicing her thought.

In that beat of hesitation that followed, Marnie's eyes locked with Tate's. Something passed between them that had nothing to do with Lance. Color stole slowly up Marnie's face as his gaze suddenly seemed centered on the taut imprint of her breasts, their fullness barely concealed behind the coral knit sweater.

Then, moving his gaze, Tate smiled a cold little smile that wasn't a smile at all. "Ms. Lee."

The instant Tate and Fran walked off, the waitress arrived with Lance and Marnie's food. Once their glasses were refilled, they tried to pretend nothing was wrong. They laughed over small incidents that had taken place at the plant and argued amiably about nothing that mattered.

Marnie made an effort to savor every bite she took,

but she could not. The pizza tasted like cardboard. Finally, she gave up and eased the plate aside.

Lance, however, didn't seem to have the same problem. He devoured his lasagna with relish.

"You're not hungry?" Lance asked, pushing his empty plate away.

Marnie casually flicked a hair away from her face. "Guess not."

"Do you mind if I finish it?"

She smiled and shook her head. "Help yourself."

"Well, the way I see it, it's a shame to waste good food."

Marnie, trying her best to forget that Tate was sitting across the room from her and that she was under his baleful eye, focused her attention on Lance. Still, she couldn't rid herself of Tate's annoying presence. She was aware of him with every heightened nerve in her body.

"Mmm, now that's pizza," Lance said at last, rubbing his stomach. "You don't know what you missed."

"Oh yes, I do." Marnie's voice was low. "I just wasn't as hungry as I first thought."

Lance leaned forward. "Look, don't let my dad get to you. Like I said, his bark is much worse than his bite."

Marnie didn't believe that for a second. Nevertheless, she didn't say anything.

The silence lengthened while they sipped their wine.

Then lowering his glass, Lance blurted, "Marry me, Marnie. Tomorrow."

Marnie stared at him in stunned disbelief.

"We could make it work," Lance went on. "I love you enough for both of us."

"Oh, Lance, you promised you wouldn't bring that up."

Lance shrugged. "Okay, so I broke my promise, but dammit, I want you so much."

"That's because you haven't had me," she countered with blunt honesty.

He flushed. "It's not from lack of trying, that's for damned sure."

Determined to make her case once and for all that marriage between them was impossible, Marnie said, "Your father came to the office the other day."

Instantly Lance tensed. "Where was I?"

"At the attorney's."

"Why didn't you tell me?"

"Because he didn't come to see you. He came to see me."

His jaw dropped open. "You. But why?"

"He told me to leave you alone."

"You're not serious."

"Of course, I'm serious," Marnie snapped.

He flushed again. "Sorry."

"In fact, he tried to buy me off."

"Why...that—"

Marnie leaned forward again and clasped his hand, interrupting him. "It was never my intention to cause trouble. Obviously that's exactly what he thinks I'm doing." She paused and withdrew her hand. "Still, I'm curious if it's just me he doesn't like or if it's any woman who gets close to you."

"Well, I have gotten myself in a couple of jams," Lance admitted grudgingly, "but I've never asked anyone to marry me."

A smile eased the tension around Marnie's lips. "And don't think I'm not honored that you asked me, because I am. But I don't love you, Lance, and I don't think you love me. And I don't think we should see each other outside the office any more.'' She paused again and drew in a shuddering breath. ''I can't afford to lose my job.''

''Did my father threaten you? Is that what this is all about?''

Marnie shifted uneasily, unable to meet his direct gaze. ''Let's just say we didn't part on the best of terms and leave it at that.''

''Well, I hope you told him where to get off, because if you didn't I intend to.''

''No, Lance,'' Marnie said emphatically. ''Enough is enough. He thinks what he's doing is right, and who am I to argue? After all, look what a good job you're doing on this project.'' Dropping her gaze, she stared at him from under her lashes. ''Let it go, Lance. Just let it go.''

Lance didn't look at all convinced. ''All right, Marnie. You win for now. But I'm not giving up. You can mark that down, and this, as well—I can handle my father because he needs me, needs me to do the job he no longer wants to do. So you see, you don't have a thing to worry about.''

No, you're wrong, she cried silently. *Dead wrong. No one handles Tate O'Brien.*

Later, when she and Lance got up to leave the restaurant, Marnie vowed she wouldn't look at Tate. She looked anyway. But he was too busy laughing at something Fran was saying to notice her scrutiny.

With cheeks ablaze, Marnie followed Lance outside onto the deserted street corner, then toward his car that was parked on a side street. Preoccupied, they walked in silence.

The night was gorgeous, Marnie thought. The sky was thickly populated with stars. After a moment of stargazing, Marnie paused, took a deep breath and wished she could stop thinking about Tate.

So caught up was she in nursing her inner turmoil that she failed to notice the car easing to the curb until it was too late.

The vehicle's door flew open, and a masked man jumped out with the quickness of lightning. Before either she or Lance could turn around, the man lunged for Lance and began dragging him toward the car.

Marnie, paralyzed with fear and shock, couldn't move, couldn't speak. Then recovering with an alacrity born of desperation, she screamed a blood-curdling scream. "Lance! Oh, my God, Lance!"

Lance fought. "Run, Marnie, run!" he cried weakly before his assailant slapped a cloth against his face.

"Let him go!" Marnie cried, tearing after them.

"Shut up, lady," the man ground out as he pushed Lance, who was now deadweight, into the front seat.

"Stop it!" Marnie shouted.

The man paid her no heed.

Physically she knew she was no match for the man's brute strength, but that didn't stop her. Suddenly and unexpectedly, she attacked him from behind, dragging her nails across his bare, tender scalp.

He swore loudly, but then recovered his equilibrium and tried to still her hands.

"Dammit, lady!"

Though her breath was lodged in her throat and hot tears almost blinded her, she refused to let go of the man. She balled her fingers into a fist and slammed them against the man's head. Once. Twice. Three times.

"You bastard, let—"

She got no further. The man whipped around and whacked the side of her head. For a split second the blow stifled Marnie's effort. But then she shook her head and charged him again, grabbing his mask. On contact, it partially split. For a heart-stopping moment, Marnie was eye-to-eye with the man.

Then sobbing, she staggered backward.

"Stop her, you idiot," the man behind the wheel shouted. "Get her, too."

With both hands now free, Lance's assailant reached for Marnie grabbing her arms with fingers that felt like steel traps.

Her breath hurt in her lungs. Her face throbbed where she'd been hit. Her arms ached from hitting him. Still, she fought like a wild, wounded animal.

She wouldn't let them take Lance. She wouldn't let them take *her*. But time was against her. She begged her body not to let her down.

The man's savage strength gave him the upper hand. Marnie felt hers slowly drain from her body. She knew it would be only a matter of seconds before she would be forced inside the car along with Lance.

Voices. Had she heard voices? Yes. And feet, feet pounding the cement. Her heart leaped.

"Help me," she sobbed, trying desperately to break his hold on her.

"Let her go!" the man's cohort yelled. "We gotta get outta here!"

Those words barely registered on Marnie's numbed mind, but what did register was the hard shove she received from behind.

"Oh, God," she whimpered, grappling to maintain her balance.

"Marnie! Marnie!"

She looked up in silent agony. *Tate!* she mouthed, just as she made contact with the pavement and felt its roughness rip the skin from her knees.

Five

"Oh, Tate," Marnie sobbed, clinging to him as he lifted her, torn and bleeding, to her feet. "Lance...you've got to help. He—" She broke off, her breath coming in short, gutsy spurts.

"Marnie, where's Lance?" Tate's voice, close to her ear, had a scraping, tearing edge to it. "Was he in the car that drove off?"

Marnie stood and stared at him as if in a stupor, waiting for her mind to function. Nothing came, nothing but horror. She was shaking. She had to make herself believe this was real. She had to control the shock reeling through her.

Tate's grip on her shoulder tightened. "Lance," he shouted. Then, his features contorting, he shouted again, "Where's Lance?"

It was the panic in his voice that eventually penetrated

Marnie's numbed senses. She finally managed to groan, "They—they took Lance."

"Bastards!"

Marnie shook her head miserably. "I—I tried to help him, only I couldn't." Her voice once again faded into a pale, childlike wail. "They—they tried to take me, too."

"Who are they?" His tone was frantic now, and he was all but shaking her.

"Two men. They—they took him and drove off."

She heard his horrified gasp. Then he ran his hands up and down her arms. "Are you all right?"

"I'm…fine," she lied, trying not to think about the searing pain in her legs.

He pushed her to arm's length. "No, you're not," he said, looking down. Blood had saturated her panty hose at the knees and was dripping down her legs.

With a muttered curse, Tate led her toward the door of the restaurant. Ashen and shaking, Marnie clung to his hand while mass confusion reigned.

The Back Porch had emptied. Its patrons were outside, wide-eyed and whispering. Passersby had stopped, as well, and were gawking. A siren screamed in the breezy night air.

Once inside the restaurant, Tate eased Marnie down onto a padded bench. Grim faced, he looked up into the hovering manager's face.

"Did someone call the police?"

"Yes, sir," the man answered. "We called the paramedics, too."

"Thanks," Tate muttered, then turned his attention back to Marnie, who was once again staring at him through glazed eyes.

Without removing his gaze from her, Tate dug into his

back pocket and pulled out a handkerchief. Then he knelt and dabbed very gently at the blood oozing from a wound.

"Oh, please, don't," Marnie whispered, feeling as if she might faint at any moment, the pain was so severe.

Tate immediately stopped. "Sorry."

"Mr. O'Brien, the police are here," the manager said from his position by the door.

"About damn time."

Tate had no more than gotten the words out of his mouth when two uniformed men walked through the door and introduced themselves as Officers Taylor and Barnhardt.

"My son has been kidnapped," Tate said without mincing words. "Ms. Lee was a witness to it."

Taylor, the older and the shorter of the two, turned to Marnie. "Please tell us what happened."

In a halting voice, Marnie told them exactly what she'd told Tate, and more. Through it all, Tate stood quietly by her side, his face looking as if it were carved out of stone. But his eyes were anything but stonelike. They were narrowed slits filled with outrage.

When she finished speaking, she peered up at him. "I—I'm so sorry. If only I'd…"

A thick, knotty artery stood out in his neck. "Don't blame yourself."

But for some crazy reason Marnie did blame herself. She knew how desperate, how helpless Tate must be feeling, and her heart went out to him.

Officer Barnhardt cleared his throat, then spoke soothingly. "Mr. O'Brien is there anything you can add to what Ms. Lee has told us?"

"Not much, I'm afraid." Frustrated, Tate ran a hand over his forehead.

"Where were you when the kidnapping took place?"

"I was in the restaurant, at the back of the veranda. By the time I heard the commotion and got down to the street, it was after the fact. I saw only the man's back as he jumped into the getaway car."

Tate paused and focused his attention on Marnie. "Look, can we dispense with the questioning for now and get Ms. Lee some medical attention?"

"Of course," Barnhardt said hurriedly. "We'll radio ahead and have someone meet you at Ben Taub."

The next hour passed in a blur for Marnie. She didn't know how she got to the emergency room, nor did she care. She just knew that Tate never left her side, and for that she was grateful.

It was only after a kind-faced doctor entered the small, sterile cubbyhole that reeked of antiseptic and applied medicine to her wounds, that she rallied.

"Sorry, Ms. Lee," Dr. Evans said when Marnie bit down on her lower lip to keep from crying out. "But these are nasty abrasions and have to be tended to."

Marnie perched on the edge of the cotlike bed and closed her eyes just as the room began to spin.

"Has she fainted, doctor?" Tate asked, his tone anxious.

"I'm...sick to my stomach, that's all," Marnie whispered.

Before Tate could respond, the door swung open and two sober-faced men walked in. The one who flashed the badge and introduced himself as FBI agent Stan Courtney was tall and thin with an abundance of rust-red hair flaring around his clean-shaven face. His partner, Agent Mike James, was short and round, with blond hair that was not long enough to be stylish, but long enough to look as though he needed a haircut.

They could have passed for Mutt and Jeff, Marnie thought, battling an overwhelming desire to laugh, to dissolve into hysteria.

Stan Courtney was the first to speak. "I know how difficult this is for you," he said, focusing his gaze on Marnie, "but I have to ask you to repeat what happened."

"All right." The words were barely audible. Once again tears flooded her dark eyes.

"Make it short, Officer," Dr. Evans put in. "She's been through enough for one night."

His lips set in a thin, taut line, Tate stepped closer, as if to protect her, but he didn't say anything. Marnie flashed him a grateful look, then retold her story.

James folded his arms across his chest. "So you got a look at one of the men."

Marnie nodded.

"Think you could ID him?"

"It—it was dark. I'm not sure." At the moment she wasn't sure about much of anything, except that this was turning into a nightmare without an end. She felt the tears well up and winked in rapid succession to keep them back.

Courtney wrote furiously, then turned to Tate. "Mr. O'Brien, we need to know everything there is to know about your son. Do you have any idea who would want to harm him and why? Is there anyone in his business or his household whom you might have reason to suspect?"

"The household is out. My son lives alone." Tate's voice was tight and controlled. "But the possibility of his kidnapping being job-related is very real."

"Oh?" Mike James chimed in. "What makes you say that?"

Tate explained in detail the project Marnie and Lance were working on.

James swung his eyes to Marnie. "Can you add anything to this?"

Marnie swayed.

"Enough, gentlemen," Tate said in a curt tone, stepping forward, his eyes fixed on Marnie's drained, waxen face.

Both agents looked as if they wanted to argue, but then they acquiesced.

"All right, Mr. O'Brien," Courtney said on a sigh, "take Ms. Lee home. But both of you be downtown in the morning. We'll cover everything from our end—wiretaps, et cetera. Within the next twenty-four hours you'll more than likely hear from the kidnappers."

"No problem. We'll be there."

During the next few minutes silence wrapped itself around the room while Marnie accepted two pain pills and a cup of water from the doctor. Then, with the help of Tate and Dr. Evans, she stood and began a slow trek toward the door.

"Easy does it," Tate murmured, placing his hand on the door knob.

"Ms. Lee."

All three stopped and turned around.

"Do you have somewhere you can stay the rest of the night?" Barnhardt asked.

"Are you saying that she shouldn't stay alone?" Tate demanded bluntly.

"That's exactly what I'm saying. They know or at least think she can identify them, so…" He let his voice play out, but the meaning was clear.

If possible, Marnie turned paler. "I…have a friend who can stay with me."

"Good." Courtney almost smiled. "And for precaution, we'll have an officer posted at your home."

Tate waved an impatient hand. "That won't be necessary."

"Why is that?"

"Ms. Lee will be staying at my ranch."

Marnie stared up at him and gasped.

"No."

"This is not up for discussion, Marnie."

"For the second and last time, I will not pack a bag and go to your ranch."

They were in the living room of her condo. Marnie rested against the bar while Tate stood in the middle of the room, his posture rigid. She didn't want, didn't *need* this confrontation. Weariness, mixed with the pain from her fall, had left her with a dull throb behind her eyes. All she wanted was to crawl into bed.

During the fifteen-minute drive to her house from the hospital, they had scarcely spoken a word to each other. Even so, she'd been aware that Tate's thoughts were as tormented as her own. Would they ever see Lance alive again?

His blue eyes seemed to drill into her. "Dammit, I'm in no mood to argue with you."

"Nor I with you," Marnie said, tears perilously close.

Her weakness and inability to function were not lost on Tate. He made an aggravated groan and stepped forward, only to suddenly stop, as if finding some last minute control.

"Either you call your friend and she comes over or you go with me." Without waiting for a reply, he strode to the phone, lifted the receiver and held it out. "What's it going to be?'' Something hard had crept into his eyes, something Marnie dared not ignore.

Trembling violently, she took the receiver and punched out Kate's number. When she heard the answering machine click on, her heart sank. Kate was on a flight.

"She's not home," Marnie whispered, suddenly feeling so exhausted she thought she might die.

"Come on, I'll help you pack."

Her face crumpled. "Please...don't..." She turned away, again struggling to keep the tears at bay. She knew she was behaving terribly and hated herself for it.

As if he sensed she was close to the edge, Tate stood where he was for a moment, his expression brooding and uncertain. "All right, Marnie, you win. I'll stay here."

She stared at him as tremor after tremor rocked her body. He looked composed, so together, so unrelenting, as if he was afraid to show that he was as frightened about Lance as she was.

He should be the one crying, not her. She knew he was hurting. Suddenly she longed to throw her arms around him and tell him that everything was going to be all right, but she couldn't because she was afraid nothing was ever going to be all right again.

His gaze left hers and he scanned the room. "The couch'll do just fine."

"I have a guest bedroom." Marnie spoke barely above a whisper.

Their eyes met again and held.

"I'll be fine here," he said tightly.

Forcing her gaze off him, Marnie made her way to the door, where she paused and turned around. "Do...you think they will..." Her voice broke on a sob.

A flicker of pain crossed his face. "I don't know. We'll just have to wait and see, won't we?"

*   *   *

Unlike Marnie, Tate made no effort to sleep. There was too much to do. Despite the hour, he called his assistant the minute Marnie left and told him what had happened. He then asked him not only to see about Lance's car that was still parked outside the restaurant, but to call and make sure Fran had gotten home. At some point amidst the confusion, he had told Fran to get a cab.

Once he hung up from talking to Neal, he sat on the couch and placed his head in his hands. Later he had no idea how long he had stayed in that position, but he didn't care. It was only after he felt the wetness in his palms that he got up and walked to the window.

Staring out into the inky blackness, he gave in to the multitude of emotions ripping through him. He cursed. He ranted. He raved. He agonized. But most of all, he prayed.

Nothing seemed to help. A terrible sense of loss possessed him.

Lance. His son. He still couldn't believe Lance had been kidnapped, even though he'd lived with this fear since he had made his first million.

Tate closed his eyes and drew on a long breath. Suddenly a memory of he and Lance fishing on the side of a creek bank came to mind. Lance had been four years old.

''Looky, Dad, what I catched,'' he'd said, holding up a fish that hadn't been much bigger than his hand.

''That's great, son,'' Tate remembered saying with a wide grin, ruffling Lance's hair. ''You're doing great.''

Tate's heart twisted in pain as guilt settled over him.

And to think he still had to tell his mother. That thought didn't bear thinking about either. She adored her grandson as much as she adored Tate.

Damn those bastards to hell! He could feel hate pour

out of his body like dirty sweat. When, not if, those slimeballs were apprehended, he'd make sure they paid. No liberal judge was going to let them off on a technicality or give them a slap on the wrist.

Meanwhile, if they so much as tried to hurt Marnie again, he'd... *Whoa, O'Brien....*

But when he'd lifted her, torn and bleeding off the pavement, he'd felt fear. He'd felt anger. But most of all, he'd felt a tightness in the back of his throat.

The feeling was crazy, he knew, and one he didn't understand or want.

Especially now.

Marnie rolled over on her side. "Ouch!" she yelped under her breath, feeling as though every bone, every muscle in her body had been pummelled with a baseball bat.

It could be worse, she reminded herself. She could have been held captive in some airless closet. Or she could be dead. That sobering thought brought her eyes open, along with all the horrifying events of the previous evening. Tate. Was he still occupying her couch?

After she'd left him standing in the middle of her living room, she'd gone to her room, discarded her bloody shirt along with her other clothing, stepped in the shower, then crawled into bed, all with zombielike coordination. It was as if she'd put her brain on autopilot and merely done what had been required of her.

When she'd closed her eyes, however, she hadn't experienced that blessed relief of deep sleep. Instead, her mind had jumped into gear.

But it hadn't been Lance's stricken face that had filled her mind. It had been Tate's. And with it had come questions she couldn't answer. Why had he refused to leave

her? Why hadn't he said to hell with her hardheadedness
and walked out?

Now, in the clarity of daylight, the answers to those
questions still eluded her.

She had always prided herself on her ability to see
what made a person tick. But in a matter of days, Tate
had succeeded in undermining that ability. And she knew
to try to understand him would be next to impossible.

Groaning, she turned toward the clock on the bedside
table and saw that it was not quite seven. With all Tate
had to take care of, he had probably left an hour ago.

Eying her robe on the end of the bed, she eased herself
up and reached for it. Until she had that first cup of coffee, she couldn't bear to think about what lay ahead of
her. After a short stint in the bathroom, she padded bare-
foot into the living area, only to suddenly stop midstride.

Tate hadn't left. He was stretched out on the couch.
She crept closer. From where she stood, she couldn't see
anything but the back of his head and an arm dangling
off the side.

Blinking against the morning sunlight, Marnie inched
still closer. It was only after she reached the end of the
sofa and had him in full view that she froze. Not only
was he sound asleep, but he was naked—at least from
the waist up.

Her cheeks on fire, Marnie jerked her eyes up to his
face. But she didn't fare much better there. A day's
growth of beard stained his tanned cheeks, making them
darker, hollow. Lines surrounded his mouth and eyes,
lines that she hadn't noticed before. Yet he looked relaxed. And defenseless. How wrong—on both counts.

There was nothing relaxed or defenseless about Tate
O'Brien. He'd written the book on energy, grit and per-
severance.

Suddenly he breathed deeply, causing his stomach muscles to ripple. Dazed, she continued to stare without conscience.

His chest, wide and covered with salt-and-pepper, wiry hair, tapered perfectly into a flat, hard stomach comprised of nothing but muscle. Her nerves taut, a breathless feeling in her chest, she stared lower, lingering on his navel, made visible by his low-riding jeans.

She wondered what the rest of him looked like and her heart pounded. Her nipples tightened, and she worried briefly that they would protrude through her gown and robe. Her limbs felt suddenly boneless.

He was attractive, dangerously attractive. A woman would be a fool to get mixed up with him. Still, like a flower drawn to the sun, she was drawn to him. Graphic thoughts of what it would be like to have his lips on hers without hurtful pressure made her insides quiver with suppressed longing.

Tate stirred again. Then, unexpectedly, as if he knew he was being watched, his eyes popped open.

Stunned black eyes locked with her shocked blue ones. The moment was electric as each forgot for a brief time the circumstances that brought them together.

Tate's eyes searched and held her. For the longest moment he didn't seem able to turn away. Rich color flooded Marnie's cheeks at the fervor in his gaze. Her lips parted on a panicked breath.

A heartbeat passed, followed by another. Then, as if reality suddenly struck him like a blow, Tate's expression hardened. "Sorry," he muttered roughly, and reached for his shirt.

An ache ripped at her insides. *For looking at me with something other than hate?* she demanded silently. Aloud she said, "Why?"

He threw her another look. "For not being up and dressed."

She strove to make her voice as light as his. "That's all right. Under…the circumstances, you needed the sleep."

"No," he said emphatically, "under the circumstances, I *didn't* need to sleep."

"Tate…I—"

His eyes were on her lips. "Save it, Marnie."

A hot flush climbed her cheeks. "I—"

He cut her off again. "While I'm at my mother's telling her about…Lance, you get dressed. I'll be back shortly to take you downtown."

"I can drive myself."

He cursed roundly. "Don't argue with me—at least not this morning. Look," he spoke now with extreme patience, as if he were talking to a child, "I know you're sore all over, so just make it easy on yourself and let me drive you. I have to be there, anyway. I've thought of something that might help them find Lance."

Her lips parted as she met his level gaze. "All right, I'll be ready."

He looked at her a second longer than necessary, then turned and walked out the door.

After locking it behind him, Marnie leaned against it, feeling the sting of tears. Lance. Her every thought should have been on him instead of on Tate and how he made her feel.

Hopefully God would forgive her, because she couldn't forgive herself.

Marnie had dreaded the second confrontation with the FBI. But since she'd wanted so desperately to be instrumental in helping find Lance, she was doing her best to cooperate. But it wasn't proving to be easy.

As promised, Tate had returned to pick her up. Determined to give her frantic mind and her sagging spirits a lift, she had dressed with care in gold linen pants, off-white shell and matching jacket.

Still, nothing short of a miracle could erase the dark circles under her eyes or reshape the downward pull of her lips. Yesterday had changed her. But then, one didn't fight off a kidnapper and not feel its effects. Her life would never be the same; *she* would never be the same.

Nor would Tate. Although he'd appeared remarkably fresh in slacks and a striped sports shirt, there had been no denying the gaunt, drawn look on his face.

They had been just a few blocks away from the FBI headquarters before Marnie broke the silence. "I guess it would be safe to assume there has been no word from the kidnappers."

He kept his eyes on the road. "No, not yet," he said tightly, "though all the phone lines in the house are being monitored."

"How's your mother?"

He faced her briefly. "Not good. The doctor had to give her a sedative."

"She hadn't heard before you got there, had she?" Marnie's voice quavered slightly; she felt another twinge of guilt because he hadn't gone home last night.

"No, thank God. So now you don't have to feel guilty any longer."

"Who said I'm feeling guilty?" she said hotly.

"Aren't you?"

A wave of color swept her cheeks. "No one forced you to stay with me, you know."

"No, that's right, they didn't." His voice was an explosive growl.

"Then why did you? Stay, I mean?" The words sounded before she could think to keep quiet.

He faced her again. His blue eyes appeared hollow, as if there were nothing inside him. "I wish to hell I knew."

That had stung, but she hadn't said anything, opting to hold onto that silence even after they had entered FBI headquarters and she'd looked around. The offices were typical. Crowded. Bustling with activity. Sterile, uncomfortable furniture. Cabinets and desks littered with files.

Now, as she stood behind the computer screen and listened to the artist's instructions, Marnie inhaled deeply and tried to clear her mind of everything, everything except the kidnapper's face. But it was no use; his features remained hazy and unclear.

"It's all right, Ms. Lee," Stan Courtney said. "Just take your time."

Marnie frowned. "I was positive I could remember what he looked like, and now…" Her voice faded as she turned anxiously toward Tate, who was standing slightly behind her.

Tate's eyebrows were also drawn together in a heavy frown that lightened only marginally when he spoke. "Maybe you're trying too hard. Or maybe the doctor's prediction came true."

"And what is that, Mr. O'Brien?" Mike James asked, stubbing out his cigarette in the ashtray he was holding in his hand.

"She is unable to recall due to the trauma she suffered."

Both James and Courtney turned their scrutiny on Marnie.

"Do you feel like that's what's happening, Ms. Lee?" Courtney asked.

Marnie dragged in a shuddering breath. "I don't know. But I...suppose it could be true." Then turning to Tate, she added, "I'm...sorry."

"Yeah, me too."

Silence fell over the small group.

Courtney coughed. "Well, we'll just have to keep the faith that you'll remember."

In spite of her efforts to appear composed, Marnie's lower lip trembled. "I just pray it won't be too late," she finally said, sick at heart. Not only had she let Lance down, but she had let Tate down, as well.

"It won't," Agent James said with far more confidence than the situation warranted. Nevertheless, Marnie was grateful and gave him a small smile.

After coughing again, James switched his attention to Tate. "If it was the plastic explosive they wanted, why not simply steal the plans?"

"Who knows what these crazy terrorists do or why they do it?" Tate said grimly. "But my guess is that the plans are no good without someone to interpret them."

"And your son can do that?"

"No."

James's eyes narrowed. "Then why the hell did they take him?"

"I'm assuming they didn't know that." Tate's tone was crisp but patient.

James blew his breath out and raked a hand through his hair. "Ah, so you think that if Lance keeps them thinking he can reconstruct the design, his chances of staying alive are good?"

"That's what I'm hoping for, unless..." Tate paused,

and this time it was he who plowed his fingers through his hair.

Marnie, watching him, had to again fight the urge to run to him, fling her arms around his neck and comfort him.

"Unless what, Mr. O'Brien?" James pressed, his eyes alert.

"Unless Lance was kidnapped for some other reason."

James's tone of voice did not alter. "And what might that reason be?"

"Lance was almost kidnapped once when he was five years old," Tate said. "It was an extortion attempt, and though the attempt was foiled, I've lived in dread of that happening again."

"I see," Courtney said, entering the conversation and gnawing at the side of his jaw. "Well either way, without Ms. Lee's description, we don't have a lot to go on."

All eyes swung to Marnie.

Her chin jutted. "I'll remember," she said. "I have no choice."

"In the meantime," Courtney said, looking at both Marnie and Tate, "I want to know all there is to know, the latest firings in the company, disgruntled employees, rivalries, forgotten enemies and grudge-bearing friends."

Three hours later they walked out of FBI headquarters.

"I'll come in with you."

Tate had just killed the engine of his Porsche and sat facing Marnie. They were parked in front of her condo.

She shook her head and reached for the door handle. Suddenly the confines of the interior were too close. *Tate* was too close. She could see the smooth plane of his jaw, see the way the hairs curled thickly on the back of his hands, smell his cologne.

"Thanks, but that's not necessary," she said unevenly. "You heard Agent Courtney. He said my place would be crawling with plainclothesmen."

"*Would.* That's just the point."

"All right," Marnie said, too tired to argue.

His eyes widened, and he almost smiled.

"Surprised, huh?"

This time he smiled for real. "That you didn't argue? Very."

The change the smile made was startling. Marnie almost gasped aloud. Instead, she averted her gaze and quickly got out of the car.

Her thoughts were elsewhere as she preceded him inside, so when she looked up it hit her suddenly.

"Oh, no!" she cried, freezing in her tracks.

"What the h—" Tate got no further.

The room was a complete wreck. The wicker furniture was slashed to ribbons, the cushions ripped, their stuffing strewn around the room like snowdrifts. There was black paint splashed everywhere. Her cassette tapes and records had been taken out of their sleeves and either bent, broken or scored with something like a fork.

Her books were off the shelves and looked as if they had been chopped with an ax and left to bleed.

"This settles it," Tate muttered savagely from behind her. "You're coming to the ranch with me."

Six

If Marnie had still harbored any illusions that she might not be in danger, she couldn't doubt her situation any longer as she stood in the guest bedroom at Tate's ranch.

A light springtime rain was falling softly, coating the leaves outside the window with a thick, shiny sheen. The weather matched her mood, she thought, swallowing the lump in her throat, the lump that had been there since earlier today when she had walked into her condo and found it trashed.

Feeling suddenly weak again, Marnie sank into the nearest chair and closed her eyes, hoping to block out the vivid pictures of the devastation that had been her home. Her efforts were in vain. The sight of her furniture slashed, her things strewn, mangled and broken, would haunt her forever.

Tears stung her eyes, forcing her to open them again. She was scared, scared that the men who had taken Lance wouldn't stop until they had her in their clutches, as well. But what frightened her as much, if not more, was that she was now under Tate's roof, under his watchful eye.

What was there about this enigma of a man that had her so out of sorts? She had enough problems without adding a fervent fascination with a man who felt nothing but animosity toward her. Physical attraction—was that at the root of the fascination? More to the point, was it sex? The *lack* of it?

Angry, she got up and walked to the window. She'd admit there were times when she was lonely, yearned for someone to cuddle against at night, to talk over the events of her day, to share her problems with. But those feelings were fleeting and far between.

Besides, she'd been hooked once, shortly before her father was diagnosed, on an older man, an attorney who turned out to be married with two children. She'd been devastated, but because of Silas she'd had to pull herself up by the bootstraps and tend to him.

In the following years she had come to terms with both her past affair and her father's illness and was content with her life. Until now. Until Tate O'Brien had entered it. And to think she'd let him lead her to his house like a docile, unsuspecting lamb to the slaughter. But what choice had she had?

When Tate had blurted that order, she had been so overwrought she hadn't been able to think clearly, much less argue.

After one more incredulous look around the condo, Tate had spoken again, his voice as cold and sharp as a razor. "Come on, let's get the hell outta here."

Once they had turned their backs on the devastation and hate, they had walked outside and stopped. Marnie had sat on the top step of the porch, while Tate stood beside her.

They had remained there for a long time, perfectly still and perfectly quiet. Then Tate, with a muttered curse, had gone next door to use the telephone.

Courtney and James hadn't let them go back inside the condo until the forensic team was through with its investigation. Marnie had waited in the back seat of the agents' unmarked car while a tight-lipped Tate had paced up and down the sidewalk, furious because they had refused to let him inside the building.

"It's mostly the living room," Courtney had said a short time later, lighting a cigarette and taking a deep puff. "Needless to say, Ms. Lee, you won't be able to stay at home."

"She's staying at my place," Tate said, looking at Marnie.

"That's a good idea," Courtney replied, his eyes shifting between the two of them.

"Why would someone want to do something like that?" Marnie asked in a faraway voice.

"That's a damn good question," Tate put in harshly.

Courtney shrugged, then flipped his unsmoked cigarette to the ground and crushed it with his shoe. "I figured they broke in to either take Ms. Lee or to scare the hell out of her. Or both. And when she wasn't home, they vented their frustrations."

Tate's face looked gray. "Or maybe it was a warning of things to come?"

"Could be," Courtney said.

"Oh, God," Marnie whispered, her gaze on Tate. "Is—is this ever going to end?"

For a moment Tate's gaze softened, as if the threadbare look on her face had gotten to him. Then his features hardened and he said, "Possibly when you remember what the piece of slime looked like."

All the remaining color drained from Marnie's face, and she flinched, feeling as if Tate had punched her in the stomach. Then she rallied, boiling fury consuming her. "Don't you think I'm trying?" she lashed out.

A deep silence fell.

Once again Courtney's eyes jockeyed between Tate and Marnie, looking as if he wanted to say something to relieve the tension, but didn't know how.

But in the end it was Courtney who broke the silence. "Look, no one's to blame here," he said, taking another cigarette out of his pocket and lighting it. Then focusing his gaze on Tate exclusively, he added, "Both your office phones and your home phones are tapped. You should be hearing something soon. Based on that, we'll make our move accordingly."

"Don't patronize me, Courtney." Tate's bitterness was tangible. "We both know the chances of my son getting out of this alive are not—"

Staring at him, Marnie started to choke.

Tate returned her stare for an aching moment, then muttered another expletive and looked away.

Before anyone had a chance to speak again, the front door opened. Mike James stood on the step. "All through in here, Stan."

Tate turned to Marnie. "Come on, let's get your things and go."

"And in the meantime," Courtney said, sounding relieved, "if it's all right with you, Ms. Lee, I'll call a firm I know who can come around and clean up the mess— they specialize in vandalized houses. I suppose your insurance will cover everything."

"I...hope so," Marnie said, getting out of the car and forcing herself to walk with Tate up the sidewalk.

Once they reentered the house, Marnie moved like a robot through the debris to her room, where she packed a bag as quickly as her unsteady hands would allow.

The trip to the ranch was made in virtual silence as she leaned her head back, pretending to rest. She didn't have anything to say to Tate, anyway, especially after his brutal comment pertaining to her inability to identify the kidnapper.

Annie met them at the door with red-rimmed eyes and a lower lip that wouldn't stop trembling.

"Oh, Tate," she wailed, "what are we going to do?"

"Everything that's possible is being done, Annie," Tate said gently, giving her outstretched hands a squeeze.

"I just can't believe it," she wailed again, resting her eyes briefly on Marnie. "I just can't believe it. My precious Lance—"

"Annie," Tate interrupted, "Ms. Lee's going to be our guest for a while. Her house was broken into and vandalized."

Annie's hand flew to her mouth. "Oh, no. You poor dear. Well, don't you fret. No one will bother you here. I'll see to that."

Tate patted her on the shoulder. "Good girl. I knew I could count on you."

Marnie dug deep for a smile. "Thanks, Annie."

The housekeeper followed them to the guest bedroom and pulled back the shutter while Tate set her bags on the chest at the foot of the bed.

"Would you care for something refreshing to drink?" Annie asked, her hand on the doorknob.

"Not right now, Annie. I just want to freshen up and rest for a while."

"Well, if you need anything don't hesitate to ask."

An awkward silence followed Annie's exit. Marnie refused to meet Tate's eyes.

"Marnie."

Startled by the unexpected use of her name, she looked up but still refused to meet his gaze.

"You'll be all right, won't you?" he asked, his voice sounding raw, as if the words were ripped from his throat.

"Do you really care?" she retorted.

For a moment they simply looked at each other, the air sizzling between them. Marnie felt a jumble of emotions too complex to analyze.

Finally Tate muttered, "I'm going to the office. I'll be back later."

That conversation had taken place over thirty minutes ago, and she still hadn't freshened up or rested. Swallowing a sigh, she stood and walked to the window and looked outside, determined to put aside thoughts of Tate and the tragic circumstances that had forced them together.

Directly in her line of vision was a well-manicured lawn that extended as far as the eye could see, a lawn littered with trees of all sizes and shapes—oaks, sweet gums and Chinese tallows.

Farther to her left was a large barn with a concrete addition and another long building. A sturdy post fence that eventually turned into barbed wire disappeared into the huge pasture dotted with Tate's prized quarter horses.

The tranquil beauty, while not awesome, was certainly heart-stopping. She watched the horses graze for a moment longer, then turned wearily away. If she didn't sit down soon, she knew she'd fall down. She couldn't remember ever being this exhausted.

She eased down onto the side of the bed and released a long, pent-up sigh.

The decor of the room, like the rest of the house, was luxurious but warm. The walls were painted an off white, and the floor was covered with thickly piled peach carpet. A queen-size bed dominated one end of the room and was topped with a peach-flowered comforter. The single chest and night stands were walnut.

Her condo was nice, but it couldn't compare with this luxury, which only emphasized the difference in her and Tate's stations in life.

She sighed again and leaned back on the bed, only to suddenly sit back up.

"Ms. Lee."

"What is it, Annie?"

"I'm sorry to disturb you, but there's someone here to see you. A Ms. McCall."

Kate!

Smiling, Marnie shuffled to the door and gladly opened it. "Where is she?"

"In the den."

"Thanks," Marnie said warmly, and made her way very gingerly down the hall.

When she reached the large room, Kate was perched on the edge of a chair, her blue eyes wide and uncertain.

"Kate McCall, you're the last person I expected to see," Marnie said, meeting her friend halfway and hugging her tightly.

After a moment Kate stepped back and asked, "Why? The minute I turned on my machine and got your message, I had to see for myself that you were all right."

Marnie suddenly felt like crying. "Well, as you can see, I'm still in one piece, though barely. But I couldn't leave my condo without letting both you and the nursing home know where I was.''

''Are you sure you didn't dream this nightmare?''

Marnie pointed to her slacks-covered knees. ''You want me to show you the damage?''

Kate shuddered. ''I get the picture. Anyway, your face says it all. If I cut your throat, I doubt you'd bleed a drop.''

''Probably wouldn't.''

''Let's sit down,'' Kate said. ''There's so much I don't know.''

As best she could, Marnie told her friend everything that had happened after she and Lance had walked out of the restaurant.

When Marnie finished, Kate's face was as pale as Marnie's. ''God, what if Lance—''

''Please, don't say it,'' Marnie cried. ''Don't even think it.''

''What does his father think?''

Marnie toyed with a strand of hair. ''We haven't discussed it. It's…something neither one of us has been able to talk about.''

''There's no word from the kidnappers yet, I take it?''

''Zilch,'' Marnie said flatly.

Kate smacked the palm of her hand. ''Of all the blessed times to get called out.''

''Don't blame yourself. Tate…spent the night on my couch.''

Kate raised her eyebrows. ''Tate? You mean Lance's old man stayed with you?''

Marnie flushed. ''If you could see him, you wouldn't exactly call him old.''

Kate's eyebrows rose even higher.

''Don't say what you're thinking,'' Marnie snapped.

"You couldn't be more wrong. Tate O'Brien wouldn't throw water on me if I were on fire."

"Then why are you here?"

"Believe me, it's not by choice. The FBI said I couldn't stay at my condo."

Kate smiled. "You can stay with me."

"How, when you won't be there?"

"Oh, but I will. I'm starting a three-week vacation tomorrow." Kate smiled again. "I'll be home every night."

Marnie's face brightened, only then to dim. "That'd be great, but it's just too risky. I'd hate to put you in danger."

Kate got to her feet. "Don't worry about that. I'm not. Look, I hate to leave, but I'm due to fly out shortly. Are you sure you'll be okay?"

Marnie put up a brave front. "I'll be fine. This place is crawling with FBI."

"Tell me about it," Kate said. "I thought I was going to have to go back home and get my birth certificate in order to get past them."

Marnie laughed. "You're just the tonic I needed, my friend."

Kate's face turned serious. "You sure you'll be okay?"

"I'll be fine. I promise."

Marnie heard the clock chime ten. Still Tate had not come home.

After Kate had left, Marnie had visited with Annie over a light dinner. Then, a cup of coffee in hand, she'd gone into the den where she'd sat, thumbing through one magazine after another. Finally she had gone to her room—to bed but not to sleep.

Marnie knew it was foolish to worry about Tate, but she couldn't help it. What if... No, she wouldn't think about that possibility. She was crazy enough just thinking about Lance and what he was going through. She didn't intend to add Tate to her list. Anyway, she knew he could take care of himself. In his present mood she pitied anyone who crossed him, herself included.

Suddenly disgusted with her thoughts, Marnie tossed back the cover and got out of bed.

"What you need is some hot chocolate," she muttered aloud.

A short time later, having consumed a cup of hot chocolate milk, she walked out the door to the kitchen, only to suddenly come to a halt. Tate was standing in the shadowy hallway, only a hairbreadth away.

"Oh," she mouthed, stunned.

His lips parted as if to speak, but nothing came out.

Suddenly fear consumed Marnie. "It's Lance, isn't it?" she whispered, clutching at him. "Something's happened to Lance."

At the unexpected sight of her, Tate wanted to run—disappear; instead he felt as if he were trapped between walls of cement.

Yet he was aware of the chiming of the small grandfather clock and the soft glow of the light left burning in the kitchen. He was aware of Marnie staring up at him out of those bottomless eyes, wide with fear. But more than that, he was aware she was touching him.

Swallowing hard, he said, "There's been no word on Lance."

"When I saw your face... I thought..." Marnie's words faded, though she still didn't move. Nor did her hand. It stayed firmly on his chest. The touch was like magic.

It affected his body as if he'd been buried inside her in a hot, withering embrace. He felt his flesh stiffen, and he winced.

"Tate?" She still sounded frightened. Her mouth was trembling, yet so soft, so kissable.

He forced himself to say something, anything. "I didn't mean to scare you."

"That's all right," she whispered.

The light behind her cast her in an ethereal glow. He could smell her hair; it reminded him of the fresh spring rain that had so recently fallen. It adhered in wisps to her cheeks, giving her a wild, tousled look.

Slowly his eyes moved over her body, lingering on the gentle swell of her breasts, the nipples visible through the thin material of her robe. They were pointed, as if begging to be stroked.

The heat rose quickly to his skin, and her hand moved on his chest, lightly like a caress. Instantly he was trapped again, trapped by his body, bound by a liquid heat surging through him.

God! How can you think about sex when your son—
"Tate?"

The strangled use of his name shattered the spell. He dropped his hands suddenly as if he'd touched a furnace and stepped back.

They remained silent for long, heavy seconds.

"What are you doing up?" he asked, sucking much-needed air through his lungs.

"I...couldn't sleep."

"Still thinking about your place?"

Marnie drew an unsteady breath. "Yes."

"No one can get to you here. This place is like a fortress."

"I know I keep asking this, but is—is this nightmare ever going to end?"

"I don't know," he said bleakly, "I honestly don't know." He turned away and stared down the dark empty hall. "If only the bastards would call."

"We're...you're at their mercy. All you can do is wait."

"Yeah, and that's something I don't do very well."

"I...know."

She moved then, and he caught another whiff of her scent. He inhaled deeply, determined to fill his lungs with it.

He knew then that if he didn't leave this second, he wouldn't leave at all. She looked so vulnerable, so frail, as if a gentle breeze could blow her away. The urge was so strong to pull her into his arms, to kiss her until she melted against him and begged for more, that it made him sick to his stomach.

"You'd better go back to bed," he said abruptly, "before you fall on your face."

"The same could be said for you." Her voice, husky and soft, flowed through him like rare, soothing wine.

"It's been a helluva day."

She nodded. Their eyes met.

He could see the steady beat of a vein at her temple. She swallowed noticeably, then backed away. "Good... night," she whispered.

She was halfway down the hall when he stopped her. "Marnie."

She turned around.

"Are...are you in love with my son?"

He heard her sharp intake of breath and knew she was

shocked by his question. He cursed silently while she looked at him long and hard, her features seemingly frozen. Then, without answering, she turned and walked away.

The moment he heard her door shut, he leaned against the wall, feeling what little energy he had left seep out of him as if it was his own blood.

What had she done to him? He wondered if he'd ever get her off the brain. She had truly bewitched him, arousing sensations in him that he had not experienced in years. This lady, his conscience kept saying, he could hurt. And she could hurt him. Either way, it was wrong. Dead wrong.

"You must be Marnie."

Marnie smiled at the woman walking toward her. Clearly in her seventies, she was thin and fragile looking, though her still-lovely face was etched with strength.

"And you must be Mrs. O'Brien," Marnie said, extending her hand.

She clasped Marnie's hand warmly. "Please, call me Edith."

"Edith, it is," Marnie said lightly. She had been curious about Tate's mother, but as yet had never had the pleasure of meeting her. She wished now it wasn't under such painful and trying circumstances.

Still, Marnie was glad of the break in her routine. Since that incident with Tate in the hallway, two days had passed. Except for the few hours she'd spent at her condo supervising its restoration, she'd been at loose ends. Hours had been spent by the pool, soaking up the healing sunshine. Today was no exception.

After breakfast, she'd wandered outside and had been here ever since. It would soon be lunchtime. Tomorrow, thank goodness, she was returning to work. Just yesterday the doctor had deemed her fit to once again assume her responsibilities.

In the meantime, however, a visit from this soft-spoken woman gave Marnie's spirits the lift they needed.

Yet Edith was anything but cheerful. Marnie didn't have to be told that she had aged since her grandson had been kidnapped. Though she was smiling, her eyes were filled with a deep sadness.

"I thought I might actually catch Tate before he left," she said, sitting in the cushioned chair opposite Marnie, "but Annie told me I was too late."

Marnie pushed her sunglasses closer to the bridge of her nose. "He's been going to the office early every morning. Since Lance—" Marnie broke off, watching as Edith's face whitened.

"Poor Tate," Edith said after a moment, her eyes swimming with tears. "This has been so hard on him."

"It's been hard on everyone," Marnie said softly.

"I know, but somehow Tate thinks it was his fault." Without looking directly at Marnie, she went on, "You know they had their differences before he...he disappeared."

Marnie sighed. "I—I know."

A silence fell between them.

"My grandson is right," Edith said unexpectedly. "You are beautiful."

Marnie squirmed in her chair. "Thank...you."

"Are you surprised he confided in me?"

"I guess I am."

"My grandson told me all about you."

"*All?*"

"He told me he was going to marry you but that Tate was adamantly against it."

An intense blush scalded Marnie's face. "Mrs. O'Brien—"

"Edith," she interrupted gently.

Marnie smiled ruefully. "Sorry."

"Look, I'm the one who should be saying I'm sorry," Edith said, leaning forward, her tone gentle. "I know I'm prying where I shouldn't, but it helps to talk about... about Lance." Fresh tears glistened in her eyes and she drew an unsteady breath. "Right now Tate and I aren't able to comfort each other, we're both so broken up."

Marnie tried to swallow the lump that rose to the back of her throat, surprised that she, too, was close to tears. She had thought she had no more tears left to cry. "If only I could remember what the man looked like—"

"Don't, my dear," Edith admonished. "Don't torment yourself. It's something you can't help. After all, you've been through hell yourself."

Try telling your son that, Marnie agonized silently. Aloud, she said, "I know, but still..."

Edith reached over and squeezed her hand. "Just keep the faith. Now, if you'll excuse me," she added, "I have an appointment. But I'll look forward to seeing you again soon."

"Same here," Marnie said with a smile.

Once she was alone again, she closed her eyes and tried not to think.

The phone became the enemy.

A week passed and no phone call. No message. No word whatsoever from the kidnappers.

Marnie made an effort to resume a normal work schedule, but it was impossible. Plainclothesmen lurked about the premises, reminding everyone just how dangerous the situation was.

Tate was in and out of the office, reminding *her* of how dangerous the situation was. Each time their eyes met, accidentally or otherwise, her pulse quickened. However, it was obvious nothing had changed between them.

He still didn't trust her and made a point not to be alone with her, especially at the ranch. She would concede the waiting was tough and that it had taken its toll on him; it had on her, too. But she hadn't behaved like a wounded animal, snapping the head off of anyone who got close to her.

In the evenings he almost never came home until late, long after she was in bed. On the two occasions he'd parted from that ritual, they had barely been civil to each other through dinner. Then he had politely excused himself and gone to his office.

But this evening she would fool him. She wouldn't be in bed. Earlier, after having returned from the nursing home—the FBI in tow—she had showered, slipped into a comfortable cotton jumpsuit and made her way into the den.

After grabbing a magazine, she had eased down onto the couch, switched on the lamp beside it and curled her bare feet under her. She knew that she must have fallen asleep because she didn't hear him until he called her name.

"Marnie?"

For a moment she sat in a confused fog. Then on unsteady feet, she stood. "Tate?"

"Who else?"

"I—I must have fallen asleep," she said, offering a hapless, halfhearted smile.

His deep stride brought him within touching distance of her.

She automatically stepped back and turned away, his closeness an all-out assault on her senses.

"Why are you still up?"

"What—what time is it?"

"Nearly midnight."

She ran a hand through her already tousled curls. She knew she must look a mess, but she didn't care.

"You should be in bed." His voice sounded rusty.

"So should you," she whispered, looking up at him now, at his pale, haggard face. He was once again dressed in faded jeans and a casual shirt, the top buttons undone to reveal a mat of wiry, dark hair.

Consciously lowering her head, Marnie gave in to the tingling sensation that ran up and down her spine, and wondered if her body trembled from the cool breeze blowing through the open French doors or from his hypnotic power.

Quickly, she jerked her face up, and when she did, her startled eyes collided with his.

"I think you'd best tell me what this is all about," he said roughly.

"I'd like to talk to you."

"Now?"

"Yes, now."

"What about?" He dragged the back of his hand across his mustache.

"I'm leaving."

He blinked. "You're what?"

"I'm leaving," she repeated, drawing a pattern across her lower lip with her tongue. "I...can't—I won't stay here any longer. It's obvious you not only blame yourself for what happened to Lance, but me, as well."

"You damn right I do," he lashed out.

A silent scream of denial caught in her throat.

"But that's beside the point," he added, his tone low and less abrasive.

Marnie clenched and unclenched her fingers. "It is not beside the point. It *is* the point."

They glared at each other.

"It's—it's insane to—to blame me," she finally whispered.

He turned away, closed his eyes and exhaled sharply. "If he hadn't been so smitten with you, he might have been more alert, more on guard."

Marnie almost strangled on her own fury. "That's the most ridiculous thing I've ever heard, and you know it. And that's the reason I'm leaving. Tomorrow. I'm going to Kate's."

"Like hell you are. You're not going anyplace."

"I don't have to answer to you! You're not my keeper. Or my jailer."

"You damn well have to answer to the authorities. They won't let you leave. Count on that."

He was right, of course, Marnie reasoned with a sinking heart. She was trapped, but she sure didn't have to like it. Her thoughts raging, she spun around and took a step.

"Oh, no you don't," he said, latching on to her arms and hauling her against his chest. "Until my son is found, you'll do exactly as you're told."

Marnie stared down at his hands digging into her arms like clamps, then back up to his face. The color ran from her face, and their breaths mingled.

Later, Marnie couldn't say when the mood changed. Suddenly breathing became an effort as she stared at Tate. Her heart rose into her throat.

Move…now. Now…. Now!

The command was urgent, but her body seemed made of lead. Only her rapid, shallow breathing proved that she was still alive.

"Marnie, oh, Marnie." Tate's voice sounded as if it had been dug out of him.

"Tate…please."

His lips, when they touched hers, were hot and hard. She clutched at him frantically as his tongue, soft and insistent, meshed with hers.

"Oh, Marnie," he groaned again, unzipping the front of her jumpsuit. When her breasts spilled into his hands, she groaned.

His kiss hardened while he tugged on a nipple, as if trying to draw the very life from it.

Then suddenly it was over as quickly as it had begun. With tormented eyes and a deep groan, he thrust her away from him.

"Marnie…I—" Tate began in a thick voice.

"Don't," she cried, backing up, her eyes on fire with tears. "Don't you dare say another word."

With that she turned and fled.

Seven

Tate dreaded going to bed, knowing he wouldn't sleep. But his body didn't seem to care; it cried for rest. Not only had he put in long hours at the plant, he had also put in long hours at the stables. Back-breaking physical work had been his stress management. But even that had its limit.

Now, stretched on the bed, he clasped his hands behind his head and fixed his eyes on the ceiling. As predicted, he was too wired to sleep. Worry played havoc with his stomach.

Why the hell hadn't the kidnappers called with their demands? It was well over a week now since they had snatched Lance from the city street. He knew the FBI was doing everything it could, but it had come up empty-handed.

His own efforts had also fallen short. He'd ordered Neal to hire the best private detectives in the state. Nothing. It seemed as if Lance had vanished. Gut instinct told him that since the kidnappers had delayed so long, the explosive was not the reason.

If only Marnie could remember what the man looked like. If only Marnie weren't involved in this mess. If only Marnie hadn't come into his life. If....

He flopped onto his side and closed his eyes, hoping to blot thoughts of Marnie from his mind. But Marnie's pale, stricken face wouldn't disappear. He knew she was right; it was ludicrous to blame her. It was equally as ludicrous to blame himself. But he did.

Suddenly he wondered if he would ever be free of guilt. Or was it something that attached itself to a person and never let go?

He had purposefully not wanted to think about Marnie or the hot, torrid kiss they had exchanged only a short while ago. Ah, but she'd felt so good in his arms, so right. Every detail was imprinted on his brain—the brush of her hair like silk against his cheek, the quivering soft-ness of her lips, the feel of her hands on his skin.

Clenching his eyes shut, he groaned as he felt his body respond.

Without warning, Marnie had become his lifeblood and cross.

Maybe he should let her leave. Maybe he would. He'd think about that...later.

Marnie paused a few feet from the door of the main office. "Mr. Anderson, is there something I can help you with?"

Sam Anderson, the tall, lanky head custodian, jerked his head up and stared at Marnie through narrow, lazy eyes.

"No, ma'am," he drawled. "I was just checking the

bolt on this door. Mr. O'Brien's orders. Said it wasn't working right.''

"Well, is it working right now?'' she asked pointedly. She had never liked this man, had never liked his insolent attitude. Maybe it was because he seemed to think he was too good for the job.

"Yes, ma'am,'' he replied, his eyes roaming over her. "It's fixed.''

"Good, then I'm sure you have other duties to attend to.''

"Yes, ma'am.'' His grin was bold. "Sure do.''

Marnie held herself erect and watched until he sauntered down the hall, then resumed her steps, a troubled frown on her face. She was certain Anderson's ear had been pressed against the door. But why? Curiosity? That was it, of course, she told herself quickly. Since Lance's abduction, emotions around the office, around the entire plant, were running high.

Dismissing the incident from her mind, Marnie walked the remaining distance to the main office. When she reached the spot where the custodian had been standing, she paused and listened. As expected, she heard voices. Tate's voice in particular. Noticing that her hand trembled slightly, she gripped the knob harder and squared her shoulders.

She had bargained on not having to see him this morning. Even so, she had tried to remove all traces of her sleepless night, but she knew she hadn't been successful. The last thing she'd done before she'd left her room was to look at herself in the mirror.

Although her khaki-striped camp dress flattered her figure and was perfect for the lovely spring day and although her hair framed her face perfectly, there was nothing else perfect about her. Her eyes were huge in her thinly drawn face, and the circles were dark and deep. Her makeup did little to hide them or the sad curve of her mouth.

While she was deeply concerned for Lance, she was concerned for herself, as well. Tate had become an obsession. And last night—heat scalded her cheeks—well, that didn't bear thinking about. But think about it she did, about the wanton way she had behaved, about the way her tongue had twined with his greedily, about the way her hands had reached under his shirt and clutched the flesh of his back, about the way she had let his fingers caress her breasts until she was ready to explode inside.

She'd wanted him then. And, God help her, she wanted him now.

Finally, with less control than she would have liked, Marnie took another deep breath and opened the door. The minute she stepped across the threshold, she took one look at Tate and stopped cold.

He was on the phone, listening, his face devoid of color. Without being told, she knew the kidnappers were on the other end of the line.

The long-awaited call had finally come.

Quickly, her eyes scanned the room, locating Stan Courtney standing reed straight to the right of Tate's desk and Mike James on the other side, standing equally erect.

The tension was tangible.

Stan Courtney looked at her and placed a finger against his lips. He need not have worried about her saying anything; she couldn't have uttered a word if she'd had to. She was too caught up in watching Tate, and her heart ached for him.

''I'm Tate O'Brien,'' he was saying, his tone clear but cold.

He listened, then said, "Dammit, I want to talk to my son."

Marnie's hand went to her throat.

Tate listened again, then suddenly, furiously, he slammed the receiver down on the hook. "The son of a bitch wouldn't tell me what they wanted, said they'd call back later with their demands and a meeting place."

"Damn!" Stan muttered, his lips white and pencil thin.

Mike rubbed the back of his neck. "I second that."

Only Marnie and Tate had nothing to say. From across the room their eyes met in silent horror.

Marnie had no intention of exploring any farther than the main barn. When she'd first started meandering through the grounds, she'd had no intention of going into the barn at all. She had intended to remain in the open air, hoping that it would soothe her troubled mind.

It had been two days since Tate had received the call, and she had made it a point to stay out of his way. He was more of a bear to be around than ever. Fear of confronting him had chased her outdoors.

But now that she had walked into the barn, she was both curious and awed. She'd known that Tate was a powerful and wealthy man with a passion for quarter horses, but she'd had no idea of the magnitude of his operation.

Once she ventured out of the barn, well-fortified with grain and hay, she wandered down a paved walkway that was lined on each side with stalls.

She paused midway and looked around. Though the first few stalls were empty, she knew she'd stumbled upon Tate's stable of quarter horses. To bear this out, the scent of horseflesh reached her, followed by a loud whinny.

All told there were between fifteen and twenty cement-block stalls with thick plywood walls and wood shavings on the floor. She remained where she was a moment longer, content just to look. Then she moved on, not stopping until she reached an occupied one. There she paused and rubbed a mare's nose.

Though she didn't know much about horses, she had always admired them, thinking them strong, friendly creatures. She had just laid her forehead down on the muzzle of the bay horse when she heard the voice behind her.

"Well, what do you think?"

Marnie swung around.

Tate was leaning against the door, watching her, though his eyes were somewhat shielded by the Stetson angled down over his forehead.

"How come you're up so early?" he asked when she didn't answer.

Marnie swallowed with difficulty, thinking how good he looked in an open-necked shirt and worn, tight jeans. "I thought the fresh air would do me good," she said, her voice quavering slightly.

"Did it do the trick? The fresh air, I mean?"

Her smile was nervous. "Yes," she said, continuing to rub the horse.

Tate moved toward her. "You a horse lover?"

"Yes, only I don't know a lot about them."

For a second he didn't respond, his eyes settling on the gentle swell of her breasts, which were obvious under the thin red T-shirt tucked inside her jeans.

Instantly, her stomach knotted as a spurt of fire darted through her.

"You don't have to know a lot about them to like them." His voice had all the roughness of sandpaper.

"Are—are all your horses quarter horses?" she asked, desperate to break the spell, the same kind of spell that had held them in its grip last night.

"Running quarters, to be exact," he said, his voice not yet back to normal.

"I don't understand."

"They're one-third thoroughbred, which makes them faster."

"Well, whatever. All I know is that they are beautiful with their barrel chests and big hips."

"Ever ridden much?"

"No, no I haven't. Very little, in fact."

"Wanna give it a try?"

Stunned, Marnie sought to catch his eyes, but he kept them fixed on the animal. Silence stretched between them.

"When?" she asked, sounding choked.

"What's wrong with right now?"

"Oh, I don't know. I…"

His eyes burned into hers. "If I promise to keep my hands to myself, will you come?"

She caught her breath.

"I won't apologize for the other night," he said roughly.

The stark desire in his eyes made her mouth go dry. "I…don't want you to."

They looked at each other for another long moment, then Tate asked in a low tone, "Well, are you game?"

Marnie slid a glance at the mare. "What if I fall off?"

Suddenly he threw back his head and laughed. "We'll cross that bridge when we come to it, okay?"

She had never heard him laugh before, not a deep belly laugh like now. It sent her blood pulsing through her veins like warm, heady brandy.

"Okay," she said on a breathy sigh.

It took them a half hour to cross the open pasture into the edge of the thicket that was also part of Tate's land. But it wasn't because Marnie was having trouble managing her mare; she wasn't. They got along supremely well, and she was proud of herself. It was because there had been so much to see that she had wanted to take her time, soak up the beautiful surroundings.

Marnie and Tate paused under a huge oak and faced each other. Marnie was the first to speak.

"This is heavenly. I can see why you're addicted."

He quirked an eyebrow. "So you know that I'm horse crazy, huh?"

"Lance told me," she said hesitantly.

"What else did Lance tell you?" He paused deliberately and looked at her with smiling eyes. "About me, that is?"

"Not—not much."

Amusement curved his full lips. "Liar."

Marnie colored and tried not to show her surprise at Tate's sudden change in mood. This was a side of him she had never seen before, and she was loath to say or do anything that would cause him to revert to his cold, cynical self.

"Come on, fess up. What did he say?"

Tate O'Brien, teasing her? Unheard of. Still, a potent excitement percolated through her as she stared at him, a smile softening her lips. "Mostly that your bark's much worse than your bite."

"And do you agree?"

An abrupt tension swept away all humor.

"I don't know," she finally said, the words coming out in a rush.

An impatience came and went in his eyes. "What's important to you, Marnie Lee?" he asked, changing the subject. "What do you want out of life?"

"A job that I find challenging and enough money to live comfortably."

"In that order?"

"No, actually money comes first," she said honestly, and waited for the fireworks.

None came. Instead he asked in a benign voice, "Because of your father?"

She stared at him, perplexed. "How'd you know…?" Her voice trailed off, and her features changed. "I'd forgotten you know everything there is to know about me," she said, disconcerted.

"Not everything."

It wasn't so much what he said that sent a tremor through her, but the way he said it.

"Oh, and just exactly what is it you don't know?"

"How you really feel about my son." His gaze never flickered. With maddening slowness his eyes wandered over her. "You never answered that question."

His voice was once again a husky, seductive lure, and she felt herself responding.

"I want an answer—now."

She circled her dry lips with her tongue. "I care about him, but I—I don't love him."

"Thanks for being honest." His face betrayed no emotion, but a muscle twitched in his jaw.

"He'll…be all right." Her voice broke. "He just has to be."

Tate toyed with the brim of his hat. "God, I hope you're right."

"And I want you to know that I haven't given up hope

of regaining my memory,'' she whispered, her voice as dry as a rustling leaf.

His eyes held hers for a long moment, revealing nothing. Then he said brusquely, ''Come on, let's ride.''

Again they rode in silence in and out of the thicket, not stopping until they reached a clearing. They sat atop their mounts and watched the sunset.

''Tate.''

''Mmm,'' he murmured without looking at her.

''I'm not sure this means anything, but I caught Anderson…''

It happened then. One gunshot. Then another. Then another. All were close. Too close.

''What…!'' Tate got no further as another bullet passed by Marnie's head.

Her horse bolted. ''Tate!'' she screamed, struggling to hold on.

White-lipped, Tate reached for the reins, but it was too late.

Suddenly the mare pitched Marnie, tossing her on the ground like a broken, discarded rag doll.

''Oh, God,'' Tate wheezed, clearing his mount and scrambling to her, cradling her in his arms. ''Marnie, talk to me!''

Marnie knew she wasn't dead. Or at least she didn't think so. But she was stiff enough to be dead, she told herself, wincing. With her eyes closed, she wiggled one toe, then another. So far so good.

What was wrong? Why did she feel as if she were trying to swim to the surface while currents pulled her under? She opened her eyes and moved them carefully across the ceiling, then around the room. Where was she?

Moonlight, spilling through the window, cast the room

in shadows. She moved again and this time felt nothing but relief; it didn't hurt.

Suddenly, with the impact of a blow to the head, she remembered. Gun shots. Someone had tried to kill her.

"Oh," she whimpered aloud, trying to swallow around the golf-ball sized lump in her throat. She couldn't. It refused to dissolve. In order to keep from strangling, Marnie let the hot tears flow.

"Oh, no...." she whimpered again. Had Tate been hurt? Had the bullets struck him instead of her?

Frantically, her mind groped to bring the entire scenario into focus. Tate couldn't have been hit because he had come to her rescue. A giddy feeling of relief replaced her panic.

She could see Tate, white-lipped and shaking, bending over her, cradling her hand on his knee, hear him cry.

"Tate," she breathed, fully conscious but dazed.

"Thank God." He'd looked up then, as if delivering a prayer of thanks. Without saying anything else, he ran his hand over her body.

"The bullet missed me...but my head is pounding." She placed a hand on her head. "What about you? Are— are you all right?"

"I'm fine," he said, his voice biting. "But the son of a bitch who shot at us won't be fine when I'm through with him."

With what energy she could muster, Marnie reached out and clutched at the front of his shirt. "Who—who would do such a thing?"

Tate didn't say anything. Instead his features turned harder and his eyes icier as if he were making a pact with the devil right there on the spot.

The look on his face frightened Marnie more than if he'd lashed out the truth. Her hold on his shirt tightened.

"You—you think he...they were shooting at us? At me?"

His jaw clenched. "No more questions. I'm taking you home."

After he'd gently secured her in the saddle in front of him, she remembered very little, only bits and pieces of the following hours.

Now, as she eased to her elbows, Marnie wondered who had put her in bed—naked, except for panties. Tate? The thought weakened her further.

Her heart rate settled; Annie had taken charge. Tate had left her in the housekeeper's competent hands.

She laid her head back but felt no comfort, other than the fact that neither she or Tate was seriously injured.

What she felt was anger, gut-wrenching anger. Suddenly she longed to run away from the nightmare that was now her life, run from the men who were trying to harm her, run from thoughts of Lance. But most of all, she wanted to run from Tate, who with one look, one touch, could make her ache like a woman in love. A familiar surge of dread swelled inside her. She couldn't love him.

Surely she hadn't been that stupid, knowing they had no future. Besides, she was just a game to him. When he finished playing, he would fold his cards and walk away.

Without warning, the room began to spin, and like a puppet whose strings have broken, Marnie's head collapsed against the pillow. Deep, wrenching sobs racked her body.

It was only after her weeping had run its course that she heard a noise. She stiffened. Then, ever so slowly, with her heart in her throat, Marnie shifted back into a sitting position and stared at the door.

As feared, a figure stood on the threshold. She gasped and squeezed the sheet to her breasts.

"Marnie."

"Tate?" Her voice was a mere whisper.

"I—I heard you crying."

She opened her mouth, but speech was impossible. She could only stare at his bare chest and jean-clad hips and tremble.

"Marnie," he whispered again.

Another sob escaped her lips.

"Marnie, don't...please." His voice sounded broken.

"Oh, Tate," she cried, "I..." She stopped and watched as he began walking toward her in slow motion. He seemed unaware that his legs were moving.

No! This was insane. If he touched her now... She had to stop him. She couldn't let him near her, especially not now, not in her weakened condition. She had to be strong.

But with each step he took, that voice of caution dwindled.

He moved closer, and her heart almost stopped beating. Neither spoke.

Tears marked her face.

"Marnie...it's all right." He stopped a foot from her.

She stared up at him for long moments, her soul in her eyes.

He needed her. He needed her *now*.

It was an all-consuming need that knew no boundaries. And, for the first time, his feelings for Marnie were not tempered with guilt. His screaming conscience had been completely stifled.

For hours after the shooting incident, Marnie had preyed on his mind. In the end he knew he couldn't settle down until he'd assured himself one more time that she was sleeping soundly.

He'd left his room and walked down the hall to hers. Without hesitation, he had twisted the knob and pushed open the door.

That was as far as he'd gotten.

His muscles had locked. The bright moonlight had perfected his vision, enabling him to see her clearly. One shoulder and one long slender leg had been free of cover. Her skin had shone like satin.

His heart had slammed against his rib cage. He had come apart inside; it was just that simple and just that complicated. For the briefest of moments his conscience had tried to rally, but it had been crushed with callous determination.

Now, as he felt himself drowning in those eyes, he tried one more time to pull back. Apologize for intruding, he told himself, and get the hell out.

The apology stuck in his throat. He couldn't take his eyes off her, off her breasts. They were full and high and porcelain-white. The nipples were small, and in the moonlight they glistened like pink pebbles.

Life filled his manhood.

Marnie moaned, seemed to be throbbing, shivering.

Tate's eyes delved lower, taking in the perfect skin, the narrow waist, flat stomach, navel, coming to rest on the top of her panties. The saliva in his mouth dried, and in his mind he was already dispensing with the fragile garment.

The light lingered on her eyes, making them sparkle like violets covered with drops of dew. He wanted to disappear inside her, but contented himself with merely looking at her and saying nothing.

She returned his stare and whispered something incoherent.

Finally, he reached out and ran a thumb across her lips—so like silk. They quivered.

"Marnie…"

Wordlessly, she held out her arms.

"Marnie, oh, Marnie," he muttered, sitting on the bed and slipping into them. "I—I shouldn't be here."

Her fingers sank into his shoulders.

"Please…don't leave me." Her cheeks were smudged with tears.

Tate groaned. Then unable to help himself, he kissed the tears from her face, tears that mingled with his own. Then he gently pushed her to arm's length, struggling for control. "Don't you understand," he cried, facing her again, "I can't just hold you. I—"

She raised a finger to his lips, hushing him. "I know," she whispered. "And it's all right."

"You mean…?"

This time she stopped his flow of words with her lips. Their bare chests touched, and he almost exploded. Blood stampeded through him, settling in his manhood. He stood and quickly discarded his jeans.

"Tate, Tate, Tate." Her tone was agony as she reached for him again and clutched him hard. Then, as if surprised to feel his hardness pressed against her stomach, she gasped.

"See what you do to me," he said thickly, holding her close once again.

They plummeted onto the bed, and in a fluid movement he rolled on top of her, positioning himself so that he could look into her eyes.

"Kiss me," she pleaded.

"Oh, yes, yes," he groaned against her mouth.

Their tongues meshed in a hot, coiling foreplay, and he began to move his hips against hers. He separated from her mouth and raised his head to again watch her face. At the rapture he saw there, all coherent thought fled. She was his, his alone.

He shifted his position, eager to gain access to her breasts while continually brushing the apex of her thighs with his strength.

She gasped again with pleasure and held him close. "You're making me crazy."

After a moment, Tate stopped, disentangled himself and stood beside the bed.

Marnie's eyes widened anxiously.

"Soon, my darling, soon," he whispered, removing her panties.

With both now free of clothing, Marnie reached for him again and opened her legs as he covered her.

"Oh, Marnie…" His groan ended in a cry as he felt her soft hand surround him.

With another muted cry, he slipped deep inside her. She was tight and he tried to hold back, but she wouldn't let him. She locked her legs around his buttocks, and instantly blind urgency claimed them.

"Marnie…" He was unable to say more. He could only feel, feel as he'd never felt before.

She moaned and clung to him.

"Marnie, Marnie…. Oh, Marnie…I want you!" The words were delivered in pulsating gasps, coming from his lips at the same time his warm seed spilled into her. Sweet pain shook their bodies.

"Oh, Tate," she cried.

I love you! God, I love you Marnie! I love you.

Eight

Marnie shifted slightly. Not only was Tate's head on her pillow, but his leg was draped over one of hers, binding them together. She feared any unexpected movement would awaken him and she didn't want to do that. She knew he needed sleep as badly, if not worse than she.

But for now sleep was the furthest thing from her mind. She was far too keyed up. Rather than sleep, she wanted to remember, to savor every moment of their passion.

She let out a quiet, forlorn sigh. She couldn't quite get past the idea that she had somehow betrayed Lance. Still, if she had it to do over again, she wouldn't change a thing. She had known Tate would be a marvelous lover, and he had more than fulfilled her dreams.

What about her? Had she done the same for him? She wanted the answer to be yes so badly it hurt. Yet, she was scared it meant nothing sacred to him, that the pas-

sion that forced them to turn to each other time and time
again during the night was just that and nothing more.

But hadn't he said he wanted her? Wasn't that a sign
he cared? Not necessarily. He had probably told countless
women that same thing.

So, in the cold face of midnight, she forced herself to
brave reality no matter how much it hurt. She'd seen the
fear in his eyes. There had been no mistaking it. It had
been heavily camouflaged with passion and lust, but it
had been there.

Swallowing her sigh, Marnie stole another glance at
him, longing to touch him, if for no other reason than to
make sure he was real.

But there *was* another reason. Somewhere along the
way, she had indeed lost her way and done the most
foolish thing imaginable. She had fallen in love, fallen
deeply and irrevocably in love with Tate O'Brien.

And while there was intense joy within her, there was
also sadness and fear. Because she loved him, she was
at his mercy. With his mouth, his hands, his body, he
could manipulate her, control her.

And Dear Lord, she didn't want him to release her,
either. It had been so good to be filled, so right to be
needed, so exciting to be burdened with his weight. She
didn't want it to end. She didn't want to live apart from
this man. Not now. Not ever.

Marnie's eyes moved from his face to the rise and fall
of his chest. Finally, for her ears alone, she whispered
tearfully, "I love you."

For now that was all her heart could spare.

"Are you asleep?"

"No," Marnie whispered, snuggling closer to Tate's
hard, warm body. "Are you?"

He caressed her back with a calloused hand. "No."

"What time is it?" Marnie asked, barely able to speak. His touch was doing strange things to her body.

"Six o'clock."

She groaned.

"I second that."

"Do we have to get up?"

He chuckled, still strumming his fingers across her back. "Not if you don't want to."

"I've been awake since midnight."

Tate moved slightly so that he could peer down at her. "You were thinking." It wasn't a question.

"Yes. About us. About you."

She felt him stiffen. "Go on."

She toyed with the crisp hair on his chest. "Actually, I was thinking about your...wife."

"What about her?" Tate's tone was taut.

Marnie knew she was treading on dangerous ground. "Were...you happily married?" She held her breath.

"No," he said bluntly. "Believe it or not, she always wanted more than I could give her."

The angry pain festering inside him sounded in his voice. Marnie ached for him.

"How did she die?"

"An accident. She'd been drinking and lost control of the car."

"How tragic."

Silence fell between them.

"What about you?" Tate's voice was as warm now as the hand covering her breast. "It's time you fessed up."

Marnie smiled. "I'm afraid I have very little to 'fess up' to."

"Ever been in love?"

Her smile slipped, then completely disappeared. "No."

"I find that hard to believe."

Marnie shifted in his arms. "Well...I thought I was once."

"What happened?"

"I found out he was married with a family."

Tate hesitated, then said, "There's been no one else?"

"No one."

They fell silent again.

Marnie's shuddering breath broke it. "About us...about last night..."

"What do you want me to say, that I'm sorry?"

I want you to say that you love me. "Are...you sorry?" she whispered.

"God no. But I didn't mean to touch you," he added in a strained voice.

"I know," she said huskily. "I didn't mean for you to, either."

Tate tipped her chin so that she was forced to look into his eyes. They were troubled. "Are you saying that *you're* sorry?"

She lowered her long, curling lashes. "No."

"Even if you get pregnant?"

Her heart missed a beat. "It's—it's the wrong time of the month."

"Did I hurt you?"

She swallowed. "No."

"It's a wonder. You're so small, so tight...."

"You didn't hurt me." Her voice was husky. "It was wonderful."

"Oh, Marnie, Marnie, what am I going to do with you?"

"What do you want to do?" She hated herself for asking, but she had to.

"I'd like to hole up somewhere and make love to you until we're both so weak we can't move."

"Oh, Tate," she whispered.

"But we both know that's impossible, don't we?"

Her heart sank. Guilt stood like a steel wall between them. And the fact that he didn't love her—she mustn't forget that.

"Yes," she said in a small voice, "I know."

They didn't say anything for a long while, content to simply hold each other.

Finally Marnie asked, "What about the gunshots? Did you find out anything?"

"Not a lot, but I will." His voice was hard. "After I left Annie clucking over you, I called the FBI. Then I went back and looked around."

"And?"

"I found a deserted campsite and two cigarette butts which forensic took in for analysis."

"Do—do you think it's related to—"

"I don't know," he said, interrupting her. "But one thing I do know, there's going to be hell to pay when I get my hands on whoever was behind that little fiasco. If they had hurt you..."

His concern brought tears to her eyes. "But they didn't, and that's what counts."

"Yeah, but it was too close a call to suit me."

"This may not mean anything, but remember before we heard the shots, I was telling you about Sam Anderson?"

Tate nodded.

"Well, I was coming down the hall and he was at the office door pretending to work on the lock, only I know he wasn't. He had his ear to the door and was listening in on the conversation between you and the FBI.''

Tate frowned. "Why?"

"Curiosity is the only thing I can think of."

His frown deepened. "I don't know. There has to be more to it than that. I'll pass the word on to the FBI and let them look into it.'' He paused and stared deeply into her eyes. "In the meantime there's something else I want to do.''

"And what's that?"

"Make love to you."

A flush stained Marnie's cheeks. Heat spread between her legs. "That's what I want, too."

While sunlight seeped through the windows and the dawn turned into day, Tate reached for her. Her body was warm, ready. He stroked her slowly, gently, creating an ache within her that only his being inside her would alleviate.

When he lifted her on top and eased her down on him, her lips parted wildly and her eyes rolled back.

"Ah...Tate," she moaned, giving in to the sensations racking her body. He filled her completely.

"Easy does it, baby."

Splaying his hands across her back, he eased her forward and took a nipple in his mouth. As he sucked on it like a greedy child, she moaned again and together they began to move.

Afterward, with him still inside her, she collapsed on his sweat-riddled chest. She was still there a few minutes later when the phone rang.

Instantly alert, Tate eased her away and reached for the receiver.

"Hello," he said, his tone short.

Equally alert, Marnie watched, suddenly uneasy.

Tate held the phone out to her. "For you—it's the nursing home."

Doing her best not to panic, she took the receiver. "This is Marnie Lee."

Moments later the receiver slipped from her hand. Her face was stark white. "It's...Daddy—he's disappeared."

"Where can he be?" Marnie asked on a wail.

"Trust me," Tate said, "it's going to be all right. We'll find him. How can we miss with the police, the FBI and us looking for him?"

Marnie sighed and rubbed her temple. She wished she could be as self-confident about finding Silas as Tate was.

Since the call had roused them out of bed, events had passed in a haze for Marnie, reminding her of the night Lance was kidnapped. After Tate had hung up the phone for her, he'd drawn her close against him and held her.

Her first thought, of course, was that Silas had been kidnapped in retaliation.

"Now, now," Tate had consoled as if reading her mind, "let's not jump to conclusions until we have all the facts."

Everything else forgotten, they had quickly made their way to the home, where they had been met by the administrator and head nurse. Both had informed Marnie that one minute Mr. Lee was sitting on the porch and the next he wasn't.

"How could he just disappear?" Marnie had demanded, looking from one to the other.

"Unfortunately, we don't have an answer for you, Ms. Lee," the administrator had said in an embarrassed tone.

Two hours later Silas had still not been found. It was as if he had disappeared into thin air—or worse, into the kidnappers' hands.

Marnie and Tate were now tramping through the woods beyond the home's lawn, thinking that Silas might have wandered there. But with each step, with each minute, Marnie's fear increased along with her frustration.

Cutting a glance at Tate, she knew that he felt the same way, in spite of his earlier words to the contrary. Worry lines now ruled his forehead.

"I...do you think they took him because—because of me?"

Tate stopped and faced her, only he didn't say anything. Instead, he touched her cheek with his finger, purposely trapping a lone tear that was trickling down her cheek and threatening to land on her blouse.

"Oh, honey," he said, "I don't think it's like that at all, though I won't say I'm not concerned. And certainly your fears could turn out to be reality, but I don't think so."

"I hope and pray you're right."

They resumed walking, and Marnie felt comforted as Tate kept his arm loosely around her shoulders. She reveled in his strength and didn't want to think about what she would have done if he hadn't been there to take charge.

Yet she knew she shouldn't be thinking such thoughts. She shouldn't depend on him. In the end she knew it would only bring her more heartache. But after last night she didn't have either the strength or the desire to put distance between them.

"Ms. Lee!"

They both froze in their tracks, recognizing the excited ring in the voice.

Marnie's eyes widened. "Oh, Tate..." She couldn't go on.

He grabbed her hand. "Let's go."

In order to avoid the undergrowth, they were forced to move more slowly than they would have liked. Even at that, Marnie wasn't prepared when a stray limb slapped her across the upper arm.

"Ouch!" she yelped.

Tate stopped midstride and swung around. "What's wrong?" Concern sharpened his tone.

"Nothing," Marnie managed to say between gulps, the stinging sensation making her sick to her stomach. "I'm all right. A limb just grazed me, that's all. Please, let's hurry."

"Whoa, hold it," Tate warned, clamping a hand down on one shoulder. "If you fall and hurt yourself, what good will you be to your dad?"

Marnie squinted against the bright sunlight. "I know, but I'm still so scared."

"I know," Tate murmured softly. "I know."

Finally they made it through the last clump of trees. Silas Lee, flanked on each side by the nurse and administrator, was standing in the middle of the clearing.

"Thank God," Marnie cried, smiling up at Tate.

With that same finger, Tate touched her cheek tenderly. "Well, what are you waiting for? Go give him a hug."

A short time later Silas was back in his room, sitting in his favorite chair by the window. Marnie stood beside him, while Tate leaned against the wall and eyed them closely.

"How long has he been like this?" he asked.

A sad smile appeared on Marnie's face at the same time her fingers slicked down the cowlick sticking up in the crown of Silas's head. "Forever."

Tate's eyebrows shot up.

Marnie sighed as their eyes met. "That's an exaggeration, of course. I know this sounds awful, but when I

try to remember how sharp, how active he was, I can't."
Her eyes pleaded with Tate to understand. "When I'm
home or at work and try to think about the good times
we had, they're murky. All I can see is the way he is
now, and it breaks my heart."

Tate's mouth was stretched into a grim line. "I can
imagine how tough it must be for you to see someone
you love stricken with this blasted disease."

"The worst part of it, he won't get any better. He'll
only get worse."

For a moment there was silence. Then Tate asked,
"Are you sure he's in the right place?"

"The very best money can buy."

"Then how in the hell did he just wander off?"

Marnie's eyebrows knitted together. How *had* he just
wandered off? Silas Lee had done what so many other
Alzheimer patients had done; he had simply walked off,
lost as if he were a newborn baby. The home staff had
been distraught, full of recriminations and apologies.
Those, however, had done little to relieve her anxious
mind.

As if sensing her torment, Tate reached out with a
steady hand and patted her shoulder. When he spoke, his
tone was less harsh. "Sorry, I didn't mean to—"

She cut him off. "Don't apologize. You're right. I'm
asking myself the same thing."

"I'd feel better if he had round-the-clock protection."

She avoided his gaze. "That goes without saying, only
I can't afford it."

"Well, I can," he said flatly.

Marnie's eyes sought his, an incredulous expression in
them. "You'd do that for me?"

His gaze didn't waver. "Yes, I'd do that for you."

Marnie licked her lips. "I'll...repay you, of course. Somehow."

"Forget it," he said roughly.

"I—"

"I said forget it."

She decided to do as he said.

"Look, I'm going to the office," Tate said then. "Will you be all right?"

Marnie smiled. "I'll be fine."

"You sure?"

"I'm sure."

He gave her a long, slow look, then moved within a hairbreadth of her. "Call if you need me," he said huskily.

"I...will."

He leaned toward her and laid his mouth against hers. Clutching at him, Marnie parted her lips beneath his.

When it was apparent neither one could breathe, Tate pulled away. "Later," he whispered thickly before turning and walking out the door.

Afterward, Marnie lost all concept of time. She had no idea how long she sat beside her daddy, holding his hand, talking to him. But when she finally got up and left, she could still taste Tate's kiss on her lips.

Where the hell was Courtney? Tate wondered with impatience. The agent had called him over an hour before and said he was on his way.

Before now, Tate hadn't had time to get anxious. The second he'd walked into the office, he'd sent for his assistant. Without mincing words, he'd told Neal to see to it that Silas Lee had twenty-four-hour protection.

Once Neal had left to do his bidding, Tate had thumbed through the stack of contracts that Marnie had put on his desk. But he hadn't been able to concentrate. Even the folder stamped in bold letters, CLASSIFIED, hadn't held his attention. Inside it were the final plans of the plastic explosive, plans that the government had approved without a snag.

Lance would be proud.

Oh, God, son, are you still alive?

He glared down at the papers strewn across his desk as if they were his enemies. Suddenly, in a fit of frustration and anger, Tate longed to rid the desk of its contents. He refrained, of course. He had always prided himself on having control of his emotions. Until now he had always had. But with his fear over Lance and his passion for Marnie, his control was being pushed to its limits.

Was he destined to begin and end every day for the rest of his life with thoughts of her? Yes, his heart answered. When he'd touched her last night, a slow burn had started deep within him. And when he'd embedded himself inside her tight softness, that slow burn had raged into an inferno, and the fire was still smoldering inside him.

He had lost control. The last thing he'd planned was to fall in love with the woman his son loved.... No! It wasn't love he felt; it couldn't be. But he knew it was. Only love could tear his soul to pieces, make him wish he were dead when he was in perfect health.

Even now, as he stood, her delicate scent seemed to have settled on his skin. The sweetness of it made him ache. He wanted her. Again. And again.

"O'Brien."

Startled, Tate jerked his head around. Agent Courtney was peeking around the door.

"Come on in," Tate said abruptly, almost rudely.

Then he cursed. It wasn't fair to use the agent as his whipping boy.

"I knocked..." Courtney broke off with a shrug. His face was almost as red as his hair.

"Sorry," Tate muttered, "I didn't hear you."

"That's understandable with all you've got on your mind."

"Have a seat," Tate invited. When the agent was settled, Tate asked, "Everything still all right at the home?"

"Was when I left."

"Good," Tate said.

Courtney's eyes narrowed. "But that's not what you wanted to talk about, is it?"

"No." Tate let out a slow breath. "It's about a man by the name of Anderson who works here as the head custodian."

The agent crossed one knee over the other. "What about him?"

"Marnie caught him eavesdropping on our conversation."

"And you think it might be more than curiosity?"

"Don't know, but it wouldn't hurt to check it out." Tate paused and reached for another folder on his desk and then tossed it to the agent. "His personnel file. We checked him out carefully, of course, but we could've missed something that your sophisticated computers can pick up."

"Never can tell. We'll get on it."

A short silence ensued.

"Do you think Lance is still alive?" Tate asked, forcing the words out.

Courtney sighed. "I wish the hell I knew."

"The waiting—that's what's so damned tough."

"I know. And what beats me is they haven't called back with their demands."

Tate rubbed the back of his neck. "That's precisely why my gut instinct tells me it's amateurs that grabbed him."

"With dumb luck on their side."

"Exactly." Tate stood and came from behind his desk. "If it had been terrorists wanting the design, they would have already moved. I think whoever took Lance has an ax to grind either against Lance or me."

"Or the company."

Tate perched on the edge of his desk. "I think they did it for the money."

"So why the delay?"

"That I can't answer."

For a long second the room was hushed.

"Tell me, Courtney," Tate said at last, "do you ever get tired of dealing with the slimeballs of the world?"

"Every day, Mr. O'Brien, every day. And speaking of slimeballs, I guess I'd better check out the one you just gave me."

Tate's lips tightened. "Let me know."

Courtney eased to his feet. "Count on it."

It was late when Marnie maneuvered her car out of the parking lot at the home and headed toward the plant. She'd decided that if Tate's car was there, she would stop and see if there was anything she needed to do.

She wanted to be near him; it was that simple. Silas's sudden disappearance had robbed her of the opportunity to think about their lovemaking last night, but the memory had teased her all day like a brightly wrapped package under the tree that couldn't be opened until Christmas day.

Now as she sped down the boulevard, vivid details raced to the forefront of her mind and she gripped the steering wheel hard to keep from whimpering aloud.

It was then that she saw Sam Anderson walk out of the convenience store across from Systems.

Afterward she had no idea why she bothered to slow down and watch him. At the time she operated purely on instinct. Maybe it was the way his eyes kept shifting from right to left as if he was looking for something or someone.

A small, nondescript car suddenly swept toward the curb and braked. Marnie continued to stare, more out of curiosity than anything else. But ever since she'd caught Anderson eavesdropping, she hadn't trusted him.

The driver, she noted, seemed as nondescript as the car. Yet there was something familiar about him, something she couldn't quite put her finger on. Perhaps he, too, worked at the plant and she'd noticed him in passing.

"You're losing it, Lee," she said aloud, pressing down on the accelerator.

It was only after she reached the plant parking lot that it struck her where she'd seen him.

"Oh, no!" Marnie cried, tearing out of the car. She didn't stop until she reached Tate's office. Without knocking she thrust open the door, out of breath.

Courtney, heading toward the door himself, came to an abrupt halt. Tate's face turned white. "Marnie?"

"I remember what the man looked like." She paused and sucked in a breath. "In fact, I just saw him. He used to work here."

Nine

The sky glittered with stars while the moon hung in their midst like a huge ball of fire in the midnight sky.

As she strolled along the edge of the swimming pool, Marnie raised her head and pulled the fresh air into her lungs. Still looking up, she tried to force herself to relax, to enjoy the beauty of the warm spring night.

She couldn't. No matter how breathtaking, how spectacular the sight was before her, she couldn't lose herself in it. Her insides were coiled as if she'd been punched in the stomach and was expecting another blow.

But then after the day she'd had, how could she expect otherwise? Even now, hours after the fact, she found it hard to believe she'd seen the man who had taken Lance. It had to be one of those quirky twists of fate; there was no other explanation for it.

The instant she had walked into Tate's office and told him and Courtney what she had seen, events had steamrolled. An all-points bulletin was put out on Walter Elliot, a former employee who had recently been fired, and on Anderson, who had not shown up for work during the past few days.

Following another sigh, Marnie stopped and slipped the oversized T-shirt over her head to reveal a bikini underneath. The bathing suit, a seductive burgundy, left very little to the imagination. For a moment she wished Tate could see her in it.

Then chastising herself for such a thought, she sat down on the side of the pool and dunked both feet into the water. Ah, heaven, she thought, feeling the water penetrate her limbs like a soothing balm. Shortly, she lifted her head and looked around, the moon providing her with adequate lighting.

By anyone's standards the haven, which included the deck and pool, was as beautiful as it was peaceful. Marnie's gaze fell on the twelve-foot-high stockade fence that surrounded it, offering the maximum of privacy even from the agents who continuously combed the grounds. Her eyes wandered back to the pool, mesmerized by its kidney-shaped beauty.

No doubt about it, Tate had the best of everything. But she felt no envy, only regret. Regret because she did not fit into his world of glitz and glamour, no matter how hard she might want to.

Suddenly, her eyes turned toward the house and Tate's bedroom. All was dark. She wasn't surprised. In Lance's absence Tate was working long hours.

On the way from the police station, she had asked him if he wanted her to help him clear his desk. He'd said no, insisting she return to the ranch, telling her she'd had enough excitement for one day.

But she hadn't wanted to leave him. The night without

him had been dismal; the thought of a future without him
was more dismal.

"Is this a private party?"

At the sound of his voice, Marnie nearly jumped out
of her skin. Turning rounded eyes on him, she noticed
he was standing to her right, clad in a pair of black trunks
and nothing else.

"Did I scare you?" Tate asked, sitting down beside
her.

"Yes."

"Sorry, didn't mean to."

Her heart was beating fast. "How…did you know
where I was?"

"I went to your room."

Somewhere close by a cricket chirped. A soft breeze
blew, filling the air with the scent of flowers. Neither
noticed, so intent were they in each other.

"You—you did," Marnie said inanely, thinking how
good he looked, how good he smelled. She couldn't stop
thinking about what it felt like to touch him.

"I thought you'd be asleep."

She leveled her gaze on his face. "I tried but I
couldn't."

"I'm not surprised. Sleep doesn't come easily to me
these days, either."

"Are—are you just getting home from the office?"
The minute the question passed her lips, Marnie wished
she could recall it. Color stole into her face.

"Sorry," she added before he had a chance to respond.
"I didn't mean to pry." Of course, she meant to pry. But
what if he gives you an answer you don't want to hear?
For all she knew, he could have been making love to his
blond friend. The thought made her ill.

"Marnie, look at me."

Swallowing, she faced him.

"You have every right to pry," he said thickly.

"No..."

"Yes." His eyes held her. "Since I met you, I haven't been with another woman."

"Oh, Tate," she whispered, looking at him, enjoying the hard flex of his muscles as he leaned back and braced himself on his elbows. "We've got ourselves in a mess, haven't we?"

"A helluva one," he echoed with a ghost of a smile.

They were quiet for a while.

"Do you think they'll catch Elliot?" Marnie finally asked, kicking the water with one foot.

"It's only a matter of time."

"I hope you're right."

"I know what you're thinking."

"You do?"

"Why Anderson and Elliot would risk being seen together in broad daylight?"

Marnie frowned. "It just doesn't make sense."

"No, it doesn't. But like I said before, you never know about sickos."

"In light of what we know, do you think it was Anderson who was driving the car that night they took Lance?"

"More than likely. And to think that sonofabitch has been working for the company all this time."

"What about Elliot?"

"Him, too, but at least one of the engineers had enough sense to fire him for not doing his work."

"So you think they got together and planned the whole thing? I find that hard to believe."

"Me, too."

"Then it has to be revenge they want instead of money," Marnie said, thinking aloud.

"Exactly."

"Well, all I can say is that you have to be slightly deranged to do something like that."

Tate's face was as hard as his tone. "It's those types who have the guts to do it."

Marnie designed patterns in the water with her feet. "I can hardly stand to think about it. When I saw him today, that whole nightmarish episode replayed itself in my mind until I thought I'd scream."

"Shh, don't think about that now. You're safe." Tate's eyes were dark with concern. "Wanna swim?"

"I'd love to," she said, though a bit shakily.

Tate stood, only to then use the edge as a spring board and split the water with a perfect dive. When his head reappeared, Marnie eased into the pool.

Side by side they swam to the opposite end, but instead of clinging to the side and resting, Tate heaved himself up and out of the water. Startled, Marnie watched as he peeled off his trunks and kicked them aside with a toe.

Her breath hung suspended as the moonlight played over his aroused body.

With his eyes fixed on hers, he got back into the water and placed his hands on her shoulders.

"Every time I'm around you, I want to touch you."

"I feel the same way."

He kissed her then, with no excuses.

"You shouldn't...we shouldn't..." she whispered at last.

"Why?"

"The agents. They—"

"Can't see us," he murmured against her lips.

"Are you sure?"

"Positive," he said, sliding the flimsy straps off her shoulders, stroking them.

"Mmm, that feels good."

"Are you happy?"

"Yes."

"Me, too."

She looked at him carefully. "Is it wrong to feel this way when Lance is still missing?"

"We're doing everything possible to get him back."

"I know, but I still feel guilty."

"So do I, but that doesn't stop me from wanting you. Does that make me an insensitive s.o.b.?"

"No," she whispered. "It makes you human."

"Maybe, or maybe it's called living for the moment. I learned to do that in Nam, thinking that each breath I drew might be my last one. I swore on the spot that if I made it out of that hellhole, I wouldn't waste another second of my life."

"I sort of felt that way when Daddy was struck with Alzheimer's."

Without warning, he unhooked her top and thrust it aside. Together they watched it float away.

He turned back to her and for the longest time merely looked at her. "Do you know your skin glows in the moonlight?"

She smiled. "No." Her lashes fluttered; he brushed his mouth against them.

Then lowering his head, he ran his lips across her shoulders.

"Mmm, your mustache tickles," she mused aloud.

"Like it, huh?"

"Love it," she gasped as he took a soft bite from her shoulder. "I've never had the pleasure before...you."

He stopped what he was doing and chuckled. "Really?"

"Really, and it's dynamite against my skin," she whispered, wrapping her arms around his neck and returning the favor.

He moaned as her mouth made contact with his skin, hot and sweet.

"Marnie, Marnie, you make me crazy."

"Good."

He bent down and tongued a nipple. When she moaned deep in her throat, he lifted his head and watched her expression as he tongued the other nipple.

She dug her nails into his arms. He had to care. *He had to love her.* Surely it wasn't just sex. But because she was still riddled with doubt, she continued to hold on to her sanity and refused to be swept away by this hunger he created within her.

She inched her hands down and cupped the cheeks of his buttocks. They felt so hard, so smooth, so perfect.

"Does riding do this for you? Keep you in such good shape, I mean?"

"That and jogging." His mouth split into a grin. "I refuse to have a beer belly."

"I can't see that ever happening. You're too… perfect," she added shyly, feeling his hardness surge between them.

"But not nearly as perfect as you," he said, moving against her.

She couldn't speak.

His hands spanned her waist. "You're so tiny here."

"Exercise," she said breathlessly.

"What about here?" He laid his hands on her hips where he began to dislodge her trunks. "Is your tight little butt from exercise, too?'' he asked, his fingers seeking and finding her warmth.

Suddenly her legs threatened to buckle beneath her. ''I don't know,'' she whispered. ''Please…oh…you're…''

''Wrap your legs around me,'' he ordered urgently, cupping her buttocks.

''Have you ever made love like this before?''

''No.''

A warm sensation curled through her, but she couldn't tell him how he made her feel. And as he expanded inside her, all coherent thoughts fled her mind.

''Marnie,'' he whispered against her neck, ''I don't want to hurt you.''

''Let's get out, then,'' she said urgently, on fire for him.

Moments later found them on the grass where Tate immediately slipped into her. Then with her fingers sinking into his back, his lips dusted her neck, then danced down her stomach.

He pressed deeper into her. She reveled in his strength, hot and pulsing, as he began to move faster and faster. Her hands held him to her while he burst within her, almost stopping her breath. Then she exhaled in one long, shuddering sigh and dropped slowly back to earth.

The smell of bacon awakened her. She stretched, then smiled, remembering. With that smile still intact, Marnie reached out a hand to the space next to her. Empty. Tate was gone. Though disappointed, she wasn't surprised.

She glanced at the clock. Seven o'clock. He was probably already at the office. Since it was Annie who was responsible for the heavenly smell, Marnie made no effort to get up. She wanted to think.

Their lovemaking that began in the pool and ended in

her bed had been more than perfect. She lay waiting for that delicious shiver of remembrance to rush through her. But this time it didn't come. Fear came instead. What was she going to do when she had to give him up?

A short time later, after having showered and slipped into a caftan, Marnie padded into the kitchen, only to pull up short.

"Tate?"

He spun around from in front of the stove and grinned. "Mornin'."

"Morning," she said, walking deeper into the room. She didn't stop until she was beside him. He looked so sexy in a pair of cutoff jeans and worn T-shirt that she almost melted on the spot. "Where's Annie?"

"She's off."

"Oh."

He laughed. "What does that mean? Don't you think I'm capable of fixing you something to eat?"

"Mmm," she teased. "We'll just have to wait and see.

He laid the fork down and pulled her against him.

Marnie angled her head so that she could see him. His lashes were damp and thick. "Why aren't you at work?"

"I will be shortly."

"You smell absolutely delicious," she said, inhaling deeply.

He nibbled on her neck. "Not nearly as good as you, and if you don't move your you-know-what to that chair, I'm going to haul your delectable body back to bed."

Weakly, Marnie moved out of his arms and sat down. "Chicken."

She made a face. "Not chicken, just exhausted."

He threw back his head and laughed, then poured her a cup of coffee.

She had just taken the cup from him and sat down

when the kitchen door opened. She peered beyond Tate's shoulder, only to feel the cup slip from her hand.

Lance! she mouthed.

"Hello, my darling Marnie."

Marnie blinked back the tears. Still they came, saturating her cheeks, dripping into her mouth. Frantically, she delved into her purse, yanked out a Kleenex and wiped her face. What was wrong with her? She should be laughing instead of crying. Lance was back. He had made an amazing escape. That was cause for celebration, not tears.

Self-flagellation did not help. She had existed under such a strain for so long that even though the crisis was over, her emotions couldn't cope.

Finally gaining some measure of control, Marnie stole a glance at Tate. They were the sole occupants of the waiting room at a small private hospital on Houston's west side. It was obvious that relief had also escaped him.

He was staring out the window, his face grim, his shoulders rigid. He had changed out of his cutoffs and was wearing jeans and a sports shirt. She longed to reach out to him, to comfort him, but he suddenly seemed untouchable.

She tried to tell herself that his aloofness was not directed toward her personally, that he was consumed with worry over Lance. Since their arrival at the hospital over two hours ago, the doctor hadn't let Tate see Lance, nor had the doctor come and talked to him.

Unable to handle the silence another minute, Marnie got up from the leather sofa and went to the coffee bar. Once there, she turned and faced Tate's back. "Would you like a cup of coffee?"

Tate swung around and leveled his gaze on her. For

an instant she thought she saw his eyes soften, but she couldn't be sure.

"No thanks. I think I'd choke on it."

Suddenly Marnie lost her desire for any, as well. Still, coffee in her stomach, she reasoned, was better than nothing.

"Wonder what's taking them so long?" she asked, gripping the cup tightly.

"Beats me," Tate said, his tone clipped. "As far as I know, Dr. Mays hasn't even let the FBI in to see him."

"Well, thank Heavens he's alive," she mused aloud.

"Yeah," Tate muttered, "but just barely."

Marnie could understand Tate's impatience and concern. When Lance had walked into the kitchen, they had been speechless. But shock hadn't affected their eyesight. They had soaked up Lance's bruised and battered face. He looked as if he'd been in a boxing match and lost. Both cheeks were black and blue. A cut shone above his upper lip. And it had been apparent he hadn't eaten a decent meal since he'd been gone. He was skin and bones.

"Oh, Lance," Marnie had cried at last, forcing her jellylike legs to move in his direction.

"Lord, son," Tate said, closing the distance between them, as well.

Tate reached Lance first and embraced him. Marnie saw the tears in Tate's eyes and looked away, all the while grappling with her own torrid emotions.

Once Lance disentangled himself from Tate, he reached for Marnie. She went willingly into his arms and embraced his weakened body.

"Oh, Lance," she cried again, "thank God you're back."

"Thank God is right," Tate echoed. "There were

times when I didn't think I'd see you again.'' He stopped for a moment and drew in a harsh breath.

"My feelings exactly," Lance said weakly. "But I finally outwitted those sonofabitches." He gently pushed Marnie away and looked at Tate. "It wasn't easy."

Tate's Adam's apple worked overtime. "No, I'm sure it wasn't," he responded in a tight voice.

There was a moment of emotion-filled silence, then Tate cleared his throat and asked, "Did the FBI stop you at the gate?"

Lance nodded. "An army of them, but I told 'em I wanted to surprise you. I think I need to sit down," Lance added, mopping his brow.

"What you need is the hospital. Now." Tate's eyes sought Marnie's. "Get the car and I'll help Lance."

Minutes later, with two FBI cars trailing behind, Tate maneuvered the car onto the highway. Lance was sprawled across the back seat while Marnie sat up front with Tate.

However, Marnie kept her gaze locked on Lance, fearing he might pass out before they reached their destination.

"Don't you want to hear what happened?" Lance asked in a strained voice.

Tate's eyes were reflected in the rearview mirror. "Only if you're up to it."

"I'm...all right," Lance said, his gaze encompassing Marnie, as well.

Marnie didn't believe him for a second, and she knew Tate didn't, either. Anyone as banged up as Lance couldn't be all right.

"All I want is for those bastards to pay," Lance added, his voice regaining some of its lost strength.

"Oh, they'll pay, all right." Tate's tone was sharp and menacing.

Marnie shivered.

"Did you miss me, darling?" Lance asked, intruding on her thoughts.

Color surged into Marnie's face, and she dared not look at Tate. "Of course I…we…did. I…" She couldn't go on; her voice broke.

"I'm glad," Lance said warmly.

"How the hell did you get away?" Tate's voice sounded suddenly disembodied.

"Most of the time the bastards were both there for meals, but early this morning only one came—Anderson. When he untied my hands and gave me the slop he called hot cereal, I threw it in his face and ran like hell."

A smile flirted with Tate's lips. "Did you give them a hard time?"

Marnie looked on as Lance tried to smile; it turned into a wince instead. "I wish. But I didn't have a chance. The minute they shoved me inside this dark hole they called a room, they both took turns using me as a punching bag."

Marnie grieved for Lance. "Oh, God, they sound like animals."

"Worse," Tate said in a cold, flat voice.

"I heard them talking. They planned to hold you up for a ton of money," Lance said, sounding drained to the bottom.

Marnie had wondered when he was going to come off his adrenaline high. It had taken longer than she had thought.

"That's what we figured," Tate said, "ruling out that your abduction had nothing to do with the explosives project. But what we couldn't figure is why they waited so long to make their demands.''

"Because the longer they held me, the more anxious you'd become.''

A frown slashed Tate's face. "And give 'em what they asked for without quibbling?''

"That's right. Elliot was the brains behind the whole thing,'' Lance said, his voice once again beginning to fade. "After he was fired, he talked his good buddy Anderson into helping him.''

Muscles bunched in Tate's shoulders. "It's a damn wonder they pulled it off. There's not enough brains between the two of them to fill a thimble.''

"That's the sweet truth,'' Lance said, closing his eyes.

While Lance slept, Tate had concentrated on getting them safely to the hospital. Now, as they waited for the doctor, his patience was wearing thin.

"Are you sure you don't want some coffee?'' Marnie asked again, sipping on hers. "It tastes really good.''

Tate stared at her in brooding silence for a moment, then said, "Positive.''

"What about your mother?'' Marnie spoke quickly. Anything, she told herself, was better than the clawing tension between them. "Do...you want me to call her?''

"I'll do it, but thanks anyway.'' Tate's features relented somewhat. "Only I want to wait until Dr. Mays comes and talks to us.''

As if on cue, the doctor strode into the room, a grin adding relief to his harsh face and lips.

"It's good news, Tate. Physically Lance is going to be just fine. There are no internal injuries.''

Tate seemed to wilt. "That's damn good news.''

"What about mentally?'' Marnie put in anxiously, taking things a step further.

Dr. Mays's features changed. "Now that's a different matter altogether."

"What does that mean?" Tate asked sharply, his eyes narrowing.

"Calm down, Tate. Don't go gettin' your dander up. Your boy's been through hell and it's going to take time. I'm…"

"Spit it out, Clay."

"All right," Dr. Mays said, fixing his gaze on Tate. "There will more than likely be mental repercussions."

Tate's expression tightened. "So what do you suggest?"

Marnie's heart went out to him, and again she ached to touch him, to comfort him. Still she did neither. She simply ached in silence.

"I suggest that he remain here in the hospital for a few days under a psychiatrist's care."

"Whatever it takes." Tate's tone was dull.

There was a short silence.

"Can we see him?" Tate finally asked, his eyes on Marnie.

Dr. Mays didn't hesitate. "No problem."

"What about the FBI?"

"No problem there, either."

When they walked into Lance's stark room a few minutes later, Lance was prone on the bed, a frown on his face. He no longer looked as weak and washed out as he had earlier. In addition, he seemed to have regained some of his confidence.

"When can I go home?" His tone now had a sullen edge to it.

Relief shot through Marnie. Flashes of the old Lance— arrogant and spoiled to be exact—meant he was rebounding. However, she didn't think Tate shared her view.

"Not for a few days, I'm afraid," Tate said, crossing to Lance's bedside. "The doctor wants to keep you here for observation."

"Why?" Lance demanded. "I'm fine."

Tate flashed Marnie a brief glance, then turned back to his son.

"No, you're *not* fine."

"Well, the only way I'll stay is if Marnie stays with me."

Thrown into sudden confusion, Marnie couldn't say a word.

"Marnie?" Lance said again, a petulant ring to his voice.

Swallowing a sigh, Marnie crossed to the other side of the bed and placed her hand in his. "I'll be here as much as I can," she whispered, knowing her voice sounded unlike her own. Dear Lord, she was trying. But with Tate watching...

"It—it was thoughts of you that kept me sane." Lance paused and tightened his grip on her hand. "You won't leave me now, will you?"

The sudden stillness in the room was like a deafening roar.

Marnie lifted her head and met Tate's eyes, eyes that were as empty and bleak as a harsh winter day. Then he looked away.

Trying to ignore the stabbing pain around her heart, she forced herself to say, "No, I won't leave you."

Marnie remained true to her word. Almost every spare moment of every day was spent with Lance. It was only in the evenings that she returned to the ranch. And without fail found Tate absent.

She had wanted to go back to her condo, but until the

kidnappers were apprehended, neither Tate nor the FBI thought that was a good idea.

During that week the blissful times she and Tate had spent in each other's arms seemed more a dream than a reality. His odd behavior not only puzzled her, but upset her, as well.

Was it guilt that kept him from coming to her, or something else? It was that "something else" that had her nearly crazy.

The situation with Lance was a delicate one, she knew, and must be handled with care and caution. But just because it was impossible to blurt the truth to Lance right now shouldn't mean that she and Tate couldn't be together.

Instead of looking on the dark side, Marnie clung to the hope that once Lance got out of the hospital, things would return to normal—Tate would return to normal. What then? Would they tell Lance they were lovers? Yes. She was willing. But she honestly didn't know how Tate felt. The uncertainty was tearing her to pieces.

In the meantime she kept her promise to Lance, though each day was more trying than the one before. Lance's personality had undergone another change, a change that was definitely unpleasant. One would think that his ordeal would have matured him, made him look at life differently. Not so. If anything, Lance seemed more self-centered, more demanding than ever.

He was responding to treatment, even though at times he was plagued by nightmares and periods of deep depression. The majority of the time, it was all Marnie could do not to shake him.

Since she'd arrived at his room two hours ago, he'd been griping about everything in general and nothing in particular.

From her chair close to the bed, Marnie said, "I've decided nothing is wrong with you other than you're spoiled."

Lance gave her a dark look. "You've been around my father too much."

She took a deep breath to ease the pressure within her. "What's with you two, anyway?"

Ignoring his question and determined to steer the conversation onto a safe subject, Marnie said, "I keep thinking Dr. Mays is going to release you."

"Yeah, me too. The food stinks."

Marnie rolled her eyes. "Surely that's not the only reason you're anxious to leave?"

Lance reached for her hand and began caressing it. "No," he said, his voice low. "The main reason is that I want to make love to you."

"Lance, please," Marnie said between clenched teeth, wanting to scream in frustration. "We've—"

"Am I interrupting anything?"

Feeling her heart sink to her toes, Marnie forced herself to turn toward the door. Tate was leaning nonchalantly against the frame, looking cool and unflappable. Marnie sensed his mood was anything but. He refused to meet her eyes.

"Come in," she finally said, removing her hand from Lance's grasp. "You're...not interrupting anything."

"Says who?" Lance put in, a belligerent slant to his lips.

"Sorry," Tate said, only he didn't sound sorry. He sounded furious, Marnie thought. His nostrils were flaring.

When he spoke, his voice was calm, though a bit rough. "I've got some good news."

Marnie didn't say anything. Nevertheless, he had her

full attention. He looked wonderful, and she yearned to touch him.

"Anderson and Elliot have been arrested," he said.

"'Bout time," Lance said.

"I second that," Marnie added, still trying to get Tate to look at her, but without success. He seemed more than ever bent on ignoring her, and each time he did, she died a little on the inside.

"Does that mean they'll go straight to the pen?" Lance was asking.

"If I have my way, the bastards will fry."

"Or at least stay locked up for the rest of their lives," Marnie added.

Tate's gaze rested on her. In that second something trembled between them.

"You're out of danger now, you know." Tate's voice was thin.

"That…means I can go home."

"That's right." Tate drew a ragged breath. "That ought to make you happy."

What about you? Marnie wanted to scream. *Does it make you happy?* "It does, of course," she murmured politely, as if she were discussing the weather with a complete stranger.

If Lance sensed the tension in the room, he chose to ignore it. "Well, it makes me happy. It makes me damn happy."

Neither Marnie nor Tate said a word.

Again their silence seemed not to bother Lance. He went on, though he only had eyes for Marnie. "Maybe now I can convince you to marry me."

The air was fraught with tension.

Marnie's eyes swung to Tate; hers were pleading. A white line surrounded his lips.

"You two don't need me." Tate's voice was flat. "I'll see you later."

With that he walked out the door. Marnie sat in pained silence, feeling as if he'd taken part of her heart with him.

"Is that all, boss?"

"Yeah, Neal. I think that about does it for now."

"Good. I'll see to these contracts, then."

The instant Tate was alone, he got up, strode to the bar and poured himself a drink. Hell, he knew it was too early in the day to be indulging, but he didn't give a damn.

He had to have something to dull the pain.

He knew it would happen. And it had. She was breaking his goddamn heart, and there was nothing he could do about it.

He should have known better than to get involved with her. Dammit, he should never have touched her to begin with.

It was too late for self-recriminations. All there was to do now was suffer. Every time he saw her and Lance together, it was as though someone jammed a knife into his heart. It was worst when Lance touched her.

He had no right to feel that way. Marnie didn't belong with him. Not only was he too old for her, but too jaded. Sure, he could give her material things—the best money could buy. But that wasn't enough. In the end he knew that wouldn't hold her. Even money, after so long a time, paled.

No, she deserved someone better. She deserved someone young, someone who could make her laugh, fill a house with children's laughter.

But was that someone his son? In the beginning he'd

been against a relationship between them, for all the wrong reasons. He'd thought Marnie was a gold digger and he'd felt Lance was too spoiled and selfish for a lasting relationship. But now he truly believed that Lance was in love. And if he, Tate, stepped out of the picture, Marnie would find happiness with Lance, as it should be.

Suddenly a bitter taste flooded Tate's mouth and he had the urge to throw the glass in his hand against the wall. Suddenly he did just that, the sound rocking the room like a small explosion. When quiet finally came, he felt no better.

Completely drained, he sat down and slumped over his desk, head in his hands.

How was he ever going to let her go? He didn't know. He honestly didn't know.

"Tate…I want to talk to you. Please."

Marnie, as she'd done once before, had decided to wait up for him, no matter how late the hour. This was her last night at the ranch; tomorrow she planned to return to her condo.

Before she left, though, she had to get some answers from Tate. If it was over between them, she wanted him to say it. If he didn't want to ever hold her again or make love to her again, she wanted him to tell her to her face.

Lance's two-week stint in the hospital was coming to an end. He was due to be released in a few more days. During that second week, Tate had remained his unapproachable self. She simply couldn't take it anymore.

Away from Tate, her life had ceased to have meaning. Things that had been important to her paled in comparison to her feelings for Tate.

Now, as she confronted him at eleven o'clock in the evening, she wasn't sure her idea was a good one, after all. If his foreboding features were anything by which to judge, he wasn't thrilled to see her.

"What about?" he asked, treading lightly into the room, then tossing his briefcase on the bar, where he mixed himself a drink.

Marnie nursed her lower lip. She had rehearsed this speech over and over, only to feel the words suddenly desert her along with her nerve. Finally she forced them out.

"You know what about. Us."

With his free hand Tate yanked at the tie around his neck. "There's no us, Marnie," he said flatly. "There never was."

She felt as if he'd speared her heart. "But—"

"Does Lance still want to marry you?"

"Yes, but—"

"Good. You have my blessings."

Ten

Marnie went pale, and the floor underneath her feet seemed to shift. He wanted her to marry Lance. *Impossible!* He didn't mean that. He *couldn't* mean that.

"What—what did you say?" Even to her own ears, her voice sounded as if she were dying.

Tate shoved a hand through his hair. "You heard me," he said tersely.

"But I don't understand...." Marnie shook her head in misery and bewilderment. There had always been that deep-seated fear that he didn't love her, after all. Still, she hadn't dreamed their relationship would end like this. Oh, God, not like this. "You—you can't mean that," she wheezed.

"I mean it," he said, his voice sounding hollow.

Marnie flinched visibly. This wasn't the same man who so recently had taken her in his arms and made love to her, deeply and passionately. This was a cold, hard stranger whom she barely recognized.

"You had to know it would end sometime," he said, his eyes never leaving her face.

Marnie refused to let him know how much he was hurting her. She lifted her chin, though it shook despite her efforts to the contrary. "Are you doing this because you think I'm not good enough for you?"

"Hell!" His disgust was obvious. "If I thought that, would I be encouraging you to marry my son?"

Marnie caught her breath and worked on ignoring the lump stuck in her throat. "I don't want to marry Lance. I've never wanted to marry Lance. He's…a spoiled rich kid who's never grown up." She paused, trembling. "Is it because Lance touched me and I didn't pull away…?"

"Look, let me make it clear right now that it's not jealousy that's causing me to end our relationship." He paused and breathed deeply. "Although, I will admit, it nearly ripped my gut to pieces."

"Oh, Tate," Marnie whimpered.

"But at the same time," he went on, as if she hadn't spoken, "I saw how right you two were together, how much happier he could make you than I."

"That's not true!"

"Face it, Marnie, I'm too old for you."

"That's ridiculous," she cried, twisting her fingers together. "Age doesn't matter when you love someone," she added, brokenhearted.

"What about children?"

"What about them?"

He snorted. "You deserve to have them, and I'm too old to start over."

"That's simple. We won't have any. Anyway, I want you, not children."

"You say that now," he said stubbornly.

She placed her hands over her ears. "Stop it! Stop it right now! Stop trying to put the blame on me. It's you who's making the excuses." She choked on a sob. "You're the one who's afraid, who can't make the commitment, who—who doesn't love me!"

"Dammit, that's not it!"

"Then what is it?" She was begging now, but she didn't care. "Lance? Is that it? Is that what this is all about? Guilt?"

Looking at him, into his smoldering eyes, she felt her senses stir with a primitive emotion only he could arouse in her.

"It's over, Marnie." He swallowed hard. "There's no other way."

"Oh, Tate," she breathed. "Don't make this the end, please. Sacrificing us for Lance won't work. He's not for me. Can't you see that?"

Tate's eyes were filled with agony. "Do you think I wanted it this way?" he muttered harshly.

She deliberately moved closer to him, aching to smell him, touch him, wrap her arms around his flesh.

"Oh, God, Marnie," he groaned. Then pulling her to him, he parted her lips with his own.

Fiercely, she clung. Coherent thoughts refused to form, words refused to come. Only the urgency of wordless, pristine need sustained her.

Then it was over. His breath ragged, Tate thrust her away and turned, his shoulders bent as if from an unbearable weight.

Tears streaked Marnie's cheeks. Oh, God, she was losing the battle. His guilt was proving too powerful a stumbling block to overcome.

"Tate..."

"Don't...Marnie." His voice sounded strangled. "It's over."

Suddenly desperate, Marnie grabbed his arm and spun him around. "Tell me you don't love me!" she cried. "Look me in the eye and tell me that."

Tate hesitated, looking as if there was nothing left inside him. But when he spoke, his tone was low and even. "I don't love you."

There was so much she wanted to say, so much she wanted to do. But she did nothing. Instead, she just stood there and watched as he turned and walked out the door.

With a muted cry she sank to her knees, harsh sobs racking her body.

Tate's cruel rejection of her had been a blow to her heart. Only her pride saw her through the dark week that followed.

She had avoided Tate, which hadn't been difficult as things at the office were under control, leaving him free to remain at the ranch.

While he'd gone on a horse-buying trip, she'd quickly and quietly moved out of the ranch and back into her condo. Kate's presence had been a godsend.

"I'd like to give that bastard a piece of my mind," she'd said as soon as Marnie filled her in on the latest developments.

Just thinking about Kate's flashing eyes and wrinkled nose brought a fleeting smile to Marnie's lips.

"Marnie."

Shaking her head and forcing herself back to the moment at hand, she turned around and faced Lance. Because of a minor setback, he hadn't been released from the hospital.

"Yes," she said, smiling at him absently.

"We've spent a lot of time together lately, right?"

"Yes," she said again, her tone guarded.

"So doesn't that prove that we'd make a great team—"

She waved her hand in silent protest. "Don't, Lance. Don't even start. I know where you're headed, and it won't work. Anyway, you promised that the word *us* would not be discussed."

Red washed Lance's face. "Dammit, Marnie, I'm not going to give you up without a fight."

She bounded out of the chair. "You have no choice," she said coldly. "The sooner you understand that, the sooner you can get on with your life."

There was a long pause, which solved nothing.

"Is he good in bed?"

Marnie's eyes widened in astonishment.

"Gawd." Lance drawled out the word. "Don't play the innocent with me."

"Lance…"

"I know about you and my father."

Marnie felt her stomach drop away. "How…long have you known?"

"I might have had a few licks on the head, but I'm not blind, Marnie." His tone was cutting.

She straightened. "I never thought you were."

"So when's the wedding?"

"There's…not going to be—" her voice cracked "—a wedding."

"So he won't marry you, huh?"

Hot, boiling fury coursed through her. "Go to hell, Lance."

He laughed darkly. "Most likely I will, thanks to you."

Marnie gasped.

As if sensing he had gone too far, he said, "Look—"

Marnie cut him off tersely. "I'm going to quit the company, so you won't have to worry about me being around." She paused and with forced steadiness walked to the door. "Then, I'll probably leave town."

"Does Tate know?"

"No, and I'm not going to tell him, either." She paused and raised a hand to her heart; she could feel the thunder of its beat. "I guess this is goodbye, Lance."

Lance stood at the edge of the bed and jammed his hands into the pockets of his jeans. "If you walk out that door, you'll be making a mistake."

She turned the knob.

"Dammit, I'm every bit the man my father is!"

Marnie spun around, her eyes flashing. "Grow up, Lance. You'll never be the man Tate is."

When she walked down the hall a second later, she could still see Lance's gaping mouth.

For the first time in a long while, Marnie smiled from the heart.

Tate knew he would pay for rebuilding the entire fence on the south side of the pasture at one whack. But he didn't care. Manual labor had once again saved his sanity.

J.D., his beer belly wiggling like a bowl of jelly, had all but threatened to quit if Tate didn't stop working so hard. Tate had just as quickly told him that he'd do what he damned well pleased on his own ranch.

Muttering something under his breath, J.D. had stamped off. Then he'd stopped, wheeled around and said, "Whatever's got you all torn up inside is gonna cause you to break your back."

Now, as Tate dropped his hammer and stood, the sun

bearing down on him with no mercy, he admitted that J.D. had been right. He didn't know how much longer he would be able to survive without Marnie. No amount of physical abuse had been able to drive her from his heart.

Was she right? Was he just using guilt as an excuse when in reality he was a coward? Was he afraid to take a chance on love again? Afraid to make a commitment? Or was the reason more pointed than that? Was he afraid to love *Marnie*, for fear she would soon tire of him? She was so young, so full of life.

And, ultimately, was he strong enough, unselfish enough, to let her marry Lance? Just the thought of them making love...well, he couldn't bear to think about that.

Yet that was a real possibility. After all, he'd more than done his part to bring it about. Still, Lance had not mentioned Marnie since he'd been home, and Tate hadn't asked.

Tears burned his eyes. He raised an unsteady hand, covering them. The sunlight seemed to pierce his brain. He fought for breath.

Suddenly the sound of horse's hooves claimed his attention. Once again shading his eyes, he peered into the distance and watched a rider approach. It was Lance.

Swallowing a tired sigh, Tate made his way toward his son. Momentarily, he grasped the mare's reins and peered up into Lance's face. "What's up?"

Without preamble Lance said, "I need to talk to you."

"Sure thing." Tate removed his Stetson and wiped his brow. "Only not here in this sun."

Silently, Lance and horse followed Tate to a huge oak that provided more than ample shade. Tate propped himself against it while Lance rested an elbow on the saddle.

"Is something wrong?" Tate asked at last, a fear of another kind festering inside him.

"I'm moving out, getting an apartment."

"You won't get any argument out of me," Tate said easily. "It's past time you were on your own."

"Marnie's leaving."

If it was his intent to shock, Lance had hit the mark. Tate went still; every nerve in his body seemed to stop functioning. "Leaving?"

"Yeah, as in the company." Lance's tone now held a note of triumph, as though taking great delight in telling Tate that. "Maybe even Houston."

Refusing to rise to the bait, though his insides were clamoring, Tate forced his expression to remain blank. "I'm...that's too bad."

Lance snorted. "Hell, Dad, spare me the rhetoric. I know about you and Marnie."

Tate suddenly felt cold inside. "There is no Marnie and me. I won't stand in your way if you still want to marry her."

"And take your leftovers? No thanks."

Blood thundered to Tate's head and his eyes iced over. "I ought to make you apologize for that remark—or better still, I ought to drag you off that horse and beat the daylights out of you."

When Lance didn't say anything, Tate hammered on, "I thought that Marnie would be better off with you, but I was wrong. Dead wrong. I love you son, but God help me, I've ruined you. And until you grow up, you're of no use to anyone, most of all yourself."

Lance eased off the saddle onto the ground where he pawed the grass. "Look, I'm sorry, I was way out of line—"

"You damn straight you were."

"About you…and Marnie—"

"That's no longer any of your damn business."

Lance turned red, but when he spoke, his voice was forceful. "Well, just for the record, I think you're a fool if you let her go."

"I couldn't agree more."

"So now can we talk, really talk?"

"Later," Tate said, spinning around and heading for his mount, which was grazing close by.

"Where you going?"

Tate didn't miss a stride. "Guess."

"Are you sure quitting your job is for the best?"

Marnie stared at Kate and smiled bleakly. "No, right now I'm not sure of anything, other than the fact that I can't continue working for Tate and keep my sanity."

They were in Marnie's condo, sitting on the couch and drinking coffee. Both their expressions were sober, as sober as the weather outside. Rain was falling. The night was warm.

"Boy, did that bastard do a number on you."

"That he did," Marnie agreed on a shaky note. "This sounds crazy, I know, but the only time I find peace of mind is when I visit Daddy."

"Have you told Tate yet?" Kate asked after a moment.

"I told Lance instead."

"So what happens now?"

"I'm—I'm going to look for another job."

"Oh, Marnie, honey, I wish I could say something, anything that would make you stop hurting."

Marnie felt numb, but she had to handle it. "Me, too, only we both know that's impossible."

Kate opened her mouth to respond only to be cut off

by the chiming of the doorbell. "You expecting company?"

Through unwanted tears, Marnie peered at the clock on the wall. "Not at ten o'clock."

"Want me to answer it?"

"Please," Marnie whispered, drawing the sash on her paisley robe tighter and struggling to regain her composure. Every time she thought about Tate, talked about him, she cried. Just getting through each day was hell.

"Marnie."

She could tell by the tone of Kate's voice that something was wrong. With her heart in her throat, Marnie swung around.

Tate stood in the shadows of the entrance hall, his eyes fixed on her. For a moment Marnie couldn't function, could hardly breathe.

His hair and mustache sparkled with raindrops under the muted lamplight. His jeans and blue shirt were wet, as well, adhering to his body like a second skin.

No one spoke; the silence was long and heavy.

Then Kate coughed and stammered, "M-Marnie, hon, I gotta run. I'll…talk to you later."

Marnie could only nod and watch as Kate scooted out the door.

Still Marnie did not move, nor did Tate. They could only stare, their eyes devouring each other.

"God, Marnie, I've…"

Marnie steeled her heart against his husky tone and the agony in his eyes. "What are you doing here?" she whispered, barely able to stem the tide of her emotions. He looked so big, so strong, so dear.…

"Lance told me you were leaving."

"He shouldn't have."

Tate smiled at that, only it never reached his eyes. "Did you think I wouldn't find out?"

She didn't answer.

"That's not all he told me."

"Oh." her voice was faint.

"He told me I was a fool."

Her eyes widened.

"Yeah, imagine that," Tate said with a cynical smile. "Imagine my son telling me I was a fool and my agreeing with him."

Marnie couldn't remove her gaze, held spellbound by what he was saying.

Her voice trembled. "I...don't know why you came, but it's late and—"

"I love you, Marnie."

For a second she thought her ears were playing tricks on her. Or was she hearing words that she had only heard echoing in the chambers of her heart?

When she didn't respond, Tate edged closer. "I love you," he said again, his voice warm, colored with passion.

Stifling a cry, Marnie reached for him, her eyes brimming with tears. When he crushed her against him, she felt his strength surge through her. "Tate. Oh, Tate...I missed you so. I love you." She didn't want to hold back or hide anything from him.

"Can you ever forgive me?" he asked desperately. "You were right about everything. I was afraid. But once a dream is shattered, trust comes hard."

Marnie pulled back. "What—what about Lance?" She had to ask. She had to know.

Tate bracketed her face with his hands and looked into her eyes. "I tried to do what I thought was best for him, for you, only it wasn't." He paused as if struggling to get the words out. "I love him, but God help me, I love you more."

The sounds of belonging rang in his tearful whisper. The firm strength of his arms was tender and gentle.

"Don't," she whispered, opening her lips to his. They kissed, hotly and deeply, their mouths speaking their hearts' desires.

"Oh, Marnie," Tate whispered, clutching her tightly, their tears mingling. "Marry me. Now."

Something eased within Marnie's heart while they seemed suspended in time.

"Hold me, Tate. Don't ever let me go."

"Never, my darling, never."

* * * * *

AND BABY MAKES
PERFECT

Prologue

Sweat trickled down his face, but Drew MacMillan failed to notice or to care until the liquid dripped into his mouth. He grimaced; the sour taste forced him to lift the tail of his T-shirt and swipe at his lips. Still, his concentration held as he stared at the newspaper article.

Houston's most eligible bachelor, Drew MacMillan, strikes out again. Engagement #2 has apparently been called off by his fiancée. Could the automobile magnate and racer be less than perfect, after all? Mmm, stay tuned....

"Damn," Drew muttered, his features twisted into a scowl. Gossip columns. They ought to be outlawed, he thought. Furthermore, someone ought to shoot the people who wrote them, this one in particular.

Yet he, like scores of others on Sunday morning, found himself reading the fat, juicy column.

Drew had awakened around seven and decided it would be blasphemy to pass up the opportunity to jog on this spring morning. April rarely saw a cool morning, and even though he normally didn't exercise on Sunday, he'd made the exception today.

He'd enjoyed the three-mile run, especially since the dogwood trees and purple wisteria were in full bloom. He appreciated the finer things in life only when he ran; most of the time he was so busy that nature's beauty passed him by.

Though dripping wet, he'd walked through the side door of his southwest Houston condo completely relaxed, his thoughts on a meeting he would have later that day with his assistant to discuss an important business deal. He'd taken a quick shower, slipped into a T-shirt and pair of athletic shorts, then grabbed a cup of coffee.

He'd sat down at the kitchen table and spread the paper. He hadn't been in the mood to read the society page, but something had drawn his gaze, a premonition maybe. When his name had leapt out at him, he'd frozen inside, as if he'd been zapped with an electric shock.

Now, as he reread the insulting words, Drew pushed back from the table, snatched the sheet containing the article, wadded the page into a tiny ball and tossed it into the nearest trash can. Garbage, pure and simple. For starters, his fiancée hadn't broken the engagement, *he* had.

Drew reached for his cup and took a sip of the now tepid coffee. He muttered another expletive, only to then hear a tap on the back door.

Before he could say anything, the door opened and his assistant, Skip Howard, sauntered over the threshold.

Skip took one look at Drew's face and grinned.

"What's got you so riled? You look like you just bit into an apple and found a worm."

Drew's brows furrowed into a deeper frown. "Funny."

"Wasn't meant to be."

Drew felt the tight coil around his belly loosen. "You're right. I did just bite into the apple—and I found the worm."

Skip laughed. "Wanna explain?"

Skip, a crackerjack second-in-command, was also a good friend. Drew respected and admired him because of his integrity and his loyalty.

To look at Skip, though, the word ordinary or nondescript jumped to mind. Everything about the man was average. Average height, average weight and average features. His deep chestnut-colored hair and heavy-lidded eyes even looked average on him. But you had to be around him only a short time before you realized there was nothing average about his mind or his sharp and sometimes caustic wit. When Skip spoke, Drew paid attention.

"You still haven't answered my question."

Drew pointed toward the trash.

Skip moved to the brass container and peered inside. "I don't see anything except maybe a spit wad."

Drew laughed a humorless laugh.

Skip shrugged, then leaned down and retrieved the paper. While he read it, Drew poured Skip a cup of coffee and set it on the table. But Drew was too restless to sit down. He propped himself against the cabinet and watched from under hooded eyes for his friend's reaction.

Finally Skip looked up, a wide grin once again fixed on his face.

"What the hell's so funny?"

Skip's grin fled. "Nothing really. It's just that you're so uptight."

"Wouldn't you be?"

"Yeah, guess so. The lady doesn't pull any punches, does she?"

"Think I've got grounds for a suit?"

Skip reached for his coffee without taking his eyes off Drew. "Why don't you lighten up, take it in stride? The publicity's good for your image."

"That's bull and you know it. That broad has attacked me personally, and I sure as hell don't want her to get away with it."

Skip lifted his shoulders in another shrug. "When you're in the limelight you should expect this kind of stuff."

Drew couldn't argue. Thanks to hard work, his two Jaguar dealerships in Texas and one in Louisiana were booming. His success had enabled him to do what he really wanted and that was race cars. His racetrack skills, combined with his reputation as a ladies' man, made him fair game for the press.

"So you think I ought to leave well enough alone, huh?"

Skip stretched his legs out in front of him and crossed his arms over his chest. "Sure do."

Drew thrust a hand through his sandy-colored hair. "What if it doesn't blow over? What if she thinks she can take potshots at me anytime she wants to and get away with it?"

"If she does, then you just might have to do something about it. Until then, my advice is just to ignore it and see if interest in you dies a natural death."

Drew knew Skip was right. Nevertheless, it galled him to sit by and let the columnist get away with what amounted to slander. Maybe Skip was right, though, and he was making a mountain out of a molehill. He'd be the first to admit that he had a low boiling point, that things got to him in the worst sort of way. But incompetence made him see red. And that lady gossip columnist was as incompetent as hell for not getting her facts straight before she printed them.

"I guess it's safe to say, you're not in the mood to discuss business?"

Skip's brisk voice snapped Drew back to the moment at hand. "No, but I don't have much choice. We can't keep Blackwell Realty waiting much longer. If we don't give them an answer soon, we'll lost the property."

Skip leaned down and reached for his briefcase. "It's a good deal, Drew, in spite of the price."

"I don't know." Drew bent over the papers that Skip spread across the table. "What if we decide not to put another dealership in Texas? I sure don't want to be stuck with the property."

"But—"

The phone rang. Drew got up and crossed the room to the buffet where it sat and lifted the receiver.

As he listened, his face turned a pasty white.

"What's wrong?" Skip demanded.

"It's John, my daddy."

"On the phone?"

Drew grimaced as he hung up. "No. That was the family doctor."

"Uh-oh, bad news."

"John's had a stroke."

"Hey, man, I'm sorry."

"Yeah, me too," Drew said, his voice lifeless.

Skip stood and gathered his papers. "Well, don't worry about things here. If the Blackwells don't want to wait for an answer, then to hell with them. You go ahead and do what you have to do." Skip paused. "Is there anything I can do?"

"No," Drew said. "Thanks."

Skip walked to the door. "Let me hear."

"Yeah."

"You sure you're all right?"

Drew nodded. "I'm fine."

Skip looked as if he wanted to argue, but he didn't. Instead, he opened the door and walked out.

Drew stood rigid, his hands balled into fists. He didn't want to go home. He was concerned about his daddy, but there was no love lost between them. He'd be the first to admit that and his daddy second. Still, that didn't alter the fact that he had to return home to MacMillan, Texas. He had his mother to think about. And he loved her very much.

He turned and headed for his bedroom to pack his bags. Dread weighted his footsteps.

One

"**I**f you want *my* opinion, I think he can't get it up." Ignoring the startling silence in the nail shop, and the uncertain giggles, Hazel Minshew went on, "Oh, what's that word?" She pursed her lips and she flapped her hand, well aware that she was center stage, and loving it. "*Impotent*—that's it."

Ann Sinclair tried to control the shock waves that coursed through her, but she couldn't. Her hand shook to such an extent that the polish applicator in her hand slid up Jewell Thornton's fat finger.

"Oh!" Jewell cried, horrified.

Color flooded Ann's face as her eyes locked on the splash of Positively Red nail polish that covered all of Jewell's finger. For a moment Ann couldn't seem to move, appalled at her lack of control.

Pauline Sims, also waiting her turn for a manicure, laughed out loud. "Goodness, Ann, I don't think I've ever seen you so flustered." She lowered her voice conspiratorially. "Us talking about Drew MacMillan wouldn't have anything to do with it, now would it?"

Before Ann could reply, Sophie Renfro, her employee and friend said, "Hey, Pauline, cut it out. You know how Ann feels about gossip, especially the garbage-can variety."

Ann cast Sophie a grateful glance while she doused two cotton balls with remover and vigorously rubbed Jewell's hand.

When Drew MacMillan's name had been brought up initially, Ann had made it a point to distance herself from the conversation. She did in fact abhor gossip and always tried her best to control it in its earliest stages. But she wasn't successful all the time; today proved that.

"Why, that's the silliest thing I've ever heard," Pauline added, batting her black false eyelashes. "I can't imagine Drew MacMillan not being able to get a hard-on."

Ann knew beauty parlors and nail shops were hotbeds for idle gossip. When she'd opened Polished Choice several years ago, she'd been determined her shop was going to be different. For the most part, it had been.

Maybe if she pointedly continued to ignore the women, they would cease discussing Drew's sex life, of all things.

"Makes sense to me," Hazel said, waving the society-page article through the air. "Why else can't he keep a woman?"

"Oh, for heaven's sake, Hazel. Get real." Both of Pauline's eyelashes were slapping her upper cheeks. "I imagine Drew's just the opposite. Why I bet he's randy as hell."

If the situation hadn't been so serious, Ann would have laughed, fully expecting at least one set of Pauline's eyelashes to pop off from sheer overexertion. But the situation was serious. Enough was enough.

"Okay, ladies," Ann said. "You've had your say and your fun. If you don't mind, I think you've raked Drew MacMillan over the coals enough. Anyway, you all know the stuff that's in the news is not worth the paper it's printed on. It's gossip and that's all. Besides, Drew MacMillan is not a topic I want discussed in my shop."

Though she spoke in her usual soft, modulated voice, there was a hint of steel behind it. Everyone heard it and wasn't about to ignore her. When Ann's violet-colored eyes darkened and her jaw clenched, she meant business.

She'd much rather concentrate on her good fortunes than the MacMillan family. She gazed around the shop and smiled to herself.

She had worked hard to obtain the success she now enjoyed as the only licensed manicurist in a town the size of MacMillan. In fact it was almost unheard of. When she'd conceived the idea, naysayers had voiced their opinions loud and clear.

"You're crazy. MacMillan's not large enough to support such a venture."

"You'll lost your shirt, young lady, just as sure as it rains buckets in East Texas."

Ann had ignored those comments and a dozen others like them, determined that MacMillan, along with the neighboring counties, could support her shop.

Thanks to the MacMillans, MacMillan, Texas, was a well-heeled town of approximately five thousand. The town bore the MacMillan name because the family owned the majority of the land that comprised it. Along with the newspaper and the grocery/hardware store, a large lumber company provided the community's lifeblood. Combined, those businesses made MacMillan prosperous.

Ann's success, however, hadn't come easily. She had overcome great odds, the main one being her poor background. She had been reared in a home where money was short but love was abundant.

The latter hadn't been enough for her brother, Peter, who was ashamed that his parents were employed by the MacMillans. Alice Sinclair had labored as a maid, while Burton had worked as a gardener and general handyman.

Even so, Peter and Drew had been best friends. Ann, two years older, used to envy her brother. She'd had a secret crush on Drew—thought he was the handsomest boy she had ever seen. But he'd never known she was alive except as Peter's older sister.

Despite the pain and heartache the MacMillans later brought to bear on her family, Ann didn't hold grudges. Well…maybe a slight grudge against John MacMillan. In fact, she wasn't sure she could ever forgive him. But Drew was a different matter altogether.

Ann sometimes wondered if she hadn't carried that schoolgirl crush into womanhood, only to dismiss the thought as both ridiculous and ludicrous.

"You're right, of course, Ann," Pauline said, bridging the long silence and breaking into Ann's thoughts, the lines around her eyes easing somewhat under her smile. "We ought to be ashamed, especially with John lying ill in the hospital."

Another moment of silence followed, as the ladies weighed the changes that would affect the town, and their livelihoods, should something happen to John MacMillan.

"I would've never thought it, but my nails look

great,'' Jewell said, eyeing Ann carefully, as if trying to read what went on behind that reserved but warm facade.

The entire time Ann had been woolgathering, she had automatically put a second coat of polish on Jewell's nails, followed by the top coat. Now she was about to put solar oil on them to seal the polish and moisten the cuticles.

Ann smiled. ''I'm glad you're pleased. I know you don't want to hear this, but next week I'll probably have to cut them or you're going to lose two, that I know of, on your right hand.''

Jewell's lips puckered. ''If I lose even one before the country-club dance this weekend, I'll just die.''

Ann knew that if she looked at Sophie, she would burst out laughing. Sophie's eyes were sure to be facing heavenward.

Keeping a straight face was hard to do, especially when Hazel put in scathingly, ''Cool it. No one's going to notice whether you lose a fingernail or not.''

''I don't know about y'all, but I'm tired of paying so much for groceries.'' Only after Sophie smoothly changed the subject did the ladies settle down.

''Whew, I don't know about you, but I'm exhausted,'' Sophie said an hour later. It was after five o'clock, and the shop had closed for the day. ''Those three women drive me up the wall.''

Ann had just cleaned her station and treated herself to a mug of coffee. She'd had two sips, but they had failed to buoy her spirits.

She focused her attention outside. She found that looking at the glories of springtime cheered her. The park across the street had more than its fair share of huge oak trees, their branches forming odd, irregular patterns. Beneath them, annuals carpeted the ground in a blaze of color.

Sophie chuckled. "I thought I'd lose it for sure when you smeared that polish all over Jewell's fat hand." Sophie's chuckle burgeoned into full laughter. "Tell you the truth, I loved it."

A smile toyed with Ann's lips. "You're bad, my friend."

"I know."

"Thanks for siding with me."

Always, Ann thought. She wouldn't have made it this far without Sophie's help and support. Sophie worked hard, then at the end of the day went home to her three-year-old whom she alone supported, thanks to a husband who had abandoned her when she got pregnant.

But Ann knew her friend wasn't destined to stay single much longer. With her fiery red hair, pixie features and mischievous brown eyes, she never lacked for male companionship.

"Hey, no way could I sit back and let them rip apart a hunk like Drew MacMillan. Why he's..."

Ann's smile faded.

"Sorry," Sophie said, an odd look in her eyes. After a brief pause, she went on, "Look, considering how close we've become since I've been working for you, don't you think it's time you leveled with me, told me what the deal is between you and the MacMillans?"

"It's not a pretty story," Ann said with a sigh.

"I'd still like to hear it."

Ann's words came slowly. "You know that both my parents worked for the MacMillans."

Sophie nodded.

"And my brother, Peter, and Drew were close. Anyway, Drew loved cars, and because he had money, he had a fast, powerful car, which he loved. The faster, the better.''

Ann paused again and leaned tiredly against the window ledge. ''One afternoon after football practice, Peter was in the car with Drew when a truck ran a stop sign.''

Sophie sucked in her breath.

Ann continued, a faraway look in her eyes. ''Drew slammed into the side of the truck, and though Drew wasn't hurt, Peter was.''

''God, what a mess.''

''You don't know the half. Drew was absolved of any wrongdoing, but Peter blamed him for the knee damage that ended his dream of playing pro ball.''

''A crying shame.''

''Peter never recovered and is still a big problem.''

''And something happened to your daddy, right?'' Sophie flushed and looked slightly embarrassed. ''I have to admit that when I first came here, I heard some gossip—''

Ann held up her hand. ''Don't apologize. For the longest time, the Sinclair scandal was the hot topic of conversation.'' She didn't curb the bitterness that laced her words.

''What happened?'' Sophie pressed gently.

''Shortly after the accident, John accused my daddy of stealing, then fired him. Though my daddy was later found innocent, the damage had been done.'' Ann blinked back tears.

''Look, if this is too painful—''

''Not too long afterward, Daddy...took his own life.''

The room fell ominously silent.

Sophie gnawed the inside of her lips. ''Oh, Ann, honey, how horrible.''

''Yeah, it was a bit much to handle,'' Ann said, and

dabbed at the tears with her fingertips. "But it happened a long time ago, and as the old saying goes, 'time is a great healer.'"

"Look, why don't we stop by Sam's and get something to eat? Maybe it'll put a little color back in your cheeks."

Ann smiled wanly. "Thanks, but no thanks. If you don't mind, I think I'll go home, take a hot bath and go to bed."

"Well, if you're sure—"

"I'm sure. You go on. I'll talk to you later."

Fifteen minutes later, Ann locked the door behind her and headed home. *Home.* That word should have made her feel better. It didn't. Her thoughts were too chaotic. Talking about the past, about Drew, had upset her far more than she cared to admit.

Would he come home to check on his daddy? If so, would she see him?

Two

Ann opened the door to her house with her mind still churning. A much-craved sense of peace settled over her, and she smiled.

The small, but adorable, house, with its living room and attached kitchen, fireplace, two bedrooms and two baths, belonged to her. That wasn't exactly true, she corrected mentally. The mortgage company had its fair share. But she was confident that one day her home would belong to her.

The living area had high ceilings and many windows. Sunlight flooded through the glass, expanding the dimensions of the room. However, its spaciousness gave way to an ordered clutter. Live plants, shelves of books, bric-a-brac and family pictures were scattered about the room, along with framed prints on the wall, a flowered, over-stuffed couch and several inviting chairs.

An air of coziness prevailed that suited Ann just fine

and fitted her long-range plans. One day, the spare bedroom would belong to the baby she had hopes of adopting. Ann wrapped her arms around herself and squeezed, a feeling of excitement sweeping over her.

A baby. A real live human being. Her baby. Hugging that sweet thought, she scurried into her bedroom, dumped her purse and briefcase, then kicked off her shoes.

Her feet sank into the soft, seafoam-green carpet as she made her way to the closet. A few minutes later, she shed her skirt and blouse for a pair of walking shorts and cotton shirt.

She padded back into the kitchen and helped herself to a glass of iced tea from the fridge. A ton of paperwork awaited her, but for the moment, she aimed to sit and enjoy the peace and quiet.

She loved her job and couldn't wait to get to work, but the constant chatter often got on her nerves. She considered herself a "people person," yet a side of her coveted the time she was alone.

She walked into the living room and sat on the sofa. She curled her feet under her and was about to sip her tea when the phone rang. Her heart jumped as it always did, especially when she was at home. For days, she'd been expecting a call from the state adoption agency; she had filled out the preliminary application one month ago.

With shaking hands, she lifted the receiver. "Hello," she said.

"Ms. Sinclair?"

"Yes?"

"This is Dorothy Sable at the state agency."

"Oh."

The woman's voice held amusement as if she expected

that reaction. "I'm calling to let you know that your application has been placed in the 'active file.'"

"Oh," Ann said again, then felt like an idiot for her tongue-tied behavior.

Dorothy Sable chuckled warmly.

"That means my name has been actually placed on the list?" Ann asked in a surprisingly strong voice.

"Exactly. The next step is an orientation meeting here in Austin."

"That's wonderful."

"So the next contact I have with you will be to set a date and time for that meeting."

"All…right."

"Any questions?" Ms. Sable asked, that warmth still present in her tone.

"Can you give me an idea how long the wait will be?" Ann asked.

"No, I'm sorry I can't."

"Thanks for calling," Ann said.

"I'll be in touch, then. Goodbye."

Ann reached for a decorator pillow and squeezed it. Her heart hammered so fast, she thought she might faint.

Reality hit. Was this something she really wanted to do? A panicked feeling upped her heart rate even higher. Did she know what she was getting into? Was she prepared for the upheaval a baby would bring? Was she willing to make adjustments in her way of life, alter it to fit a baby's needs? Was she willing to give up her independence?

"Yes, yes, yes!" she whispered aloud, struggling to ward off the tears.

She took several deep breaths and cautioned herself against getting too excited or getting her hopes up. Not only was the waiting period interminable, but the odds of the adoption actually happening remained chancy, despite the active status of her application.

Single-parent adoptions were uphill battles, or as Sophie had put it, ''They're no piece of cake.'' Certainly such adoptions were not looked on favorably because the demand for newborn babies far outweighed the supply. She knew that. Too, she must keep in mind the orientation and home visit. They were both crucial. She mustn't lose sight of either of those variables.

Yet she couldn't squelch the excitement that made her slightly giddy. But she was scared. Lord was she ever.

What would it be like to be a mother? Would she botch the job? Would the missing male figure cause her to rear a dysfunctional child? How would the lack be felt? The thought beat like a dull throb inside her, like a bone bruise that wouldn't heal.

Still, she knew she had to try. Why? Her life was remarkably on track, considering what she had suffered. But she wanted more. She wanted someone to love.

Following her daddy's suicide, she'd had to glue her shattered heart and soul back together piece by piece. She'd also had the responsibility of helping her mother regroup. When it had become feasible to leave her mother, she'd gone to Tyler and enrolled in business school, only to find that she didn't like it.

One of her college friends had suggested she try beauty school—in light of the fact that she was continually cutting and fixing someone's hair. The thought had excited Ann, and after enrolling, she found she loved it. She also found she liked giving manicures even more, challenged by the opportunity of transforming ugly hands and nails into beautiful ones, like hers. She'd been blessed with slender fingers and long, strong nails, which drew envious comments.

After she'd returned to MacMillan and worked as a beautician, she longed to own her own shop. That had been neither feasible nor practical as her mother had become stricken with cancer. The responsibility to care for her had fallen on Ann's shoulders. Her brother had been no help. She had worked as well as nursed her mother until her death.

Ann had put in longer, more grueling hours at work to fill the void, and soon had managed to save enough money to rent a building and set herself up in business.

Her shop had done so well that now she was in the process of expanding into a full salon: beautician, masseuse and skin-care expert.

But a successful career wasn't enough. She was lonely, unfulfilled. She wanted to get married. She wanted a husband, a strong and caring man who shared her hopes and dreams.

So why hadn't she found one? Though not beautiful in the true sense of the word, she knew she could hold her own among the female population, having been endowed with clear skin, violet-colored eyes and a cap of black hair.

Her one drawback, she thought, was her breasts. Her stature was slender and petite, and no matter how little she ate, her breasts remained persistently a touch too generous.

Still, some—especially a man—would consider that more of an asset than a deterrent. Maybe the reason she hadn't found the right partner was that she had no interest in casual sex. Sex, for her, was tied to deep feelings. She never did anything halfway, which was why she often got hurt. What she wanted was to give herself fully to one man, who would risk, as she was willing to, the gamble of commitment.

As ludicrous as it seemed now, when she'd been young and naive, she'd often dreamed of Drew declaring his undying love for her and asking her to marry him.

That stroll down fantasy lane had stemmed from a brief encounter one afternoon when snow had covered the ground, a rarity in East Texas. She had gone outside for some reason and had come upon Drew and Peter, who were mauling each other with snowballs. Suddenly a snowball had landed against her right temple. She'd lost her balance and dropped to the ground.

While both boys had run towards her, it was Drew's hand that had reached out to her.

"Sorry," he said, grinning devilishly. "Are you hurt?"

"No," she said, and gave him her hand.

The contact sent a burst of adrenaline through her veins. But when she made the effort to put distance between them, she inadvertently leaned into the strength of Drew's hard frame.

Sparks shot through her. Stepping back, she felt as if her nerve endings had been burned. "I'm...sorry," she murmured.

Drew smiled at her, his eyes twinkling. "No problem. Glad you weren't hurt."

She'd thought of that moment often through the years. That was the first time she'd realized she had a crush on Drew, and wished he'd pay attention to her instead of to Peter.

But that was not to be, and early on, those foolish, girlish hopes had died a natural death.

No, she feared the man of her dreams didn't exist. That was why she took matters into her own hands concerning a child. At thirty-one, her biological clock was ticking, and Ann felt she must race against time.

A child. She was so busy delighting in that wonderful thought, she failed to hear the doorbell until its rings turned so persistent that she couldn't ignore them.

"I'm coming," she called, dashing across the room and swinging open the door.

"Where were you?" Sophie said without preamble.

Ann smiled. "Congratulating myself, actually."

"Oh? Something happen I should know about?"

Sophie skirted past Ann and marched into the living room. "Well, tell me. Don't keep me in suspense."

"I got a call from the agency."

Sophie's eyes lit. "All right!"

They both giggled, then hugged.

They broke apart finally, only to keep their silly grins in place.

"What are you drinking?" Sophie asked.

"Oops, sorry. My manners aren't what they used to be. It's tea. Want a glass?"

"After today, how about two glasses, one for each hand and dashed with a jigger of bourbon?"

Ann chuckled. "Sit down. I'll be right back."

A few minutes later, they sat facing each other from opposite ends of the sofa.

"So what else did the lady say?" Sophie asked.

Ann leaned over and set her empty glass on the coffee table, then explained.

"So, no baby right away, huh?"

Ann released a heartfelt sigh. "Maybe not for another year or two."

"Jeez. That's too damn long to wait."

"I know, but that's the rule, especially when you're a single parent."

"Sounds like they make it near impossible."

"Almost but not quite." Ann laughed. "Remember, I'm 'active.'"

Sophie laughed back. "Whatever you say."

"By the way, what brought you to my doorstep? Not that you aren't welcome anytime," Ann added hastily, "but—"

"You're right. I did stop by for a reason." Sophie's face sobered. "You don't know, do you?"

"Don't know what?"

"John MacMillan died a little while ago."

"Oh, no."

"It was on the six o'clock news, but I see you don't have your TV on."

"And haven't had."

"I knew you'd want to know," Sophie said, draining her glass, then standing up.

Without saying anything, Ann stood also. When she'd learned that John MacMillan had suffered a life-threatening stroke, she hadn't been able to muster much sympathy. She'd always thought of him as a cold, taciturn man who alienated his own family, most of all his son.

Now that she'd learned of his death, her emotions were mixed. On the one hand, she felt sadness—on the other a sense of justice. She knew she shouldn't think ill of the dead, but John MacMillan's insensitive actions had left a deep scar on her heart.

"The town'll be in a tizzy," Sophie commented.

"I'm sure." Ann felt dazed and rubbed her forehead. John MacMillan dead. That didn't seem possible. His presence had lorded over MacMillan for so long, the town wouldn't be the same without him.

"So, are you going to the funeral tomorrow?" Sophie asked.

Ann watched Sophie closely. "If I do, it won't be out of respect for John, that's for sure."

"That's understandable."

"But Mrs. MacMillan was kind and helpful to my mother. Out of respect for her, I feel I should go."

"What about Drew?"

"What about him?"

Sophie shrugged. "You two always got along, didn't you?"

"Why is it that everyone, including you, stares at me when Drew's name is mentioned?" Ann's tone was sharper than she intended, and immediately she regretted the outburst, although Sophie didn't seem to take offense.

Sophie held up her hands, and her lips quivered with the need to smile. "Whoa, I didn't mean anything by that. Really I didn't. It's just that when his name comes up, you seem to tighten up, get an odd look on *your* face."

"Oh, all right. Maybe I do. At one time, I envisioned us waltzing off together into the sunset and living happily ever after."

Sophie laughed outright. "Sounds good to me."

"Well, dreams have a funny way of not coming true. Anyway, I've recovered from the blow, so you needn't worry."

"I believe you." Sophie headed for the door. "If you want me to, I'll go to the funeral with you."

"Fine. See you tomorrow."

Ann twisted the lock behind Sophie, then leaned against the door and breathed deeply. If Drew hadn't already returned to MacMillan, he would definitely do so now. And she was certain to see him.

So what? It wouldn't make any difference to her one way or the other. She was over him, for god's sake.

Though she knew she could never have Drew or even another man like him, she could have a complete and happy life. Her baby would make that happen.

For the first time in a long while, that thought failed to comfort her.

Three

"John MacMillan will be sorely missed by young and old alike...."

The minister's voice droned as he sang the praises of the town's most important citizen. But Ann couldn't bear to listen to the words another minute. She closed her eyes and willed herself to concentrate on something else.

She and Sophie had not attended the funeral inside the largest Baptist church in town. There hadn't been room for all the mourners. Consequently, loudspeakers had been placed outside so the overflow crowd could hear the service.

Ann had opted only to attend the burial ceremony at the cemetery on the outskirts of town.

Now, as she stood beside Sophie, she pinned her eyes on a bumblebee that hovered over a huge wisteria close by. The smell of the flowering vine wafted past Ann's nose. She breathed deeply of its delicate sweetness.

Weather-wise, the day was perfect. No clouds marred the sky, and the temperature hovered around the seventy-degree mark.

The bee flew away, and Ann faced the minister once again. She felt like a hypocrite. But out of respect for Janet MacMillan, she had felt both duty- and conscience-bound to attend.

Because she and Sophie had arrived only minutes before the service began, she hadn't seen the family. She knew, though, that Drew wouldn't be far from his mother's side. Janet MacMillan was in fragile health herself.

While the minister continued to heap praises on John MacMillan, Ann's thoughts centered on Drew. How was he feeling? she wondered. Sad? Numb? Frustrated? Probably all three, she speculated, knowing of the constant battle between father and son.

Only after Sophie nudged her hand did she notice that everyone's head was bowed and that the minister was saying a prayer. Flushing, Ann lowered her head and shut her eyes tightly. She prayed for forgiveness for her fidgeting and her wandering mind. She shouldn't feel guilty, though. John MacMillan had been a tyrant, and nothing anyone could say or do would convince her otherwise.

Relief rushed through Ann as the minister finally said, "Amen."

The crowd dispersed immediately, except for close friends and family members. Ann wanted a word with Janet MacMillan, but she couldn't bring herself to intrude. Anyway, she wasn't sure how she'd be received, considering it was no secret how she felt about John, though she didn't seem to have garnered any condescending stares for her presence.

"Do you want to speak to any of the family?" Sophie asked in a low voice. "If you do, I'll wait in the car."

"No, no, I don't think so." Ann played with a loose strand of hair. "I'll stop by and see Mrs. MacMillan one day next week."

"Ah, there's Maxine," Sophie said, craning her head. "I need to talk to her a minute. I'll see you in a minute."

Ann nodded, then turned and made her way toward her car, which was parked quite a way from the cemetery. She didn't know what made her twist her head at precisely that moment, but she did, and Drew filled her vision.

He stood slightly off to himself, and was leaning stiffly against a tree. Janet, nearby, was surrounded by friends.

Even yards away, Ann could see the changes the years had wrought. He looked older than his twenty-nine years. But he was still handsome, more so, actually, than she remembered.

He had picked up weight, which complemented rather than detracted from his six-foot-plus frame. Another obvious change was his hair. The blond streaks seemed to dominate, maybe because the gray was mingled with them. His dark tan, along with the blue suit that matched his eyes, depicted a larger-than-life macho man with the power to win women's hearts and break men's jaws.

To her dismay, every fiber of her being prickled with awareness. She hated herself for that weakness. A schoolgirl crush was one thing, but to react this way now was totally unacceptable.

As if Drew sensed he was being scrutinized, he swung around. Their eyes connected. Ann was positive he didn't recognize her. His eyes appeared blank, only to then narrow in surprise.

Ann's heartbeat quickened as he uncoiled his frame

and narrowed the space between them. She wished she could read his thoughts. But as their eyes continued to hold, she experienced the same jolting shock of emotion she had had that snowy day long ago when he'd lifted her against him.

"Ann? Ann Sinclair? Is that you?"

She reeled under the put-down. How could he not recognize her? Had she changed that much? She thought not. It just proved how little she had meant to him.

Swallowing convulsively, Ann said, "Hello, Drew." She was relieved that her voice sounded natural, even if she trembled inside.

He didn't extend his hand. For that she was grateful. Something told her not to touch him....

His face was sober, and the lines pronounced. Yet the twinkle in his eyes she remembered so well remained— "a twinkle that could charm the birds right out of a tree," her mother used to say.

"It's been a long time," Drew said, angling his head to one side and gazing at her.

"Yes, it has."

"How've you been?"

"Fine. And you?"

"Till now, fine."

His tone was a mixture of sorrow and anger, though his gaze held steady on her, and Ann felt a rush of heat envelop her. Granted, the afternoon was warm, but the flush inside her had nothing to do with the weather. Drew's nearness brought on the attack to her system and made her want to shed the jacket to her suit.

"How's your mother?" she asked awkwardly, unable to bring herself to say she was sorry about his father.

"She's holding up about as well as can be expected. The shock's been doubly hard on her heart, though."

"She's a special lady," Ann said.

"How's Peter?"

Ann's chin lifted. "Do you really care?"

"As a matter of fact, I do."

"Sorry, I didn't mean to be rude."

"Yes, you did."

Ann's sharp comeback died when she saw the smile tug at the corner of his lips.

"Okay, so I did," she said a trifle breathlessly.

She didn't understand the tension that simmered between them. Maybe it was the past rearing its ugly head. More likely, though, it was her reaction to him.

"I should get back to Mother," he said.

"Of course." She paused. "Look, about John—"

His jaw tensed. "I understand, believe me. After the number he did on your family—"

Ann nodded, feeling her throat tighten.

"Maybe I'll see you around," he said finally.

"Maybe."

He stared at her a moment longer, then pivoted on his heel and strode off.

When she joined Sophie in the car, Ann's breath still came in short spurts.

"You aren't leaving today, are you, son?"

A pang of guilt stabbed Drew; his stomach lurched. He bent down and squeezed his mother's cold, limp hand.

"You know better than that, Mamma." His tone was gentle. "Even if I didn't have the estate to settle, I wouldn't leave you."

Janet MacMillan raised watery eyes, the same color as her son's, and smiled. Before her first heart attack, she'd been a strong, lovely woman. While still lovely, with a cap of thick snow-white hair and almost flawless skin, she was far from strong. Her illness had taken its toll. That, combined with the death of her husband, caused Drew grave concern.

"I know you have your own life, and that—" She broke off, her lips trembling.

"Shh, Mamma. Everything's taken care of. I'm not going anywhere, except maybe to Daddy's office."

Unfortunately, his mother had the knack of reading his mind. She knew he hadn't planned to stay in MacMillan. But he was trapped. Even if his mother didn't need him, MacMillan Investments did.

"Drew," she said softly, her eyes still troubled.

"Shh, you just rest. We'll talk later."

That conversation had taken place a little while ago, after the housefull of well-meaning friends had paid their respects and left.

Now, instead of going straight to the office as planned, Drew stood at the grave site of his father and stared down at the immense number of flowers that covered the fresh dirt.

He wished he felt something besides this pit of emptiness inside. He wanted to cry, but the tears wouldn't come. He felt as though a rock was lodged in his throat. He had been home only one day when his daddy had died. John had been in a coma and hadn't even been aware of his presence.

Drew paused in his thoughts, shielded his eyes from the harsh sunlight, then gazed around. Where earlier the cemetery had been crawling with people, it was now eerily quiet. Only the hum of a small plane above offered any break in the silence.

He looked back at the grave and wished things had been different, wished he could have been close to the man whose life was now a closed chapter. But no one had had that privilege, not even his mother.

John took and never gave. With Drew he'd been the most unbending. He could never accept his son's brash, happy-go-lucky nature, nor his penchant for living dangerously.

From the time Drew had been a mere child, cars were his favorite toys. That never changed. But what galled John the most was Drew's disinterest in joining the family business. On the day he left for college Drew told John he couldn't care less about MacMillan Investments. They'd quarrelled and had barely spoken since.

"It's too late, now, Dad," Drew whispered in the wind. "But for whatever it's worth, I wanted you to love me. Only you never did, did you?"

He stared at the grave a while longer, then grimfaced, he turned and walked to his car.

Only after he drove through the main street of Mac-Millan did his mood lighten somewhat. Memories both good and bad swept through him, especially the times he and Peter had dragged Main Street when Drew's daddy was out of town. Old Sheriff Becker had been too chicken to tell his old man.

Thinking of Peter made him think of Peter's sister. Good golly, he couldn't believe the Ann Sinclair who used to bug him and Peter was the same as the Ann Sinclair he'd seen earlier.

The change was miraculous. She'd turned into a heart-stopper. When he'd approached her, his breath had caught in his throat. Where once she'd been skinny and shapeless, she was now model thin and shapely.

But her exquisite looks weren't all. Something else about her struck him. Was it that fresh, untouched look

that piqued his interest? She didn't appear to be aware
of how she affected people.

He wondered what she did in MacMillan? And if she
was married? When he realized where his thoughts had
taken him, he muttered a curse. What the hell was wrong
with him? He never intended to seriously involve himself
with any woman again.

He coveted his free time and wanted to spend it on the
racetrack. Someday he intended to qualify for the Indy
500. That desire to compete overshadowed his desire for
a permanent relationship. Besides, he'd learned how
painful love was. He'd learned that from his daddy, and
he'd programmed himself not to care.

He simply had not been able to give of himself to the
woman he had fancied himself in love with. Time, devotion, love—they had wanted it all. He didn't know how
he knew or even what possessed him to think such a
thing, but instinctively he knew Ann Sinclair would most
certainly demand all of the above. And more.

A bird screeched overhead. The obtrusive sound jerked
Drew's thoughts out of that emotional minefield, only to
turn once again to his daddy's grave. He suddenly felt
drained to the bone for the lost opportunities and the
might-have-beens.''

The only way to heal himself was to finish the job here
as soon as possible and get the hell back to Houston, to
what he knew best. Fast cars and fast women. And not
necessarily in that order.

Four

Frustration tightened like a band around Drew's gut. He felt completely overwhelmed as he stared at the stack of papers and folders on his daddy's desk, most of which he hadn't even sorted through.

John's personal and company lawyers had just left. Instead of providing Drew with straight answers and firm facts concerning his daddy's assets and liabilities, they had given him the runaround. He sensed their hesitancy didn't stem from negligence but rather from ignorance. John had kept them in the dark about much of his business dealings. The only one who seemed to know anything was the business manager, Timothy Pollard, who was presently, and Drew suspected conveniently, out of town on business.

Drew's lips narrowed until they almost disappeared. As soon as Mr. Timothy Pollard returned, he would have a lot of questions to answer. Until then, Drew knew he'd just have to sift through the papers and try to glean the state of affairs as best he could.

The phone jangled. Still distracted, he lifted the receiver and muttered a terse, "Hello."

"Got another burr under your butt, huh?"

Drew eased back in the chair. "One thing about you, Skip, you cut to the heart of the matter."

"Always. See no reason to pussyfoot around."

Drew laughed. "What's up?"

"When you coming back?"

"Not anytime soon. Dad's affairs are in a mess. He wasn't nearly as efficient as I'd thought."

"Has anything been finalized?"

"The will's being probated. He left everything to Mother, of course, but she's in no condition to oversee it."

"Well, if there's anything I can do on this end, just holler."

"What about papers that need my signature?"

"There's a stack of 'em."

"Fax them to me."

"The Dallas firm is going to give you a reprieve about the property. Their attorney called a little while ago."

"That's good news," Drew replied. "Or at least I hope so. Get all the facts you can about the area, traffic, etcetera."

"Will do."

"I'm planning to drive down the first of next week, for the day at least."

They said their goodbyes. Drew twisted in the chair and stared out the window. The day held the promise of both sunshine and humidity. He longed to be on the racetrack; it was all he could do to stifle the urge. But Janet depended on him, and he couldn't let her down. Nor did he want to. His mother had made life bearable for him through his childhood. She had done everything in her power to protect him from John's emotional abuse.

Thoughts of his mother brought a smile to his lips. She was the epitome of the genteel Southern lady, liked and respected by everyone in town; the outpouring of love and concern had been proof of that.

Suddenly, unbidden and unwanted thoughts of Ann Sinclair sprang to mind. In many ways her demeanor reminded him of his mother's. He'd thought about Ann a lot since he'd seen her at the cemetery a week ago today.

He wondered again why he was so intrigued by her. He couldn't answer that, except to admit her quiet beauty stirred something inside him. That in itself was crazy because he made a point to stay away from women like Ann Sinclair. Her kind were not for one-night stands, and that was all he was interested in.

He expected his women to know the score, sexually and socially. Innocent, unsophisticated women had never appealed to him. Since he'd sworn off commitments and marriage, anything serious made him nervous. *Ann* made him nervous.

Disgruntled with his thoughts, Drew swung around in his chair and decided what he needed was a cup of strong coffee.

Ann placed the receiver back in its cradle and laughed aloud. Another important call. More good news. She couldn't wait to tell Sophie.

Before the call had come, she'd been busy reviewing her ideas for renovating the supply room. If she was going to handle a skin-care line, additional space was a necessity. The room she and Sophie worked in didn't have a spare inch anywhere.

Ann gave her manicurist table the once-over. Satisfied that everything was in order, she looked up. Like her house, her shop was her creation and equally as charming. She seldom patted herself on the back for anything she did. On the contrary, she was far too hard on herself, expected too much.

But today, during the quiet hours before the shop opened, she once again admired her handiwork. One wall was decorated with a patterned wallpaper that enhanced the thick peach carpet on the floor. The remaining walls were painted white, allowing her to splatter them with posters and pictures, in all colors, sizes and shapes, that pertained to her profession.

Two brass-and-glass étagères held various nail and hair products for sale. Positioned throughout the shop were pots filled with live plants and baskets filled with peach potpourri.

Two other rooms completed the shop. One was the pedicure room; the other was the room she hoped to renovate.

If only her personal life were as rich as her professional one, she'd have it made. Ann frowned as she sat back down. Since the funeral, thoughts of Drew Mac-Millan had haunted her. Seeing and talking to him at the cemetery had shaken her more than she cared to admit. She had forgotten just how good-looking he was. And when he'd looked at her...

She heard the key turn in the lock and waited until Sophie closed the door behind her before she said, "Guess what?"

Sophie dumped her purse beside her station, then said, "You heard?"

"How did you know?"

"I didn't," Sophie replied. "Just a wild guess."

Excitement shone from Ann's eyes. "They're definitely interested. All Natural is sending a rep by to visit with us, to inspect the shop."

"Really!" Sophie's tone reeked with shock and awe.

"Really."

Sophie clapped her hands. "Way to go. Their product is so popular and top of the line. How'd you do it? You must've laid the charm on thick."

"Actually, I don't know why they were so receptive. You know, I thought calling them was a long shot, but I had to try."

"Well, the gamble paid off."

"Not yet. We still have to prove that we can sell a bundle of their products. That means we have to advertise like crazy."

"Right," Sophie said. "Starting today, between customers, I'll work on some stuff."

"Me, too," Ann said, looking down at her book. "Uh-oh, I'm afraid that's out for today."

Sophie crossed to her table. "Ditto. My book is nearly full already. If we have many walk-ins, we're going to be in trouble."

"Just the kind of trouble I love," Ann said, then winced as she thought of the two pedicures she had scheduled, along with two sets of nail tips to apply.

"So, I guess it's to work," Sophie mused aloud.

"And none too soon. Here comes Ms. Riley."

The most popular hangout on the square bore the proud name of The Coffee Cup. The sign was so old and faded that for years Drew had expected it to fall and land on someone's head, but to date, it hadn't budged.

The place buzzed. Drew saw a booth in the far corner and slipped into it, but not before several curious stares and nods were thrown his way. A smiling blond waitress took his order. While he waited for his coffee, he peered out the window, willing his mind to stop spinning.

It was then that he heard his name, followed by teeters of laughter. Curious, he buried his head against the cushioned bench and listened. He hadn't noticed who occupied the booth behind him; he hadn't cared. Until now.

More laughter. He waited. The booth was occupied by several women, he decided as two giggled while another spoke in guarded tones.

The waitress chose that moment to bring his coffee.

"Will there be anything else, sir?"

Drew forced a smile. "No, thanks."

She stared at him a moment longer; curiosity burned in her eyes. Much to his relief, she didn't say anything, merely turned and scuttled away.

Immediately, the booth behind him reclaimed his attention.

The women were whispering. Finally one's voice rose slightly above the others. "Did you see him at the funeral?"

"You'd have to be blind if you didn't," another said.

"I know you shouldn't be aware of things like that at a funeral, but he looked absolutely gorgeous."

Another woman laughed. "You won't get an argument out of me. Drew MacMillan can eat crackers in my bed anytime he wants."

Drew smiled. Mmm. So far so good.

"Why, honey, if Sam heard you say that, he'd kill you."

Drew's smile widened. They were getting braver; their volume level had increased. Drew could hear them now without straining. He just hoped no one else could. Yet he couldn't help but be amused at what he was hearing.

"You two are terrible. He looks good all right," a high-pitched voice said. "But I'm still not sure he can perform."

Drew's smile disappeared along with his smug good humor.

"Oh, for heaven's sake, don't believe everything you read."

"Well," one exclaimed, "if he's really impotent..."

Drew recoiled as if he'd been slapped. He'd heard enough. Without bothering to finish his coffee, he threw a couple of bills on the table and stalked toward the door.

A few minutes later, he walked into the kitchen of the MacMillan mansion, fury pounding through his veins.

Rebecca Cribs, the housekeeper who had been with the family since before he was born, stood in front of the sink. The large airy room smelled of fresh-baked bread.

"You're either sick or mad," she said bluntly, her too-large bosom shaking slightly. "Which is it?"

Because of her devotion and long-standing with the family, she took liberties and got away with them. She was fiercely loyal to the family and would defend and protect them at all costs.

"The latter." Drew's voice quivered with suppressed anger.

"I see. Want a cup of coffee?"

"No thanks. How's Mother?"

"God bless her, she's sleeping. I just checked on her."

"Good," Drew said, then fell quiet, struggling to regain control of himself.

"You sure you don't want to tell me what's got you in such a snit?"

Drew couldn't help but smile. "Ah, Becky, my girl, what would we do without you?"

She blushed at the compliment. "Hope you don't have to find out."

Drew's warm humor vanished. "I just came from the coffee shop where I was being discussed."

"Doesn't surprise me none."

"What does that mean?" he asked, an ashy taste in his mouth.

Rebecca stopped what she was doing and faced him. "You know how people talk, especially about your family. It's not ever going to change."

'You've heard the gossip, haven't you?" Drew asked.

"Yes, but I didn't pay no attention to it. Just filthy gibberish, that's all it is."

"Damn!"

"Watch your mouth. Why, your mamma would have a conniption fit if she heard you say that."

"You won't tell on me now, will you?" Drew's tone was cajoling once again.

A smile added wrinkles to Becky's face. "No." She paused. "I bet I know where that nasty tale got started."

Drew tensed. "Where?"

"Polished Choice."

"What the hell is that?"

"A nail shop. You know, where women go for manicures. Ann Sinclair owns it."

Drew felt his breath lock, as if his throat had iced over. "Well, I'll be damned."

"It's just like a beauty shop...."

Drew no longer listened. He crossed to the door and swung it open.

"Where do you think you're going, young man?" Rebecca demanded in a huffed voice. "It's dinnertime."

"Don't worry. I'll eat later. There's something I've got to do."

With that, he strode out the door and closed it firmly behind him.

The remainder of the day passed in a blur. Both Ann and Sophie did indeed book back-to-back appointments. Ann suspected the dance at the country club this weekend contributed to the rush. Also the local foundry had rehired a hundred workers. The local paper had reported that one factory was awarded a government contract.

Whatever the reason, Ann was thrilled. She loved the hustle and bustle that went along with a busy shop. More than that, the increased business meant she could soon begin her expansion.

"I'm outta here," an exhausted Sophie announced at seven o'clock.

"Whew, I won't be far behind," Ann said. "I don't remember when I've been so tired."

Sophie paused at the door. "See ya."

Ann began readying the shop for tomorrow when she heard a knock on the door. A frown puckered her forehead. Who in the world would knock at this hour? Could be anyone who had seen the light still on in the shop, she guessed. Well, she wasn't about to do a manicure at this late hour, not as tired as she was.

She unlocked the door and flung it open. Drew stood on the porch, slouched against the pillar.

Ann felt her mouth go slack before shock rendered her speechless.

Five

Drew barrelled across the threshold, stopped midway in the room, turned and announced, "I'm going to sue the hell out of you."

As calmly as her jerking muscles would allow, Ann eased toward him, a stunned and perplexed look on her face. "Whatever are you talking about?"

He curled his lips into a sneer. "Don't play the innocent with me."

Aghast, Ann stared at him. She stood close enough to him to sense his strength. The cords in his neck stood out. His shoulders, which needed no padding, bunched.

The hint of a beard showed through despite his morning shave. His high cheekbones, along with the crook in his nose, the latter a trophy from his football years, were also more pronounced.

He wore a pair of black jeans, a casual shirt and boots. And though he appeared calm, Ann knew better. He was madder than hell, which made him that much more sinfully attractive.

"Stalling isn't going to do you any good."

Ann manufactured a brave, cool smile. "I still don't know what you're talking about. You come in here like something wild, and start flinging around accusations that—"

"Save it," he said rudely.

Ann jutted her chin and clenched her fists until her knuckles felt as if they would pop through her skin. But that didn't halt his bold, appraising gaze. It toured her hidden curves with insolent deliberation. The deep brilliance of his eyes, which she remembered from youth, had lost none of their disturbing sensuality.

She lowered her head and concentrated on removing a thread that clung to her slacks. When crossed, Drew's easygoing personality ceased to exist. Apparently she had crossed him in some way, or at least he thought she had. He liked his own way, she thought, remembering moments when he and Peter would have a heated disagreement. He would pour on the charm one minute, only to turn meaner than a junkyard dog the next.

Despite that, Ann gave in to the forbidden temptation of seeing how far she could push him. She lifted her chin defiantly. "This is *my* property, and I could demand that you leave."

"Wouldn't do you any good," he said with arrogant self-assurance.

Ann saw red. Just who did he think he was? She grappled to speak, but choking anger made it impossible.

"Somehow, I thought you were different." He snorted. "But you're not. You're just like all the rest of the women I know. You just can't control your tongue."

"Control my tongue!" Ann's voice matched her body

temperature. "For heaven's sake, stop talking in riddles."

"Nasty rumors." He loomed over her. "Does that ring a bell?"

"You're way off base," she flung back.

He smiled, but it didn't last. "You can stand here and tell me that my name *wasn't* discussed in your shop?"

The heat drained from her face. Ah, so that was what this was all about. The society-page article and its consequences were rearing its ugly head. Again. And both times involved her.

"Look," she finally said with a shudder, "I won't deny you were talked about, but—"

"But what?"

"Please, just let me finish, okay?"

"I'm listening."

"If there was anything said about you outside these walls, it didn't come from me. As far as what others say—well, I can't be responsible."

"Do you have any idea how it feels to overhear that kind of garbage?"

"Don't you think you're being a tad dramatic?" she asked lightly, trying to put his conversation in perspective. "Surely you have better things to do than worry about what people say about you?"

He broke contact with her eyes. "Some things yes, others no."

She'd have to concede he was right. When a man's sexuality was questioned, he did tend to lose his objectivity. Still, she wasn't about to take the blame for some scatterbrained women who had discussed him with such zest. She had warned them to keep their mouths shut. If only she'd made that warning stronger.

"So, what did you contribute to the conversation?"

Ann blinked in confusion. "What?"

"You heard me."

He was deliberately baiting her, and she knew it. Well, she wasn't about to be a party any longer to the need to have his ego massaged. True, he'd just lost his daddy and was going through a tough time. But that didn't give him the right to take his frustration out on her.

She turned and walked to the window, unable to think with him so close. The late-evening sunlight spilled into the room and created weird designs across the carpet.

Finally, Ann faced him again and said with saccharine sweetness, "All right, if I've caused you to suffer unduly, I apologize."

Suddenly tired of the whole fiasco, Ann deliberately yawned, then raised her arms and stretched, unaware that her breasts teased the thin material of her blouse, leaving no doubt as to their generous fullness.

The sharp intake of Drew's breath made her realize what she had done. The gaze that had searched her face now moved to her breasts. And lingered.

The atmosphere in the room was charged.

Desperate to diffuse it, Ann began, "I think—"

"Prove it?" His voice was gruff.

"Excuse me?"

"Prove it?"

"How?" she asked with uncomfortably hot cheeks.

Drew hesitated only a second. "Cook dinner for me."

What was he doing? Playing another silly game? Daring her? A little of both, she guessed. But why? He had gotten what he'd come for—an apology, albeit a back-handed one.

"Say tomorrow night?" His eyes probed. "At eight?"

She felt as if she were on a roller coaster. Her stomach heaved, and she had trouble catching her breath. Sexual stares and innuendos weren't totally foreign to her. She'd received her fair share. But never with the same intensity that Drew looked at her now. It seemed as if he could see through her clothes, to her naked flesh.

She moistened her lips with her tongue. "Tomorrow night," she croaked. "At eight."

His eyes focused on her face, then he turned and sauntered out the door.

If Ann hadn't been leaning against the windowsill, she would have collapsed. What on earth had come over her? Involving herself with the likes of Drew MacMillan was tantamount to stepping on a lighted firecracker; it could only burn her. It was but a matter of time until he returned to Houston for good.

Even so, she found she couldn't stymie the dangerous excitement that bubbled inside her. If nothing else, the evening would be interesting.

"How far back did you want them?"

Drew stared at his daddy's secretary, Rose, with unseeing eyes. His thoughts were splintered in so many different directions that he couldn't concentrate on any one thing for long.

"The financial records, sir? How far back?"

"Sorry, Rose," Drew said, forcing himself to smile at her. She was a plain woman, in her early fifties, whose loyalty to his father had probably bordered on fear.

Now, as she waited patiently for his answer, the lines around her mouth seemed to have intensified. Her fear now stemmed from worry over losing her job. Well, she was right. The whole lot of employees had better worry. The company's finances and holdings should have been in better shape than they were. He aimed to find out why they weren't.

"Five years back. And Rose, what's the word on Tim Pollard?"

The company's business manager was still missing. Drew felt sure he was key to part of this mess.

"Actually, he did call before you got here." Rose paused.

"Go on," Drew prompted with uncharacteristic patience.

"He's...back in town."

"Why wasn't I told?"

"He said he'd contracted some kind of contagious virus and couldn't come back to the office for at least another week."

"How convenient," Drew said sarcastically.

Rose flushed. "Shall I call him back and—"

Drew cut her off. "No, don't bother."

Once she had gone, Drew transferred his attention back to the stack of papers in front of him. How much longer could he jockey his thoughts between here and Houston? With each day that passed, it became more difficult. His car dealerships alone needed his undivided attention. Now he was seeped in a mess far beyond his imagination. To think that his daddy, who was supposed to have been the consummate businessman, could have let his business deteriorate to such an extent was untenable.

Lamenting over spilled milk wasn't the answer, Drew reminded himself sharply, but tackling the ledger was.

Instead of figures, however, Ann's face swam before his eyes. He slammed the folder shut, closed his eyes and cradled his forehead in his hands.

Insane! Or maybe stupid. He still couldn't believe he'd asked Ann to cook him dinner. Of all the dense things he could have done or said, that one topped the list.

He'd made his first mistake by going to her shop. But

dammit, his pride had been at stake. His manhood. And still was. God, what were people thinking about him? What were they saying? Usually he couldn't care less what people thought of him. They could go to hell if they didn't like what he did or said. He hadn't even let his old man intimidate him.

But the idea that someone might believe that rubbish and think that he was impotent—

A renewed wave of disgust rushed through him. What did Ann think?

"Knock it off, MacMillan."

But nothing short of a brain transplant could stop him from thinking about Ann. Erotic thoughts, at that. When she'd lifted her arms, and he'd seen those burgeoning breasts…

In that heated moment when their eyes had met, everything had changed. Something had given way inside him.

That insane feeling hadn't resulted from the sexual fireworks between them. That was part of it, all right. He wouldn't deny that. But the way she'd stood up to him after he'd stormed into her shop like a caged tiger turned loose was to her credit. She'd thrust out her chin and faced him squarely.

No, he couldn't blame sex alone for the turbulence raging inside him. It went deeper, scaring the hell out of him.

Six

"I'll have to say that was one of the best, if not the best, meals I've ever eaten." Drew smiled lopsidedly as he lowered himself next to her on the couch, all the while rubbing his stomach.

Ann felt herself blush, even though she knew his compliment was due to part baloney and part charm. Nevertheless, it pleased her. She would hate to think she'd spent hours in the kitchen for nothing.

"I'm glad you enjoyed it," she said, embarrassed by the breathless tremor in her voice.

But then it had been there ever since he'd rung the doorbell and she'd let him in. She hadn't known what to expect from herself or from him. All afternoon she'd been in a tizzy, cleaning the house, cooking, making sure everything was perfect. Thank heavens, business had been slow at the shop, which had allowed her to leave at noon.

Once she'd finished the other chores, she'd started on preparing herself. She'd soaked in a hot bubble bath, washed and dried her hair and had taken extra pains with her makeup. She'd pondered what to wear, had finally chosen a pair of red silk slacks and matching capped-sleeved blouse. The outfit had been an indulgent splurge, and she knew she looked her best in it.

She'd tried then to put the evening in perspective, reminding herself that he wanted nothing from her except a meal. When the evening ended, he would walk out the door and that would be it.

But when he'd grinned at her from across the threshold, her bones had turned to rubber.

"Hi," he'd said.

She didn't move, but managed to say, "Hi."

He cocked his head. "Are we dining outside?"

"No, of course not," she said, and shook her head.

He laughed. "Well, then, don't you think you'd better ask me in?"

Ann felt her cheeks turn scarlet before she stepped aside to let him enter. "Sorry."

"God, it smells like heaven in here," he said, inhaling deeply.

"It's homemade bread."

"You made it?"

She nodded and joined him in the middle of the living room.

"I didn't know anyone did that anymore."

"I don't very often."

A strand of sandy hair fell over his brow. Her finger itched to brush it back. Instead, she moved slightly, out of harm's way.

"Is dinner ready?"

"I take it you're hungry."

An awareness passed between them, holding them both motionless.

Drew cleared his throat. "I haven't eaten all day."

"It's…it's ready when you are."

They'd gone straight to the brightly decorated table where he'd consumed two huge helpings of chicken, salad and homemade bread. The conversation had remained light and impersonal. Ann had been too nervous to eat much, but had enjoyed watching him make the most of the meal.

To her relief, there had been few awkward moments. Those had come only after she would laugh at something outlandish he'd said. She'd catch him watching her with a strange expression in his eyes, one that not only disconcerted her but made her feel warm all over.

Now, as she watched him continue to massage his stomach, his legs sprawled before him, she couldn't seem to stop herself from staring.

He had on a pair of jeans and a yellow shirt that magnified his blue eyes and dark tan. She thought of the hard-tone muscles under his clothes and swallowed, feeling the way she had years ago when she had a crush on him. But that was absurd. When he left, her heart would settle along with the rest of her and she'd see him for what she knew he was: an eternal ladies' man who had no intention of making a commitment.

"Not only can you cook, but your tea is the best." He proceeded to drain his glass.

She moved to get up and refill it.

He held up his hand and broadened his smile. "Keep your seat. I'll do it." He then took her glass from her.

"You won't hear an argument out of me." Ann eased back on the couch. "You sure you wouldn't rather have a beer?"

"Nope. When I leave here, I'm going back to the office to do some paperwork."

"Ah, so you need a clear head?"

"Right," he said with a disarming grin.

If he didn't stop grinning at her like that, she wasn't sure she could be held responsible for her actions. While he ambled into the kitchen, Ann felt her breath released from her tightened throat. She went limp as a rag doll. God, she had to get hold of her frayed emotions....

She heard his footsteps and forced a cool smile onto her lips. But the minute he came into view, that smile faltered. The closer he came, the louder her nagging conscience: *you're lying to yourself.* His physical power dominated the room, shrinking its size. He wouldn't be able to simply walk out of her life without repercussions, she thought with a sinking heart.

Her blood pressure wasn't up because of fear of further confrontation but because he was here with her.

He returned to his seat beside her on the couch, then held out her glass. "Don't say I didn't ever do anything for you."

Later, Ann suspected the accidental touch hadn't been part of the game plan, but it happened, nevertheless. The soft, but exquisite graze of fingers sent a current through her entire body.

Drew seemed to feel it, too. He flinched visibly, then changed the subject.

"What do you hear from Peter these days?"

Ann's face clouded. "Not anything, actually."

"Does that bother you?"

"Yes and no," she said with a sigh.

"Is it true that he's been in trouble with the law?"

"Yes." Bitterness colored her tone. "I hear from him when he needs something."

"That's a damn shame. He had…has so much potential."

"True. But Mamma always said he didn't have a backbone."

"I tried to help, you know."

"I know, but he resented it." Ann looked at her hands. "I keep hoping, praying, that one of these days he'll straighten up."

"Maybe he will," Drew said, his eyes on her.

A short silence ensued.

"Look, the evening was great, but I've got to go." He sounded desperate, yet he made no move to get up.

"So, I'm vindicated?" Ann said, returning his stare.

His lips tightened. "Go ahead and say it."

"What?" she asked, feigning innocence.

He grinned sheepishly. "That I acted like the world's biggest jackass."

"I didn't say that."

"But you thought it."

"Well…"

He chuckled. "God, I can't believe I came charging into your shop blaming you. But when Becky told me those quacking biddies had heard it at your place, I lost it."

"Well, in defense of yourself, you'd had a week from hell. John dying, worry over your mother, then hearing someone accuse you of being im…" Her voice faltered, and she couldn't go on.

"*Impotent*. That's the word," he said with a teasing glint in his eyes.

She flushed, but couldn't control her tongue. "Only you're not…" Again her voice faltered.

"I may be a lot of things. But that I'm not." His eyes bored into hers.

"I'm...glad."

He laughed at her response. "Me, too."

She liked to hear him laugh, even if it was at her expense. It originated in his chest and ended in his eyes, lightening them even more.

She liked everything about this man—his deep, husky voice, the way his hair begged for a trim, the way he smelled....

But he wasn't interested in her.

Or so she told herself, until the laughter stopped and his eyes met hers. Something sizzled between them, something alive and vital. An ache began deep inside her, and her nipples throbbed. But he never looked at her breasts. He never got the chance.

She leapt to her feet and walked to the middle of the room.

He cleared his throat. "Uh, tell me what you do?"

She swung around. "Do?"

"Yeah, you know. Your work."

"Oh." She relaxed. "I turn ugly nails into beautiful ones."

He shook his head. "And you actually make a living doing that?"

"A good one, too. And I have plans to make it even better."

"How?"

She explained about her expansion plans.

"Sounds like you know what you're doing."

"What about you?"

He shrugged. "I guess you could say I live to race."

"I can see you haven't changed."

"Nope. Cars are in my blood."

"Bet you didn't think you'd be selling them for a living, though?"

"Hell, no. I figured in the end, my old man would haul me back to the ranch, so to speak, and put me to work in the lumber mill."

"Only he didn't."

"It wasn't because he didn't want to, believe me. When I told him I had no intention of taking over the family business, he went berserk. Anyway, this college buddy of mine was a car nut like me and wanted to own his own business—used cars, that is. He needed some bucks. So I took my grandmother's trust fund and went in with him. Later he bought me out, and I bought a new car business."

"And now your success enables you to play?"

"If you call racing a game, then I guess it does."

"So when do you race again?"

His features dimmed. "Not anytime soon, not with the mess Dad's estate's in."

"I'm sorry," Ann said for lack of anything better to say.

"Yeah, me, too." He stood abruptly. "Speaking of work. If I don't get outta here, it's never going to get done."

She walked him to the door. Once there, they faced each other. Suddenly there was nothing to say. Throughout the evening, conversation had flowed. But now it seemed to dry up.

"Drew?"

For an interminably long moment they stared at each other.

Drew reached for her, pulled her hard against him. Stillness. Nothing but their breathing and the sound of crickets chirping outside. She felt that incredible heat building inside her again.

Her lips parted, only to be crushed beneath his. It was

as if her touch had set him on fire. His tongue invade
her mouth—hot and wet and fierce.

Ann locked her hands around his neck, sinking he
fingers into his hair even as she feared his energy migh
consume her. Still, she clung to him. Her breasts shoo
with raging emotion. She felt a heavy sensation in he
thighs.

The taste of lust was on his lips. He devoured he
mouth as if he were no longer in control of himself.

He pulled away then, struggling for breath, and lifted
his head to suck air deep into his lungs.

Ann heard the loud thump of her heart. Or was it his

"Damn," he muttered.

Ann turned away and closed her eyes. Tears of shame
and mortification seeped out and down her cheeks. How
could she have lost control so easily?

"Look, I'll be in touch," he said, his voice sounding
like rough sandpaper.

"All right," she managed to get out. But she couldn'
bring herself to look at him again.

A few seconds later, she was alone.

Seven

Drew scrutinized Tim Pollard. With black hair, round face, thick glasses and slightly oversize ears, he reminded Drew of an owl.

But how Pollard looked wasn't the issue; his stupidity was. How Pollard thought he could continue to take money out of the MacMillan till and not get caught went beyond Drew's reasoning.

Besides examining the ledgers, Drew had checked out Pollard personally, certain he'd find a change in Pollard's life-style. He'd turned up zilch, except for one thing. Pollard had a girlfriend. The pillar of the local church fooled around on his wife with a teller at the bank.

A niggling in the back of Drew's mind told him Pollard's liaison with the teller meant something. But Pollard's bank account hadn't shown anything. The balance had fluctuated very little, if any, over the past few years. He'd just have to keep digging.

Still, Pollard was a hard nut to crack. Drew had called him into the office thirty minutes ago and had been questioning him since.

But the business manager gave no sign that he was intimidated in the least, except that he seemed to have a penchant for running his finger around his collar as if he were choking to death.

"I have been a valuable asset to Mr. MacMillan," Tim said primly, bridging the lengthy silence. "And I don't appreciate your insinuations."

"Well, I don't like what the company's bank account insinuates, either." Drew's tone, while calm, was cold and unyielding.

Tim flushed and again dug his finger between his neck and collar. "I assure you the books are in perfect order. Have them checked."

"I intend to, Mr. Pollard."

When Pollard walked out of his office a few minutes later, Drew cursed silently and rubbed his tired eyes. What a mess. What a bloody mess. He was not an accountant and didn't profess to know the finer points of that trade. However, his gut told him the MacMillan Investments should be showing more of a profit. As he'd told Pollard, the books simply didn't add up.

He knew who could help him, if anyone could. His own accountant in Houston. That was a start anyway. Along with the ledgers, he'd box the invoices, statement and daily cash receipts that Pollard had been responsible for and take them with him.

Drew rubbed his eyes again and tried to ignore the burning sensation behind them. He'd been awake half the night. His mother had had another "incident" with her heart. She'd refused at first to go to the hospital, saying that if she were going to die, she preferred to do so in her own bed. He'd argued, of course, and in the end had won. He had remained by her side at the hospital all night and because her condition had greatly improved this morning, he'd brought her home.

Becky had assured him that she would call him if there was the slightest change in his mother's condition. But nothing could put his mind at ease. It was on a collision course. *He* was on a collision course.

Ann Sinclair was the culprit.

He couldn't shake her from his thoughts. He couldn't get that kiss off his mind. It had been five days since he'd darted out of her house like a scared teenager on his first date. But her response to him had both excited and shocked him. Cool on the outside…hot on the inside.

He still hadn't been able to justify his actions or lay the entire episode to rest. So what if he'd kissed her and she'd kissed him back? Happened with women all the time. No big deal. But it was a big deal. He hadn't wanted to stop there.

When she'd trembled in his arms, and when she'd stirred against him, he'd felt the vibrations clear down to his toes. His heart had raced, and the banked fire in his gut had roared to life.

And her mouth. It had been waiting for him—hot, moist, hungry. The burning inside him had almost leapt out of control. His baser instinct had been to lower her to the carpet, free her breasts and suck those taunting nipples that had bored holes in his chest. But he hadn't wanted to stop there. He'd wanted to jerk off her pants and bury himself inside her hot flesh.

Suddenly he couldn't breathe. Something crushed his chest. Fear? Gut-deep fear, that was what it was. He didn't want to get involved, for god's sake. What was more, he wasn't about to get involved.

He was determined to stay the hell away from her. He already had enough problems. He didn't need extra baggage.

Yeah, that was the answer. But could he do it? He closed his eyes and contemplated the whole damn problem. Finally he came to a decision. Only problem was, he didn't like it.

Disgusted, Drew slammed his hand against the desk.

Raising a Responsible Child by Dr. Don Dinkmeyer. Ann had purchased the book before coming home from the local bookstore.

She eyed the book, even lifted it to her chest, as she'd done several times since she'd gotten home from work. She'd eaten a bite, showered, then slipped into her gown.

She'd been so tired and the bed had looked so inviting, she'd plopped down and hadn't budged.

That had been hours ago. But she hadn't slept nor had she read the book with any real interest.

"Drew," she whispered aloud, despising the twist that darted through her.

During work hours, she did just fine. She kept thoughts of him repressed because they were too painful. But at night, she wasn't as lucky. She thought about her wanton behavior, and she wanted to die.

Ann leaned over and switched off the lamp. She lay against the pillows in the darkness, and listened to the pounding of her heart—and felt her cheeks blaze.

She'd practically swooned at his feet, as though she'd been starved for a man. She hadn't been, of course. Yet when his tongue had tangled with hers, wet and frisky, common sense had deserted her. She had to admit that.

And Drew MacMillan, of all people. A renegade, a

ladies' man, a velvet-tongued charmer. He was everything she *didn't want* in a man, in the father of her child.

She bolted out of bed and crossed to the window. After
opening the miniblinds, she peered outside. A light rain
caressed the windowpane. The streets would be as slip-
pery as black glass.

The way Drew drove, she hoped he'd stay off of them.
Stop it! Stop thinking about him, she told herself. But as
before, her mind and heart seemed determined to take
that dangerous turn. No rest for the weary, she told herself.

For years she had kept her personal life on a tight rein,
buried her desires. How could she let Drew change that?
How could she have veered out of control so easily? So
quickly? Well, she wouldn't do it again. Drew MacMillan
was off-limits.

Holding on to that comforting thought, she padded
back to bed, lay down and jerked the covers over her
head.

"Oh, Ann, they look absolutely gorgeous."

Pleased with the praise, Ann smiled. "You really think
so?"

"Oh, gosh, yes," Kay Townsend responded. She held
out all ten fingers and admired the set of acrylic nails,
painted a stunning pink. Ann had adhered the false nails
to Kay's natural ones.

"But the question is, can you fix hair with those
claws?" Ann asked.

"Like a charm."

"I'm going to hold you to that promise," Ann said, a
teasing warmth in her voice.

She had only that morning hired Kay as the first of
many beauticians for Polished Choice, or so she hoped.

After hours, she had interviewed several girls from Mac-Millan who were fresh out of beauty school as well as several from nearby towns. She'd wanted to make sure she found just the right person. Her and Sophie's relationship was such that a third person had to fit in, had to have the same work habits and share the same level of enthusiasm.

Though tall and rather gangly, Kay had a style all her own that began with a mop of long blond hair that Ann guessed was not altogether out of a bottle. More importantly, Kay had an infectious smile and gift of gab that was necessary to make a success of her profession.

"When do you think I'll be able to start?" Kay asked.

Ann also rose, then hesitated. "I'm afraid I can't answer that. The carpenter has promised he would work on Sundays and Mondays while the shop's closed. I figure he should be through in about two weeks." She paused with a grimace. "But you know how that is. I've never had much luck with carpenters sticking to their word."

"We can always hope."

Kay walked toward the empty room that was soon to be her new workplace. Ann followed. They stood just inside the doorway.

"I've dreamed of this time for two years," Ann said, her voice shaky. "And now that it's about to become a reality, I'm both scared and excited."

Kay smiled. "Ah, don't be scared, just be excited. Everything's going to be hunky-dory. You wait and see." She faced Ann without the smile. "Are you sure you don't want to move your station in here?"

"Heavens no," Ann exclaimed. "Anyway, you're not going to be alone."

"I'm not?"

Ann chuckled. "Well, there won't be another body."

She paused. "But hopefully, All Natural skin-care products will share your space."

"Really?"

"I'm keeping my fingers crossed. A rep is due soon to look us over."

"Wow. 'All Natural.' I'm impressed."

"Don't be—because I might not pull it off. I'm afraid they might demand a higher volume than we can produce. But it doesn't cost anything to dream."

"Do you mind if I stop by and monitor the progress?" Kay asked, inching toward the front door.

"I'll be disappointed if you don't."

Once Ann was alone, she made the shop ready for the day. Sophie was due any minute, and so was her first customer, Mabel. And if Mabel so much as mentioned Drew, Ann was going to pop her in the chops.

Now, wasn't that a delightful thought. Ann flipped the sign on the door and chuckled aloud.

The hours that followed passed quickly, despite the fact that Ann wasn't booked solid nor was Sophie. Still, Ann had a zillion things to do before five o'clock, when she had a pedicure scheduled.

"Sophie, I'll be in the pedicure room. Agnes Gaits will be in shortly."

"Well, I'm outta here, okay?"

"All right. See you in the morning."

Despite her unsettled night, Ann didn't feel tired. Nervous energy propelled her, but she didn't care. As long as she could work without forbidden thoughts of Drew interrupting, she was content.

She even hummed a tune while retrieving the foot-massaging machine from the supply closet. The buzzer on the door sounded.

''Come on back. I'm setting up.''

''For what?''

Panic flared inside Ann like a fever. She would have known that gravelly sounding voice anywhere. Every nerve prickled with awareness. Darn her traitorous body. *Darn him!*

She spun around.

The expression in his eyes was unreadable.

''How'd you get in here?'' she demanded in a mangled voice. She clutched the massager to her chest as if it were protection from her quaking insides.

He grinned that lazy grin of his. ''Walked in, actually.''

''Funny,'' she said, mustering a weak, wobbly smile, determined to show him she was in charge.

''What'cha doing?''

Eight

Drew's tone, lazy as his lopsided grin, brought to life the same "something" she'd felt when his tongue had stormed her mouth. She completely forgot his question as she lifted rounded eyes to his.

His grin faded, and his eyes narrowed.

Neither one said a word, neither moved, as they both remembered the last time they were together.

Drew shifted, then cleared his throat, though he never took his eyes off of her.

Her cheeks on fire, Ann bent down, determined to hide her embarrassment. She placed the massager on the floor and made a big deal out of plugging it in.

Why was he here? she ranted silently. She figured he didn't want to see her any more than she wanted to see him. *Liar!* You want to see him, only you know in the end you'll be the one that gets hurt.

Why didn't he stop tormenting her and leave her

alone? He was here now and apparently had no intention of leaving. So she'd just have to make the best of an impossible situation and take charge.

"Mind explaining what you're going to do with that?" he asked.

Ann straightened. "It's a foot massager."

"Whatever you say."

In spite of herself, Ann smiled. "Hey, don't knock it. Next to acrylic nails, it's my biggest money-maker."

He still looked blank but made an attempt to fake it. "Uh, how so?"

Ann's smile strengthened. She felt at an advantage for the first time since his surprise visit. "This is used for pedicures," she said with confidence.

"And that is?"

"Oh, come on. You're putting me on. Surely you know what a pedicure is. Anyway," she went on, indulging herself and him, "pedicures are manicures of the feet. I do everything to feet that I do to hands."

"What's this gizmo?" Drew pushed away from the doorjamb and moseyed toward a sturdy white wooden bench that resembled an animal, a giraffe to be exact. He touched it while his gaze met hers. His mouth twitched with amusement. "This is strange, you'll have to admit."

"This gizmo, as you call it, is where I sit."

He crossed his arms, spread his legs slightly and rocked on his heels. He had on jeans, as usual, and a green knit shirt that stretched across his muscled chest. God, but he was good-looking, Ann thought, her mouth going dry as cotton.

"And they sit in that chair in front?"

"Er…right," Ann said, and collected her scattered senses. "And after I cut or file the nails, remove the excess skin from their heels, etcetera, they soak their feet, then dip them in hot, scented wax. The polish comes next.''

"So some lucky woman's about to get the works, huh?''

"Who said it was a woman?''

Drew looked stunned. "You mean it's a man?''

His expression was priceless. Ann chuckled. "Would that be so terrible?''

"You mean you'd actually do all this to men's stinking feet?''

She laughed out loud this time. "Of course. Their feet don't smell any worse than some women's.''

"I don't give a damn. A man shouldn't get his feet 'done.''' He paused. "I wouldn't be caught dead in that chair.''

"Never say never,'' she responded airily.

He eyed the "gizmo" with distaste. "In this case, never is never.''

"If it'll put your mind at rest,'' she said with false sweetness, "my client today is a woman. I just wanted to get your reaction.''

"Well, you got it.''

A twinkle appeared in Ann's eyes. "However, I do have several male clients.''

Drew snorted.

Ann heard the buzzer again. "Look, my lady's here.'' She paused. "Was there…er…something you wanted?'' she forced herself to ask.

"Yeah, would you like to go with me to Houston tomorrow?''

"Why?'' she asked, her tone wary.

His gaze didn't waver. "No reason, except I'd like the company.''

Ann's mind raced. "Well, I…''

"If I promise to keep my hands to myself, will you come?"

A short silence.

"All right, I'll go," she whispered. So much for good intentions, she thought, her heart hammering wildly.

"Good. I'll pick you up about eight."

"So what do you think?"

Ann picked up on the "little boy" eagerness in his tone, despite his efforts to appear nonchalant. She smiled and gave in to the urge to rattle him a bit. "I think exactly what you thought I'd think."

He frowned. "What the hell kind of answer is that?"

She laughed. "Oh, all right, it's a showplace. Now, are you satisfied?"

"Completely," he said with his usual arrogance.

Ann rolled her eyes, then surveyed the surroundings with critical intent. She could find nothing to criticize.

They had left MacMillan around eight o'clock. When Drew had arrived at her house, she'd had butterflies the size of elephants in her stomach. She hadn't as yet come to grips with the idea that she had agreed to this lark. She despised the effect he had on her; his presence made it impossible for her to remain strong. How would she handle being closed up in the car with him for two hours? What would they talk about?

She needn't have worried. He'd striven to put her at ease. After pleasantries had been exchanged, he'd slipped in a cassette of Cher's latest album and they'd listened to it. The strains from the Jag's elaborate stereo system were like none she'd ever heard.

The tension, however, had remained. She was aware of every move he made, no matter how small or insignificant. So when he'd let her out at Town and Country Mall to shop, relief had washed through her.

He'd come after her only thirty minutes ago. Now, they were at his Jaguar dealership.

"I wanted everything to be just right," Drew said close to her ear, "so Mother had a friend whose daughter was an interior decorator." He waved his hand. "The showroom is her handiwork."

In more ways than one, Ann thought cattily. Jealousy, wild and fierce, rushed through her. With an abrupt twist of her head, she forced herself to take in the details that surrounded her.

The showroom floor, though tastefully decorated with plush gold carpeting, huge decorator buckets filled with live plants, and paintings positioned on the paneled walls, actually paled in comparison to the automobiles.

To the side of the main showroom were small offices. A long hall, she suspected, led to Drew's office and the service department beyond. But again, it was the auto-mobiles themselves that made the showroom come to life, added to the refinement.

Ann tried not to show her awe as she inspected the sleek machinery in front of her. She placed her hand on the side of the cranberry-colored Jag and felt as if she were stroking velvet.

"Nice, isn't it?" Drew said from close behind her.

Chill bumps danced across her skin. Without looking at him, she stepped closer to the car. "That's hardly the word."

"Want to sit inside?"

He opened the door and released the new-car scent. Ann inhaled deeply. "It even smells expensive."

"It's supposed to."

She angled her head to one side and peered at him. "How much does one of these jewels sell for?"

"This one, the XJ6 4.0, goes for thirty-three, four."

Ann gulped. "As in dollars?"

His lips twitched. "Good ole American hard, cold cash."

"What about the one over there?" She nodded toward the steel-blue one that revolved under a spotlight.

"That little beauty goes for over forty."

"It must be nice, is all I can say."

Before Drew could respond, a man walked up. Drew introduced him as Skip Howard. They talked for a moment, then Drew turned to Ann. "I need to sign some papers."

"No problem."

"You'll be all right?"

That intimate look again. Her blood pressure shot up, and she ran her tongue over her lips. "Of course."

His eyes delved into hers a second longer. "I won't be long."

He wasn't. Thirty minutes later, they left the dealership and were once again closeted in the car. Ann shifted sideways so that she could study his profile. Instead, her eyes fell to his hands, and she watched as they effortlessly guided the steering wheel. Skill and energy seemed to flow from each finger. She wondered what those fingers would feel like caressing her naked flesh, exploring her body's hidden secrets.

"So what did you do while I was at the mall?" she asked suddenly, desperately, and was rewarded that she had successfully covered the cracks in her voice.

Drew turned and gave her a quick look, his eyes crinkled at the corners. "Met with my accountant."

"Mmm, sounds interesting."

He laughed, then eased a hand off the steering wheel and rested it on his thigh, a thigh that appeared rock hard underneath his casual slacks. "No, it doesn't. It sounds boring as hell."

His laughter added another dimension to the camaraderie they found themselves sharing. Ann angled her head. "Was it? Boring as hell, I mean?"

"No, in light of the fact that I'm trying to nail Pollard's butt."

"Tim Pollard?"

"One in the same."

"Whatever for?" Ann stared at him in amazement. "Why he's one of the pillars of the community. And if I'm not mistaken, a good friend of your family's."

"You're right. My mother went to school with him and thought of him as a close friend. No 'hanky-panky,' mind you, just good friends."

"And isn't he a deacon at church?"

"Front row, amen corner." Drew's voice was thick with sarcasm.

"He must've done something terrible for you to turn on him like this."

"If my suspicions prove correct, you bet he has."

"I can't imagine. Why, he looks like he'd be too scared to do anything wrong." Tim Pollard's face sprang to mind, and she shook her head. She'd always thought of him as a benign being. "Are you sure you're not mistaken."

"I shouldn't be telling you this, but I think he's been taking money from the till."

"You're kidding?"

Drew shot her a sharp glance. "Would I kid about something like that?"

"No, no you wouldn't."

"He's embezzling, pure and simple."

"But how? How could he get by your daddy? I can't imagine a man like John MacMillan not taking care of his business."

"Nor can I."

"Despite all his other faults," Ann said bluntly, "I'd always admired his business savvy."

"Apparently, he had total confidence in Tim Pollard."

Ann let out a pent-up breath. "I'm here to tell you I'm shocked."

"How the hell do you think I feel? I thought everything would be in great shape, that it'd be a breeze to settle his estate. Then, as soon as Mother stabilized, I'd head back for the bright lights."

Her life would be much simpler if he had, Ann thought. "Only it hasn't worked out that way," she said.

"Not hardly. I guess Dad just got complacent and didn't see any reason to question Pollard. I don't know. Anyway, today I took a ton of stuff to my accountant for him to go through. Maybe he can confirm what I suspect."

"What are you going to do if you find out it's true?"

Drew laughed without humor. "Have the sonofabitch arrested, that's what."

Ann had no doubt he would, thinking again how easygoing he was until crossed. Then there was hell to pay. She shivered.

"What's wrong?" Drew asked.

She forced a smile. "Nothing."

"Surely you don't think I should just slap his hand and let him off the hook?"

Ann chose her words carefully. "No. It's...just that

it'll be an awful scandal. I was thinking about his wife and two children.''

A muscle tightened in Drew's cheek. "He should've thought about them before he got greedy.''

"I know," Ann replied, her tone still troubled.

He looked at her strangely for a moment. "So what about you?" he asked, changing the subject. "What did you accomplish?''

"Shopped.''

"For clothes?''

"Uh-huh.''

His eyes slowly looked over her. It could have been her imagination, of course, but she was certain they lingered on her breasts as he said, "What are you, a size four?''

She saw the heat in his eyes and could hardly get her breath. "A two, except for—" She broke off, appalled at her near slip of the tongue, at what she was about to admit.

"Your breasts," he said softly, though his voice had a scraping edge to it.

Ann's tightly clogged lungs clamored for air. "You're out of line.''

"I know.''

She tore her gaze from him, stared out the window and fought for composure.

After a moment Drew said in a cooler tone, "So what did you buy?''

Relief made Ann weak. She sagged against the door. "I didn't shop for me.''

"Then who did you shop for?''

"The baby.''

"Baby? Whose baby?''

"Mine.''

Nine

"*Yours!*" His jaw dropped like an anvil. "What the hell?"

Ann couldn't suppress a quick smile. When she'd blurted her news about the baby, she hadn't realized how it must have sounded. Women were openly bearing children out of wedlock these days, and while not totally accepted by society, it no longer had the stigma attached it once had.

But that wasn't what had brought about his flabbergasted reaction, she surmised. It was the thought that she had a child and hadn't bothered to tell him.

"Actually, they're for the baby I'm hoping to get," she said, breaking the heavy silence.

Drew continued to stare at her as if she had indeed gone off the deep end, his blue eyes dark and inquiring.

"Don't look at me like that," she said.

"Get? You said get." He didn't bother to conceal his impatience.

"If you'll just give me time, I'll explain." Ann's impatience now matched his.

"I'm listening."

"I want to adopt a child." She smiled again. "In fact, I've applied to a state agency."

"You can't be serious."

Ann's smile disappeared, and she stiffened. "Rest assured, I'm serious."

"Why, that's the craziest thing I've ever heard."

"I don't recall asking for your opinion."

"Surely you haven't thought this through."

Ann gritted her teeth. Her eyes flashed. "Of course I've thought it through. Adoption is the best for me."

"Well, in my opinion, that's taking a big risk." His tone was harsh. "Oh, I know they screen the babies, but in the end there always seem to be problems."

A chill passed through Ann. "I happen not to agree."

"If you want to have a baby, why the hell don't you just get married and have your own baby?"

Her face turned ashen, and she clasped her hands together. "Why don't *you* mind your own business?"

"I just don't get it," he said, removing a hand from the steering wheel and raking his fingertips through his hair.

"I don't care if you get it or not." Fury shook her voice.

Drew took his eyes off the road again and gave her another long, probing look. "You're really serious about this, aren't you?"

"Yes."

"Why?" His voice sounded strained.

"I want a baby, a child, that's why."

"Can't you have one of your own? I mean, is there something wrong?"

His question hit her with the subtlety of a baseball bat over the head and shattered her control. Blood rushed to her cheeks. "Go to hell."

He eyed her oddly, then smiled, a smile that spread into laughter. "I still think you're crazy, but if that's what makes you happy...."

Ann kept her eyes straight ahead. How dare he treat her like this, as though she were a nitwit? It was all she could do to keep from reaching out and smacking his smug face. "Don't you dare make fun of me."

"Look—"

"Forget it. I don't think we have anything else to say to each other."

Drew swore aloud, then faced the road and said no more.

Ann lifted her shoulders up and down, then crossed her right hand to her left shoulder and massaged it. She couldn't remember when she'd ever been so tired. Part of her fatigue stemmed from physical labor and part from mental stress.

The last customer had gone for the day, even though it was only four o'clock. Ann was alone; Sophie had walked to the café across the street to grab a bite to eat. Four boxes of supplies had arrived earlier, and Sophie had promised to help her check them in and stock them on the shelves.

"Ugh!" Ann muttered, when she caught a glimpse of the boxes stacked inside the beautician room.

She got up from behind her worktable, stretched, then continued to rub her shoulders. Boy, was she tired. The weather was terrible; rain had fallen all day. Maybe that was why business had been so good. Both she and Sophie had been busy.

She was thrilled, of course, but it had been an effort to be cheery and chat with the customers. She'd felt slightly brain-dead all day.

Oh, who was she trying to kid? She'd been in a state, not just today, but ever since Drew had made her feel like a fool for wanting to adopt a child.

Damn him.

It was three days after the fact, and she still hadn't forgiven him. She doubted she ever would. Things happened for the best, her mother had always told her. Well, she was certain this was for the best.

A home and family weren't in his vocabulary. And a child... Obviously that was a dirty word. In spite of the hard core of anger inside her, tears stung Ann's eyes. Why did he have to be so handsome? So charming? But such a cad.

She dashed the tears from her eyes, stiffened her spine and headed toward the boxes. If she ever wanted to get home and soak in the tub, she'd best stop feeling sorry for herself and get to work.

And face a few facts. Drew MacMillan had never been part of her life, and he never would be. She was going to have to come to terms with that.

Ann was halfway to the room when she heard the buzzer indicating that the shop's front door was open. Knowing it was too soon for Sophie to return she stopped and swung around.

"Hello, sis."

"Peter?"

"One in the same."

Ann blinked twice to make sure her brother wasn't a

ghost. But he was no ghost; he stood before her in the flesh. Months had passed since she'd seen him. He hadn't changed, except maybe his weight. He looked heavier, which wasn't a plus to his already sturdy frame. Other than that, his hazel-colored eyes still had that dull, mistrusting glint in them, and the lock of dark hair that continually fell across his forehead was there, as well. His perfect white teeth were his best feature, but they weren't in evidence as he wasn't smiling.

"What…what brings you back?"

"Now, is that any way to greet your long-lost brother?"

"No, it isn't," she said flatly, feeling the threat of tears again. "I should be hugging you. But you've made that impossible, haven't you?"

He sneered. "Don't start that bull. I'm not in the mood."

"What do you want?" she asked coldly.

"Money."

"How stupid of me. Why else would you be here?" Ann vacillated between tears and anger.

Peter came toward her. "I'm in a jam."

"No!" she cried. "Don't come any closer."

Peter's mouth twisted. But before he could say anything, Ann added, "This well has dried up."

"Dammit, I need money to pay off a loan shark."

"Have you ever thought about getting a job?"

"A *job*." Peter spat the word as though it were a dreaded disease. "There's no time. I need the money now."

"Not from me you don't."

He took a step closer. "Now, see here—"

"I don't have the money, Peter. Even if I could give

it to you, I wouldn't. What cash I had is in that room in there.'' She pointed toward the beautician room. ''So you see, you'll have to go elsewhere for help.''

Peter's features turned menacing. ''I bet I know where you can get the money.''

''Oh, and where is that?'' she demanded sarcastically.

''Your boyfriend.'' His lips curled with contempt.

''My boyfriend?'' she echoed blankly.

''Yeah, Drew MacMillan.''

Her nerve endings rang in warning, rendering her speechless. Then she recovered and laughed. ''Whoever gave you that information is dead wrong.''

''I don't think so. He's loaded. Get it from him.''

Ann gasped. ''Didn't you hear what I said? Anyway, where did you get the idea he'd give *me* money?''

''Word has it around town that you're his latest 'bimbette.' And I believe it.''

Ann swallowed around the tightness in her throat. ''How…how long have you been here?''

''Long enough.''

''Well,'' she said, ignoring the alarm that shook her voice. ''You can forget it. And just to set the record straight, Drew MacMillan is the last person I would approach for money. Even if I were to ask, he wouldn't give it to me.''

''Damn you, I'm in no mood to play games.''

The uneasiness inside her dissipated. Only pity and a numbness remained. ''I'm not, either. You disgust me. Just go. Just get out of my sight.''

''Not until I get what I came for.''

''Oh, for heaven's…''

Peter bolted toward her, his face a thundercloud.

Ann couldn't move; her limbs were paralyzed. Her heart pounded, and her lungs clamored for oxygen.

The buzzer sounded.

Frightened of her brother for the first time in her life, Ann went weak with relief.

"Ann, what on earth—" Sophie broke off. Her eyes darted from Ann to Peter.

"I'll be back," Peter said tersely. Then he whipped around and skirted past Sophie. He slammed the door behind him, and the room seemed to rock.

"Whew!" Sophie exclaimed, her eyes huge in her small face. "What was that all about?"

Ann bit down on her lower lip to stop it from trembling. "You don't want to know."

"Yes, I do."

Ann took a long breath before she said, "That was Peter."

"Your brother?"

"My brother."

"Good Lord. You all right?"

Ann nodded mutely.

"Want to tell me what this is all about?"

"Oh, Soph, it's a long, heartbreaking story. But the short of it is, since he couldn't play football, he's drifted in and out of trouble and from one job to another." She paused and stared into space. "And to think he was once such an adorable kid."

"Unfortunately, adorable kids sometimes grow up to be hellions. So, what does he want from you?"

"Money, which I refused to give him."

"This just hasn't been your week, has it? First Drew made you see red, now this."

Ann hadn't intended to tell Sophie about her day spent in Drew's company, but after he'd upset her so and after she'd moped around the shop for two days, Sophie had pulled the truth out of her.

"I guess you can't win them all," Ann finally said with false bravado.

"Ah, blow 'em both off. We both know that men are pains in the royal rear." Sophie shrugged. "Feed 'em fish heads and rice, my daddy used to say."

"Oh, Sophie, you're the best friend a person could have."

"Think so, huh?"

Ann laughed through her tears. "I know so."

"Then come here, you little idiot, and let me give you a hug."

Ten

"Will that be all, Mr. MacMillan?"

Drew lifted the floral box filled with a dozen long-stemmed red roses and smiled at a retired ex-teacher of his who worked part-time at the florist. "That's all today, Ms. Epps. But I'm sure I'll be seeing you again, soon."

She chuckled. "You young boys are all alike, a new girl on the string every day."

Drew's lips twitched. "Well, I'm hardly a boy, Ms. Epps, but thanks for the compliment anyway."

A few minutes later, Drew sat in his Jag and eyed the box on the seat next to him.

Would she accept the roses? Would she see him? The latter was what he worried about and not the damn roses.

He owed her an apology, pure and simple. But that wasn't the only reason for the flowers. Wherever he turned, he saw Ann's face. And tasted her lips, just made for kissing. After sampling those, he'd known he couldn't stay away.

So why had he acted like a jerk and taken issue with her about adopting a baby? She wanted a kid? Hell, let her get one. It was no sweat off his back, nor was it any of his business.

He didn't want to marry her, but he sure as hell wanted her.

Following their disagreement, he'd tried to tell himself she didn't matter, that he'd get over the aching in his gut. He'd worked on his daddy's business, gone through the motions of doing what had been required of him, but it hadn't worked.

He wanted Ann so much it made him physically ill, sick to his stomach. That loss of control angered him. He couldn't remember when something had gotten to him this badly, when he'd been so emotional or so undisciplined. But then he believed she was only a passing fancy, that this obsession would either temper or fade altogether. It hadn't. At first, she presented a challenge to see what smoldered beneath her calm facade, and he took pride in never backing down from a challenge. Even so, he capitulated with the ease of a child being offered a new toy.

Maybe if he slept with her, he'd lick his fixation once and for all.

He nosed the Jag in the direction of Ann's house, his burden much lighter.

Ann's head pounded. It felt as if two snare drums were battling inside. As she let herself into the house, one thing was on her mind: relief.

She tossed her purse on the couch, then dropped her

tote bag on the floor. It was then she realized she wasn't alone. She spun around. Her heart dropped to her toes.

"What are you doing here? What do you want?" she demanded in what she hoped was a strong voice.

Her brother sat on the couch in the shadows, nonchalantly, his legs sprawled in front of him. He appeared not to have a care in the world. Ann knew better. She saw that look in his eyes—the same look he'd had as a little boy when he hadn't gotten his way.

Well, he was sadly mistaken if he thought she was going to placate him. He hadn't been able to bully her in those days, and he wasn't going to now. He should have realized that at the shop. Still, she felt another tiny ripple of fear. Stop acting silly, she scolded herself. He's your brother, for god's sake. When it comes down to it, he's not going to hurt you.

"I see you finally got home," Peter said, watching as Ann ventured deeper into the room.

"I asked you what you wanted." Her tone was cold and flat.

"Same thing I wanted when I came to the shop."

Ann lifted her chin. "And the same thing still applies. I don't have the money, and even if I did, I wouldn't give it to you."

Peter stood, then yawned.

"My God, Peter, look at you. Unshaven. Dirty. How can you do this to yourself? You need help."

"I didn't come here for a sermon," he hissed, closing the distance between them. "I told you to ask Drew. By god, he owes me!"

"You poor misguided fool." Pity shone from Ann's eyes. "Join the real world. People like Drew don't owe anyone. They owe *him*."

"If I don't get the money, I'm going to be in real trouble."

"Oh, Peter," Ann said dully, "how many times have I heard that?"

"It's different this time," he said in a faint, slightly cajoling tone.

Ann squared her shoulders and prayed for strength. He'd duped her so many times, hurt her so deeply, that she had to remain strong. If she kept bailing him out of trouble, he'd never learn. But the thought of anyone hurting him, physically, didn't bear thinking about.

"Sis…"

"Get a job, Peter. That's the only answer. Tell them you'll pay them back a little at a time."

"Dammit, there isn't time for all that. I have to have the money within a week."

"The answer is still no," she whispered, blinking back the threat of tears.

"Where's your purse?" Peter's angry eyes swept the room. When he spotted her purse on the couch, he rushed toward it.

"What are you doing!" Ann cried, and dashed after him.

By the time she reached him, he had her purse open and was rummaging through it.

"Stop it!" She jerked on his arm. "I told you I don't have the kind of money you need."

Peter's eyes glittered dangerously. "Where's your checkbook?"

"No!"

"Yes!" He dropped the purse, reached for her and shook her.

"Peter…no!" she cried again.

"What the hell!"

They both froze at the sound of Drew's voice. She and Peter had been so involved in their argument that they hadn't heard the door open. "Take your hands off of her," Drew said.

His tone of voice gave his words a more ominous ring than if he'd shouted them.

Peter's arms tightened around Ann. "Go to hell!"

Drew tossed aside the flowers and lunged for Peter.

Peter let go of Ann; she stumbled backward. Drew shoved Peter against the wall.

"Don't, Drew!"

Drew stopped in midaction. He dropped Peter—as if he were a sack of garbage. But Drew didn't back away. He remained in front of Peter's face and said with icy softness, "If you ever lay a hand on your sister again, you'll be sorry."

"You don't scare me," Peter replied, his tone sneering.

But Ann knew he was scared. A pulse thumped in his Adam's apple, and sweat covered his face. One on one, Peter was no match for Drew.

"What are you doing here, anyway?" Drew demanded. "Hope it's not to ask for money."

"It is," Ann put in. "He's after money for his gambling debt. I already told him I didn't have it, but he wouldn't take no for an answer."

"Well, you'll damn well take no for an answer now and get out of here."

Peter's expression darkened. "You can't order me around. It's for Ann to say whether I go or not."

"I suggest you rethink that last statement," Drew said, his tone once again even, but with that ominous ring to it.

"Stop it, both of you! Stop it right this minute." Tears

blinded Ann, and she wiped them away with an angry gesture.

Peter looked at both of them for a moment, then stomped to the door, walked out and slammed it behind him.

Ann couldn't speak, nor could she move. Her bones felt too brittle. She could only stand there while the tears washed her face.

"Don't," Drew groaned, then strode toward her, stopping close enough that their breaths mingled.

But he didn't touch her. He looked at her, and she saw raw, naked desire in his eyes. She trembled violently, and he drew her into his arms.

"Shh, don't cry," he said, holding her against him for the longest time. Only after she sighed and nestled closer did his lips slowly but hungrily trail across her cheek, drinking the tears, possessing her mouth.

Like a frightened doe on the run, Ann's heart beat inside. His tongue meshed with hers in its quest to inflame and conquer.

"Drew," she murmured weakly, half in protest, half in submission, but he wasn't listening. His attention was focused on tugging her blouse free of her jeans and getting to the flesh underneath. She heard his sharp intake of breath when he unclasped her bra and his hand came in contact with her breast. His hand couldn't contain its fullness as she swelled under his touch.

Moisture flooded Ann's body, and she sagged against him, the tug-of-war on her nipple almost more than she could stand.

He pressed the length of him against her, and she felt his hardness. "God...I want you...." He choked out. "Now."

I want you, too, she cried silently, only not like this,

not in the heat of the moment. "No...I can't." Ann broke out of his arms. "No...I can't," she gasped. "No... please...not like this."

She needed his comfort, needed to feel his arms around her. The time had been so right for that. But for anything else, the time had been so wrong. Lust was not the answer. That wasn't what she wanted from Drew. Not a quick, meaningless roll in the hay. And for Drew, that would be all it would mean.

He let her go. The arms that dropped to his side were as tight as steel bands; the muscles shuddered as if he was suffering withdrawal pains.

"Dammit, Ann, I..." He couldn't go on.

Their eyes locked. Questions hung in the air, thick and heavy. Questions neither dared voice.

"You...you don't have to say anything," she whispered. "I...understand. Please just go."

"You sure you'll be all right?" Drew asked at last, though his voice sounded rusty and his breathing wasn't quite right.

"I'll...be fine."

His eyes continued to probe hers for a long moment.

She shifted her gaze to the pathetic bouquet that she only vaguely remembered him tossing aside.

"Thanks...for the flowers," she said just as she reached the door, hating for him to leave her but knowing there was no other way.

He swung around; his lips hinted at a smile. "The flowers look kind of sad, don't they?"

"Water will take care of that."

They fell silent, but sparks still flew between them. Her skin felt scorched from them.

"Why...did you bring them?" Ann asked in a barely

audible tone, her eyes finding his once again. "The flowers, I mean."

He gave her his heart-tugging, lopsided grin. "My way of apologizing for acting like an ass the other day."

Ann looked startled. Drew apologizing? She couldn't believe it. "I think we both got out of line. We'll just leave it at that, okay?"

"You're sure you'll be all right?" he repeated.

She could feel his body lure her, pull at her. She hugged cold hands to her side. "I'm…sure."

Only she hadn't been sure. She hadn't been sure about anything, she told herself later, in bed, as she stared at the ceiling. She wouldn't ever be sure of anything, not as long as Drew remained in MacMillan.

Another sliver of pain darted through her head. But she simply didn't have the energy to get up and take anything. So she lay still and gave in to the flood of emotions that assailed her. Confusion? Desire? Need? Which one described what she felt toward Drew?

The emotion she had taken pains to bypass inadvertently jumped to the forefront of her mind. Love? The thought stabbed her like a sharp knife. No, absolutely not. He was just a forbidden temptation, a forbidden fling. When she fell in love, it would be with someone whose goals and life-style matched hers.

Anyway, she had better sense than to do anything that stupid.

Eleven

Ann knew she was a glutton for punishment. Continuing to see Drew proved that. But she was smitten. No, she was addicted to his volatile personality and lopsided smile. She couldn't reconcile her out-of-character behavior, so she refused to dwell on it.

She simply savored the time spent with him. Since the night of the brouhaha with Peter, she had gone to dinner with Drew, then to a movie in nearby Lufkin. Though he hadn't touched her—he'd gone out of his way to avoid doing so—the electricity had been there, exposed, ready to burst into flames without warning.

The intimacy had alarmed her, and excited her. Waking each morning had never held such pleasure. Her liaison with Drew hadn't been all that contributed to her happiness; she'd gone to Austin for the orientation session at the agency.

She hadn't told Drew; it hadn't been necessary. He'd

spent the same two days in Houston. Besides, she hadn't wanted anything to mar her trip. The experience had been one she'd never forget.

The meeting had begun with Ann and several couples being introduced to the agency staff, followed by a panel of prospective birth mothers. But what had impressed her the most, had been the tour of the facility with emphasis on the maternity wing.

"Take a good look," Dorothy Sable had said with a smile. "Because this is the last time you'll be allowed in this section."

"Why?" Ann asked shyly.

"By then there might be a chance that you'd come in contact with the birth mother of your child."

When Dorothy said "your child," panicked excitement shot through Ann.

Afterward, they had returned to the meeting room for a question-and-answer session. In all, it had been a wonderful day, and she was reassured that she was doing the right thing.

The only shadow in her life was Peter. Despite her efforts not to, she constantly worried about him. He was her brother, after all, her only surviving kin, and the thought of some creep breaking his leg or worse, caused her deep pain and remorse. Had she done right in refusing to bail him out of trouble again? Drew had assured her that she had. Still...

Now, as Ann pilfered through her tote bag for her ledger, thoughts of Peter kept intervening. She had closed the shop early because of the funeral for another of the town's leading citizens. Her two customers scheduled for late afternoon had canceled.

Tonight she was to have dinner at Drew's house, and her exhilaration was building. But first things first, she told herself, taking everything out of the bag, certain she'd brought home the ledger.

When she didn't find it, she pursed her lips and thought for a moment. Her mind's eye saw it at the shop, on the desk in the pedicure room.

"Drat," she muttered, knowing she'd have to dash back to the shop and get it. She had to post today or get further behind. Without any more fuss, she made the short trip downtown.

When she first opened the door, she didn't notice anything amiss or even different. What she did notice, however, was an eerie quiet.

She paused on the threshold, switched on the light to counteract the cloud cover outside, then gasped. "Oh, no!"

The shop's interior looked like war-torn Beirut. Judging from where she stood, the room appeared as if nothing had escaped the intruder's vengeance. Tears blinded her as she stood helplessly silent. Who could have done this? Who could have wrought such stark destruction? And for what?

Unwittingly, thoughts of Peter rose to her mind. Oh, God, no, please don't let him be responsible. If that were the case, she didn't know how she would survive the blow.

Finally, Ann decided that wallowing in self-pity was not the answer, and she forced herself to cross the room to the phone. Blinking back tears, she dialed the police, then Drew. She groped for the chair, sat down and swallowed the huge lump in her throat. The tears she'd tried to hold back soaked her face.

"Oh, Drew, you can't mean it?"

Drew stood by powerless and watched his mother's

self-control crumble. "I don't have the proof yet," Drew said, easing down beside her on the couch. "But I expect to have it soon."

"But...Tim Pollard...why, he's been a family friend forever."

"I know, Mamma," Drew said. He took her cold hand in his and squeezed it.

He hadn't planned to say anything to her about the mess until he had proof one way or the other. But Janet had been feeling much better lately and had gone to the beauty shop. She'd heard the gossip.

His mother had confronted him with what she'd heard, and he'd had no choice but to be honest with her.

"I'll just pray that it won't be true," she said in an unsteady voice.

"Me, too, Mamma, me too."

"So is Ann coming to dinner?" Janet asked, changing the subject and sounding much stronger.

Drew got up, peered down at her and smiled. "Yep."

"Good. I always liked her. Thought she was made of the right stuff, especially in light of what she's been through."

The maid appeared just inside the door of the den before Drew could answer. "Mr. MacMillan, there's a phone call for you. The lady says it's urgent."

"Thanks, Maggie," Drew said with a frown, and strode to the phone nearby. "MacMillan here." He listened, and the color slowly left his face. "I'll be right there."

"What was that all about?" Janet asked.

"I'm afraid Ann won't be coming to dinner, after all," he said tersely. "Her shop's been broken into."

"Well, for heaven's sake," Janet said, and placed her

hand to her chest. "Who would do a thing like that in MacMillan?"

"Don't know." Drew's tone was frigid. "But I aim to find out or see that the police do." He bent down and kissed his mother on the cheek. "I'll call you later."

Drew arrived at the shop at the same time the police did. Ann stood by the door, tracks of dried tears on her face. He longed to pull her into his arms, but of course he couldn't. He had to settle for taking a cold limp hand in his and warming it.

"Oh, Drew," she whispered, her bottom lip quivering. "I can't believe this."

"Shh, take it easy."

"Ma'am, I'm Officer Riley. I need to ask you some questions."

Drew removed his hand from Ann's and introduced himself to the young, green-eyed rookie.

Recognition lit his eyes. "Gee, Mr. MacMillan, I'm pleased to meet you. I keep up with you on the racetrack. I think you're a real fine driver."

"Thanks, I appreciate that," Drew said, with enough impatience that the officer realized he was off base.

'Sorry," he said, red-faced. "Now, Ms. Sinclair, is there anything missing?"

"No, not that I can tell."

"Do you know anyone who would do this?"

Drew sensed her hesitation, but only for a moment.

"My...my brother and I had a disagreement." She took a deep breath.

Drew knew what it must have cost her to implicate Peter. And like her, he didn't want to believe that his childhood friend could do anything so vindictive, so desperate. Yet he had to keep in mind that Peter had tried to manhandle Ann. If he'd do that, he'd do anything. And if he turned out to be the perpetrator here, Drew would like nothing better than to thrash him within an inch of his life for putting Ann through hell.

Drew stopped his thoughts from wandering and paid attention while Officer Riley asked Ann several more questions. Another officer dusted for fingerprints. At last he and Ann were left alone. Ann folded her arms across her chest as if to protect herself from the evil that had penetrated the premise.

"I feel so violated," she said, and stared at him, her lashes glazed with fresh tears.

"Anyone would in this situation," he responded.

Drew guessed she was about to break. She was holding herself together by a mere thread. Again, he steeled himself not to haul her into his arms and promise her that everything was going to be all right.

"And I feel so awful about implicating Peter, like I'm betraying him."

"Hey, stop beating up on yourself. You had to tell the truth."

"But what if he didn't do this?"

"Well, if he didn't, and that's a big if, mind you, then he'll be exonerated."

"I wish it were that simple." She let out a deep sigh. "He'd never forgive me."

"There's nothing to forgive," Drew said, deciding he'd best take her home before she retracted everything she'd told the police.

"I'm—"

"Come on," Drew interrupted brusquely, "let's get out of here."

Ann gripped her hands together. "I can't just leave this mess."

"Yes, you can. I'll take care of it. The insurance company needs to be notified. And I'll call a buddy of mine right now who owns a janitorial service out of Lufkin. My guess is that he'll have a crew here first thing in the morning. He owes me a favor."

Ann's eyes were huge in her pale face. "All…right, but tell him to contact me. I'll need to help supervise." She paused, surveyed the damage, then folded her arms over her chest as if to ward off a sudden chill. "Dear God," she whispered, "what a mess. What a miserable, infuriating mess."

"Whoa, don't crash on me now," Drew said again, still refusing to touch her. "You've been doing great. As soon as I make that call, we'll go. We'll get your car tomorrow."

Ann didn't say anything, nor did she talk on the way home. Only after she entered the softly lamp-lighted room did she turn to him and say, "Thanks…for coming to my rescue. I'm fine now."

She was still visibly shaken, her tone unconvincing. Drew stifled a groan. "You're welcome—that goes without saying. But you're not fine."

An awkward silence followed.

He broke it. "Mother's sorry you couldn't come to dinner, and about the break-in, of course," Drew said, scrambling to counteract the heat building in the room. Or was the heat inside *him?*

"Tell her I'll take a rain check on dinner," Ann responded, a slight tremor in her voice.

"Look, I'd better go and let you get some rest." The lines around Drew's mouth deepened, and he spoke in a bleak, throbbing whisper.

Something flashed in Ann's eyes. Was it panic? He didn't know.

"Sleep. I wish that were possible."

He remained silent and stared at her, at her throat where her pulse beat as steadily as a tiny drum. "I'll call you later."

"Don't go, please."

He shoved his hands through his hair. "Do you know what you're saying?" he asked in a harsh, ragged voice.

"Yes," She reached out then and splayed a hand across his chest.

Her touch, even through his clothing, sent sparks blazing through him. His loins tightened.

Her gaze was wide and questioning. "Drew..."

What willpower he had left completely deserted him. He yanked her against him and ignored the warning bell that clanged inside his head. Don't think, Drew. Make the most of the moment.

He'd already partaken from the forbidden fruit and he'd just as soon die than stop now. He was tired of the ache in his gut from wanting to touch her like this, to explore the delights her lips had hinted at the other night. He had never experienced the raw desire that he felt for her.

How could he have backed himself into such a corner? How could he need her above all else? Before, he'd needed no one but himself.

"I tried not to want you," he whispered, his eyes filled with longing. "But by god, I do. I want to touch you. I want you to touch me."

His lips covered hers, and Ann collapsed against him, having lost the will to walk away. They were trapped in a fire of their own making. Everything else was of no importance. Recriminations would surely follow. But for now, the rich taste of him was all there was.

Her mouth parted and received his tongue; she felt it

war with hers. Her back arched, and her breasts crushed against him. He was her lifeline; she must have his strength, his power. Yet her legs felt weighted down, as if she were standing in concrete. A throb developed between her thighs, and she had trouble breathing.

Drew opened her blouse. His hands surrounded a breast and kneaded it. An animal cry tore from her, and she moaned as his lips trapped a nipple and sucked. She wanted to know his body, to bring him the same pleasure.

When she tugged at his shirt, he pulled back and muttered, "I'll do it. It'll be faster."

Clothes were discarded, and once they were naked, Drew grabbed her with a fierceness that both thrilled and terrified her. But after they sank to the carpet and her fingers boldly circled his hot hardness, the terror fled. Only heady anticipation remained.

"Ann, oh, Ann," he groaned, as he entered her moist flesh with throbbing urgency.

They cried out simultaneously, and Drew stroked deeper. Pinpoints of ecstasy swept through them as their liquid union plunged them into a vortex that neither wanted to end. Their feverishness was edged with a painful holding back.

Ann was filled; her hands clutched at his back and buttocks. "Oh, yes, yes!"

His mouth sank into the hollow at her throat, the sides of her neck, her ears before halting on a breast where he again assaulted its fullness with his tongue.

Ann almost fainted with pleasure. Her eyelashes fluttered, and she whimpered as she gave into the friction that centered in her lower belly. Her hips convulsed inward again and again, and she felt the answering tautness in him. She gripped him until her fingers turned white.

Then he made a guttural sound and spasmed while they both hovered on the brink of ecstasy before tumbling headlong into that endless moment.

Twelve

Exhausted but sated, Ann rested her head against Drew. His heart hummed in her ear; its cadence beat the same pace as hers. It was as if this oneness she now felt with him gave her insight as to how his mind worked; his likes and dislikes, what angered him, made him happy, made him sad, and frightened him. To indulge herself like this was absurd, she knew, but for the moment, she couldn't stop.

She wanted to know everything about this man who made her body hum as none other ever had or ever would. But she was a realist. This moment in his arms was merely plucked out of time, never to be repeated. She prayed she was wrong.

"Are you awake?" he asked.

"Barely." She spread her hand across his stomach. The hairs there tickled her palm. He placed his hand over hers. Their coming together so suddenly, so urgently, had erased the awkwardness, the shyness.

"Ann."

"Mmm." Even his deep, coarse voice had the power to stir her.

"Did I ever tell you how sorry I was...am about your daddy?"

Ann went still, and her heart constricted. She hadn't expected this. "No, no you didn't."

"Well, I am."

"Thanks," she whispered, the one word scraping past the raw spot in her throat. She tried not to think about her daddy, for doing so always brought on tears and regrets.

"I tried to tell my daddy that he was making a big mistake." Ann felt his muscles tense under her hand. "But as you and everybody else know, you couldn't tell John MacMillan a damn thing. He thought he knew it all."

Drew paused, shifted his position slightly so that he could look into her face. "You know, the worst part about it is he went to his grave feeling the same way."

"No," Ann whispered. "The worst part is that the two of you never reconciled."

"I tried, but he never budged." His voice was a monotone, expressionless. "Everything had to be his way or not at all."

"That's too bad."

"If it hadn't been for my mother..."

He didn't have to say anything more. Ann understood. "Mine, too. She was my rock until she got sick. If medical science is right about stress causing cancer, then Mother was a clear-cut case. Peter's escapades kept her tied in knots."

Drew's eyes were bleak. "I'm sorry as hell about that, too. I'd give anything if that accident hadn't happened."

"The accident wasn't your fault. And I don't blame you for my daddy or Peter. Life just decides to kick us in the teeth sometimes, and we never know why."

"Deep down you think Peter trashed your shop, don't you?"

"Yes, and it tears me up to think that he is so desperate." Her eyes glazed over. "Maybe if I'd given in and helped him one more time."

"Don't...don't say it—don't even think it. He's got to learn that he can't run to you every time he gets in a jam."

"You're right. But when I think of my beautiful shop..." Her voice broke.

His hold tightened. "Hey, your shop's going to be in good shape, you'll see. You'll have to replace some supplies and that glass stuff for sure. But at least it'll be straight and clean. You can bet on it."

"Poor, poor Peter."

"Yeah, maybe if I'd been the one hurt that day this would have never happened. I never planned to play pro ball."

"What is this, true confession time?" Ann teased, hoping to remove that bleakness from his eyes and to lighten the dark mood that had settled over them. Yet she'd glimpsed a side of Drew she'd never seen before. His sincerity and vulnerability touched her.

As if sensing he'd shown too much of his inner self, he switched on his I-don't-give-a-damn-charm and grinned. "You're right, enough of this confession malarkey. We've got more important things pressing."

"Such as?"

His eyes darkened as he circled a breast with the tip of one finger. "Beautiful. So beautiful."

"They're too big," she said with a boldness that shocked her.

"Never."

"Is that supposed to be a compliment?" she asked huskily.

"They're perfect." He put his lips to her nipple.

She squirmed.

"Feel that?"

"Yes, down to my toes. Oh...."

He chuckled before moving his mouth to her face, to the corners of her eyes that were sensitive and smooth as silk. He kissed her there, then, with a heart-felt sigh sank his head between her breasts and licked the rising tops of her breasts.

"Oh, Drew," she whispered, arching toward him, wanting him again.

"Don't you think we ought to find a bed?"

They hadn't moved since they'd drifted to the thick carpet.

"Do you?" she asked, finding it hard to concentrate as his mouth continued to do strange things to her body.

"No," he said thickly. "I'm not sure I could walk, anyway."

"Me, either. But aren't you uncomfortable? I mean..."

He chuckled again. "You needn't worry about my knees because this time, you're going to be on top."

With that, he pulled her over him. Ann sucked in her breath, and her eyes widened when he lifted her and slid high into her. Her thighs parted, then closed around him.

He muttered incoherently, positioning his hands at her waist while they both moved.

Ah, perfect. The sensation of what they were sharing

jarred something loose inside her, like running nude on the beach on a moonlit night. Ann's heart soared as she hurled tempestuously toward the ultimate ending, the sweet meshing of flesh and emotion into one.

He cried out suddenly and heaved, and she felt him shudder as he thrust higher into her. She heard her own cry the instant everything inside her shattered, as if she'd just walked blindly into a mirror.

"Oh, Drew," she sobbed, and fell against his chest.

Later, they did make it to her bed and actually slept. Now sunlight eked through the blinds and awakened Ann. At first she felt disoriented as she stretched and experienced an unfamiliar soreness. Then she remembered. Her eyes popped open, and she sat straight up in bed.

Drew walked back into the bedroom, his discarded clothes clutched in one hand. Her mouth went instantly dry. He was still naked. And though she had touched every part of that rock-hard body, the sight of him in full view sent her pulses skyrocketing again.

"Good morning," he said without modesty, as if he made a habit of parading around naked.

"Hi," she murmured.

"I'd about decided you were going to sleep all morning," he said, a glint in his eyes.

"Er…what time is it?"

He glanced at his Rolex. "Eight."

"Eight!" she exclaimed. "I have a set of 'falsies' to put on at nine."

"Come again?"

Ann's cheeks turned scarlet. "Oh."

Drew laughed outright. "I can't believe you're embarrassed."

"Actually, what I meant to say was that I have a set of false nails to put on a lady."

Her prim tone garnered a deep-throated chuckle from Drew.

She returned his smile, only to then feel it fade, thoughts of the break-in intruding. "Do you think I'll be able to work?"

"You may have to run to the store and buy some supplies, but other than that, I don't see why not."

Her face cleared somewhat. "The storage closet wasn't touched. I'm positive I have some polish in there."

They were quiet for a moment.

"'Falsies,' huh?" Drew said at last, and scratched his head. "That's a good one. Yeah, I'll have to remember that."

"Oh, you!" She threw a pillow at him. It hit him square in the face, then ricocheted to the floor.

He looked at her, stunned. "Bull's-eye."

They both laughed. Then the laughter died as a more potent, more powerful emotion took its place. An intimacy that surpassed words blazed between them, merged them as one, again.

"Ann…"

"Yes?" she whispered achingly. Her body stiffened against the tumultuous emotions he always created in her.

Drew looked away, and the spell broke. But he was affected, too. A pulse hammered in his jaw; the hand he slipped through the arm of his shirt shook.

Yet Ann couldn't bring herself to ask the question that hovered over her like a dark cloud threatening to blemish the moment. Would she see him again? Or was this the typical one-night stand that he was so famous for?

Don't whine, Ann, she ordered herself brutally. After all, she reminded herself, she had known the score when she'd chosen this path. She knew she was flirting with heartbreak. Even if they both wanted a relationship, it wouldn't work. She was settled; he was unsettled. He was wealthy; she was just the opposite. He lived on the edge; she walked the straight and narrow. He broke the rules; she followed them.

He pulled on his jeans and buckled his belt. Her gaze focused on his hands, hands that had explored the roads of her body, slowly, thoroughly, with a delicious wantonness.

It hit her then. She had done the worst thing imaginable. She had fallen in love. Or possibly, she had loved him all along. Her stomach lurched, and the only reason she didn't cry out was that she bit her lower lip.

"I'll be by the shop later, okay?"

He stared at her, his eyes smoldering with passion.

"Okay." The word came out a mere whisper.

He turned his back on her and walked toward the front door.

"I love you." There, she'd said it, spilled the words like a glass of forbidden wine.

Only he hadn't heard her. The room beyond was empty.

Thirteen

"**W**hat are you doing here?"

The words shattered the long-standing silence.

She whirled and faced him with startled eyes. "Jeez, you scared me," she said. She placed her hand over her heart as if to quiet it.

"Didn't mean to," Drew moseyed toward her. "I thought the shop was closed on Mondays."

"It is, but Kay, my new hairstylist, is fixing a lady's hair." Ann pointed to the back. "They're in there."

"That doesn't explain what *you're* doing here."

Ann shrugged. "I'm straightening, something I've been doing since the break-in."

Three days had passed since that eventful day and night. She had been hard at work ever since. Though the janitorial service had done an exemplary job, only Ann knew exactly where her supplies belonged. Thank goodness, the insurance had been quick to pay, enabling her

MARY LYNN BAXTER 273

to replace the glass displays and other items that had been broken.

Drew had even helped her, or tried to, on one occasion. But he'd ended up being more of a hindrance than a help, especially when he'd kept nuzzling her neck every chance he got. Finally, she'd chased him out. Telling him she'd never get anything done with him around. But he'd seen the glazed look in her eyes and had sensed the rapid beat of her heart and knew she wanted him as much as he wanted her.

Now as he stood over her, he asked, "You planning to work all day?"

She paused and looked at him. "Probably."

"I don't think that's a good idea."

She raised her eyebrows. "Oh?"

He shrugged. "For starters, the weather's great and I don't want to work."

She gave him the once-over. "I can see that."

He had on a blue T-shirt, cutoffs and deck shoes. He grinned, then shrugged again. "I told you I'm not going to work."

Ann didn't respond, and his eyes tracked her as she took bottles of nail polish out of a box and placed them on a glass shelf.

He had to admire the way Ann met crises head-on. She didn't try to ignore or run from them. Maybe that was because she was organized and wanted everything perfect, a trait that became more evident as he watched her perform her task, her features pinched in concentration. Her hand moved with sure even strokes, in the same manner she'd stroked his body....

"So," he said quickly, into the mounting silence.

Ann peered at him from under a screen of lashes while

a smile toyed with her lips. "So you don't want me to, either, huh?"

"Ah, finally the lady catches on."

Ann threw him an exasperated look before making her way to the pedicure room.

"Hey, where're you going?"

When she didn't answer, Drew followed her, mesmerized by the way the outfit she had on emphasized her derriere. The long fuchsia top failed to cover the enticing curve of her rounded buttocks.

He went hot all over.

"So what did you have in mind?" she asked just inside the room.

"This," Drew muttered, and grabbed her and pushed her against the wall.

"Drew!" she gasped, startled.

"Shh," he whispered, nudging her lips apart. "I've been wanting to do this ever since I walked in the door."

"Stop it," she pleaded, and wiggled against him. "Kay might see us."

"So what?"

He bent his head.

"Drew…" His name drowned in the hot moistness of his lips.

Ann sagged weakly against him and whimpered, even as she kissed him back. Only after his hand cupped a pulsating breast did she push him away and step out of harm's reach.

Drew sucked air deep into his lungs but still couldn't speak. He sneaked a look at her and finally managed to say, "What are those called you have on?"

She glanced down. "My…pants?"

"Yeah."

"Leggings."

His gaze skimmed over her again, devouring, posses-
sive. "Nice."

"Er...thanks."

He heard the breathless quality of her voice and knew
that he affected her the same way she affected him.

"Let's get out of here," he said, stifling a groan.

"And go where?"

"Oh, say a ride in my Jag." His eyes crinkled at the
corners. "Ah, come on, be a sport."

Ann hesitated. "Oh, all right. Let me tell Kay."

A few minutes later, Ann sat buckled beside him. He
didn't start the car. Instead he stared at her for a long
moment. "There's something I want...have to ask you
about the other night," he began, his voice sounding cot-
tony, unused. He coughed and cursed himself as she visibly tensed.

But he had to say what had plagued him for days. He
wanted to get it off his chest so as not to ruin the day.
"I hope there're not going to be any repercussions...."

"Don't you mean you hope I'm not pregnant," she
said bluntly, her face losing its color.

He exhaled deeply. "Yes, that's what I mean. But I
blame myself. I should've taken precautions, only..." He
let his sentence trail off, thinking that he'd been in too
damn big of a hurry to bury himself inside her.

"You don't have to worry," she said, staring straight
ahead. "It was the wrong time of the month."

He frowned. "I didn't think there ever was a wrong
time of the month."

"I just finished my period." She faced him with wide
unsettled eyes. "So you see, you're safe."

"And so are you, right?"

"Right," she said with a slight catch in her voice.

Drew gripped the steering wheel. Dammit, he knew

she wanted a baby. But not his, for god's sake. Panic surged through him.

"I thought we were going for a drive."

Her flat voice prodded him out of his thoughts. He twisted the key and listened as the Jag's engine purred instantly. Still, he couldn't let the subject go. There was something niggling at the back of his mind. "I know you want a baby, Ann, but..."

She jerked her head around. "I know what you're thinking," she said rigidly, "but don't. I want a baby, but not yours."

He cursed at his fumbling again. "Sorry, I was out of line."

"Yes, you were."

Following a long silence, he reached over and stroked her cheek. "It's all right if you wanna knock me up side the head."

A smile flirted with her lips.

"Forgiven?" he asked, that devilish glint back in his eyes.

She faced him and smiled for real. "Yes, you big idiot."

He chuckled and gunned the engine. "You're gonna love this."

"I guess you're planning to show off."

"Like you've never seen before."

She rolled her eyes. "Did anyone ever tell you you're a cocky 'you know what'?"

A deep rumble came from his gut. "At least once a day."

"You're bad."

"I know." His warm gaze slid over her and rested on her breasts. His gut knotted at the same time her breathing turned shallow, as if she could read his mind.

MARY LYNN BAXTER 277

"Don't...you think we ought to go?" Ann's face was flushed.

"Yeah, right."

Drew punched a button and the car's roof glided back. The sunlight poured through and danced across their skin.

"You couldn't have asked for a more perfect day for an outing."

"It is nice." Ann took a breath of fresh air. "And I needed the break."

Drew steered the car onto the highway. "You got that right."

"Where are we going?"

"Where do you want to go?"

Ann lifted her dainty shoulders. "This is your party, remember."

"We'll just drive for a while." He winked at her. "I'll show you how a Jag can perform."

They traveled in silence for a while, each lost in their own thoughts.

Finally, Ann asked, "Have you proved your case against Tim Pollard yet?"

"No. I'm still waiting to hear the final word from my buddy in Houston."

"I hope he can help."

"Me, too," Drew replied grimly. "I know the SOB's guilty, only I can't prove it. The company's just got to be more solvent than it shows."

"Have you told your mother?"

"Yes, and it shocked her."

"I can imagine."

"Meanwhile, dealership business is on hold." He didn't bother to curb his frustration. "I'm ready to get the hell back to Houston and stay."

"I'm sure," she said softly.

Only I don't want to leave you, he thought. Of course he couldn't say that aloud even as he felt her beside him like an extra beat of his heart. He cursed himself for being a fool.

What was happening to him, inside where he was so vulnerable? Strong, capable and loving was Ann Sinclair. She cared about him; he knew that. He had taken advantage of that, too. Ignoring the consequences, he had indulged his own needs. He wished it were that simple; it wasn't. The feelings she evoked in him were something new. And because he was waging war with himself, he was at a loss as to what to do.

"Mmm, this was a great idea," Ann mused, shattering the silence.

He faced her just as she tossed her head and laughed. He clamped down on the urge to touch her, experiencing that all-too-familiar kick in his gut. "Told you."

She grinned saucily. "You would."

Drew laughed.

They were now on a deserted road that seemed to stretch forever. He smashed the accelerator. The car shot forward.

"Drew!" Ann shrieked, her white knuckles curling around the edge of the seat.

"Drew, what?" he mimicked, excitement leaping from his eyes.

Ann's hair billowed around her face like a black silk cloud. She scraped a dozen strands off a cheek and out of her mouth before she could speak. "How...fast are you going?"

"Not fast enough, that's for sure."

Her excitement matched his. "You come alive behind a wheel, don't you?"

"It's almost as good as sex."

Ann snapped upright. "That's disgusting."

The wind tossed his laughter at her. "But truthful."

She gazed heavenward. "What you are is hopeless."

"Want me to show you what this lady can do?" He patted the steering wheel.

Ann hesitated. "All…right."

Drew shoved the Jag into another gear, then bore down on the pedal even more. The wildflowers and cattle grazing on the side, even the tall pines, blurred in the wake of the car's lightning speed.

But Drew scarcely noticed. He was on a high that nothing could touch, except sex. He smiled inwardly and stole a glance at Ann. He'd meant it when he'd told her racing brought the same feeling. Her response had been so prim, but he'd seen the smile hovering over her lips.

"Drew, don't you think you should slow down?"

He flashed her another quick look. "Hey, we're barely getting started."

She smiled, but it didn't stick. "Surely not. Surely this car can't go much faster." She sounded out of breath.

"Oh, but it can. I'll show you."

"No, I don't think that's a good idea."

"Ah, come on, where's your sense of adventure?" he demanded, watching as the speedometer climbed.

"Drew…please…stop," she begged in a whisper.

"Relax, baby, and enjoy the ride."

"I can't."

"Yes, you can. Trust me, okay?"

She seemed to take him at his word, and for a while they sped along the highway with the wind roaring in their ears.

"I was right, wasn't I?" he said, keeping his eyes straight ahead.

Silence.

Drew whipped his head in Ann's direction. Her face was a greenish gray, and her backbone was as rigid as an iron bar. "My God, are you all right?"

"Stop...stop the car," she choked out, "or I'm going to be sick."

A few seconds later, Drew wheeled the car into the shoulder of the road. His brow was knitted in concern.

"Are you all right?" he asked again.

"N-no...no," Ann stammered.

The abject fear in her eyes cut him to the bone. "You weren't kidding. You were scared." He opened his mouth to apologize only—

"Don't you ever pull a stunt like that again!"

The cold fury in her voice stunned him. "Hey, don't you think you're overreacting?"

"Overreacting!" she shrieked. "You're crazy!"

He tried to hold down the anger building inside him. "I know what I'm doing," he said patiently. "I'm a professional at this."

"I don't care."

Drew reached over and touched her shoulder. "God, you're uptight."

She shook off his touch. "I may be uptight, but I'm not stupid."

Something in his eyes turned savage.

"Take me home."

Her words hit like a strap across raw flesh. His flesh. He flinched.

"I want to go now." A tear crawled down her right cheek.

"With pleasure," he said in a low, terse voice.

Fourteen

"They're too short," the woman wailed, and glared at Ann.

Ann prayed for patience. "But, Jessica, you sat here and told me to cut them off."

"But not completely," Jessica countered huffily.

"I had no choice. To make them look decent, I had to even them up, and that meant taking the majority of the length." Ann forced a smile. "They look lovely. Really they do."

"Well, I guess they do at that." Jessica's pained features relaxed. "How much do I owe you? I've got to get home. Elmer's going to kill me as it is."

Ten minutes later Ann was alone. She wilted against her chair and rubbed her right temple. A dilly of a headache was coming on. Jessica was typical of her day. She looked at the time. Six o'clock and she was just now finishing. Or just about. She still had to ready the shop for the next day.

On the other hand, she had no reason to hurry home. Nothing waited for her there except emptiness, the same emptiness she carried inside her. She had existed in a kind of limbo since her verbal skirmish with Drew.

She feared their relationship was severed for good. So face that and let it go, she told herself fiercely, getting up and stomping to the closet to get a broom. Let *him* go.

The harder she swept, the harder her mind worked. It was for the best that he'd swept out of her life, the same as he'd swept into it. But she missed him. Dear Lord, did she ever.

A week had passed since he'd pulled into her driveway after they'd ridden home in stony silence from the outing that had started with such sweet promise.

Scuttlebutt had it that he'd gone back to Houston to race. Ann leaned on the broom and felt a shudder pass through her. What if he had a wreck... No! She wouldn't allow herself to think about that. But she couldn't control her thoughts; they ran rampant down that forbidden track. If the way Drew drove was an indicator, Drew wasn't afraid of the devil himself.

Another shudder shook her, as she remembered the Jag's hair-raising speed and the sick fear that had soured her stomach. She never wanted to experience anything like that again. But that was what Drew craved, that dangerous excitement, that living on the edge.

White-faced, Ann moved to the closet and replaced the broom. How could she have fallen in love with him? How could she have been so reckless?

Ann had counted on love, if it ever happened to her, to evolve slowly, to invade her heart quietly, with little or no fanfare. She had likened love to a tiny seed that must be watered and fed in order to grow and mature. She had always scoffed at the notion of bells and fireworks going off as a result of a look, a touch. No longer—having experienced exactly what she'd ridiculed. But never in her wildest imagination had she expected love to dominate her mind and senses to such a degree that everything else took second place.

Possessed.

That said it all. But even that failed to describe the churning inside her, the need that controlled her every thought, her every move. And the internal void was more noticeable than before.

With an effort, Ann held the tears at bay and finished her tasks. Then loaded down with her tote bag and purse, she walked to the door. The phone rang.

"Damn," she muttered, only to feel her heart leap. Maybe it was Drew....

She dropped her burden and hurried to the phone. When she lifted the receiver, she didn't know which pounded louder, her heart or her head.

"H-hello," she stammered.

"Ann, is that you?"

While she was disappointed that the caller wasn't Drew, she was thrilled it was Dorothy Sable from the adoption agency.

"Did I catch you at a bad time?"

"No, of course not," Ann said hastily. "I was just about to go home."

"Would you rather I call you there?"

"Heavens, no."

"Well, this will only take a minute."

"It's always a pleasure hearing from you," Ann said,

and grabbed the edge of the manicure table to steady herself.

"What I'm calling about," Dorothy said, "is to ask if you'd be willing to take an older child, a two-year-old for example? I know you'd prefer a newborn, but as we told you up front, they are almost always reserved for couples."

"And I told you I'd take my chances and wait."

"Correct. Do you still feel that strongly?"

Ann didn't hesitate. "No, no I don't. I'll be willing to take an older child, especially if it'll speed up the process."

"I can't promise that, of course, but it'll certainly help."

Red tape, Ann thought, tons and tons of red tape and more to look forward to. But then that was part and parcel of dealing with the state. Ridiculous, that was what it was. Yet she had no choice. She had to play by their rules or not at all.

"Ann?"

She heard the question in Dorothy's tone. "That's fine. Really it is."

"Good, then, I'll be in touch."

Once the receiver was back on the hook, Ann released her grip on the table and sank into a chair. She was thrilled, of course, and ached to share her good news with Drew. A grimace tightened her lips as she axed that thought. First, he couldn't care less; he thought she was crazy for wanting to adopt a child. And second, she doubted she'd see him again except in passing.

Maybe if she hadn't reacted so violently to his fast driving, tempered her fear... No! She couldn't hide her feelings. If she was happy, her friends knew it. If she was upset, they knew that, too. Like it or not, she had to be herself.

Ann switched off the light and went out the door, feeling more alone than she ever had in her life.

"You didn't hear a damn thing I said, did you?"

Drew raised sheepish eyes to stare at Hal Ackerman, his accountant friend. Instead of sitting at his massive desk, Hal leaned on a filing cabinet behind it and returned Drew's stare. Grim humor straightened his full lips.

"No, I didn't," Drew admitted bluntly.

Hal rubbed his protruding stomach. "It's clients like you who give me heartburn."

"Not hardly. It's all that greasy food you put away that does that."

To label Hal overweight was an understatement. Drew bet he tipped the scales at two-ninety. But his physical malady had no bearing, thank goodness, on his mind. It was as sharp as Drew remembered.

"You wanna discuss this another day?" Hal asked.

Drew squirmed in his chair, uncomfortable under Hal's intense scrutiny.

"No, dammit. I made a trip to Houston just to see you."

"I don't know what it is, but something's got hold of you and is chewing on you real good."

"Mind your own business, okay?"

Hal grinned. "You haven't changed a bit."

"Neither have you."

Although they didn't see each other often and had gone their separate ways out of high school and college, they had once been good friends and knew each other well enough to take certain liberties.

Hal laughed. "Somehow I don't think that's a compliment."

Drew snorted.

"It's got to be a woman," Hal said, his laughter deepening. "Always is."

Drew had no comeback, because Hal was right. This past week without Ann had been hell. He'd thought about little else. The more he'd cursed himself for his lack of control, the worse he'd felt. His need for her was so strong it had the potential to become an obsession. Up until now, he'd taken racing seriously, never a woman. Ann was certainly playing havoc with the order of his life.

"Yeah, it's a woman, all right. I can tell by the look on your face."

"Lay off, Ackerman," Drew warned, though his gruffness had a soft edge.

"Suit yourself."

"So what were you saying?" Drew asked, all business now.

"I was asking if you'd checked Pollard's bank account to make sure he hadn't built up a surplus?"

"Other than the fact that he's messing around with the teller, I found nothing out of the ordinary."

Hal yanked at his mustache. "He's putting the cash somewhere, and two will get you five that that sweet darlin' at the bank is obliging him in more ways than one."

Drew shot straight up. "You mean you found something?"

Hal patted himself on the back. "Yep."

"I'll be damned. Then I was right, the SOB is guilty."

"Guilty as sin, most likely."

"How's he doing it?"

Hal pushed away from the filing cabinet and crossed to his desk. "Invoices," he said, pointing toward the boxes lining the walls that Drew had carted there.

"So when can I go to the authorities?"

"Soon," Hal replied. "I'm still loading my guns, so to speak."

"Just say when," Drew said, and got to his feet, then headed for the door.

"Where're you off to in such a hurry?"

Drew stopped midstride and turned around. "Back to MacMillan. I've got some pressing, unfinished business I need to take care of."

"Wouldn't have anything to do with the woman, now would it?"

"When did you get to be such a nosy bastard, anyway?"

Hal's belly laugh rang in Drew's ear all the way down the hall.

"I'm coming. I'm coming."

Despite the doorbell's insistent ring, Ann paused and stared briefly into the mirror on the wall. She bared her teeth, determined to make sure there was no grain of pepper lodged between them. She had just swallowed the last of a boiled egg.

Satisfied that none was there, she reached for the door and opened it. Drew's tall, imposing figure faced her. Ann's tongue clung to the dry roof of her mouth. She couldn't say anything nor could she move. Surprise robbed her of both functions.

"Can I come in?"

Was she mistaken or had his voice sounded unsteady? "Of...course," she said, stepping aside. She leaned against the door for support when he walked past her.

His cologne swamped her senses, made her weak. He looked so good, and she was so glad to see him she would forgive him almost anything.

"I figured you'd tell me to go to hell," he said. They stood in the middle of the room, an arm's length apart.

"I'm not in the habit of telling people to do that."

He smiled, though it lasted only a second. "No, I guess not."

A short silence intruded.

"Why are you here?" she asked. Her voice sounded rusty.

"To apologize." His eyes delved into hers. "Again."

Ann tried to pull her gaze away, but couldn't. "Look—"

"I know what you're thinking," he said, a muscle twitching in his jaw. "I'm a real bastard and don't deserve another chance."

"I—"

"Let me finish. You're right, I am. And while I'm not sure I can change that, I'm willing to try." He shoved his hand through hair that needed a trim. "I don't know what the hell's happening between us—" he broke off and looked at her through tortured eyes "—but I don't want to stop seeing you."

He seemed to droop visibly, as if that long speech had exhausted him. Yet he didn't take his eyes off her.

"I...don't want to stop seeing you, either." Ann's heart sang inside her chest.

"Then come here," he muttered thickly.

With a cry that was both laughter and sobs, Ann ran headlong into his arms.

Fifteen

"It was so nice of you to keep me company, dear."

Janet MacMillan's soft voice sounded weak—though it was stronger than it had been two days ago when she'd been rushed to the hospital.

"The pleasure's mine," Ann said. She reached for the delicately veined hand and held it. "My...mother thought so much of you."

"No more than I thought of her. She was a fine lady."

"Thanks." Ann turned away. She feared Janet would see the tears that sprang into her eyes.

"So you and my son have been seeing a lot of each other." It was a statement, not a question.

Ann swung around and felt color steal into her face. "Mmm, that's right."

Janet squeezed Ann's hand. "Good. He needs a steadying influence."

Ann laughed. "Think so?"

"I know so. That son of mine thrives on danger. And speaking of my son, when is he due back?"

Ann glanced at her watch. "Anytime now, actually."

"I hope the doctor tells him he can take me home," Janet said, her eyes fluttering shut.

Ann disengaged her hand, then eased back into her chair. She had her doubts about Janet's release, for today anyway. When Drew finished at his office, he would have to tell his mother that the doctor preferred she remain another night.

Ann had been working late at the shop when Drew called and asked if she'd meet him at the emergency room. As soon as she'd hustled her last customer out the door, she'd driven to the hospital in Lufkin. A grim-faced Drew had met her at the entrance. His mother had had another attack, and while not critical, she was in pain.

She and Drew had waited for the doctor, hands locked tightly, which was something they had done a lot of the past two weeks. Following his apology for his reckless-ness in the car, they had been inseparable, especially dur-ing the evenings when they would play tennis or jog to-gether, then drive to Lufkin to dine. But the majority of their time had been spent in each other's arms making love.

He only had to come near her and she would melt. But though the physical attraction was a heady part of their burgeoning relationship, it wasn't all. She loved his laughter and yes, his arrogant charm.

Drew, however, had never once told her he loved her; and she had convinced herself that he did. She'd also convinced herself that despite their differences, they had a future.

No one could be that attentive, that loving, if love wasn't the motivator. Or was she fooling herself, hoping for a miracle that might not happen? No. He had to love her. He just had to.

Now, as she heard the door open, she twisted around. Drew smiled before easing himself cautiously to the bed and mouthing, "Is she all right?"

Ann nodded, glad she was sitting down. Just looking at him made her go weak in the knees. He looked sensational, as usual, in black jeans and a white shirt that called attention to his tan and whipcord strength. She feared he could hear the thundering of her heart.

Janet's eyes opened. "I wasn't asleep."

Drew winked at Ann, then leaned down and kissed his mother on the cheek. "How're you feeling?"

"Fine. I'm ready to go home."

"Doc says maybe tomorrow."

Janet's face fell. "Talk to him, please. I know Kyle—he's known to change his mind quite often."

"Well, he knows what's best for you," Drew said soothingly. "So just don't ruffle the waters, okay? You scared the hell out of me as it was."

"Don't swear, Drew," she said primly.

His lips twitched as he looked at Ann. She hid a smile. "Yes, ma'am," he drawled.

"You two have something better to do than baby-sit me, I know. Anyway, I'm expecting Elizabeth any minute."

"Oh, Lord, let's get out of here, then," Drew said quickly, and reached for Ann's hand. "That ole biddy'll talk the horns off a billy goat and back on again."

"Drew MacMillan!"

"All right, I take that back." He leaned over and kissed her again. "We'll see you later."

"Take care, Mrs. MacMillan," Ann said softly, then followed Drew out the door.

The instant they got into the car, Drew reached for Ann and kissed her hard on the lips. "Mmm, you taste as good as you smell."

"I try," Ann said, when she recovered her breath.

"I've been dying to kiss you all afternoon."

"Same here."

He cranked the Jag and made his way onto the street.

"Where are we going?"

"To Mother's."

Ann raised her eyebrows. "We are?"

"Yep." He reached over and caressed a cheek. "Thought we'd grill steaks, jump in the hot tub, then make love till we can't walk."

"What if I'm not hungry?"

A red light caught them; he faced her with smoldering eyes. "I hope it's food you're talking about."

"As a matter of fact it is," she said, purposefully circling her lower lip with her tongue.

Drew sucked in his breath. "If you know what's good for you, you'll behave yourself."

Red tinted her face.

He chuckled. "I love it when you do that."

"I hate it," she said petulantly.

He laughed outright, then said, "So we'll skip the food and go straight to bed."

"You're insatiable."

"So are you."

She threw him a look.

"Only I'll admit it. The more I have of you, the more I want."

Ann's mouth went dry. "Same here."

They both fell silent.

"What about the housekeeper?" Ann asked at last.

Drew shifted positions. "Gave her the evening off."

"I don't know about you, Drew MacMillan."

"That's what keeps you coming back for more," he said arrogantly.

Ann laughed then was silent. She realized he was absolutely right—and that she loved him. But for now, the latter thought was her secret. No matter what the future held, the moment was hers. She wasn't about to waste a second of it.

"Drew, put me down. I'm too heavy."

"Like hell."

Ann giggled and sank closer against him while he climbed the stairs.

He had never felt so alive as he did when she was in his arms and he was inside her. Her fingernails scored his back while her moans rent the air. That high far surpassed anything he'd ever felt on the racetrack.

He hadn't thought he would ever find a woman who could make him feel that way. Admitting it, though, had a definite downside. It made him vulnerable and powerless—emotions he swore he'd never feel.

That was before Ann, before he'd sampled the delights of both her mind and her body, just as he was about to do again.

He reached his bedroom with haste and immediately stood her on her feet. Wordlessly, she stared at him, then placed a hand on his cheek.

Thunder clapped outside, and lightning danced around the sky. Neither could compare with what her gentle touch did to him. He shivered as he inhaled the warm, sweet smell of her. His need was so hot, so potent.

She unbuttoned his shirt, then slid her hand across his chest, sending another current through him.

He folded her against him and felt himself harden. He

kissed her greedily and whispered, "I want you. I want you so much it's tearing me to pieces."

With trembling hands, he finished undressing her. She returned the favor with an excited awkwardness that was both sensuous and titillating.

"Love me," she said urgently, fitting her body to his as smoothly as the pieces of a puzzle. He embedded his fingers in her hair and sank his lips onto hers. They fell across the bed, their limbs tangled.

"I'm on fire," she whispered.

"And I ache."

He heard her whimper as he stroked her breasts with his tongue, then moved down her flat, smooth belly to the moistness between her thighs.

Minutes later, she placed her hands on either side of his head and pleaded in an agonized whisper, "Please, it's my turn."

He didn't have the willpower or the desire to refuse her. Her mouth, her lips and tongue were every bit as persuasive and primal as his in her effort to please. He heard himself moan and slip toward that edge, no longer in control.

"I want you," she pleaded. "I need you now!"

He entered her, and she cried out, her body shifting to accommodate him. He slid all the way up her. His own release came almost instantly, and then he heard her murmuring softly in sync with his own body's rocking movements.

He held onto her, reluctant to let go, as if she might be a delicious dream that would disappear. She sighed and squirmed closer. He touched her hair, her face, her lips with his fingers, determined to memorize each delicate feature.

"Was I too fast?" he asked, his breath fanning her cheek.

"No. You were perfect."

"Will I ever get enough of you?"

Ann made a tiny little sound in her throat. "I...hope not."

"You always smell good. What's the name of your perfume? I aim to keep you well supplied."

"It's Red Door."

"Hey, I'm serious."

"That's the name. Honest," she said.

"Helluva name for a fragrance, is all I can say." He slapped her playfully on her bottom.

"Ouch!"

"Ouch! You've got to be kidding. That didn't hurt."

"Wanna bet. Turn over and let me do the same to you—then we'll see."

He leaned over and tweaked a nipple. "I've got a better idea. Come on."

"Where're we going?" she asked, giving into the tug of his hand.

"You'll see."

They climbed together into the tub filled with hot, churning water, they faced each other, their legs entwined.

"God, this feels good."

"Mmm, it does, doesn't it?" Ann echoed his sentiments.

"But not as good as you." His lips closed over hers. Ann moaned.

The phone rang. Their bodies tensed, then broke apart.

"Damn!" he cursed.

Ann giggled.

"I'd say to hell with it," he said, standing, "but I'm afraid it may be the hospital."

She purposely batted her lashes. "Don't worry, I'm not going anywhere."

He flashed her a hot glance, then climbed out of the tub.

When he returned, his features appeared cast in stone.

"Your mother?" she asked, frowning.

"No. It was the sheriff's office. They picked up Peter."

The officer, Mickey Hargrove, whom both she and Drew knew from their high school days, shoved his wide-brimmed hat farther back on his head and eyed Ann. "He admitted he broke into your shop."

Ann shuddered. Drew cursed.

During the ride to the station, she'd sat stoically beside Drew. Her heart had lain like a lump of lead in her chest, just the opposite of how she'd felt only minutes prior when she'd anticipated a romp in the water with Drew. Her comedown had been like a slap in the face, convincing her that no matter how hard she wanted to, she couldn't escape reality. And her brother was definitely reality. The cold, harsh kind.

Peter, she'd learned from Drew, had been picked up at a woman's house on the outskirts of town.

"Uh, what do you want to do, about pressing charges, I mean?" Mickey asked.

Ann shook her head. Drew had asked her that same question; she hadn't known the answer then, nor did she now.

"I'd like to see him first."

"Sure."

"Is....is he all right?"

"He is now. He was a sight for sore eyes, but I made him clean up." Mickey nodded toward a room off the main one. "He's in there."

"Thanks, Mickey," Ann said. Still, she hesitated.

"I'll go with you, if you want me to." Drew's hand circled her elbow.

She flashed him a watery, grateful smile, even though she knew his presence would exacerbate the situation. But she needed his support.

Peter sat slumped in a chair; his head was bent, resting on his hands. When he heard the sound of scuffling feet, he jerked his head up.

Ann held her breath and waited for him to curse her and create a scene because Drew was with her. He did neither. Instead, his dull eyes rested on them, then he turned away, his face pale and gaunt.

Ann's heart turned over. So much potential, so much waste. If only things had been different. They weren't, though, and she had to face the untenable situation head-on.

She ventured closer to Peter and forced herself to ask, "Why, Peter, why?"

He looked at her, his features contorted. "You wouldn't help me."

"And that was your way of paying me back?"

"Something like that."

Ann fought back the tears. "You...you must hate me...."

"Sis...please." Peter drew a deep breath. "Are...are you going to press charges?"

"Do you think I should?"

"Yes," he said simply.

Drew stepped closer but remained silent.

Again Ann felt his strength and was grateful for it. "You're right, I should. Only I'm not going to."

Peter stared at her as if he hadn't heard her correctly, then his shoulders visibly relaxed. "Thank God," he croaked.

"But you're going to have to play by my rules." Ann's voice brooked no argument. "First, you're going to seek professional help."

"And I know just the right person," Drew put in. "There's a counselor in Nacogdoches who's the best."

"Dammit, Drew, I don't need a shrink."

"Yes, you do," Ann cut in forcefully.

"You also need a job," Drew added. "I'm willing to put you to work at the lumberyard."

Ann's eyes sought Drew's, and for a second it was as if they were the only ones in the room. Her look expressed her heartfelt thanks.

But when she turned back to Peter again, she saw that his face had turned paler. Ann sensed he was choking on Drew's offer, but this time he had no alternative and he knew it.

"All right," he said without looking at either of them. "I'll do it your way."

"But that's not all, Peter."

Ann's soft, but still firm voice brought him back around. "Whaddaya mean?" Peter demanded.

"I mean that I expect you to pay for the damage you did to my shop. I may not be pressing charges, but you're not about to get off scot-free."

He nodded.

"Also, once a week, I expect you at the shop after work to clean it. I haven't hired a cleaning service. For now, you can fill that bill."

"Anything else?" Peter asked in a dull tone.

"No...that's all."

"Why don't you come back to the house and stay with me tonight?" Drew offered, relieving some of the tension in the room.

Peter shook his head. "Thanks, but I'll go back to Sandra's, where I was picked up."

"Let's get out of here, then," Drew said.

But no one moved—at least not Ann or Peter. They stared at each other for a long moment, then Peter said in a pain-filled voice, "Sis...I'm...sorry."

"Oh, Peter," she whispered, crossing the room straight to his arms. "It's going to be all right. You'll see."

A short time later, Drew walked Ann to her door. He reached out and tipped her chin. Their eyes locked. "You sure you don't want me to stay with you?"

"No," she said huskily. "I think I need to be alone."

"You sure?"

She smiled against his hard chest. "Yes, I'm sure. Anyway, we both could use a good night's sleep."

He chuckled. "Touché."

"Call me."

"That goes without saying."

He kissed her then, and she clung to him for a minute. When they pulled apart, Drew said, "I have a favor to ask."

"Anything."

"I'm racing this weekend. Will you come and watch me?"

Ann forced herself not to react outwardly, though her heart wrenched. Was this a test? Somehow she thought it was. So she had to try. She loved him. Wasn't that reason enough to lend her support to something that was so important to him?

"Yes," she whispered, backing out of his arms and staring at him. "I'll come."

Sixteen

"**B**y the way, did I tell you you look good enough to eat?"

Ann cut her eyes at Drew, who had one hand on the Jag's steering wheel and the other on her knee. She placed her hand over his; their fingers curled together. "No," she said, "but it's always nice to hear."

And it was, especially as she'd chosen her clothes carefully this morning. She knew the red cotton jumpsuit with white piping trim was a perfect foil for her black hair and alabaster skin. White sandals, silver earrings and a bracelet completed the outfit.

The day of the race finally arrived. In spite of her reservations, she was excited. That excitement stemmed from spending the entire day with Drew and partly from the news she was eager to share with him.

Since they had gone to the jail to confront her brother, so much had happened. Two days afterward, she and

Drew had driven Peter to Nacogdoches to meet with the counselor. Ann had been impressed with the tall, clear-spoken doctor. His overall manner depicted complete confidence in his ability to help someone like Peter. Once the sessions had begun and Peter attended in good faith, Drew put him to work at the lumberyard.

Though still concerned for her brother's well-being, Ann had tried to put things in perspective. The call from the adoption agency had certainly helped. Her first home visit was scheduled for next week. She'd found it hard not to blurt out the news to Drew, if for no other reason than to test his reaction.

But she hadn't. She planned to tell him tonight, after the race, when they were snuggled in bed.

She studied him. As usual, she felt a warm feeling invade her body. She loved him with her whole being, and with each passing day she was convinced he loved her, too. Soon he would say the words she longed to hear.

She averted her gaze to his racing gear. The flame-retardant suit seemed to mock her. Her stomach lurched. *Flame-retardant.* The words and their meaning weighed heavy on her heart. No, she told herself. No gloomy thoughts today.

Drew looked at her and said, "What's wrong?"

"Wrong?"

"Yeah, wrong." He frowned. "You looked like you just thought of something distasteful."

She made herself smile. "Didn't mean to."

He kept his eyes on her another minute, as if he wanted to take issue, but he didn't. Instead, he crooked his head so as to peer at the sky. "I'm holding my breath the bottom won't fall out."

Ann also craned her head. "How can you even think that when there's not a cloud in the sky?"

"Hell, in East Texas anything can happen."

"True, but you've got to think positive."

He gave her a self-conscious shrug. "Nerves, I guess."

"You're nervous?" Ann teased. "I don't believe it."

"Well, believe it," he said flatly, only to smile then. "But it's a good kind of nerves, gets the adrenaline flowing."

"Do you realize I know zilch about racing?"

"Well," he drawled, "that's because you've never asked."

"I'm asking now. So tell me."

"My car is what you call a top-fuel dragster. It has a long snout in front, and the rear is a miniature airplane wing."

"Sounds like something out of *Star Wars*."

He flashed her an indulgent smile. "It's flashier, actually."

"Figures," she said ruefully.

He laughed.

"How fast will it go?"

"Are you sure you want to know?"

Ann's face clouded. "No, but if you don't tell me, I'll imagine it's worse than it really is."

"It travels over two hundred and fifty miles per hour."

"Oh, my. I wish you hadn't told me," Ann said with a small voice, battling a sick feeling in her stomach.

"Are you all right? You've got that funny color again."

Ann straightened and forced a lightness into her tone. "I'm fine."

"And pigs fly."

She gave him a scathing glance. "So I guess you sit practically on top of the engine. I might as well get all the bad stuff in one lump sum."

"It sits right behind me, all right, but I'm cocooned in the cage."

"Cage?"

"Cockpit. And by the way, the starting line is called Christmas tree."

"That's weird."

He chuckled. "I thought you'd get a kick out of that."

"All this is carefully regulated, isn't it?" she asked anxiously.

"You bet. The National Hot Rod Association is the sanctioning organization that makes the rules and makes sure we abide by them."

"That's good to know."

He reached over and again trapped her hand in his. He brought it to his lips. Shivers danced down her spine. Only one look, one touch, and she went off inside like a firecracker.

"You're going to love it," he said with an answering light in his eyes. "I suspect you're going to like it so much that you'll want to watch again."

"Tacky, tacky."

He dropped her hand at the same time a belly laugh tensed his stomach.

She reached over and yanked his ear in retaliation.

"Remind me to pay you back for that." His eyes honed in on her. "Later."

"Is that a promise?" She barely recognized her voice.

"Count on it."

They finished the trip wrapped in a cloak of warm euphoria. Only after Drew pulled into the racetrack parking lot in Baytown a short time later did the silence break.

"Do I get a kiss for luck?" he asked hoarsely, running his eyes over her.

"Oh, Drew," she whispered, and dove into his arms. "Please, please be careful."

The sun sparkled in the sky like a huge jewel. Perched on the bleachers among thousands of cheering, flag-waving fans, Ann waved her banner and clapped with the crowd. She eyed the track and was shocked. Drew hadn't told her it was only a quarter of a mile in distance or that it was straight, not a circle as she'd thought. But then she hadn't asked him about it, apparently he'd assumed she knew.

The announcer came on the loudspeaker and named the cars and their positions. When Drew's was called, she again questioned the sanity of what she was doing.

A day after she'd told him she would watch him race, she'd been traumatized with fear. How could she sit and watch him blatantly endanger his life? She hadn't known the answer then, and she didn't know it now. Nevertheless, here she was, mingling with the jubilant crowd, determined to fulfill her promise no matter what the cost to her peace of mind.

Drew knew what he was doing, didn't he? And it was only one race, for Pete's sake. She would soon ridicule herself for her foolishness. Meanwhile, she would hold close the thought that Drew was a professional. And pray.

Two cars took their position—Drew's and one other. She chanted, "Drew, Drew," along with the crowd. Her man was a favorite.

Ann felt the tension and the excitement mount. She had absolutely no saliva left in her mouth.

"Ladies and gentlemen," the announcer cried over the loudspeaker, "are you ready?"

"Yes," the crowd screamed in response.

Since both men had an outside lane, neither had the

advantage. But Ann felt sure that wouldn't make any difference to Drew. She had a clear view of him, and that was what counted. She locked her eyes on Drew's brightly painted dragster and waited, her heart in her throat.

"Start your engines!"

The flag shot up. The gun boomed. Ann watched as Drew wrapped his hands around the steering wheel and nailed the pedal.

Suddenly, brutally, his engine exploded in flames.

Drew!

Ann bolted out of her seat and tried to scream, but raw fear closed her throat. She could only stand and stare in horror. The pit crew stampeded toward him. The fire-fighters and the medical crew did, too. Waves of fear washed over her, leaving her body paralyzed.

Was he dead? Dear Lord, *no!* She saw him then, not being lifted onto a stretcher, but climbing out of the cockpit on his own volition.

"Thank God," Ann whispered.

The crowd roared and whistled in relief while two men got on either side of Drew and, after lifting him, carried him toward the pit.

With tears blinding her, Ann felt for the chair behind her, positive she was going to faint.

She must have cried out because the man next to her dropped back into his seat and stared at Ann. "Lady, you all right?"

Ann couldn't say a word. She took deep gulping breaths and tried to regain control. The frozen feeling in her heart, the building pressure in her stomach, her limbs shaking as if she had the palsy, and the rank taste in her mouth were all standard symptoms of panic.

"Lady, answer me!"

"Please," she whispered through bloodless lips, "take me to the man who...who was hurt."

"You with him?"

Ann could only nod.

"Jeez, come on, then, I'll see what I can do."

Ann never knew how she found Drew or how she ended up along with him in a cubbyhole in the makeshift infirmary. She thought his pit-crew manager had probably intercepted her and taken charge. She just knew that she now stood across from Drew, her eyes taking in the scratch on his forehead and the extreme pallor of his skin.

Yet, he was smiling as he came toward her. "Sorry, I didn't make a better impression. That's what I get for wanting to show off. Maybe next time I won't screw up." He reached for her.

She slapped at his hands and stepped back.

"Ann...?"

"Don't...don't you dare touch me!"

A hard shudder raked him. "For god's sake, don't look at me like that. See, I'm fine. Just a mild concussion."

"Oh, is that all?" She laughed, only it came out a sob. "Just a mild concussion! How...how can you toss that off as nothing?" She heard her voice rise with each word, approach the level of hysteria, but she didn't care. "Damn you! You...you could've been killed. And for what!"

"Hey, take it easy. You're blowing this way out of proportion."

"Oh, really. Oh, that's great. Well, I happen to have been there and watched while your car blew up."

"Well, I happened to have been in the car, and it's no big deal. Accidents come with the territory."

The terror that Ann had experienced earlier was nothing compared to what she felt now. Outrage and shock and disbelief. An excruciating pain ripped through her insides. She feared she would throw up on the spot. How in the name of God could he treat a near-miss on his life so lightly?

"You can't handle it, can you?" His voice sounded as if the life had gone out of it.

"No, I guess I can't."

"Can't or don't want to?"

His penetrating blue eyes seemed to read her soul. She steeled herself against their magnetic pull for understanding. "Maybe a little of both."

"I see."

"No, I don't think you do."

A muscle in Drew's cheek throbbed. "If I thought something like this would've happened, I would never have insisted you come. But since we can't predict the future, you'll have to accept what happens and go on. The way I see it, life's one big gamble, anyway."

"Not to me it isn't."

Drew smiled a cold smile. "You're right about that. If it's not a sure thing, you aren't interested, right?"

"What I think or feel isn't the issue here," she said.

"Oh, but it is. You know the word that best describes you is *coward.* You're a coward, Ann Sinclair."

"That's not true!" she countered.

"Yes, it is. The thought of taking a chance absolutely blows your mind." His eyes were stormy. "The bottom line here is, you're afraid."

A warning went off in her brain. But she refused to heed it. She had to say the words crowding her throat or choke on them. "I'm not afraid of taking chances that count," she threw back at him. "Such as commitments to the important things in life."

The silence that followed was stark. Both were trapped in the fragility of the moment. Every word, every gesture, every sensation became important, threatening.

"It's not going to work, is it?" Drew said in an emotionless voice.

Ann's pulse pounded in her ears. "Not if you don't want it to," she whispered.

Tension stiffened his jaw, and he didn't say anything.

Something cold settled in the bottom of her stomach. "Oh, I want it to, all right," she said, feeling herself break apart inside, "but I'm greedy. I want it all—a home, children, but most of all a husband who's a man and not a spoiled little boy with a penchant for danger."

Drew's face crumpled, then twisted bitterly. "In that case, I guess you'd best hightail it back to that safe, boring world where *change* and *excitement* are dirty words. Personally, I no longer give a damn."

Ann reeled.

"I'll have my manager drive you home."

The abrupt slam of the door rocked the trailer.

The fear, the sickness she'd felt before in no way rivaled the blinding agony that bent her double.

Was it over? Was *he* over? Bile stuck in Ann's throat as she stood transfixed and watched her dreams, her hopes, disintegrate. You always did want what you couldn't have, a voice taunted.

"No…!" Another agonizing pain ripped through her.

Seventeen

——————

"You sure you aren't sick?"

Drew was sick all right, but he wasn't about to admit it. He glowered at his assistant. "Hell, no, I already told you that."

"So you did." Skip scratched his head. "Something's got you riled, that's for sure." He paused. "It's not your mother, is it?"

Drew's features relaxed somewhat. "No. For the time being, she's doing okay."

"That's good news. I also have some more good news."

"Shoot."

"If you still want the property, it's yours."

"I want it," Drew said without much enthusiasm, which garnered another strange look from Skip. He ignored it and went on, "Go ahead and start the paperwork rolling."

"Right." Skip walked toward the door. "Oh, I almost forgot, Hal Ackerman called and said he was on his way here."

"'Bout damn time," Drew muttered. "Tell Wendy I'll see him immediately."

Alone, Drew stood and walked to the window, his stride jerky, like that of an old man. He cursed himself, and while he had the urge to shove his hand through the plate-glass window, he didn't. Resorting to unnecessary violence was not the answer to his stupidity.

He'd told Ann he didn't give a damn. A sneer stretched his lips. Famous last words. He gave a damn, all right, only he hadn't recognized that until it was too late.

Though he kept the highway hot between MacMillan and Houston, he spent the majority of his time here at the office. He felt he could cope better. Besides, his dealerships had gone without his attention long enough. Since his mother was doing as well as could be expected, and he'd gotten his daddy's business better organized, except for the Tim Pollard debacle, he'd felt free to concentrate on his own bailiwick.

Or so he'd thought. The lines deepened in his forehead at the same time the door opened behind him. He swung around and watched as the accountant waddled across the threshold.

"Your secretary told me to come on in," Hal said by way of a greeting.

"Want a cup of coffee?" Drew asked.

"Naw, just had one, but thanks, anyway." Hal's eyes narrowed on Drew. "You sick?"

An expletive scorched the air. "What is this? First Skip, now you. No, dammit, I'm not sick."

"Hey, I didn't mean anything by that." Hal's nonchalant smile seemed to lengthen his mustache. "It's just that you look godawful, like maybe you've been chasing the bottle.''

"Give it a rest, okay?"

Hal shrugged. "Whatever you say."

"So tell me what you've come up with." Drew perched on the edge of his desk.

Hal shifted his massive body weight into action. He set his briefcase down. "I've got proof."

"Proof that'll nail his butt?"

"To the prison floor."

"Good."

"Is that all you can say?"

Drew raised his eyebrows as he stood. "What would you like for me to say?"

"How should I know," Hal said darkly. "Shout hallelujah, or better still, why not jump over the desk?" Hal's attempt at humor fell on deaf ears as Drew strode back to the window and stared outside. "Just show some emotion," Hal added.

How can you show emotion when you're dead inside? Drew wondered. Ann, sweet Ann. She was the best thing that had ever happened to him, and he had let her go.

He ached for her, ached to feel her naked against him, ached to kiss her beautiful belly, feel her breasts against his cheek, hear that purring sound that was all her own.

Her image surged to his mind with such vividness that it was all he could do to collect his thoughts and pay attention as the accountant walked over to him, a sheet full of figures in his hand.

"Here's the proof," Hal said.

Drew shook himself and faced Hal, though he felt vulnerable, exposed. "Were you right?"

"Yep. The receipts don't match the deposits."

"So the little weasel's been pocketing the money."

"With the help of his sweetie at the bank."

"Sonofagun!" For a moment Drew's eyes returned to life. "She's been depositing the money in her account."

"I'd stake just about anything on it," Hal responded. "Let me make sure I got this straight. Pollard helps himself to the money, then adjusts the deposits accordingly. And because he was confident he'd never get caught, he didn't bother or didn't know how to adjust the cash-register tapes."

"I'd say that's it in a nutshell," Hal said.

Drew folded the paper and shoved it into his shirt pocket. "Anything else I need to take to the authorities?"

"That about covers it."

"I had confidence in you from the beginning, my friend."

"Why don't I think that's a compliment?" Hal asked at the door.

Drew actually smiled. "Well, it is. You did a helluva job. Thanks."

"As always," Hal said, and sauntered out the door.

Drew hadn't wanted to go home, but he had no other place to go. He'd gone the bar route, only booze hadn't helped to ease the yearning inside him. Rather, it had intensified it, made him less human.

It was twelve o'clock and raining like hell. He'd stayed at the office until he was so weary, he'd had trouble driving home.

But the instant he'd opened the door and walked inside, it had hit him, as he knew it would—the desperate hunger to see her, to hold her. Again, he longed to feel Ann's arms around him, feel her warm, seeking lips against his, feel the solidness of her body. The craving was so bad it gnawed in his gut, like a virus that kept lingering.

He trudged into the bedroom, stripped quickly and fell on the bed. Nights tore him up. The loneliness was unbearable.

How could he have loved her and not known it? He guessed he'd fought so hard *not* to love her that he hadn't recognized the symptoms. He'd told himself that if she couldn't love him as he was, his goals and dreams included, then a relationship between them was doomed. And it was better to know that now than later.

This way he could start to rebuild his life. He still had what was important to him—his work and his love of racing. He would be fine.

Only he wasn't. He was miserable.

He loved her so much that his life had changed. Where once it had been challenging and exciting to wake up, now it was a drag. The color had gone out of everything. He missed her so much that his whole body throbbed.

"Ann," he said, his face against the pillow. "Ann."

He rolled back over, squeezed his eyes shut and gave in to the pain of losing her. He thought again about how she'd said, "I'm not afraid of taking chances that count. Such as commitments to the important things in life." He knew then, with the certainty of death and taxes, that he couldn't go on like this. He had to have her back.

She should be celebrating, Ann told herself. Her life, as she'd planned it, was exactly on course. Unfortunately, the course had changed. When she'd first mapped it out, Drew hadn't been a part of it.

She'd planned to expand her shop, employ a beautician and add a skin-care line, which she had firmed up just three days ago. And while she hadn't planned on her brother's reappearance, she was glad, especially as he'd responded to counseling and made a conscientious effort to become a responsible citizen.

But the enthusiasm was gone; the joy of accomplishment was missing. When Drew went out of her life, a light switched off inside her, plunged her into the dark—a dark from which she couldn't seem to emerge.

Even now as she waited for Dorothy Sable to pull out of her briefcase a raft of papers that needed signing, Ann felt that darkness taunt her with its menacing presence. Yet, she wanted this child, maybe more than before. It had become her lifeline; it was all she had left—the thought of someone to love, and to love her.

Still, a child wouldn't completely alleviate the dark void inside her. Only Drew could do that. Dear Lord, had it been only three weeks since they had parted? It seemed more like three years. She couldn't remember the last time she'd slept through the night.

Dreams wreaked havoc with her sleep. Often they were colorful, sexual dreams about Drew. Sometimes she awoke, sat straight up in bed, panting and clammy with perspiration, positive he was beside her, only to be devastated to find that he wasn't. Her overactive mind took its toll on her body.

Sophie had summed it up quite adequately. "If you don't start eating, you're going to dry up and blow away. You look like a walking corpse."

"I'm trying, really I am," Ann said.

"Pooh, you're not, either." Sophie fell silent a moment, then added, "Look, I know you're having a tough time since Drew...but you can't keep your feelings bottled inside forever."

"I know," Ann said through a haze of tears. "Just bear with me a while longer, okay?"

"If you want a shoulder—" Sophie paused and patted hers "—you got one."

"Thanks, I'll keep that in mind."

That conversation had taken place right after the breakup and still, Ann couldn't bring herself to open her heart and bleed on anyone, not even to Sophie.

"Ann?"

She breathed deeply, and forcing a smile, turned around. "Sorry. My mind was wandering."

"You seem upset." Dorothy looked concerned. "Is there something I should know about?"

"No," Ann assured her hastily, and smiled harder. "Pressures at work, you know," she finished lamely, praying that Dorothy wouldn't question her further.

Dorothy didn't. She returned Ann's smile and said, "It's a good thing you have your work. So many women who are waiting for a child don't have anything to occupy them."

"While I might not have that problem," Ann said softly, "the waiting is still nerve-racking."

"I know, and we're sorry. Unfortunately, the time factor remains the biggest drawback for adoptions."

"How long will I have to wait?"

Dorothy rose, her eyes sympathetic. "I wish I could say we would have a child for you anywhere from a year or two years. Or six months from now."

"The latter's not very likely, though, is it?" Ann asked wistfully.

"No, but it's not impossible, either. So, let's hold on to that thought, shall we?"

Ann nodded as she walked her guest to the door.

Dorothy extended her hand. "Take care, and I'll be in touch."

* * *

Rain slapped against the window. Ann tossed back the cover and got out of bed. But she didn't feel rested. As usual, she hadn't slept. She padded to the window, opened the miniblinds and stared at the sky.

Lightning streaked across it, then left only darkness in its wake, the same darkness that had set up permanent residence in her soul. With a sigh, she turned away from the window and eyed the bed. Today was Monday and she didn't have to work. But returning to bed was futile.

If only she had her child. That wasn't the answer, and she knew it. Only Drew could fill the emptiness in her life. So what was the answer? Certainly not surrounding herself in self-pity.

Again their bitter exchange rose to haunt her. Lord knows, she'd thought of little else.

Was Drew right? Was she a coward? Absolutely not. She was willing to gamble on single parenthood. Why, then, hadn't she given their relationship a chance? Was it because she feared she couldn't live up to his expectations, satisfy him? But if she didn't try, how would she know? She wouldn't.

But the real question was whether she could accept him for what he was, not for what she wanted him to be. Her heart gave a decided lurch. She thought for a second she might be having a heart attack; no, it was her conscience.

Had she been wrong to try to change him? Like a fist to her stomach, the answer rang clear. Yes. His recklessness, his irreverence for the status quo, were the things that made him special, made her love him.

Shaking all over, Ann dashed to the closet. She knew what she had to do.

Eighteen

Yesterday's storm had passed. Sunlight spilled onto the pavement in front of the car and created a harsh glare as well as aggravating the insufferable humidity.

The back of Ann's blouse was damp. But her problem was nerves, not the weather. She inhaled cool air-conditioned air deep into her lungs, then lowered the window and killed the engine. A waft of soggy air slapped her in the face.

She shook. This would never do. Now that she was here, several yards from Drew's condo in southwest Houston, fear threatened to render her useless.

Her watch said seven o'clock. She'd gotten off to a later start than she'd anticipated. Her plans had gone astray. She'd had two appointments she'd wanted to cancel but hadn't because both clients spent a lot of money in the shop every week.

Too, she'd gone by the dealership, thinking she might

find him there, only to learn that he was at home nursing a cold.

The neighborhood was quiet. And the condos that lined the drive were elegant. The air was rich with the smell of money. From where she parked, his condo filled her vision. It appeared deserted, but then so did all the others on the street.

She breathed deeply. Her heart was banging so badly, she couldn't move. She needed time to collect herself.

It wasn't that she didn't want to go through with confronting Drew. She had no choice. She didn't want to live another day without him. She might have to, though, and the reality rooted her to the seat. She didn't know what she would do if he rejected her.

While her stomach turned somersaults, she opened the door and got out. She stood beside the car and took another deep breath. Then she looked to make sure her blue silk shirt and slacks were not mussed. She wanted to look her best. So much was at stake.

By the time she reached the door, a calm had settled over her. What she was about to do was right; and that resolve gave her the strength to push the doorbell.

No response. Only silence greeted her.

She pushed the bell again.

Heavy footsteps finally reached her ears. She clasped one hand around her purse and waited.

The door swung back on its hinges, and Drew filled the empty space. New lines scored his face and accentuated its gauntness. And his body was leaner. But his eyes hadn't changed, except the devilish tinkle was no longer there.

"What...?" His words halted—as if someone had landed a suckerpunch to the gut. Disbelief settled over his face. And something else, something she couldn't decipher.

He set his lips in a rigid line, and Ann's body tensed. Oh, God, he wasn't glad to see her, she realized. She'd made a mistake. She felt herself dismantling inside piece by piece, and there wasn't anything she could do to stop it.

A pitiful moan escaped her lips, and she stepped back. That was when she saw it. The fixed control slipped from his features; naked misery took its place. Ann's steps faltered.

"Don't...go," he said in a gravelly voice. He held out his arms.

She launched herself into them and sobbed against his chest, "Oh, Drew, hold me."

He strained to bring her closer, savoring the moment, thinking maybe he'd died and gone to heaven.

"I love you, I love you," he whispered. "I was coming to tell you that, only I got sick."

Ann raised her face. "That's why *I'm* here. I love you, too, and couldn't stand the thought of living another day without you."

His mouth found hers with a tempered fury. "This isn't enough," he said frantically. "I want all of you. Now."

Ann wordlessly grabbed his hand and placed it on her breast. He led her to his bedroom.

With the late-afternoon sun barred from the room by the blinds, Ann and Drew roughly, quickly discarded their clothes. When the articles pooled at their feet, they reached for each other.

"Oh, God, I dreamed of this moment," he ground out against her lips. "But I didn't think it'd ever happen."

"I missed you so much, so much." Her voice held agony and ecstasy. Her eyes held promise.

"Marry me."

She made that purring sound he loved so much. "Just say when."

"Tomorrow."

"What about your mother?" Her eyes were closed, but her lips were curved sensuously.

His gentle, but impatient fingers plucked a nipple. "What about her?"

"Shouldn't…shouldn't we include her? And Sophie? And maybe Peter?"

His lips took small tender bites along her neck. "Only if tomorrow suits them."

Ann whimpered and leaned helplessly against him. "Why the hurry? I promise not to leave you." Her tongue moved down his chest in long strokes.

Her heart set him on fire.

"Not ever," she added, a tremor running through her.

"Anything you say," Drew said hoarsely, and dragged her backward onto the bed.

Her lips were hot and sure beneath his, parting so their tongues could entwine. Then, shifting within his arms, she flattened herself against him. He was so hard he hurt.

He couldn't wait. He had to have her now. He shifted, placing enough distance between them so that he could position himself above her.

But she stopped him with her hand. Her violet eyes glowed as her flawless naked body inched its way upward to cover his. Her moistness instantly enveloped his thickness. He struggled for breath. She smiled at him and brought her breasts close to his lips. He took one in his mouth, then the other.

"Ah, Drew, Drew," she said in a prolonged whisper,

beginning to move. With each stroke, everything, especially the past, ceased to exist.

Ann awakened and tried to move. She couldn't. Her body was still tangled with his.

"Hey, you," she whispered, "wake up."

"Mmm, I'm awake."

She sought his face, her eyes luminous and huge. "Will you forgive me?"

"Whatever for?"

"For trying to change you. When you race, I...I promise I'll be strong."

"Oh, baby, baby," he said, cradling her close to his chest and rocking her. "You're something else."

"I'd rather have you for one day than not at all."

"We'll have lots of days. Do you think I'd honestly do anything to jeopardize that?"

"I...hope not."

"Count on it." Drew's eyes narrowed in sudden pain. "I'm the one who should be apologizing for being so pigheaded and unbending. Hell, anyone in his right mind would've reacted the same way you did."

"But I'll do better next time," she said.

"Just be yourself, honey."

"Even if I get upset?"

"Even if you get upset."

"Oh, Drew." Her lower lip trembled.

He tongued it again before whispering, "I love you."

"And I love you."

He held her for a long moment, then said, "If you want to leave the adoption application on file, I won't object."

Like spring rain on wild flowers, his words fell delicately into the silence. Ann hugged them close, then pulled back and sought his eyes. "Thanks for that. And

I want you to know that I love you even more for having said it.''

''So how 'bout we start making our own baby,'' he muttered thickly.

Tears clumped her lashes as she smiled a beautiful, radiant smile. ''I can't think of anything I'd rather do,'' she whispered. He groaned and covered her body with his.

Epilogue

Ann decided that pinching herself wasn't the answer. But she was tempted, if only to prove that she was alive. And well. And pregnant.

I'm going to have a baby!

After leaving the doctor's office, she had gone straight home. That had been over an hour ago, and her feet hadn't touched the ground yet. But dogging the heels of her elation was apprehension. With only eight months of marriage to her credit, what would Drew's reaction be?

She hoped and prayed he'd be as happy as she was. She had no reason to suspect otherwise as their marriage was as close to perfect as it could be. Too, he'd told her he'd wanted to make a baby even before they were married.

A giddy, indulgent smile crossed her lips as the thought struck her that almost all newlyweds feel this way. But she knew she and Drew had something special.

From day one he'd made her blissfully happy, which was not to say there hadn't been disagreements and adjustments. There had. But because their love was strong, they had weathered them together.

Both their professional lives had remained on track, which accounted for part of their well-being. With Drew's help, she'd expanded her shop. Business couldn't have been better.

Drew continued to experience growth in his car dealerships, as well, though he'd turned over day-to-day management to his assistant.

And while he still raced, his desire had tempered somewhat as the family business continued to take up more of his time. With so much happening right in MacMillan, they had decided to stay.

Tim Pollard had confessed and was serving time in jail. When the news had broken, gossip was rampant, but soon the citizens had tired of that scandal and searched for another one.

Thank goodness, her brother hadn't been new fodder for the gossipmongers. Therapy had helped him tremendously. He worked every day and had paid off the loan shark. He was learning to feel good about himself.

Ann found she had very little to complain about. She coveted her happiness and felt she'd earned it. At this moment, she coveted it even more, knowing that a tiny life was growing inside her.

Suddenly noticing the time, Ann made a face. She had to get going. Still, she didn't move. Her gaze was locked on the snow-flecked Christmas tree that dominated one corner of the den of the MacMillan mansion where they lived.

Drew had wanted to build her a new home, but she'd opted to live here instead, at least for the time being.

Besides, she loved the stately old home and its treasures, and took pleasure adding her stamp to them.

Two months into their marriage, Drew's mother had become completely bedridden and, with a live-in companion, occupied her own apartment in the rear.

The lights on the tree twinkled at Ann. She laughed aloud, then placed her hand on her stomach. A baby. What a delightful Christmas present.

Finally, Ann forced herself to move. Drew was expected home for lunch. Every Monday he came home at noon; the habit had developed into a special time for them. Sometimes they ate; sometimes they made love instead.

She scurried into the bedroom where she took off her clothes and slipped into a baggy pair of knit pants and a top.

A short time later, she stood at the kitchen cabinet preparing a salad and humming at the top of her lungs.

"Gotcha."

Her heart jumped, then settled when she felt familiar arms encircle her.

She leaned against Drew's chest and looked up at him. "Don't you know it's not nice to sneak up on people?"

He grinned and nuzzled her neck. "You're not people—you're my wife."

She twisted in his arms and faced him. "Somehow I fail to see the logic in that."

He leaned down and planted a hot, hard kiss on her lips. "Mmm, you taste delicious," he whispered when he pulled away.

Ann wrinkled her nose. "So do you."

That devilish glint appeared in his eyes. "How 'bout feasting on each other, then?"

Ann feigned shock. "The very idea. And miss out on

my wonderful salad?'' She laughed. ''Not a chance. Anyway, I have something to tell you.''

''Oh?'' Drew turned her loose, leaned against the cabinet, crossed his arms and with caressing eyes, watched her.

Ann licked her dry lips. ''I went to the doctor today.''

He stood straighter. ''And?''

''I'm…I'm pregnant.''

A hush descended over the room.

''Are you sure?'' His voice sounded scratchy.

''Yes,'' she said. ''You…you aren't sorry, are you?''

''Sorry? Of course not, silly. I can't think of anything better than our child inside you.''

''Oh, Drew,'' she cried, flinging her arms around his neck and squeezing him.

He lifted her and swung her around the room. She squealed in delight. Once he settled her back on her feet, he stared at her.

''Isn't there a certain matter you should take care of?''

She gave him a perplexed look. ''What?''

''The adoption agency.''

Ann's mouth fell open. ''Gosh, you're right.''

He chuckled. ''Since we're going to have our own baby, you really ought to think about canceling your application.''

''I—'' The phone stopped her answer.

Drew groaned. ''Great timing.''

Ann laughed, then crossed to the phone. She lifted the receiver, winked at Drew, then placed her hand across her stomach.

Desire simmered in his eyes.

''Hello,'' Ann said, weak-kneed.

She listened, while the high color seeped from her face.

"Honey?" Drew said, stepping forward.

She covered the receiver with her hand. "It's…it's Dorothy Sable…"

Drew paled.

"She…she wants to know if we can come and get a two-year-old girl…says she's ours…if we want her."

Drew cleared his throat roughly. "Do we want her?"

"Do we?" Ann whispered, and stared at him, knowing her heart was in her eyes.

Drew grinned his brash, cocky grin. Two babies. Hell, what could be more perfect?

* * * * *

EVERYTHING BUT TIME

This book is dedicated
with love
to the faithful customers of D & B Book Store

Chapter 1

The door chimes pealed loudly and insistently.

"Damn," Danielle Davis muttered under her breath, her blue eyes darting from the image in the mirror downward to the gold watch circling her slender wrist. Seven o'clock. It was much too early in the morning for a casual visitor and much too early for bookstore customers, she thought, fighting back the twinge of fear that twisted through her like a dull knife.

The hairbrush slipped from her clammy grasp. It was the clatter of it hitting the glass cosmetic tray that forced Danielle to move. Shaking her head in disgust for letting her imagination run wild, she pivoted on her heels and rushed out of the room, suddenly afraid that the continuing sound of the doorbell would wake up Ann.

She had just stepped on the top step of the carpeted staircase when a chirpy voice called up to her.

"I'm up, I'll see to the door."

Thank goodness for Jusie, Danielle thought as she

turned away from the stairs and made her way down a short hall where she paused and poked her head around the door on the right. If it weren't for Justine Evans, who was both friend and housekeeper and at times guardian angel all rolled into one, she would not be able to survive much less work in her bookstore full time or teach night classes at the university.

Danielle tiptoed across the room, coming to stand beside the twin bed and peered down at her two-and-a-half-year-old daughter, Ann, who was sleeping dead to the world.

Looking at her, Danielle marveled anew at how fortunate she was to have been blessed with such a miracle. Tears burned the back of her eyes as she took in the tiny, delicate features: the rose-flushed, heart-shaped face; long, thick eyelashes which fanned over deep green eyes, complementing a perfectly shaped nose and a silky mop of black curls.

Automatically Danielle's finger reached out and captured an errant curl dangling across the tiny forehead and moved it aside. If only she weren't her father made over.... No! Don't think like that, she berated herself. Don't think about *him!*

Ann stirred, burying her teddy bear up under her chin. This action brought Danielle out of her wandering thoughts. Sighing deeply, she leaned over and grazed Ann's cheek with her lips before hurriedly exiting the room.

She met Jusie at the head of the stairs.

Her housekeeper's almond-shaped brown eyes were pensive and a frown wrinkled her forehead. ''There's a man to see you. If I didn't know better, I'd say he looks like he's one of those FBI agents or Internal Revenue dudes,'' she whispered conspiratorially, although it was impossible for him to hear their conversation.

Seeing Danielle's face suddenly lose its color, Jusie's frown deepened. "Want me to tell him to get lost?" Before Danielle had a chance to speak, however, Jusie went on, bobbing her gray curls up and down, "Huh, the way I see it, seven o'clock isn't the time to conduct any business.''

Danielle shook her head, making an effort to swallow the lump in her throat. "It's...it's all right, Jusie, I'll talk to him. If you'll show him to the office and then get us some coffee, I'd appreciate it.'' She tried to smile, but it was impossible; her lips were too stiff.

Jusie looked as though she would like to have argued, but seeing the stubborn set of Danielle's shoulders, she thought better of it. Instead she spun around and took her more than ample frame back down the stairs.

Danielle stood for a moment chewing the delicate lining of her lower lip, trying to ease her churning insides. *Cool it, for heaven's sakes! You're making a mountain out of a molehill.* It was probably just a salesman making an early call. Oh, hell, who was she trying to kid? She knew it was no salesman. It was trouble spelled out with a capital T. She might as well go downstairs and face the music. But why now? After all this time.

For the past three years, Danielle's life had settled into a pattern. She loved her work, owning and managing a small but lucrative bookstore across the street from the university campus in the quaint East Texas town of Nacogdoches, Texas. Adding to her pleasure was the convenience of having her business in the same building as her home. By being frugal she had saved enough money to buy an old two-story house and remodel it, making the upstairs into an apartment and the downstairs into a bookstore. It was an ideal setup, allowing her to be close to Ann while she worked.

It was the first time in Danielle's life that she had ever had a home and family. Or had roots. To Danielle, creating a home filled with love and security for her daughter and herself was the most important thing in life. Having been reared in an orphanage with no knowledge of her parentage, she'd had a hard life. She had learned at an early age that she could count on no one but herself. As a result she was fiercely independent and maintained an aloof shell around her which few could penetrate. Now that she had finally attained a happy home atmosphere, she was resentful of anyone or anything that tried to interfere with it.

Smoothing her hands down her corduroy skirt, she breathed deeply and began a slow but determined descent down the stairs. Without hesitation, she twisted the knob and opened the door that screened the stairs leading up to her private apartment. For once she did not pause to glance at the racks of paperback and hardcover books that graced the numerous racks in multicolored splendor. She marched through the maze as though someone had a gun pointed to her head and was threatening to pull the trigger at any given moment.

The door to her office was open. She paused long enough on the threshold to view the tall stranger standing in front of the bookshelves decorating one complete wall of her office. She judged him to be in his late fifties, and he still appeared to be in excellent physical condition. Although he was dressed immaculately, dapper was not the right word because he was too tall and thickset. His hair was slightly gray, but his skin was tanned and healthy as though he kept in shape through rigorous exercising. He was casually thumbing through the pages of a book when he looked up and saw her standing in the door. He seemed to tense, although his ready smile belied this.

"Good morning, Ms. Davis. I'm Tony Welch from the U.S. Marshal Service." In two long strides he was standing in front of Danielle with his hand extended.

Danielle had to squelch the urge to turn and run. But somehow she managed to stand reed straight as his thick fingers made contact with her long slender ones. Although she tried, she could not disguise the way her nerves were jumping chaotically throughout her system. Her trembling hand spoke for itself. The moment he uttered the words, U.S. Marshal, it was only by a supreme effort of self-discipline that she was able to rigidly brace her sagging body.

She quickly withdrew her hand and linked it tightly with her other one and gave him a plastic smile. "What can I do for you, Mr. Welch?" she asked, knowing that she was being impolite by not asking him to have a seat. But she was not interested in exchanging pleasantries with the stranger. She just wanted him to state his business and get out of her house and out of her life as quickly as he had come into them.

Tony Welch's dark eyes narrowed slightly at her frozen tone, but he smiled, showing uneven teeth through his thin lips. "First of all let me apologize for disturbing you at this ungodly hour of the morning, but when you hear what I have to say, perhaps you'll understand."

Danielle had her doubts, but she kept her face expressionless and moved not one muscle as she waited him out.

He suddenly shifted his gaze away from hers. Danielle followed his eyes as they rested on the gaily striped couch in the corner of the room. He turned back to face her. This time his voice had an exasperated edge to it. "Do you mind if we sit down? What I have to say will take a while."

Danielle felt a heat brush her cheeks at being caught red-handed with her rudeness. Yet she could not bring herself to apologize. "Of course, I don't mind," she said, gesturing toward the comfortable couch. "My housekeeper will be in shortly with coffee." That was as close to an apology as he was going to get, she told herself defiantly.

He smiled. "Thanks. A cup of coffee sure sounds good, especially on such a cold damp morning." He lowered his frame easily onto the couch while unbuttoning his coat, allowing him the freedom to stretch his arm across the back of the cushion. "Does it always get this cold in East Texas?" He smiled again, obviously trying to put Danielle at ease. "It's a helluva lot colder here than it is in D.C."

Danielle worked at making her voice sound normal, but she was afraid that her words came out sounding strained and unnatural. "This...this is the first January since I've been here that the weather has been this cold," she murmured tersely.

A silence followed her words.

"The minute I stepped off the plane, the chill cut clear through to my bones," he added, continuing to indulge in meaningless small talk in spite of the edge to her voice.

She nodded stiffly before turning her back and covering the short distance to stand in front of the ceiling-to-floor window behind her desk. For a moment, she watched the barren oak tree limbs bobbing up and down in the blustery wind. The weather was a duplicate of how she felt, she thought, dreary and extremely unsettled.

Suddenly she could not wait another second to find out

why this man had intruded upon her life. She was tired of inane chatter; she wanted action.

Twisting around, she began coldly, "Mr. Welch, I'm sure you didn't come all this way just to discuss the weather. So if you don't mind—" She halted in midsentence when she noticed Jusie standing inside the door balancing a tray laden with a coffeepot and two cups and a plate of steaming doughnuts. Although she knew that Jusie's homemade delicacies were delicious, food of any kind was the furthest thing from her mind. Her stomach revolted at the idea.

She flashed Jusie a weak but reassuring smile before quickly introducing Tony Welch. He stood up as Jusie set the tray in the middle of Danielle's desk and smiled at her politely. Jusie then turned to leave, but not before bestowing upon Danielle a questioning look.

"Thanks, Jusie," was all Danielle said to her housekeeper's retreating back before focusing her attention once again on Tony Welch. "How do you like your coffee?" she inquired, stifling the urge to sling the hot liquid in his calm face, only to be suddenly appalled at her vicious thoughts.

Tony Welch sat back, crossing one leg over the other, and watched Danielle. He had not missed the play of disruptive emotions that flickered across her delicate features, but it did nothing to take away from the pleasure of looking at her. He appreciated gentle beauty when he saw it, and Danielle Davis was exceptionally attractive.

She had soft blue eyes; they were a stunning combination with her blond hair and fair skin. In spite of her past and the difficulties she had overcome, they were expressive, very open. The eyes of a woman who had endured the trials of life, yet had not gained much knowledge of it. He could see himself reflected in them as she held the cup of coffee out to him. Suddenly he hated himself and his job for having to bring more pain down on those fragile shoulders. But he had to do it. If not him, someone else...

As he reached for the cup, wide blue eyes collided with his. "You're right," he said gruffly, turning away. "I didn't come here to talk about the weather."

"Exactly why did you come?" Danielle demanded quietly while lowering herself into her desk chair where she could keep her gaze pinned to this man who she knew was about to bring fear and uncertainty back into her life.

"You're needed in Washington, immediately," he said without preamble. He tried to ignore the way she flinched as though he'd struck her.

"Go on."

"I'm here to take you back with me, if possible, today. If not today, then first thing tomorrow morning."

"Why?" The simple word was barely audible.

"The Russian agent that has so effectively and easily escaped the FBI's clutches for the last three years is finally in custody." He paused and eyed her closely. "Or at least we think he is. And that's where you come in. As you well know, you're the only one who can identify the gentleman." The way he sneered the word "gentleman" was not lost on Danielle. "You remain the only link that can tie up this entire nasty mess."

Although her legs felt as though they were made of jelly, Danielle got up out of the chair and stood glowering down at him. Suddenly this nice, soft-spoken man had become her enemy. He was here to pull the rug out from under her well-ordered life, a life that she had paid dearly to obtain. And she had no intention of giving up without a fight.

Dots of color stained each cheek as her eyes bore into his. "Mr. Welch, I..."

He held up his hand, aborting her flow of words. "Before you say anything else, I want to assure you that within the next forty-eight hours you will be on a plane on your way back home. And I also want to stress that neither you nor your daughter will be in any danger. You have my word on that."

Danielle did not believe him. Sheer terror had replaced the fear inside her, causing her stomach to churn violently. He had no idea what he was asking. She felt herself begin to slowly unravel on the inside, a feeling she had hoped never to experience again. But this time she would fight them to the bitter end.

Ignoring the silent plea in Tony Welch's eyes, she said coldly, "I'm sorry, but there's no way I can comply with your ultimatum. My daughter is ill with a cold, and I have no one other than myself to operate the bookstore. Plus, I've just begun teaching a class two nights a week at the university." She paused, nervously sweeping a wisp of silky hair off her cheek. "Surely there is another way this can be handled without me having to go to Washington." This time her eyes were pleading with him to understand. And she knew that her voice was heavy with panic, but she could not help it.

"There's no other way. I assure you."

"But couldn't...couldn't an artist do a drawing of his face or take a picture of him and let me identify him that way?" She was grasping at straws; she realized that, but she was desperate. She would also do anything to keep from having to take one step away from home.

He shook his head, a regretful look on his face. "I'm afraid not. My orders were to escort you in person and that's what I have to do."

Danielle remained silent, her soft, rounded eyes imploring him to back down even though she was in reality butting her head against a brick wall. When the government had taken over her life three years ago, it had done so with a swift precision. But then they had disappeared, leaving her to live a normal life. Fool that she was, she had begun to think that she would never hear from them again....

"Ms. Davis, surely you want this man behind bars, so you'll be truly free. The last remaining shadow will have then disappeared from your life, and your past will finally be laid to rest." His voice was soft, soothing, yet persuasive. Spoken like a cool professional, she thought, using psychology to get her to do exactly as he wanted her to do.

Danielle swallowed the panic that was threatening to choke her. "All right, Mr. Welch. You win. I'll accompany you to Washington, but I expect you and the rest of your cronies to live up to your end of the bargain."

Tony Welch rose and buttoned his jacket, signaling that the interview was over. "Again you have my word on that, Ms. Davis." He sealed the promise with a tentative smile.

Danielle folded her arms and began rubbing them, trying to circulate the blood through her suddenly stiff limbs. "I'm going to hold you to that promise," she said soberly; yet there was an edge of hostility in her voice that could not be ignored.

"Don't worry, everything will be fine." He paused for a moment. "Just to prove I'm not your enemy, why don't we plan to leave early in the morning instead of today. That should give you ample time to make arrangements regarding your work and your daughter."

She couldn't quite bring herself to thank him, but she

did manage to flex her lips into a small smile. "I'll be ready."

He inclined his head before making his way toward the door. He then stopped and turned around. Danielle had not moved. She just stood there staring at him with those haunted blue eyes, looking tragically alone and defeated. He had to squelch the urge to tell her to forget the whole damned mess, that he'd never bother her again. He cursed inwardly before he spoke. "Don't bother to see me out," he said brusquely. "I know the way."

The moment Danielle heard the front door of the bookstore slam, she covered the short distance to the couch and collapsed onto it. Immediately the tears began to flow. She could have stopped breathing more easily than she could have stopped the liquid pain from saturating her cheeks. How could she possibly endure returning to the place that had brought her so much heartache? But then she bitterly reminded herself that she had no say in the matter. The die had been cast a long time ago.

The East Texas day dawned clear and crisp. The moment Danielle opened her eyes to the insistent clamor of the alarm clock, the events of yesterday and the nightmares of today came tumbling down, threatening to crush the breath from her. Finding the courage to get up, she flung aside the covers while thrusting to the back of her mind the heavy sense of dread and impending doom. Swiftly, she padded to the bathroom.

Thirty minutes later, she was dressed in a milk chocolate lightweight wool suit with a multicolored blouse giving the outfit a warm splash of color. But nothing could overcome the drawn look or the dark circles that played havoc with her fragile beauty. Danielle eyed her flight bag sitting by the door draped with her caramel-colored all-weather coat as though it were an evil object to be shunned. She shivered unconsciously as she walked out of the room, switching off the light behind her.

She went straight to Ann's room. Thank goodness her daughter was now sleeping soundly. It had been after two o'clock before she had gotten Ann to sleep. She had rocked the fretful child until she was exhausted, both mentally and physically. As she leaned over now and laid the back of her hand against the chubby cheek, Danielle was relieved to see that Ann's fever had broken and that her breathing was almost back to normal.

She felt Jusie's presence, behind her as she laid her lips against Anna's cool cheek, fighting to keep the tears at bay.

Jusie laid a comforting hand on Danielle's shoulder. "She'll be fine."

Danielle turned around and into the arms of her friend. "I...I know," she gulped, wallowing in the strength of Jusie's hold. "It's...it's just that I've never left her before." She pulled away and blinked back the tears. "I can hardly stand the thought of doing so now."

"Don't you worry your pretty head about this child. You just take care of your urgent business and come home. You know I love you and Ann more than anything, that I'd die before I'd let anything happen to either of you."

"I know, and I love you dearly for it, too."

Jusie smiled. "Well, let's just say we're both lucky and let it go at that." Then her smile suddenly faded. "That man is downstairs waiting."

They hugged each other again before Danielle turned and walked out of the room without a backward glance, having learned the hard way that it never pays to look back.

* * *

It was a solemn-faced Danielle that boarded the plane two hours later at Houston's Intercontinental airport. Tony Welch had opted to rent a car and drive the hundred and eighteen miles to Houston rather than take a small plane out of the local airport. They had made the entire trip in silence. Danielle had been in no mood to talk and had not encouraged him to do so either.

Now as the Boeing 727 sped through the sky, she stared out the window at the white clouds that reminded her of white cotton balls landscaping the heavens. From time to time she was aware of Tony Welch's eyes boring into the back of her head, but she continued to ignore him, fighting to overcome the misery that had a stranglehold on her heart.

"Ms. Davis, would you care for a drink?" The sound of his calm voice forced her to turn around. Both he and a smiling flight attendant were eyeing her intently. The marshal had a canned Coke sitting on the tray in front of him.

Danielle hesitated before answering. "No...no, I don't think so. Not now, but thanks anyway." She smiled at the attractive attendant. "Maybe later," she added.

"Are you sure?" Welch asked softly. "Nothing like a caffeine fix to revive the sagging spirits." He grinned, obviously hoping to tease her out of her pensive mood.

But Danielle wasn't buying. She knew that if she accepted a drink, she would be forced to make polite conversation with him, and she did not want to. She wanted to be left alone, to try and stamp out the terrible sensation of impending disaster she felt; to try and make sense of the changes that were taking place.

"I'm sure," she answered at last, feeling his eyes heavy upon her. She turned away.

As if sensing that she was in no mood to talk, Welch

shifted in his seat and said, "Maybe a little shut-eye will do us both good, help pass the time."

"Maybe so," she said, fitting her head snugly against the cushioned seat and the wall of the plane and closing her eyes. However, sleep refused to come. Even the steady hum of the plane's engines failed to quiet her jumbled thoughts. Why did her past have to resurface now? she asked herself in silent anguish. Hadn't she suffered enough?

She had worked long and hard to overcome the crippling liability of having been reared in an orphanage. She had been left on the doorstep of the home when she was only a few days old, or so she had been told. Her parents had never been traced. Even though the home had met her physical needs, her mental and emotional needs had suffered.

When she had reached eighteen, she walked out and began working night and day, sometimes doing three jobs to work her way through college. When she graduated, she obtained a job in one of the most prestigious law firms in the D.C. area. A firm which handled top secret government contracts. But after two years with the firm her happiness had skidded to a screeching halt, plunging her into a living nightmare....

"Ms. Davis, wake up, we're getting ready to land."

Suddenly her eyes flew open, and for a moment she searched the cabin of the plane while she groped to get her bearings. Then she heard the low timbre of her companion's voice and her whereabouts came toppling down upon her with a vengeance.

"Are you all right?" he asked soberly, though his brows knitted together showing concern.

Danielle struggled to sit upright, straightening the folds

of her pleated skirt as she did so. A fleeting, but reassuring smile briefly flexed her lips.

"Yes, I'm fine. It's been a long time since I slept this soundly." She paused, pushing the silken weight of her hair away from her face in a nervous gesture. "Staying up half the night with my daughter must have taken more of my energy than I realized," she added.

But that was only partly the truth. It was the dread of what she would face today that had kept her eyes wide open after she had put Ann to bed. Just the thought of having to look at the Russian agent again, even through a screening room, made her blood run cold. However, she did not want this stranger to know how she felt. She had already lowered her guard and let him see how frightened and uneasy she was. She did not want or need his pity. She was perfectly capable of handling it alone. That was one aspect of her life that had not changed, would never change. Loneliness remained her silent companion.

"Ms. Davis, isn't that great." Again Tony Welch's voice pulled her out of her gloomy thoughts just as the giant plane made rough contact with the runway and ground to a halt.

With clammy hands, Danielle unfastened her seatbelt. "I'm...I'm sorry, I wasn't paying attention."

Tony Welch smiled. "The pilot just announced the sun is shining brightly. Maybe that's a good omen." He paused slightly before adding, "For both of us."

"I hope you're right," she said softly, but the tension in her voice mocked her words.

It was time to go. She could not postpone it any longer. Slowly she rose, and stepping in front of Tony Welch, she began her slow descent down the crowded aisle.

With each step she took, however, her nervousness increased. Oh, God, she thought frantically, could she mus-

ter the courage to set foot on Washington soil? It had
been so long. There were so many memories.

Suddenly she stopped, unable to go on. She gripped
the handle on her overnight bag until she felt the leather
cut into the soft flesh of her hand.

"It won't be long now and it'll all be over." Tony
Welch's reassuring voice prodded her into instant action.

Somehow she managed to regain her composure to get
out of the plane into the waiting government car. Neither
spoke as the driver sped away from National Airport and
merged into the traffic. The sounds and smells of the city
permeated her senses as they sat in silence while the
driver maneuvered the nondescript vehicle the fifteen
miles from the National Airport, across the bridge and
into the downtown area. Nothing had changed, she noticed as they eased past the impressive Lincoln Memorial
and the enduring Washington Monument before turning
onto Constitution Avenue.

There was a time when she truly loved the multicul-
tured city with its beehive of activities, all centered
around the hustle bustle of making this country function
as a united nation.

But the only emotion she felt now was one of emptiness. All the glamor and hype meant nothing. Instead her
mind was filled with getting this ordeal behind her as
quickly as possible and returning to the quiet sanity of
her uncomplicated lifestyle.

Why, then she wondered, was she plagued with the
nagging doubt that her life was about to make another
ninety degree turn?

Marshal Luke Cassidy's office was on the fourth floor
of the district court building. Two entire floors were oc-

cupied by the U.S. Marshal Service, for which he was totally responsible.

Cassidy's desk was facing the window so that the panorama of the great city moved constantly before him. He found the scene below him powerful food for thought: Aesthetically he loved it for its typical mixture of beauty and ugliness. The city, reflecting the harsh bright sky above, its outer boundary cut by jagged horizons of tall buildings, the glimpse of trees, was part of the reason he loved this job, accepted so readily the tremendous burdens that rested on his thin shoulders.

But today he wasn't feeling so proud. For a little of nothing, he'd chuck the whole thing and walk out without a backward glance. He had spent an hour studying the file on Danielle Davis, refreshing his memory about this woman who in the last three years had been left alone to continue her life in a normal fashion.

The only significant change during that time was the birth of her daughter, born seven months after she came under their protection. She had refused to answer questions concerning the birth. And they had not pressed her to do so. As long as circumstances, whatever they were, posed no threat to her safety, his office did not interfere.

It was unfortunate for her that things had to change.

With a sigh, Cassidy closed the file before glancing sideways at another file laying inches away. Just looking at the words "Confidential—Top Secret" stamped on the front caused his blood to boil. "God-damned incompetence," he mumbled aloud, looking down at his watch. It was one-thirty; she should be there any moment.

Suddenly the buzzer on his desk announced both Welch and Ms. Davis.

Cassidy buzzed back. "Send them in."

When she entered his office, he hastily circled the

desk, his hand held out to her, a tall, neat man, with a thin Irish face and dark brown eyes, a mop of curly hair clipped short and combed back from his face, the air of authority prevalent.

"Good afternoon, Tony. Ms. Davis. Have a seat, won't you?"

He hadn't remembered her being so pretty. Had she always had that stunning silver blond hair and those beautiful blue eyes? They pierced his heart when she looked at him.

"Do you smoke?" he asked, reaching in his left suit pocket for a pack of cigarettes.

"No, thank you," she said politely.

He noticed that her hands were shaking.

"Tony, I know you've got things to do. I want to speak to Ms. Davis alone. I'll send for you later."

"All right, sir," Tony Welch said, speaking for the first time. Then he turned to Danielle. "I wish we could have met under happier circumstances." A sad smile touched his lips. "If I don't see you again, good luck."

Danielle watched him go, suddenly wishing that she could follow him. There was something about this room, this man...

"Ms. Davis, I've never been one to beat around the bush or take up one's valuable time with senseless babbling, so I'll speak bluntly." He sat down and then leaned forward, looking at her, a hard glint reflected in his eyes. "Unfortunately there's been a change in plans."

For a moment Danielle's eyes brightened. "I'm...I'm afraid I don't understand." Dare she hope that this ordeal would be over before it had even begun?

He made a savage gesture. "Of course, you don't. And the hell of it, I don't either. But due to circumstances beyond my control, the Russian agent is no longer in the

FBI's custody.'' His mouth had tightened into a bitter line.

''In that case,'' Danielle said, staring at him, ''…in that case, Mr. Cassidy, what am I doing here?''

''I wasn't informed of this until you and Welch were boarding the plane. Shortly before you came in, I was going over the details of what happened yesterday,'' he added tersely.

She lifted a hand to her throat. ''Where…where does this leave me?''

''Here, I'm afraid.''

For a moment there was a long silence.

''No!'' She shrank back a little, away from him. She didn't want to listen to him anymore. Staying was an impossibility; there was no point in discussing it.

''There's more,'' he continued bluntly.

''Please don't.'' Danielle made a movement as if she were going to leave.

''Ms. Davis.'' The firm tone of his voice stopped her cold. ''We have strong reason to believe that your cover has been blown, that the agent and his counterpart can identify you.''

Danielle's bag clattered to the floor. She turned so white that Cassidy bounded out of his chair, afraid for a moment that she might collapse. He bent down and gave her back her purse before placing a hand on her shoulder.

''I'm sorry,'' he said. ''I know how you must feel. It's a damned mess.''

''It can't be true,'' she whispered. 'It just can't be true.''

''I've got the proof right here—in this folder.'' He picked up the manila envelope and slapped it against his leg before pitching it back on his desk. ''But we know that Letsukov is still in the D.C. area. Our security has been so tight, there's no way out. We've tied up all the mass transportation routes as well as launching a full-scale manhunt for him and his partner, a man by the name of Zoya.'' His eyes glistened dangerously. "It's only a matter of time before we have them both under wraps."

"Oh, my God," Danielle whispered, sinking forward, as the blinding tears came with a rush. "What about…my daughter? Is—is she in danger, too?"

"No, absolutely not. But to alleviate any concern on your part, we're sending a deputy marshal to stay with your child and housekeeper until this mess is cleared up."

In spite of Danielle's effort to hold her chin steady, it began to wobble again uncontrollably. "Please…can't I just go home?" Her face was whiter than tissue paper.

Cassidy did not move. He waited, letting her cry. If she didn't, he was positive that she would have fainted.

After she had composed herself somewhat, Cassidy went on, "I understand how you feel, but it's imperative that you remain under tight security until the Russians are apprehended."

"No!" She shivered, trying to pull her coat closer. She felt cold, as if all the windows in the room were open.

Cassidy acted as though she hadn't spoken. "Our top man is on his way up now. You'll be under his protective custody in a retreat in the mountains of Virginia while the FBI is combing the area." He paused significantly. "Will you cooperate?"

Danielle looked directly at him; her eyes were swollen, her makeup smudged. She looked ill. "Do I have a choice?" she demanded bitterly, before getting up and walking dejectedly to stand in front of a window.

"No," Cassidy said to her back. "I'm afraid you

don't. But I can promise you we'll—'' He paused, the insistent knock on the door claiming his attention.

"Come in," he bellowed.

Danielle heard the door open but didn't turn around.

"Dammit Cassidy, I told you to get someone else for this assignment!"

Suddenly every muscle in Danielle's body froze. She felt as though her whole body had been immersed in freezing water.

She would recognize that voice anywhere, even though it had been over three years since she'd last heard it. Oh, God, no! It couldn't be. Surely it wasn't Keir McBride, the only man she'd ever loved.

For a split second, she did not think she could move. Then on legs barely supporting her, she turned around, positive that her exhausted mind had failed her.... But it hadn't. Eyes that were the exact replica of her daughter's stared back at her.

He stood tall and stiff, disturbingly unfamiliar, yet aching familiar.

Then his harsh words effectively sliced the silence. "Dammit to hell, Cassidy, what kind of game are you playing? This woman's not Danielle Davis, she's Erin Richards!"

Chapter 2

Keir McBride made it his business always to be in control of any and every situation. Vietnam had taught him that—the hard way. He could break a man's neck with his bare hands; he could walk for miles with almost no water and no food; he could adjust to scorching heat and bitter cold. He was an expert with weapons. He was a natural marksman.

In Washington, he was known to be a silent man, too silent, one who rarely smiled. He was widely envied and respected but not well liked. His skill with a rifle and his accuracy with a pistol had earned him a top-seated position in the agency.

When a job reeked of danger, he was their man. His rise in the ranks of the U.S. Marshal Service had been swift and sure. He had gained the reputation as being tough as nails and always in charge. There was nothing he couldn't handle.

But the office staff and field investigators would be

astonished if they could see him now. The sight of this woman was almost his undoing.

Although he continued to stand as if cast in concrete, his green eyes narrowed into tiny pinpoints of steel as they categorized everything about her.

Yes, he told himself, *it's Erin all right. His Erin. No, goddammit, she's not your Erin. Not anymore. She's your past. Natalie's your future. Remember that!*

The years had wrought no change. Oh, maybe she was somewhat thinner, and there were dark smudges under her eyes that he hadn't remembered. They made her seem more fragile than ever. But her hair was the same. Its fine silvery strands had always reminded him of trapped moonlight and still did. And the graceful lines of her slender body were unmistakable, the way her blouse outlined the gentle curves of her breasts...

Oh, God, why now? he groaned silently. Why did she have to show up now just when he had managed to glue himself back together and put his life back on track?

When he had discovered that she was missing, he had reacted like a madman. He'd hired the best private detective in the area to track her down. Nothing. She had vanished as though the earth had opened up and swallowed her, leaving a dead silence and a hole in his heart as big as the Grand Canyon.

And now here she was standing before him in the flesh, looking cool and composed and lovely as ever, even in the face of danger. Damn her to hell! Suddenly, a new surge of anger tore through his jagged nerves, sending his temper to the explosive point.

"McBride, sit down," Luke Cassidy barked, effectively slicing into the heavy silence. "If you'd read her god-damned file, you'd know what was going on." Then his eyes narrowed shrewdly, not missing a second of the

scene being acted out before him. "I won't take the time
to find out how you two knew each other. That's not
important now. But what *is* important is getting Ms. Davis out of the Washington area."

By sheer force of will Keir removed his eyes from
Danielle's face whose composure was no longer intact;
her mouth was slightly open now and her eyes were
glazed with shock. He turned toward his boss, his eyes
like cold chips of ice. "Who the hell had a chance to
look at a file? I was told to report immediately to take a
top priority assignment. I was given the bare facts and
nothing more. If you'll remember correctly, you promised me two weeks off." He paused. "And if you'll also
remember, I was to have gotten married this week."

Another profound silence settled over the room, leaving each occupant stranded to cope with tangled thoughts
and emotions. It was almost as if they were puppets dangling from a string, only to have the string suddenly
break, leaving their thoughts scattered in different directions.

Cassidy actually looked disconcerted. "Er...sorry
about that, my boy, but I needed you to handle this case.
I promise I'll make it up to you and Natalie when we
have that Russian bastard back in our clutches." He almost smiled. "I'll even throw in the champagne. How's
that for a bonus?"

Danielle could not head off the horrified moan that
escaped through her trembling lips. She clawed at the air
for her next breath.

The shock of learning that her life was in danger on
top of having Keir walk through the door after three
years, only to brutally announce his wedding plans, was
too much. Questions with no answers began swirling
around in her head, making her feel dizzy and disori-

ented. Surely Keir McBride, the rich playboy and the only son of a renowned senator could not be a U.S. Marshal? It was ludicrous! Unbelievable!

She had reconciled long ago that she would never lay eyes on this man again. After all, wasn't she a totally new person with a new name, a new life, a new identity? Chances of their paths crossing were one in a million. How could fate play such a dirty trick on her after all she had been through?

While she was still reeling from the possible repercussions of those unanswered questions, the vision of Ann's tiny face leapt in front of her face. *Oh, God,* she whimpered in silent agony, *the baby. Their baby!*

Suddenly the room began to spin as the floor raced up to meet her. "Oh, God..." she said again, fighting the black void that was closing in around her.

"Dammit, man, she's fainted!" Cassidy's voice thundered through the room just as Danielle's body made contact with the carpet.

Although Keir was the first to reach her, it was Luke Cassidy who lifted her slight frame into his arms and carried her to a small couch in the corner of the room.

Keir stood transfixed, his eyes locked on Danielle's lifeless form, his own breathing coming in short gasps while his heart was pounding violently. What the hell was the matter with him? Suddenly out of the blue the truth reached out and slapped him in the face. *You're afraid to touch her, you bloody fool!*

Gut-wrenching fear surging through him kept him immobile. Suddenly he saw the entire situation slipping beyond his control. The thought of being cooped up with her for days, maybe weeks... Oh, God, it didn't bear thinking about. Luke would just have to replace him, that's all. Sweat popped out on his face as he looked down at her still form, her hair spread like silver thread over the cushion.

"McBride, for chrissakes, buzz Amy and tell her to get in here pronto with coffee and a brandy. And tell her no calls. I don't want us disturbed."

Cassidy's order yanked Keir out of his stupor. Glad to have something constructive to do, he jammed a finger down on the buzzer and in a clear authoritative tone gave the secretary the message. It seemed only a matter of minutes before she was coming through the door.

Danielle was beginning to come around when she felt someone touch her shoulder. It was a light hand, not the heavy hand of Cassidy, nor Keir's gentle one. She would have known Keir's touch anywhere, anytime.... She shivered and raised her glazed eyes upward. A girl was beside her, holding a glass in one hand. She had a pleasant face, with curly brown hair and a calm voice.

"Drink this," the voice suggested. "It'll make you feel better." Danielle did as she was told, feeling the fiery liquid scald her stomach. Gradually the tension began to ease. She noticed with relief that she had been left in peace. Immediately she began pulling herself back together, soothing her tumbled curls back into order and adjusting her skirt. Cassidy was sitting at his desk shuffling through papers, and Keir was standing with his back to her, staring out the window.

Her eyes flickered to Keir. She could see the display of muscles as he held himself stiff and straight as an arrow. God, what an impossible situation. He hated her, she knew that. And she didn't blame him. But then she wasn't without her own bitter memories, either.

Why then did she have the sudden urge to dart across the room and fling herself in his arms and beg him to hold her, to tell her everything was going to be all right?

Of course, that was impossible. It was over between them. However, she did not regret it. Could not regret it. Because of Ann. The only good that had come out of their affair was the perfect child they had created. Again she was blinded by sheer mindless terror. What would Keir do if he ever found out about Ann? He must never know....

"Ms. Davis, are you feeling better now?"

Cassidy's level voice claimed her attention, drawing her up with a start. "Yes...yes, I'm fine now, thank you."

"Are you up to traveling?" he asked.

Taking his gaze off Danielle, Keir swung around on his heels, his eyes zeroing in on his superior. "Replace me, Luke," he clipped savagely. "Get someone else to take care of... Er...I mean..."

"Dammit, man," Cassidy growled, "her name's Danielle. Danielle Davis. Don't forget that again. Surely I don't have to remind you how dangerous a slip like that could be?" Luke Cassidy had a way of spitting out words as though they were bullets.

Keir's tanned skin turned a shade paler, indicating his superior's words had hit their mark; but again his gaze returned to Danielle.

Luke Cassidy's eyes narrowed as they bounced back and forth between Danielle's pale figure and Keir's grim, unyielding one. "As I said before, I don't know what the hell's going on with you two. And furthermore I don't give a damn. But what I do give a damn about is Ms. Davis's safety." His eyes shifted to Keir. "You're the best man for the job. It's that simple. And I have to think I can depend on you to put personal feelings aside and do what you've been trained to do." He paused. "And haven't I already promised that when this is all over, I'll personally guarantee you get your time off?''

Keir felt himself drowning, but he was determined not to go under without a fight. "What about Tanner?" There was desperation underlying his words.

"Tanner's out of the question." Although Cassidy's voice had not risen one iota, it was nevertheless encased in steel. His mind was made up.

"Don't I have anything to say about this?" Danielle chimed in softly, turning troubled eyes squarely on Luke Cassidy's face. "After all, it's my life that's in danger."

Cassidy frowned, but his eyes softened considerably. "I'm afraid not, Ms. Davis. Believe me, I have your best interest at heart. And Marshal McBride is the best we have. I'm afraid you two are stuck with each other for the time being anyway." This time his voice brooked no argument. The subject was closed.

If it would have done any good or accomplished anything, Danielle would have simply sat there and cried for the injustice of it all. But tears no longer came easily to her, not those kind of tears. Self-indulgent antics were for the weak. She had never been able to afford that luxury; it was too late to start now.

So instead of crying, she stood up and squared her shoulders as though the weight of the world rested on them. "If...if you don't mind, I'd like to go someplace private and make a telephone call."

With each step she took toward the door, Danielle could feel Keir's eyes boring into the back of her head. In her mind's eye she could see his fierce eyebrows clamped together at a savage angle and his lips thinned to an almost invisible line. The total picture bore the distinct stamp of cold hostility.

She just prayed that she would make it to the door and out before her legs caved in beneath her....

The snowflakes were spiraling downward from the azure sky, their different sizes and shapes giving the early afternoon an ethereal quality that no artist, no matter how talented, could capture on canvas. But Danielle was oblivious to the haunting beauty of the winter day. She was too caught up in her own misery.

She was sitting beside Keir in a blue unmarked Chevrolet on their way to the undisclosed destination in the mountains of Virginia. She had noticed vaguely that Keir had taken Route 7 out of the city; beyond that she knew nothing.

They had gotten off later than planned, but they'd had to wait for Cassidy's secretary to go shopping and buy Danielle several more articles of clothing. Also Keir had had to make arrangements for the heat to be turned on in the cabin and food to be delivered. She was aware of him with every fiber of her being. His physical presence was too positive to ignore. His massive body filled the seat to suffocation; he smelled of the strong brand of cigarettes he smoked. His hand on the steering wheel was veined and powerful. Hands that had transported her to the heights of passion and beyond time after time. Her eyes fluttered shut against the blinding pain of those memories. She sat carefully so as not to touch him.

She shuddered just thinking about the moment in Cassidy's office when Keir had walked into the room. How she had managed to hold herself together was beyond her. Even now she could still hear the violent curses that had followed her out the door and into the adjacent room where she had phoned Jusie and explained her change of plans.

Jusie had been upset, but had assured Danielle that everything would be fine, that Ann was fine but missed her mommie. Having to explain the presence of a U.S. Marshal invading their home had been a different matter altogether. Finally, however, she had convinced Jusie that it was just a precaution and nothing more. And she had prayed that it was true.

But convincing Jusie had in no way equaled the contempt that had oozed from Keir's eyes when he had come upon her and had demanded in a terse voice, "Finish your call and come on. It's time to get the hell out of here."

Those had been the only words he had spoken to her, and they had been traveling now for about fifteen minutes.

With a sigh, she sat forward and began pulling off her coat. It was stifling in the small car. Suddenly a hand shot out behind her and latched onto the collar of her coat while she struggled out of it. She kept her gaze averted, but she felt rather than saw him flinch as his arm grazed her breast.

After that he moved very little. Her imagination might be running away from her, but it seemed as if he'd rather be uncomfortable than shift his body against hers.

She had a ridiculous impulse to burst into tears; it was like a nightmare. It couldn't be happening to her. For she had known the minute she saw him, even after three long years, that she had never gotten him out of her system. He had left a mark on her, a mark that had dulled, but never quite been erased over the years. But she must never allow him to know this. She must keep her guard up at all times. Because nothing had changed—their being together was still an impossible dream.

A brittle silence had settled between them, stretching

her nerves to the breaking point. She knew that it would take only one word and the quiet would explode in their faces.

Against her better judgment, she ventured another look in his direction. Time had definitely wrought a change in his physical appearance, she thought. He had aged; gone was the flippant, happy-go-lucky charm that had amused her so easily—an emotion that up until she had met him was a rarity for her. Amusement was an underused commodity at the orphanage.

But now it seemed as though *his* face would break if he smiled. The grooves around his mouth were deeply carved, meant to endure. But the craggy imprint of his face that had been written on her brain with indelible ink was no different: the strong defiant chink, square jaw, the black unruly hair now interwoven with silver threads were unchanged. And those same startling green eyes still had the power to drive through her, straight to her soul.

If one were to consider his features separately, he wouldn't even fall in the category of nice looking, much less handsome, but the combination made him potently attractive. And with his tall, ruggedly built body, he radiated a male grace that few men could boast.

Yes, three years had changed him physically, but everything else was the same, she reminded herself bitterly. He was still the wandering nomad, flitting from one dangerous job to another, placing his life on the line daily. But then she remembered that at least in one respect he had changed—he was planning to get married. She couldn't help but wonder if his fiancée had the power to change him, to make him settle down where she had not.

"Why didn't you come and ask me for help?"

Danielle was shocked by his unexpected and startling question. She answered before she thought.

"Hah! How could I when I didn't even know where you were?" she choked. "If you'll think back a moment, you'll remember that you were off on another of your jaunts, taking care of, and I quote, 'important business.'" She made no effort to mask the sarcasm that punctuated each word she flung at him. Nor could she ward off the stinging sensation behind her eyes. Damn him! *This is an impossible situation,* she told herself frantically, *and getting worse with each twist and turn of the mountain road.*

Keir sighed deeply, seeing the rage in her face and the way she was trembling. Suddenly he had the urge to pull the car off the road and haul her into his arms and whisper in the delicate folds of her ear that everything was going to be all right, that he'd take care of her, that nothing or no one would ever hurt her again.

Damn, he was sweating. And in the dead of winter, too. He gripped the steering wheel until his knuckles began to turn white and he began to lose the circulation in his hands. *You ass, McBride! Where's your god-damned pride? Stop thinking about the way her mouth tasted when it hungrily searched for yours or the way her breasts filled your hand...*

She was not for him. She hadn't wanted him the first time around, so what made him think she'd want him now? It was over. Finished. He must think about Natalie. Damn, why couldn't he get his head on straight before something happened that he would regret for the rest of his life?

But before he could do that, he knew that he had to hear her side of the story from her own lips. He'd force her to tell him if he had to.

Keir rubbed his hand wearily across the back of his head. "Would you mind giving me the details?" he asked soberly. "I only know what Tanner told me when he summoned me to Cassidy's office this morning, and that wasn't much, just the hard cold facts and he showed me pictures of the Russian agents. It was enough to allow me to do my job and nothing more. Of course, he assumed I'd either read or would read your file."

Danielle was aware of what it had cost him to bury the hatchet for a moment and talk civilly to her. Even some of the inner tension seemed to have drained from him, she thought. His jaw was less rigid and his eyes were no longer shooting sparks at her.

"Oh, Keir, I don't know," she said, experiencing another jolt of raw panic. "I'm not sure I can even talk about it."

"Please try," he encouraged lightly.

"I...I still have terrible dreams, awful nightmares about that horrible day." She twisted her hands together. "I...I just don't think I can talk about it...."

He stared at her broodingly, remembering his own trauma, how he had nearly gone berserk when he found out she was missing. "Please," he said simply.

A deep sigh shook her slender frame. "Why are you making me do this?" She looked down at her fingernails and then up at his face, noticing for the first time a tiny scar at the corner of his right eye. Even at a distance she could see the way the flesh was roughly drawn together. Just another battle scar, she thought harshly. "It...it won't change things, my explaining, that is."

"I know," he answered bleakly, "but at least it will clear a few things up in my own mind." A muscle in his jaw began to jump, and suddenly she knew that he had reverted to his old hostile self.

Although her tongue felt weighted with lead, she decided that she had nothing to lose by telling him the whole terrifying story, except maybe make her night-mares more real, more intimidating. "I...I had decided to stay and work late," she began, her voice low and shaky, "the night after you...you stormed out of my apartment."

She kept her head averted, not wanting to see the dark cloud that she knew would have settled over his face at the mention of that night. "I...I didn't know it at the time, of course, but no one knew I had planned to stay after hours. Anyway, I was on my way to the office of my boss, John Elsworth, to get a file. I had just turned the corner and was getting my file key out of my pocket when I heard muffled voices. I looked up and saw that Elsworth's door was open." She paused and closed her eyes fully for a moment, her long lashes throwing a veil over her cheekbones.

"Go on," he prodded, afraid that she wasn't going to continue.

Her eyes opened gently, though she still did not look at him. "I took a couple of hesitant steps up to the door and was about to knock and let my presence be known when I...I heard Mr. Elsworth say and I quote: 'This highly classified information was just sent over this morning. It's hot stuff and your government had better be willing to pay through the nose for it.' End of quote. As you can well imagine, I was horrified. I couldn't have moved even if I'd had a block of dynamite planted under my feet. But I must have gasped aloud, because both men whirled around and saw me staring at them, a terrified expression on my face. The...the last thing I remember before turning and tearing back down the hall was the murderous glint in both their eyes."

She paused again, this time to try and control the vi-olent tremor that was raking her body. For a moment, she thought she might be sick. How humiliating if she had to ask Keir to pull off the road.

But her instant pallor was not lost on him. Suddenly he hated himself for putting her through this, making her dredge up the past. Damn, but she must think him an inhuman bastard, or worse, he thought angrily. And in this instance, she wouldn't be far from wrong.

Danielle suddenly pressed her hands against her stomach and sucked her breath deep into her lungs. Cold sweat doused her body. She forced herself to concentrate on the steady hum of the engine, hoping it would lull her stomach back to normal. But luck was not with her. Keir began to glide the Chevrolet around a hairpin curve and by the time the road had straightened out, it was too late. Her insides were churning upside down. "Keir...I'm..."

Glancing up and into the rearview mirror to check the traffic, he nosed the car across the highway and onto the shoulder, bringing it to a dead stop, loose gravel flying under the wheel. Then as quick as lightning, Keir's arm shot across her and yanked open the door.

The cold mountain air slapping Danielle in the face did nothing to stop her from losing the contents of her stomach. A short time later she sat up and lobbed her head back against the seat in silent agony, unable to gather her scattered wits together. Too many things had happened in too brief a period, and she was exhausted.

Although he never said a word, Danielle felt him slide across the seat and suddenly stop within a hair's breadth of her. Instantly her heightened senses were aware of him. She could feel his warm breath misting her face as the elusive smell of his cologne wafted by her nostrils. If she so much as moved at all, their thighs would have adhered to one another.

For a breathless moment, there was a stifling, agonizing silence.

Danielle did not move, did not breathe.

"God, I'm sorry," he groaned, taking in the chalky white skin and the way her thick lashes clumped together into wet little spikes. He held his body as tight as a guitar string, crushing the desire that threatened to erupt within him. It was happening all over again. She was bewitching him. But he couldn't move, no matter how much he wanted to. He was drowning in the sensations of her.

The awareness seemed to stretch between them like a silent scream.

As though pulled by a force beyond her control, she glanced up at him, her eyes round and shadowed, her lips so stiff she could barely speak. She ran her tongue over them and said, "I'm sorry...if I disgusted you." Her voice was just above a whisper.

His eyes were dark and probing. "Disgusted me? I don't think anything you could do would disgust me."

Danielle's eyes widened further. Had she heard him correctly? Suddenly another surge of panic rushed through her. She was insane to allow her emotions to get out of control. There was too much at stake. But oh, God, every bone in her body ached for his touch. It had been so long...

Unconsciously she moved. She would shrink away from it all, just as some blossoms fold and close at darkness. It was the only way she could cope....

He sensed her withdrawal. He could not control the harsh breath that ripped through his lungs. "Don't be alarmed," he ground out harshly. "I wasn't going to touch you." He was surprised to find that he was trembling, and cursed himself for allowing her to get under his skin.

Danielle shook her head. "I'm not alarmed," she murmured softly, but the moment was shattered, never to be recaptured.

There was another long silence as Keir abruptly returned to his side of the seat and flipped the ignition switch, gunning the engine into full power. His face once again looked as though it were hacked out of stone.

Danielle did not know how long they traveled before his cool voice penetrated her numbed senses. "Are you up to finishing your story?" he asked without looking in her direction.

"Yes," she replied dully, breathing deeply, wanting to put this horror show behind her as quickly as possible. "I don't remember ever having been so frightened in my life"—*except when I was having your child all alone,* a hyper little voice inside her head whispered—"as I was when I grabbed my purse and raced out of the building only minutes ahead of Elsworth. I jumped in the nearest taxi and told him to take me to an out-of-the-way motel. There I registered under a fake name and bolted myself in the room. I never stopped pacing the floor the entire night. I was terrified."

She paused a brief second and worried her bottom lip with her teeth. "Every time I heard the slightest noise, I just knew it was Elsworth coming after me. The next morning I went straight to the FBI's office without returning to my apartment. I knew if I didn't, my life wouldn't be worth a nickle."

"Did you have any trouble getting them to believe you?"

"I couldn't believe my luck. As you well know, Elsworth was a powerful man. It was a known fact he had several senators in his hip pocket. But after spilling my story, they informed me that Elsworth had been under surveillance for months on suspicion of espionage for selling high technology secrets and endangering the security of the United States and that my secret testimony to the grand jury would put both him and the Russian agent, Letsukov, behind bars for life.

"However, the Russian managed to elude the FBI and suddenly my life was in immediate danger. After that, it was a living hell." For a moment her voice faltered. She pressed her knees together to stop their shaking. But it made the shaking worse. "I decided to cooperate with the FBI and the U.S. Marshal's office, agreeing to disappear with a new identity: a new name, a new job and a new place to live."

Keir knew that he had pushed her to the limit. Pain and despair were written into the delicate lines of her face. "God, Erin..."

"Don't call me that," she hissed, swinging around to face him.

"Old habits die hard," he said harshly.

"Tell me about it," she countered.

"Why didn't you call me?"

She laughed without mirth. "I picked up the phone and was going to do just that when I remembered you were gone."

"Dammit, you could have at least gotten in touch with me later and told me what had happened."

"Why?"

"Goddammit, you know why!"

"It was over between us, remember? You had slammed out of my apartment the night before."

"Only because you all but kicked me out." His jaw was clenched to the breaking point. "God, you have no idea what my life was like when you disappeared without a trace. I was a raving lunatic when you couldn't be found. I couldn't imagine what had happened to you, where you'd gone. And your tracks were so damned well covered. I thought it was because of me. In spite of the hellacious row we'd had, I called you the moment I got back to the States.'' He ignored her whimpered cry and went on, ''I was convinced we could work something out.''

''Why are you telling me this now?'' she cried, turning away from him, her shoulders shaking. ''It's…too late.'' She paused, tugging painful fingers through her hair. ''We…we can never go back,'' she added in a whisper.

Although their relationship had been doomed from the start, it was only during the times she spent locked in his arms that she experienced life at its finest. He had courted her, wooed her and, above all else, had taught her how to love. And when they parted, he had taken a portion of her heart with him.

After a short pause, Keir said, ''When the detective I hired was unsuccessful in tracking you down, I chucked everything and went to work full time for the government as a U.S. Marshal doing undercover work.''

''What do you mean full time?'' she asked, unable to mask her astonishment.

''The times I pulled my disappearing act, as you called it, I was on special assignment for the government. Of course, I wasn't allowed to tell you, but even if I could have, you wouldn't have understood. Would you?''

Oh, God, all that time he had been working for the government. That thought had never even crossed her mind. At times she had thought there might be another woman. And for one crazy moment, she had wondered if he was in trouble with the law. But a spy. Never.

''No,'' she said at last, ''it wouldn't have made any difference. You were determined to do as you pleased no

matter what I said. And you haven't changed. Chasing danger was always more important than I was, anyway."
And avoiding responsibility, she added silently, thinking of the hours of pain and loneliness she had suffered in the hospital bearing his child.

When she had discovered that she was pregnant, she almost went crazy. But never once did she consider doing anything about it. For the first time in her life, she would have someone who truly belonged to her. That was her only salvation during those lonely hours, weeks and months without Keir. Without that hope, she doubted if she could have survived.

"Goddammit, that was my job!"

She placed her hands over her ears. "Stop it!" she shouted. "What good is dredging up the past? All we're doing is making matters worse. I've about had all I can stand. Just leave me alone!"

She made an effort to tune out his fierce expletive, resting her head once more against the seat and closing her eyes, letting the numbness settle over her, feeling like her soul was withering and dying within her.

. If only things could have been different, she agonized silently. If only she hadn't overheard that conversation that had changed her life so completely. If only she had known he had called her that fateful day. If only he wasn't getting married. If only she wasn't harboring the secret of having borne his child. If only...if only...

Chapter 3

The snow was coming down thicker and faster now. It took all of Keir's concentration to keep the car on the slick road. The miles from D.C. to his cabin stretched interminably as his eyes swept across the Blue Ridge Mountains that seemed to hover around him like a brewing storm. This feeling merely added to his restlessness.

Not only were the close confines of the car hard to endure, but coupled with the presence of Er...no, goddammit, he reminded himself brutally, Danielle... His insides were crawling. Her perfume filled his nostrils; he could never have dreamed her scent.

He turned and looked at her. So soft and pale and lovely, he thought. Her soft curls caressed her shoulders like a silk scarf. Suddenly he flinched visibly at the dangerous path his thoughts were taking. His mouth drew into a thin, straight line, and once again his long fingers curled tightly around the steering wheel.

How was it possible to feel nothing but contempt for

her on one hand and want her so badly on the other? he wondered. An irrational anger rose up into his throat.

Like a man possessed and hating himself for what he was feeling, he delved into his shirt pocket and jerked out a cigarette. He was trying hard to shake the nasty habit of smoking, but right now he needed something to occupy his hands. He reached out and ground his index finger against the interior lighter and, after a second, held the tip of it to the cigarette. He pulled on it deeply and hungrily. Clearly still not in control of his emotions, he glanced down at his watch, checked the rearview mirror and then looked back at her. She had not moved. Was she asleep? Or was she feigning sleep in order to mask her own chaotic emotions?

He forced his eyes back on the winding road before impatiently crushing the half-smoked cigarette into the ashtray. God, if he didn't get control of himself, he wouldn't make it through the rest of the day. He hoped that the FBI wouldn't bungle the job this time and those Russian bastards would soon be behind bars and this fiasco over. And what could be a highly volatile and dangerous situation would instead turn out to be boring and routine.

The thought of Danielle's life being threatened in any way made his blood run cold. But he wouldn't think like that. After all, it was his job to see that nothing happened to her. He had to keep a cool and level head and not allow his personal feelings to color his judgment, and remember that his life was no longer intertwined with hers.

But underneath all those reflections and emotions was a layer of fright unlike any he'd ever known before. He kept trying to avoid that fear. He had nothing to be afraid of, he insisted. But he knew better. He was afraid of the truth.

Every bone in his body suddenly felt strained to the limit. Everything seemed to be failing him. His mind could dwell on nothing but her and his dilemma.

Not being able to stop himself, his eyes rested for another brief second on her pale features. Suddenly his mind became a wilderness of memories and impressions and he was frightened by an acute shortness of breath. God help him, but he still could not think of her as Danielle. When he had first met her she had been Erin....

He remembered the party as though it had been yesterday. It had been a bore. It had been like dozens of others he'd attended: too many people crowded into several small rooms, the air stale and clogged with smoke and loud and unruly laughter, a constant ebb and flow of new arrivals, departing couples.

As a rule he didn't allow himself to be ramrodded into attending these affairs, but his father had been insistent. "You need the exposure, son," Raymond McBride had said, "especially if you plan on following in your old man's footsteps and becoming senator of Virginia when I retire. The law firm that's throwing the party handles the paperwork for some of the government's biggest contracts and there will be several important bigwigs present," he'd gone on to say.

At least the food wasn't bad, he thought as he helped himself to an indulgent portion from the buffet and wedged himself into a corner. He hated to admit it, but he was bored, bored listening to the uninspired dialogue and watching a cast that felt obliged to overact. He ate absently, his eyes moving over the faces—some overly animated, others empty—before coming to rest on a woman in the far corner of the room by the door. She stood listening to a tall, earnest-looking man who had her undivided attention, bending slightly toward her, as if for emphasis, as he spoke.

The words were lost to him, the music was far too loud, but he stared, intrigued by the way the woman made a conscientious effort to pay attention. Every so often her eyes left the face of the man and searched space for an exit she might discreetly slip through.

She looked soft, Keir thought. She was of medium height, slim in a black cashmere sweater gown, with a string of pearls falling midway down her breasts. Her hair was a fine silvery color, swept away from her face, flattering and emphasizing her exquisite features. He was intrigued. He shifted closer to get a better look at her.

She could have been drinking any of several concoctions; the liquid in her glass clear. From time to time she took a sip from the glass in her right hand and regarded her companion over the rim. Keir settled more comfortably and continued to study her. On the middle finger of her right hand was a plain gold dome ring. She had on gold loop earrings that dangled when she moved her head. She was perfect, Keir decided, while he continued to eat, without tasting the food. He felt less isolated now, having someone to focus on.

The effects of his meeting with his father earlier in the day still clouded his mood and squeezed at his insides. In his mind he reran the scene with the same effect and disappointments. His father, glowering at him from under bushy gray eyebrows, his green eyes sparkling, but cold, saying, "Why don't you want to go into politics? Don't you think it's about time you settled down and quit hopping the globe and got a real job? Why *can't* you turn your flight service over to your partner and let him run it? Dammit, I want to retire and I want you to take my place in the senate chamber.''

Keir's temper was still boiling on low simmer just thinking about that conversation. It made him furious to think that his father thought he never did an honest day's work in his life. His air-cargo business netted over two million dollars a year, yet that wasn't good enough. And he enjoyed every minute of it, being the free spirit that he was. Working on the inside at a desk or being at the beck and call of another person had never appealed to him. His job allowed him to travel all over the world. But more important, it served as a cover so that he could adequately perform his special assignments for the government. A fancy word for spying, he added with a grim twist to his lips. But he could not tell Raymond McBride about these top secret assignments. He could tell no one.

His thoughts shifting, the sweet, but determined lined face of his mother rose to haunt him. ''I agree with your father—why don't you listen to him? Don't you think you've sown enough wild oats? You're thirty-five. It's time you thought seriously about marrying Natalie and settling down. She'd make a perfect politician's wife, don't you think?''

He shuddered, suddenly finding his thoughts terribly depressing. Why the hell had he given in and come to this party, anyway? But he knew. It was his mother's tears. They got to him every time, and she damn well knew it.

He carelessly thrust aside his empty plate, and when he shifted his gaze, the woman's eyes were on him. Even from a distance he could read the sadness that tinted their startling blue color. She appeared unhappy, out of place. Mildly flustered, he busied himself lighting a cigarette. When he next looked back, her companion had returned.

She was holding a fresh glass of clear liquid, and her eyes were no longer turned in Keir's direction.

She had a magnificent body for a woman of such slight stature. It was impossible to determine her exact age, but he'd guess her to be anywhere from twenty-five to thirty years old. With that settled in his mind, he retrieved his drink from the top of the mantel where he'd left it and went on inspecting her. She had a graceful neck, slender hands, generously curved breasts, narrow waist and hips, lovely slender calves and ankles.

She fascinated him. Who was the man? Her husband? he wondered. She wore no wedding ring, but nowadays that didn't mean anything. His eyes refused to leave her. He'd rarely seen a woman so well put together, so appealingly sexual. Certainly different from Natalie, he thought with a slight twitch to his conscience. God, he knew Natalie loved him and was merely waiting for him to pop the question. But he couldn't do it, not yet. Commitments were not for him. At least not now.

Someone touched him on the arm. He swiveled with a start to see a long-time friend of his father's, Ed Watson, grinning up at him.

"How's it going, eh, Keir?" Watson asked, giving Keir's arm a squeeze.

"Couldn't be better." Keir smiled easily enough, though slightly put off by Watson, especially his political ambitions. He was always playing a role, tried too hard. Fear of becoming this type of person was one of the reasons he, Keir, kept resisting the pull into the political arena. He was too much his own person to be a yes man to anyone. Even to his own father.

"So how's business?" Ed was asking, his mouth stretched into a toothsome grin.

"Same old one and two," Keir answered coolly, waiting impatiently for Watson to move on, on to a more productive prey. To someone who could do him some good.

"How'd your old man manage to get you to this shindig? You look out of place as hell," Watson said, still grinning.

"I am. In fact, I was just thinking about leaving," Keir replied pointedly. And he was. He'd had enough.

Watson patted him on the arm. "Well, in that case, I guess I'll catch you later."

Keir watched in disgust as he crossed the room, bulldozing his way into a small group where he began talking with frenetic animation. Keir took it all in for a moment, then made his way through the crowd, spying the bar, suddenly needing a refill. And after that he planned to go home.

It was the perfume, a rich, heady scent, and then his arm inadvertently pressing into a woman's breasts that alerted him. Raising his eyes, he found he'd collided with the woman in black, who was now only inches away and was staring at him with rounded, suspicious eyes.

"Sorry," he said, trying in vain to put a safe distance between them. "I didn't spill anything on you, did I?"

"No...no, not as far as I can tell," she answered in a mellow tone before dipping her head to glance at the front of her dress. Then she looked up at him as though she still didn't trust him as far as she could throw him.

His pulse suddenly elevated. Her coolness struck a challenging chord within him. The touch-me-not expression in her clear blue eyes was saying "Get lost, Mister." But he was never one to back down from a challenge, especially where a beautiful woman was concerned.

"Good," he said disarmingly, then eased his lips into what he hoped was his most engaging grin. "I'm not always responsible for my actions at these affairs.'' His eyes were twinkling. ''Sometimes a man will do most anything to break the boredom, even go as far as sloshing a drink on a lady's dress.''

She lifted perfectly arched eyebrows. ''And is that what you did?''

Keir laughed, both embarrassed and elated. ''No, actually it was an accident, but I'm awfully glad it happened, nevertheless.''

She wasn't smiling, yet. But there was a faint upturn at the corners of her mouth. A little more and she would have openly grinned. Keir held his breath, completely spellbound by her and by his sudden stroke of luck.

''Why is that?'' she asked, lifting her glass to her mouth. She held it there, waiting for his answer.

Adrenaline pumped through his veins like liquid fire, giving him courage. ''Truthfully?'' he asked, the evening suddenly coming alive. He was beginning to enjoy himself.

''Oh, of course! Be truthful.''

He was aware that she was mocking him in her own cool way, but that did not deter him. ''Because it's given me the golden opportunity to talk to you,'' he said bluntly before pausing, trying to gauge her reaction to his bold statement.

For a moment, she looked disconcerted, then she gave him a begrudging smile. ''At least you're honest.''

Her smile dazzled him. ''Would you like a refill?'' he offered, determined to keep the conversation alive. He had watched her throat as she swallowed, emptying the contents of her glass. Her skin looked like cream-colored satin. He felt slightly dizzy from her perfume; it seemed to be in his mouth and at the back of his throat.

"Please," she said, giving him her glass. "I'm drinking Perrier with a twist of lime."

"Don't go away," he whispered, prepared to force his way through the crowd.

In a moment he pushed his way back through the crowd, drinks in hand, feeling an interior warmth spread pleasantly through his chest and belly. It was an anticipatory rush that had him smiling as he moved toward her, holding out her drink.

"Thank you," she said as she closed her hand around the glass, her eyes on his.

"By the way, I'm Kcir McBride," he said, a boyish tilt to his lips.

She hesitated a moment as though weighing the consequences of telling him her name.

"I'm Erin Richards," she said.

"Glad to know you, Erin Richards." He smiled at her again. Her rounded breasts under the black dress drew his eyes.

"Are you with someone?" he asked.

She shook her head, lifting the glass to her mouth. "No, that was my boss I was talking to a moment ago."

So she'd been aware of him looking at her. That was a good sign, he told himself. "What brings you to this party?"

"Actually, I had no choice," she answered softly. "I work for the firm that's hosting this affair and I was told to be here." She appeared suddenly uncomfortable. "But I hate being closed in with all these people."

"My sentiments exactly. Would you like to leave?" he asked, glancing around.

"Yes," she said simply, although she avoided his eyes.

"Have you eaten?" he asked as they walked down the front path a short time later.

"I'm not hungry. How about you?"

"Me neither. A drink somewhere?" he pressed, hoping that the evening wasn't going to end so soon.

"No, I think not." She seemed uneasy as they reached his Mercedes and he opened the door for her. "I have an early appointment in the morning."

Disappointed, he opened the door on the driver's side and eased himself behind the wheel. Once again her perfume overwhelmed his senses.

"Where to?" he asked, trying to control his rising sense of frustration.

"If...if you'd like, we can go to my place," she began hesitantly. "I have a bottle of wine.... I can open that..."

"Great" he said and cranked up the ignition. He felt as if something had been settled. Without words, without the need for them, his future had just been decided.

"Your apartment is nice. It suits you," he said, looking at her poised just inside the doorway. Suddenly he longed to hold her and kiss her on the mouth. She had a perfectly shaped mouth, and he was intrigued by the way her lips moved when she spoke.

She smiled up at him as she slipped off her jacket and draped it across the back of the nearest chair.

Her every movement attracted him. She had a natural grace and moved well, long thighs shifting smoothly under the black fabric. He could almost feel the warm, sleek inner length of her thighs.

"Coffee?" she asked. "Or wine?"

"How about both?" He smiled and changed the subject. "This is really a super apartment."

"Thanks. I worked long and hard to get it exactly as

I wanted it. Go ahead, look around while I get the coffee started.''

He sank down on the beige sofa and gazed contentedly at the room, taking in the plants, the prints on the walls, the wicker furniture, the shelves filled with books.

She returned a few minutes later and sat down at the far end of the couch, crossed her legs and extended an arm along the back of the cushions.

''The…the coffee's perking,'' she said uneasily, as though she wasn't used to inviting strange men to her apartment.

He liked that about her. In fact he liked everything about her: the reserve she wore like a second skin that he was certain masked the shyness underneath and the underlying sensuality that had first charmed him, then aroused him. It was nothing overt, but all the more powerful because she was unaware of it. She was cut from a different bolt of cloth than the women he was used to.

''Tell me about yourself,'' he demanded softly, hoping to put her at ease.

She shrugged, turning her blue eyes on him. A man could lose himself in those eyes, he thought.

''There's not much to tell.''

He smiled. ''Let me be the judge of that.''

She began fingering the strand of pearls around her neck. ''Well…I grew up in an orphanage just outside the city.'' She paused as though to test his reaction to her confession. When he showed none, she went on. ''After leaving the home, I worked my way through college, finally getting a degree in business law. The Elsworth law firm gave me my first job. That was four years ago; I've been there ever since.'' She smiled. ''See, I told you my life was unexciting. I'm a homebody, but I'm happy.''

"That's all that counts," he said, looking again at her eyes, and then her mouth.

"And you?"

He sighed, shifting his gaze. "My life's as different from yours as night and day."

She appeared surprised. "Oh, how's that?"

"I'm the controlling partner in an air-freight company, which means I travel a great deal." A grin spread slowly over his mouth. "It's in my blood. I can't seem to settle down for very long at a time."

She frowned. "I couldn't handle that. As I said before, I like my home."

"You sound like my mother. If she and my father had their way, I'd be married with two kids and campaigning for the U.S. Senate seat my father hopes to turn over to me in the near future."

Her frown deepened. "Is Raymond McBride your father?"

"The one and the same."

"I'm impressed. He's a powerful man."

Keir laughed. "He'd love to hear you say that."

Then suddenly Keir realized that the mood had changed. She seemed distant, as though she had said too much, been too friendly.

"I'll get the coffee," she said, breaking the short silence.

"Sounds good."

He did not take his eyes off her as she rose and walked out of the room. She moved like liquid flowing from one point to the next. He reached to undo his jacket, again with a sense of matters having been settled. He wanted to spend time with her. He wanted to knock down that wall of reserve. He wanted to hold her slim soft body and listen, with his eyes closed, to her voice gently breaking the darkness. He wanted someone to relax with, to laugh with, to love.

She checked the coffeepot, then stood for a moment, leaning against the cabinet, trying to bring herself under control. She could not. She was too aware of everything about Keir McBride, almost of his very breathing. There was something incredibly magnetic about him.

God, what had possessed her to let him bring her home and then to ask him in for a drink? It was totally out of character for her. She had never done anything so rash in her life. Was it because he was so different from the stuffy lawyers she was used to dating?

Or was it because, when he'd brushed against her on his way out of the room, she'd felt a small shock, almost electric? Or was it simply that she liked the look of him, his craggy features, his boyish smile, the resonant depths of his voice, his probing eyes?

He stared at her until she felt naked.

But she knew that she would be a fool to become involved with this man. She was no match for him. *You're out of your league, lady; he devours women like you. Keep that in mind!*

Anyway, after having learned who he was, who his father was, she knew that she could not allow him to stay. They were from two different worlds. After he drank his coffee she would ask him to leave. Yes, that would be the wisest move on her part, she reassured herself. She was just too lonely, too vulnerable to allow him to stay....

Keir watched her closely as she returned to the room, once again robed with her cool composure.

"How do you take your coffee?" she asked, avoiding his eyes.

"Black, please."

A silence fell between them while she poured the brew into matching china cups and then handed him his, careful not to touch him.

Keir knew that the pleasant moments they had shared were gone. But there was always tomorrow, he thought as he took in the dark shadows coloring the tender skin beneath her eyes. It was time for him to go home. It was late, and hadn't she told him that she had to get up early?

He placed the cup on the table and looked at her softly. "It's time I went home. I didn't mean to keep you up so late."

"That's all right," she murmured, placing her half-full cup down beside his. Then she smiled. "Thank you for bringing me home."

He stood up and she followed suit.

"My pleasure," he said.

They walked to the front door, an awkward silence accenting their footsteps.

At the door he turned and looked down at her. He didn't want to leave. Instead he longed to close his hand gently over her rounded, cashmere-covered breast, to kiss her honeyed lips, to ease her into his arms and feel her breasts cushioning his chest while he tasted and explored the slick interior of her mouth.

She returned his burning gaze with wide, uncertain eyes. "Please...you'd better go."

"I can't," he groaned, "not until I do this."

At first, her lips trembled as he placed his mouth over hers. Then her arms slipped up and around his neck. Involuntarily.

His kiss deepened, easing her mouth open. His heart

was pounding as his tongue slid into her mouth. She tasted so sweet, so good; he thought he'd explode from wanting her. But instinct held him in check.

He tore his mouth away, breathing hard. "When can I see you again?"

"Tomorrow," she whispered.

He eased himself away and kissed her once more on the side of the neck. "Until tomorrow."

Tomorrow was the first day of many days they spent together. They couldn't seem to get enough of one another. Somehow he had managed to persuade his partner to make his runs, thus freeing him to be with her. Keir was completely at her mercy. He wooed her with flowers, phone calls and long intimate dinners at her apartment and his.

But never once during those early days together did he take her to bed. Because she was different, he treated her as such. He wanted to gain her trust, to prove to her that he was not going to make love to her and then, having gotten what he wanted, walk out and leave her. She'd made him aware of feelings inside him that he never thought were there. Up until then a woman was a toy, a means of relief, something to show off, spend his money on. But this woman was different.

So for nearly two weeks, he kept a tight reign on his emotions. Then the night he planned to woo her into his bed, he received the dreaded phone call. He left that same day for South America.

The days dragged by, each seeming longer than the other. He thought that he would never get back to her, and when he finally did, he was unsure of his reception. He was like an eager boy when he knocked on her door. His palms were sweaty and his heart was in his mouth.

The moment the door swung back, they devoured one another with their eyes.

"Darling…" he began huskily.

"Oh, Keir, I thought you'd never get back. I missed you so much," she whispered, tears darkening her eyes.

He crushed her to him, dizzy from relief at having her in his arms. It was pure magic.

"Please…promise me you won't ever leave me again."

He smoothed her silky curls. "Shhh, let's don't talk about that now. We have something much more important to take care of."

He took her hand in his and led her gently into the bedroom where he began slowly to undress her. She looked up at him, her eyes misty and trancelike; he thought he had never seen anything more beautiful.

As his hands sought and found the zipper on her dress, he paused, drawing her closer, and laid his lips against the throbbing sweetness of hers. He could feel her erect nipples through the sweater, the tips wonderful and hard.

"Oh, God…" he murmured hoarsely.

Her hand reached up and spanned his face. "I…I feel the same way," she whispered. "I feel as if my insides are on fire." She rubbed her cheek against his, all of her so remarkably soft and sweet-smelling.

It was almost more than he could bare. Her eyes, on his face, big and soft, sent his heart pounding, threatening to crack his rib cage.

With graceful precision, they undressed one another, fondling the clothing, the snaps, the buttons, as though everything were flesh.

When she was naked, Keir knelt, his hands everywhere on her.

"I…I hope I please you.…"

"Oh, my darling," he groaned, "you do please me. You're perfect."

With his tongue, he traced her curves, the spaces of her body, her breasts, the hollow below them, the line of her hips, her navel, the skin along the inside of her thighs before lowering his head to their parted sweetness.

A whimper, then a low cry escaped her. She felt as though she were lying back in water while constant dizzying waves washed over her again and again.

"Please…" she whimpered, drawing him up to lie beside her.…

"You're beautiful," he said, peering down at her. "And so is your body."

"Take it, it's yours."

Her soft plea filled his mouth as he bent to kiss her. He loved the feel of her lips, the shape and feel of her mouth, the impossible softness of her breasts, which were beautifully formed—small and round with full, pink nipples. He lowered his head to kiss her breast, easing a nipple between his lips, and she shivered, her fingers weaving through his hair.

She closed her eyes and examined the sensations, feeling herself starting to lose control. After a time, she pleaded, "Now…please…now."

Her body was small and tight around him. He whispered, "Easy, easy," as he felt her muscles relaxing in order to bring him in.

"I…think I'm falling in love with you," he murmured, feeling his carefully built defenses and control systems going haywire.

"I know I love you," she said clearly before moans of pleasure claimed them both, rendering them speechless.

He spilled deep inside her when it was time. He heard her answering cry as they rode the crest together.

The months thereafter were perfect. Again Keir postponed as many trips as he could in order to be with her. They spent their time loving, laughing and talking, learning about each other.

It was only after he began fulfilling his obligations to his company and to the government once again that their relationship began to deteriorate.

She could not understand why he was gone for long periods of time, and he could not tell her. She always stopped short of nagging him, though she showed her displeasure by retreating into her cold shell, closing him out. And there were other problems as well. The fact that he had money and a father who was important gnawed at her. She wanted no part of the hoopla associated with politics. She was quite vocal about that.

Then things went from bad to worse. They began to try and change one another. She tried to mold him into the way she wanted him to be, to make him into something he was not. She wanted him to give up his airfreight business and get an eight-to-five job, come home to a tidy brick home with a white picket fence and dote on her. She assumed that his long absences were connected with his freight company. He, on the other hand, wanted her to trust him, to share his life with him the way it was.

Yet, he loved her and couldn't imagine life without her. Finally he was positive that he had her convinced that in spite of their problems, they could make it.

He walked into her apartment one evening after he had been gone for two weeks on a dangerous assignment. He was exhausted, yet hungry for the sight of her, hungry to hold her, to make love to her.

She was standing in front of the window, her back to him as the door closed behind him with a click.

"Darling..."

She swung around, her hair glistening like spun silver in the muted lamplight.

He knew the minute he saw the mutinous expression on her face that something was wrong. He fought off the fatigue along with the sinking feeling in the pit of his stomach.

"Keir...I don't want you to stay." She clamped down on her lip to still its trembling.

"What...what the hell does that mean?" he demanded harshly, taking a step forward. "Don't do this.... God, we only have tonight as it is." He paused, his breathing hoarse and uneven. "I have to leave again in the morning."

"No! I don't want to hear it." She wrapped her arms around herself like a shield. "And don't come near me. I...I can't take living like this any longer," she said, flushing deeply.

"What are you trying to say?" His voice was dangerously low.

"That...that it's over." Her eyes glistened with unshed tears. "I...can't, won't, take second place in your life a moment longer. I'm tired of sharing you with your work, of never knowing where you are, when you'll be home. I...I can't take it anymore. I need security, which is something you obviously know nothing about," she said bitterly.

"Are you telling me you don't love me?" His face changed as he looked at her, disbelief mirrored in his green eyes.

"No…" She hesitated for a moment, searching for the words that would once and for all end the barbed-wire tangle of their lives.

He closed his eyes, his jaw rigid as a spasm of pain flitted across his face. "Erin," he pleaded, his hand coming toward her. "Goddammit, don't do this to us!"

She shrank back against the wall, biting her lip. "Can't you see? All we're doing is hurting one another." She paused and looked at him with her round, haunted eyes. "I'm…I'm sorry, it was a mistake," she whispered.

"A mistake!" Bitter fury made the word sting. "You selfish little bitch!"

She went deathly pale at the insult, but bent her head against the pain his words had inflicted.

"If it's my job…" He was all but begging now. "Maybe we could work something out."

She shook her head, her throat burning. "It's…it isn't just that. It's everything. We're so different…I'm afraid…" Her voice stopped in her throat.

Finally she said quietly. "Sometimes love just isn't enough."

He swore then; violence burned in his voice. "She doesn't want to get involved," he whispered menacingly. "Because it's disturbing. She might have to give up something, make a sacrifice, take a chance. You're a goddamned fake, Erin."

She turned away. "Please, just go…."

"But then why should I waste any more of my life on someone who's afraid to love, to take a chance. May God help you," he said quietly, almost as if he were talking to himself.

He turned and walked out the door and out of her life without another word.

* * *

It was only through his work that he was able to push aside the pain and disillusionment which at times almost made him suicidal. After losing her, he chucked everything—his business, his political ambitions, and went to work full time for the government as a U.S. Marshal. At times he didn't care whether he lived or died.

But with the help of Natalie and pride in his work he was able to put the past behind him. He could almost believe he was truly happy. If not happy, then, at least, content. Until now...

Something alerted him, drew him sharply out of the chasm of his dark thoughts. He glanced quickly at Danielle, taking in the steady rise and fall of her chest.

Still his sharp wit told him that all was not right. He raised his eyes and peered through the rearview mirror. Lines of worry ruled his forehead as a seething oath flew from his lips.

Suddenly he ground down on the gears without mercy. The car lunged forward and around a curve at a daring rate of speed.

Danielle's eyes sprang open as she fought to maintain her balance. "Keir?..." The rest of her sentence was strangled in her throat as she was once more hurled against the door, the tires screeching and whining around another curve.

She stared at him, wild-eyed, fright pounding through her veins. "What's wrong?" she cried.

Ignoring her cry, Keir's arm reached over and frantically released the lock on the glove compartment. Danielle watched in shocked disbelief as he pulled out a gun.

She panicked. "Keir, for God's sake!"

"Be quite and get down." His voice was as cold as steel and just as hard. "We're being followed."

Chapter 4

Danielle did exactly what Keir told her not to do. Danielle's head twirled around instantly and stared wild-eyed out the back window.

"Dammit," Keir hissed, "I told you to get down!"

"But...but...I don't see a car behind us," she stammered, relief beginning to replace the alarm his words has sent shooting through her. Obviously he was mistaken. They virtually had the highway to themselves. Now maybe he would pick up the piece of cold metal that rested like something evil on his thigh, she told herself. She tried not to stare at it, but her eyes were pulled toward it like a magnet. She shivered before slinking down lower in the seat.

"Take my word for it," Keir said tersely, "we haven't lost them. It's two men in a dark blue sedan, and they've been tailing us for no telling how long." And if he had kept his mind on his business, he would have spotted them earlier, an inner voice taunted.

He shifted his gaze back to the rearview mirror, purposefully blocking from mind Danielle's chalky face and bloodless lips.

"Well, for the moment at least, it does appear that we have shaken them, or else they're lying low with something else up their sleeve." His voice held an ominous note, making her more aware than ever of the danger surrounding them.

He reminded her of an animal, sharp-witted and cunning, who seemed to spring to life when he scented danger. In his own way, Keir was as dangerous as the persons following them.

"Who do you think it is? Letsukov?"

"More than likely, or someone he's hired to do his dirty work."

The lump in her throat seemed to grow larger with each passing second. "What...what are we going to do?" she asked, though how she managed to push the words through her swollen throat was anybody's guess.

Keir did not answer for a moment, but she could feel the sudden tension in him.

Then he spoke grimly, "Try to lose them, if at all possible. I know this highway, and the roads that jut off from it, like the back of my hand. There's a short cut through to the other highway a few miles ahead, and if I can keep enough in front of them, I can take that cutoff. Between the approaching darkness and the thickening snow, we're certain to be invisible."

"Whatever you think best," she said, twisting her head to stare out the window. Keir was right, the snow seemed to be growing thicker, but thank goodness it wasn't sticking to the road—yet. That would have brought them to a virtual standstill. She watched as it swirled around the headlights like white rain. Keir was forced to slow down to a mere forty miles per hour, the road becoming slicker and more treacherous by the minute. But even forty was too fast for safety, she thought apprehensively.

The longer they traveled, the more her stomach curled with fear. Surely at this slow rate of speed, the blue car would catch up with them. Suddenly feeling claustrophobic, she cracked the window just enough to allow a stream of air to pass through. It was raw and cold.

There was a kind of unnatural hush over everything. There was no sound except the soft, steady purr of the engine. She was conscious of a strange sense of isolation, as though she and Keir were out of this world and drifting through space together. Time and distance seemed to have receded from them. She couldn't have said whether they had driven five, ten or fifteen miles.

"Keir," she said desperately.

"Yes."

She bit her lip nervously. "How...much farther before we turn off?"

"About another mile," he said, forcing a moderate tone to his voice while trying to ignore her frantic sigh that put a squeeze on his heart.

"Are they behind us now?" she asked, looking neither to the right or left.

"We picked them up again about a half mile back."

"Oh, God, Keir, I'm scared," she whimpered, biting down on her bottom lip to keep it from trembling.

"Tighten your seatbelt," he ordered crisply, slamming the gun under his leg with his right hand. Then suddenly he pushed down on the gears, doing an intricate dance between brake and accelerator. The car went into a violent skid turn. The world seemed to dip and move out of control as the Chevrolet started to slow and the tires completely lost their grip on the road's surface.

Then Keir felt a shudder as the wheels suddenly righted themselves and regained their hold on the highway. He shifted again, building speed, feeling confidence grow with every second.

He had made up his mind in a matter of seconds. He reasoned that it was now or never. He had to lose the car before he reached the cutoff or it would be too late. Damn the blasted snow, he cursed silently as the car slid along the wet, uneven track. But he held his speed, gripping the steering wheel so tightly that every bone in his body felt jammed.

But it paid off. When next he looked in the mirror, the twin beams of the chase car did not seem to have grown any larger.

"Thank God, we've lost them again," Keir said, keeping his eyes glued to the mirror. "Now if our luck will just hold for another five minutes, we'll ditch those bastards once and for all." There was an ugly underside to his tone.

Turning toward him, Danielle searched for his shadowed profile. She was amazed at how calm and composed he was. This was a side of Keir McBride she never knew existed. But then, she reminded herself, he had changed. There was a coldness, a hardness within him that had not been there before.

She had always heard the phrase "nerves of steel"— well, in this case, it fitted Keir to a T. Not once during that harrowing spin in the road when the car threatened to topple over on its side, did he so much as flinch. It appeared that Luke Cassidy was right, she thought. If you were flirting with danger, Keir was the man to have on your side. Why then was that thought so unsettling?

Suddenly Danielle was jarred out of her reverie as Keir

made another sharp turn, the car lurching and bumping over potholes.

"Won't they finally figure out that we've turned off somewhere when they can no longer spot us in front of them?" she asked, trying to ignore the eerie darkness surrounding them while trying to control her rising fear, which refused to be suppressed.

Keir shifted down to a lower gear. "Probably, but there are other roads and cutoffs on both sides of the road. So by the time they turn around and come back to look for us, we'll be long gone."

"What do you think the chances are that they'll find the...cabin?" There was a feverish edge to her voice as she sought frantically for his reassurance.

"Slim," he said, bringing the car to a sudden halt. "And you'll see why when we get there. It's easier to get into Fort Knox than anywhere around the cabin." He turned his head around and began craning his neck, looking back toward the highway.

They sat silently listening for the sound of a passing car.

"What...what do we do now?" Danielle whispered, unable to stand the quiet another moment.

"Pray that the snow still isn't sticking so that we can get through here to the other highway. Hold tight."

He changed gears and nosed the car deeper onto the primitive mountain road. It was a nerve-wracking experience. The ground was painfully uneven, strewn with rocks and dotted with branches from fallen trees. It was impossible to see more than a yard or two beyond the headlights. The wheels lurched and slithered, tilting perilously on a frozen patch of snow, before threatening to stick altogether in a pool of mud and slush. Keir zigzagged this way and that, dodging obstacles before swinging the car around to face back toward the highway.

"Dammit to hell!" he whispered in a rage, slamming his fists into the steering wheel.

"What's...wrong now?" Danielle managed to eke out above the pounding of her heart.

"The god-damned road is closed. This is as far as we can go." He switched off the lights and the engine and added grimly, "And we'll be lucky if we can get out of here without a tow truck."

Her mouth was bone dry. She licked her lips several times before she could speak. "Why did you turn here if you knew—"

"Give me credit for having a little sense," he said savagely. "Of course, I didn't know it was impassable. It's been years since I used it, but I assumed it was still clear."

"As long as they don't find us..." she said shakily.

"Listen!"

"I don't hear anything."

"I do. Listen," he said again.

Then she heard it. She sat motionless and listened to the faint, steady purr of that other car, as it cruised slowly past them. She could feel the raw, cold air now like a heavy, smothering, icy weight pressing down on them, and cutting them off from the warm, real world of lights and firesides and warm, friendly people.

Danielle's ears were stretched to their limit. At the moment, she was aware that the snow, blanketing the sky, lent them their only protection. It blotted out the light. It provided a protective cloak over dark deeds.

She could feel Keir, taut and ready as a coiled spring beside her. He was close to her, yet disturbingly remote. She longed to slide her hand into his, but she knew that to him it would be a meaningless, irritating gesture. He wasn't conscious of the need for human contact. No matter how tightly her hand clung to his, he would still be alone. He wanted it that way.

He was shut away from her in his grim, silent fortress. She could not reach him. She could not tell what he was thinking or feeling.

Danielle could see the lights of the other car, like round, tawny eyes, looming through the falling snow. Her heart thudded, as though it were planning to stop beating at any given moment. The suspense was sapping all her endurance. She felt like a terrified animal, cowering in a thicket, watching the approach of hunters. Only it was a worse fear even than that because it was not for herself alone. She feared for Keir as well.

The lights were upon them. The hum of the engine sounded abnormally loud in her overstrung ears. Then the car passed by…and she heard Keir draw a quick, deep, breath.

He said in an unnaturally light tone, "Well, it seems that for the moment, anyway, we've drawn a reprieve."

Terror struck anew within Danielle. "Do…do you think they will come back?" Visions of Ann's tiny face popped into focus. Suddenly she wondered if she would ever see her daughter again.

"They'll be back, no doubt about it. They'll search every road until they find us."

"What do you suggest we do now?" she asked, no longer attempting to mask the tremor in her voice. This could not be happening, could it? Surely she would wake up and find this was nothing but a bad dream. If someone had told her two days ago that she would be stranded on a lonely mountain road with Keir in the midst of a snowstorm playing chase with two "goons" in a blue car, she would have laughed. Things like that just didn't happen in the "real" world. Did they?

"This area used to be flooded with campers, myself included," he said at last. "This was my old stomping ground when I was a kid. And if I'm not mistaken, there used to be a hulled out place in the side of the mountain, sort of like a cave, not far from here." He paused again and she could almost see his mind clicking. "Even though they will spot the car, I'm hoping they'll decide against tracking us down in this kind of weather."

"Whatever...whatever you think best."

"Follow me, then!" he said abruptly, reaching across her once again to the glove compartment, his gun already secured in its holster. This time, he reached in and lifted out a small flashlight. "We'll use this where we can."

Danielle remained silent, fighting back the hysteria that was beginning to bubble just beneath the surface. In an effort to keep from making a terrible situation worse, she made a big deal of slipping her arms into the sleeves of her all-weather coat and buckling the belt securely around her. She had just pushed her fingers into a pair of leather gloves when she felt rather than saw Keir's eyes on her.

"Do you have anything to put on your head?"

"No...but I'll be all right." Why this idiotic warmth? Because he had shown concern for her?

As though sensing she spoke the truth, he opened the door and slid out into the darkness. "Come on! It's scarcely the right time or season for hide-and-seek, but you might find the alternative even less enjoyable."

Danielle scooted out after him. He put his arm around her in a hard impersonal clasp. The darkness seemed to stalk them and engulf them. It was pitch black. She couldn't see anything. It was a terrible feeling; the soft wet flakes stung her face without her seeing them. She swallowed hard, fighting against a panic-stricken sense of being clawed at by something unknown, something evil.

"Scared?" Keir asked, close to her ears as he switched on the flashlight and she shivered.

"Me? Scared? Of course not, I'm just coming apart at the seams, that's all. But that's minor, wouldn't you say?"

A low throaty chuckle sounded close to her ear. "Oh, I'd say that's normal under the circumstances. When we get out of this mess, I'll disappear and let you have your nervous breakdown in peace." She had guts, he thought. He'd have to give her that.

If the entire situation weren't so bizarre, she would have been tempted to laugh. But his statement, she knew, did what it was intended to do and that was to ease the tension that encompassed them like an air-tight bubble.

Then, impersonally, he nudged her forward. Heads bent against the driving flurries and the wind, they trudged over uneven ground, teeth chattering as the cold invaded their bones.

How long they continued on their nightmare journey through the darkness, Danielle could not have said. She was too intent on keeping her balance as they stumbled over unseen rocks and debris, trying to avoid being scratched and ripped by low overhanging branches while slithering through the crisp, stiff earth. Suddenly it all seemed to her painfully symbolic of what her future life would be. Barren, lonely, empty, no security, just endless suspense and struggles and misgivings. Certainly no love to brighten the darkness.

Keir said nothing to her, nor she to him. They were locked in a vacuum with one another seething with distrust, suspicion, derision and resentment. It was as though all the warmer, more endearing human emotions had been frozen in him. And in her.

The ground was even rougher than it had looked when the car had lurched and bounced over it. She stumbled again and again and would have fallen if Keir hadn't had his arm around her. There was nothing chivalrous or tender in his hold. His touch was fiercely impatient, as though he resented the entire undertaking, which of course he did and made no secret of it.

"Not much farther now," he said, his grip like a vise as he urged her steadily forward.

Her breath was coming in short, sharp, painful gasps by the time they collided with what felt like solid rock. Keir gave a stifled curse, and she winced at the pain which shot up her leg from the unexpected impact.

"Let's stop here," Keir said jerkily. "I think these rocks will provide us with enough cover."

"Are you sure we're far enough away?"

"Yes, as I said before, I don't think they'll venture too far from the road. And they know I'll have a gun."

"Would...would you use it?"

"You're damn right I'd use it." His voice was deadly calm and matter-of-fact.

Danielle shivered, falling against the rock, his words sending a barrage of chills through her that had nothing to do with the weather.

"It's like trying to eliminate bees," he went on, as if he were pursuing his own train of thought, completely oblivious of her. "One can kill them easily enough, but it seems pointless when there are so many of them. The most effective way of exterminating the hives is to kill the queen bee."

Another chill raked Danielle's body.

"Somehow I get the impression you're not referring

to the Russians,'' she said faintly. ''You actually hate and despise me, don't you?''

Keir moved away from her almost violently, as though she had stung him.

''Keep quiet,'' he ordered roughly.

Danielle crouched against the rock, trying to control her ragged breathing. There was a prick of tears at the back of her eyes; tears of impatience and vexation at her own weakness. She could not have gone much farther without a rest, and he must have guessed that. She knew that he thought her weak. Mentally, she might be a match for him, but physically she never would be.

''The car's coming back,'' he said suddenly in a low whisper.

Danielle knelt on her knees and peered over the top of the rocks. She saw the headlights. The car was crawling along now. It stopped. Danielle heard the click of the door. Then two beams of light pierced the darkness, half shrouded by the dense sheets of fat white flakes swirling around them.

It seemed like forever before those moving lights came to rest on the government car, but they reached it eventually. They reflected off the chrome on the hood and bumper first. Then they shone inside the car.

It was a nerve-wracking, eerie ordeal to crouch on the damp ground, against a cold, hard rock, watching those two lights, but unable to see the hands that were directing them. The lights flickered inside, over and around the car, but only a few paces beyond it. Evidently, the prospect of plunging about on a deserted mountain road looking for them did not appeal to the hunters.

Danielle wondered what was going through their minds. Somehow, trying to second-guess them helped to keep her own stark terror at bay. Were they thinking that perhaps they were wasting their time on such a night? Or were they thinking instead that she and Keir were already on their way back to the main road?

The snow, which had been their enemy, was now their friend. They could have been within a few yards of their pursuers and they might have failed to spot them. They must have realized that the light continued to bob up and down on the car for a minute or two longer. Then the lights moved away, back toward the road. In a moment Danielle heard the engine of the other car crank up again.

"Hot damn, we outfoxed them!" Keir said abruptly.

The gleeful satisfaction of his tone jarred Danielle's frayed nerves. It was nothing to him that she was scratched and bruised and exhausted from the mental and physical strain of the last few hours. All he cared about was outwitting those "bastards," as he called them. This was just a dangerous game to him, and he was enjoying playing it to the hilt. *Damn him!*

"You're…you're not the same person, just not human," she said, her voice shaking.

"I'm glad you discovered that. It will save both of us a lot of trouble," he announced calmly. "Can you make it back to the car, or do I have to carry you?"

"I can walk. You don't have to do anything where I'm concerned," she murmured bitterly. As she headed toward the car every bone in her body ached, but she'd go to hell before she asked him for help.

Shortly they reached the car, Keir before her.

He opened the door on the driver's side and peered inside. Then he motioned for Danielle to get in. Without daring to touch him, she skirted around his massive frame and scooted across the seat, far to the other side. But Keir did not follow her. Instead he slammed the door shut and began stalking around the car. In a matter of seconds, he jerked open the door and slid into the seat, bringing another rush of frigid air with him.

"Dammit, they've let the air out of one of the tires and broken out a front headlight," he said explosively. "Damnation!" he repeated as the match he was holding burned down and scorched his fingers. "What a friggin' mess. I wish to God..."

"That you'd never laid eyes on me again," she said, finishing the sentence for him.

"I didn't say that," he countered violently.

"You didn't have to. It's more than obvious," she said sarcastically.

"Don't push..."

"Well, believe me, you don't wish it any more than I do," she cried, swinging her head around, her eyes shooting darts at him through the darkness. Somehow she had managed to make it to the car on fairly steady legs, but now they were trembling convulsively and she sat wallowing in a heightened sense of frustration, doubt and fear. But one thing was certain: She almost hated Keir McBride. How could she have ever felt guilty about keeping Ann a secret from him? This cold, hard, cynical man was not father material. How could he have changed to the point that she hardly recognized him?

"Well, sitting here in the warm car won't get the job done," he said harshly.

"Can I help?" she offered begrudgingly. "Maybe hold the flashlight?"

He hesitated, then said, "Sure?"

"Yes, I'm sure," she said wearily. "It's my fault we're in this godawful mess. The least I can do is help get us out of it."

"Then let's get to it," he clipped, opening the door

and waiting for her to get out, although he was careful not to touch her.

They worked in total silence. Even if they had wanted to converse, it would not have been feasible. The cold robbed them of not only their speech, but their reflexes as well. The flashlight shook violently in spite of Danielle's efforts to hold it steady. And Keir's muffled curses sliced through the air as he strove diligently to change the tire.

Finally, the task accomplished, he dropped the jack and stood up, grabbing the light from Danielle's hand. "Hey...here, steady! Are you feeling faint?" He put his arm around her again roughly. "You'd better get in the car."

Too numb to fight him, Danielle leaned against him while he opened the door and then felt herself gently pushed into the warm interior. He got in after her and quickly slammed the door.

Danielle sat stiff as a rod, her teeth chattering unmercifully. It was as though every bone in her body was knocking against the other.

"Here, lean against me," Keir suggested abruptly, while unbuttoning his top coat and fitting her next to his body's warmth. He then drew his head back to rest on his shoulder. She winced.

"What's the matter? Have you hurt yourself?" he asked.

"I...I jammed...my shoulder against that rock...." she said faintly.

"You didn't hit it hard enough to dislocate it, did you?" His hands trailed impersonally along the sensitive area.

Did she detect concern in his voice? In his touch? No,

of course not, she told herself. She was merely hallucinating. That was all.

Suddenly she felt her coat being slipped from her shoulder as strong, lean fingers reached up and began probing gently. "Is it painful? Here?"

Even through the fabric of her blouse, Danielle could feel the callused points of his fingers. They were firm, yet gentle. It sent familiar, disturbing little tremors through her, reviving sensations she thought were long dead and buried. She should have resisted even his most impersonal of touches. To let it continue would be playing with fire....

Then as suddenly as he had pulled her toward him, he pushed her away, though not roughly.

He lit a match and held it up, cupped in his hand. They stared at each other over the small, clear light. The naked hatred in those deep green eyes of his was like the thrust of a sword. She might have shrunk from it, but beneath it, submerged in those deep waters, she glimpsed other emotions...fear...and desire.

"You're lovely as ever!" he whispered in a strange, harsh tone. "And just as dangerous."

"Not dangerous to you, Keir, not anymore," she taunted.

"No. You're right. Not to *me*. I don't believe in rehashing the past."

"Do you believe in anything?"

"Oh, yes, I believe in the devil. And I believe in justice...in retribution," he whispered bitterly.

"Nemesis? I don't know why I find it strange that you'd serve that god. But who are you to deal out retribution?"

"What else is there?"

She grimaced painfully. "You could try having mercy. We all need that, including yourself."

"I've never asked for it and I don't believe in it. Mercy? That's another word for weakness."

"And heaven forbid if you should succumb to that like us other mortals."

"You more than anyone else should know the reason for that."

He lit another cigarette. Over the flare of the match, his eyes shone with an unnatural, gleaming brilliance. His lips curled upward into a mocking, derisive smile.

Blocking out the wrenching pain of her sudden movement, Danielle shoved herself against the door on the passenger side, his words having sent a dreadful ice-cold shock through her.

She kept her eyes averted as he began inching the car slowly forward on the snow-riddled ground. Her head throbbed, her shoulder ached and her eyes felt as though someone had thrown a handful of sand in them. Oh, God, she thought, if only she were home with Ann, soaking in a tub of gloriously hot water....

"You might as well get some sleep," Keir said at length. "It'll more than likely be dawn now before we reach the cabin, provided we don't run into any more trouble, that is."

Danielle did not bother to answer him. As far as she was concerned, there was nothing left to be said. The battle lines had been drawn. Now all that was left was to choose the weapon, and no doubt that would soon follow. And he told her to sleep. Sleep. How could she even think about sleep with danger lurking around every corner and her mind a seething cauldron of emotions. But she soon found that her battered body had other ideas.

Her eyelids began to droop as the warmth enveloped her like a cocoon....

Keir knew when she had fallen asleep. He was glad. No point in both of them having to suffer a sleepless night. He was used to wasting as little time in sleep as possible; but this was one time when he wished he could sleep, emptying his mind of all chaotic thoughts and responsibilities. But this night he was not going to have even the few hours of rest he required. His mind raced; he couldn't slow it down.

He shifted his weight in the seat and, lifting one hand off the steering wheel, massaged the tight muscles at the base of his neck. Then he put it back quickly, since it was extremely rough going on the slick path, made even more hazardous by only one headlight. But so far so good, he thought, seeing the main road coming into view.

Removing the same hand from the wheel again, he reached for his shoulder holster and slowly drew out his revolver. He gave it its favorite place on his thigh as he nosed the car cautiously into the clearing. Closing his hand around the cold object, he looked right and then left before making the turn onto the highway. His stomach tied in knots, he eased the car slowly down the deserted stretch of concrete, his ears alert to the slightest unusual sound, his eyes searching through the inky blackness for any signs of company.

Satisfied that the ''goons'' had indeed abandoned their hunt, he slowly eased his foot down on the accelerator. But still he was forced to drive at a snail's pace. The road was a sloshy mess, and any sudden or wrong move could send them hurling down a ravine or into the side of a mountain.

He chanced a quick glance at Danielle. She was sleeping like a baby. Feeling the knot tighten in his stomach, he quickly forced his eyes back to the road.

But he could not lay his thoughts to rest. He began to analyze the situation, turning in his mind, looking at it from every angle. Were they truly out of danger? Was the cabin as impenetrable as he thought?

He didn't care about himself. He was not particularly impressed with danger. Other people had tried to best him in that field and had lived—briefly, in two cases—to regret it.

If he were honest with himself, he would have to admit that the single cause of his fear was Danielle—God, would he ever get used to calling her that?—worry that the Russians would get their hands on her.

Well, he would have to stick with her like a second skin. But that was going to be sheer punishment. As it was, he had to fight like hell to keep a torrent of images at bay: the haunting smell of her perfume, the feel of her naked body against his, the shape and texture of her breasts and belly and hips and buttocks....

He ground his teeth together to stifle the gut-wrenching cry of agony from passing through his lips. He rubbed out his cigarette in the ashtray and adjusted his seat back. He didn't look at Danielle again; he stared straight ahead....

Danielle jumped suddenly, as though an alarm had gone off in her brain. She sat up in the seat as if thrust forward by a spring, only to moan as a searing pain shot through her shoulder.

It took her a moment to realize where she was. But when she turned and saw Keir's haggard face and day's growth of beard, the horror of the past night returned to her.

"Feeling any better?" he asked, thinking she had never looked lovelier, all disheveled and sleepy-eyed.

She avoided his gaze as she licked parched lips. "A little stiff, but otherwise fine."

"And the shoulder?"

"It...smarts only when I move suddenly," she said, taking in the lines of strain around his eyes and mouth. *If only... Stop it! Don't think like that. Don't let your guard down.*

"It's probably just a deep bruise." His eyes were once more on the road.

"I...I take it there was no more trouble," she said hesitantly.

"So far, so good. I hope we've seen the last of our friends."

"Are we nearly to the cabin?" she asked, having drawn the conclusion they were no longer on a main road.

"Approximately two more turns and we'll be there." Danielle saw the muscle in his jaw suddenly clench before he added, "And from the way things are looking, we'll be stuck with each other a lot longer than either of us will like."

Danielle's heart sank to her toes, and what little color had returned to her face quickly vanished. Even as she told herself that he was toying with her, trying to upset her, she could not shake the sense of dread his words evoked.

Somehow she had to dredge up the strength to lay the painful memories of yesterday aside and take one day at a time.

Somehow.

Chapter 5

Even with her emotions stretched to their limit, Danielle could not help but be impressed by the scene before her.

For a moment everything was forgotten: anger, frustration, fear, as her eyes surveyed her secret hideaway. It reminded her of a painting on a postcard, or better still, a magical fairyland come to life off the pages of a book. She was enchanted.

The house itself was nestled in the side of a mountain, tall pines flocked with snow surrounding it. Suddenly it dawned on her anew just how isolated they were from civilization and how totally dependent on Keir she was.

There was not a sound in the white wilderness. It belonged exclusively to them and any wild animals that were lucky enough to survive. Danielle sat transfixed and watched as the elusive dawn brightened the sky.

Would she truly be safe here, locked in this winter wonderland? She paused in her thoughts as her eyes rose and swept across the wide expanse of mountains surrounding them like crystal clouds. Or were there more unseen dangers lurking amongst all that beauty? She shivered.

"Might as well get out and get acquainted with your home away from home," Keir said flatly. "We're here now, and there's not a damn thing either one of us can do about it."

The hard, distant tone of his voice brought her sharply back to reality. The air hung heavy with the chill of the passionless tone of the few words he'd spoken. She tried to ignore the cold sweat of anxiety that caused her hands to shake, hampering her from opening the door. After several attempts, she finally managed to jerk the handle upright. But before she got out, she turned toward Keir.

"Well, at least the house is large enough so that we won't have to intrude on one another's privacy," she said tightly before planting her feet firmly in the snow and slamming the door behind her. It sounded like a bullet bouncing off its target in the early morning silence.

She waited for Keir at the door, cradling her arm against her side, easing the pressure on her throbbing shoulder. Her vulnerable mouth was twisted in pain, tears dangerously close.

Keir watched the play of emotions across her finely drawn features as he dropped the two carry-all bags at his feet and inserted the key in the lock of the heavy wooden door.

"I'll take a look at that shoulder after we've gotten cleaned up and put something to eat in our stomachs."

She refused to look at him. "Why, I wouldn't dream of putting you to all that trouble," she said, ice dripping from her voice. "Anyway, I don't need your help, thank you."

Keir's brow lowered to shadow his eyes. "I wouldn't

be too sure of that—Danielle,'' he said, his voice filled
with contempt and a deadly sneer that caused a chill to
feather up her spine. ''Remember, you're at my mercy.
I'd keep that in mind if I were you.'' Suddenly he twisted
the doorknob and flung the door open. Then with a mocking bow and a sweeping gesture, he indicated that she
should precede him through the door.

Clutching her purse as though it were a lifeline, she
took a hesitant step into the heavenly warmth, the heat
lapping over her like waves. She paused inside the front
entrance and gazed around, scrutinizing everything in one
detailed sweep: a formal foyer leading into one spacious
family room beautifully designed in cedar and aspen paneling with a loft balcony overlooking it; a great moss rock
fireplace separating the family room from the dining
room and adjacent to that two full-length sliding glass
doors with access to an outdoor deck. The formal dining
room also had a loft and moss rock fireplace. Both rooms
had high, sloping cathedral ceilings.

Danielle knew immediately that this was no ordinary
cabin; this was a luxurious trilevel mountain retreat
aimed to please, with every conceivable comfort in mind.
And it belonged to Keir's family. Was this where he had
planned to spend his honeymoon? she wondered, sudden
nausea sending nasty tingles through her body.

''Let me check the phone, then I'll show you to your
room,'' he said brusquely, carelessly dumping his coat
on the nearest table and lifting the receiver of the phone
that occupied a portion of the table. After a moment, he
slammed it down, his face dark as a thundercloud. ''The
damned thing's dead.''

She stared at him horrified. ''You...you mean we're
completely cut off from everything?'' she asked, sick
with fear at not being able to check on Ann.

"That's right, he said abruptly, then added, "Your room is this way."

They moved down the foyer together and up a short flight of stairs, so close they touched as they walked.

"Who were you talking to on the phone in Cassidy's office?" he asked suddenly. They had come to a halt in front of a door which Danielle could only assume led to her bedroom. "Was it your lover?"

He said "lover" as if it were a contagious disease that she might have contacted. "That's none of your business," she snapped as she moved quickly, fearing his touch, his probing.

His breath, as he leaned his face into hers, was as cold and impersonal as his eyes. "I wouldn't be too sure of that, if I were you. Everything about you is my business. Especially if you value your beautiful skin, that is," he goaded in that same deadly tone.

Again she flinched, backing into the door.

"And damn you, stop looking at me as if you thought I was going to pounce on you. I don't like this setup any more than you do."

"I find that hard to believe," she taunted, pivoting on her heels and walking into the room. She paused in the middle, holding her breath, praying that Keir would not follow. She had decided long ago that he was enjoying this. He was being handed on a silver platter the chance to punish her and seek his revenge. And he was not about to let the opportunity pass. But she didn't know how much longer she could hold out against his jabbing barbs. As it was, her legs were barely supporting her.

He stalked into the room behind her. "What do you find hard to believe?" he asked in menacing undertones.

The blood pounded in her head. For heaven's sake why

didn't he just go away and leave her alone? She kept her back turned while the silence reached a screaming pitch.

"Answer me, damn you!"

She held her silence. He was determined to pick a fight with her, to take his frustrations out on her, but she was tired of being his whipping post. Her back conveyed exactly that as she walked farther into the room, placing considerable distance between them.

The room was lovely, decorated in several shades of green with its own bathroom. Out of the corner of her eye, she stared at the bathroom longingly, wanting nothing more than to soak her weary limbs, especially her shoulder, in the shower and try to pretend none of this was happening, that she was home cuddling Ann in her arms, reading her a book or telling her a story.

She felt his breath on her neck. A bolt of terror struck her mind, like lightning splitting the sky.

"I'm not leaving until you answer me!"

She swung around to face him, now goaded into retaliating. "Get out!" she hissed.

"No!" He grabbed her arm, stared at her, his face contorted with anger, contempt. His eyes were piercing, his mouth a harsh line, his nostrils flaring.

"You're hurting me," she cried. "Stop it." She was shivering uncontrollably.

Her cries fell on deaf ears. He neither stepped back nor relieved the pressure on her arm.

"So you're finding it hard to believe that I'm not panting to have another taste of your delectable body?" he bit out between teeth which snapped like a steel trap. The strong brown hands moved up to encircle her throat as if he would like nothing better than to throttle her. The hard masculine face grew darker by the minute. This was the second time today she had seen that look on his face.

Danielle twisted her head, jerking herself free. "That's not what I meant and you know it," she flung at him savagely, her eyes blazing with fury as her anger soared.

"Are you sure about that?" His question was an unsteady whisper as his mouth began to travel along her uplifted neck toward her chin, while a hand slid under her blouse, across the silky underwear, searching, finding a warm breast, filling his hand with its thrusting fullness. She went rigid against him, her throat flung tautly back to avoid his kiss, deeply aware that he was seeking her lips.

"No!" She groaned. "Get your hands off me."

"You're a little liar. You want it and you know it."

In a split second it happened. It was instinctive; there was no thought behind it or she would not have dared to hit him. But her hand came out and struck him hard across the face.

"How dare you talk to me like that!" she spat. And because he moved in closer: "Don't you dare touch me again. I don't want you near me.... Go away."

Keir might have let it end there if she had said something else. He would have endured her physical abuse, let her slap his face because she wouldn't have been the kind of woman she was if she had accepted his last insult. But it was the cry of revulsion that gnashed at his nerves and sent his temper soaring.

He had been forced into a situation that he was not at all certain he was capable of handling. He had been pulled off a much-needed vacation; he'd had to postpone his wedding. For what? To protect the woman who had told him once that his love wasn't enough.

Everything was going wrong. His carefully laid plans to remain aloof, to keep his distance, had broken down. Goddammit, she was like poison within him. She remained hostile and defiant, forbidding him to put his hands on her. Her words, *Don't you dare touch me,* continued to haunt him. All the way from Washington, throughout their long ordeal, with inhaling her scent and the feel of her body against his, he had wanted to do just that.

Suddenly he clamped his hand around her waist and drew her against the rock hardness of his chest. He bent her against his braced body and forced her head back. Her mouth fell open at the surprise and pain of his hold. She moaned in protest as his mouth came down on hers, hungrily, forcing her trembling lips apart, demanding surrender.

"Dear God," he groaned against her lips. Lust for her was like a grenade in his belly. Anything at all would cause the pin to be pulled. He was remembering how it felt to have her spread under him, to hear her moan, crazy to have him.

She refused to surrender at once; she moaned and writhed and made little sounds under his mouth, but then she suddenly went limp, her lips softening in unwilling response. It was as if she were suspended, as if time had ceased to exist. She had the feeling that she was swimming in a waterway above her head and was slowly being overcome. Nothing was real but the pressure of his body against hers; her arms were lax as they hung down, free and useless; his fingers were teasing a nipple to life while he continued the assault on her unprotected mouth.

The sensations of sight and sound escaped her. She clung to his arms, rising and falling with the rhythm of his kisses, feeling the vestige of control slipping as her arms moved upward, as if they belonged to someone else, and slid around his neck. *No!* she thought wildly. She had to stop him. Stop herself. *Think of Ann!*

But she was lost in the feeling of his warm, muscular chest under her palms. Through the thin material of his shirt the heat of his body communicated itself to her skin, and a pulsating sweetness began to throb deep inside her, a feeling that had lain dormant for three long years. Her stomach and her mouth went dry as his hands became unbreakable chains against her hips.

"Please," she whimpered before his tongue swam back into her mouth.

She was drowning. No amount of self-analysis could pry her arms from around his neck. There was never a time in the past when she had lost herself as she was lost now. She had no defense against the fire his tongue was stroking inside her mouth.

It was Keir who stopped. He pushed her away from him. Already, without conscious intent, they had both moved near the bed. Another moment and he would have pulled her down on it. He was pale, scrubbing the back of his hand across his mouth bitterly, his expression more forbidding than ever.

Danielle looked up at him, her face colorless. Tears had seeped under her lids and run down her cheeks. Recoiling in shock, she stared at him in utter disbelief.

"You're just the same!" he bit out harshly. "You haven't changed! You still don't care who you hurt. But now we know where we stand; I can take you any time I like. And I like, so be careful. Be very careful."

She shrank away, shivering convulsively, her hands held in front of her like a shield. "I didn't ask you to touch me," she countered sharply. Her emotions were churning with such a mixture of anger and pain from his unexpected verbal thrust and manhandling that she didn't pause to question why Keir's words and actions still had the power to create deep and lasting wounds within her.

Suddenly the room began to spin in front of Danielle's eyes; she struggled for her next breath.

Keir stood totally still, watching her. He saw her face turn deathly white. "I didn't mean to hurt you," he said slowly. "But dammit you pushed me too far." He paused, making a helpless gesture, his jaw tightening in angry frustration before he pushed himself away from her and headed toward the door.

He stopped in the doorway and turned around. Danielle sat exactly where he had left her, trembling violently.

"I'll get you something to drink. What would you like?"

"Hot...tea." She did not recognize her own trembling voice. "If you have any, that is." She watched him walk out the door, heard him moving around in the kitchen, listened to the noise of glasses and cups and his heavy tread as he returned. *I should move from here,* she told herself. *I should get away from the bedroom, get off the bed. If he touches me again...*

"Here, drink this," Keir said. He put the half-filled cup of tea in her hand and watched while she sipped it cautiously. "I'll leave you now and let you get some sleep."

She gazed up at him, the hot liquid dulling her exhaustion. "Why...why did you stop? Why did you let me go?"

"You're a job I have to do, nothing more," he said grimly. "But I wanted to show you that I'm not the same gullible person I was three years ago. Now you know. You needn't be afraid. I won't touch you again."

"You made me hit you," Danielle whispered dully as though she still couldn't believe it herself. "I've...I've never struck anyone in anger like that, ever." After seeing him again, being thrown together in a dangerous situation from which they had narrowly escaped, she had expected to experience a painful nostalgia. But nothing she had imagined had prepared her for this instant emotional reaction whenever he simply got near her. When he had touched her, seared her lips with his, her flesh had melted beneath his fingers exactly as it had years before.

As he watched her carefully, she could feel the insistent probing of his eyes even though she averted her face. She was past caring now. All her energy was going into fighting her own rising desire. And she hated herself for this weakness of the flesh.

It was worse, she thought. His absence had managed to feed the flame of passion for him. But she knew that she could not keep on like this indefinitely. If she did, she would have to be taken out of here in a straightjacket.

She had to get control of herself, put things in their right perspective. She had to look at Keir as her protector, nothing more, and stay out of his way, praying that he would keep his promise not to touch her. And through it all, she must cling to thoughts of her child, her home, her work. To hell with Keir McBride.

His heavy sigh brought her back to reality. She stared into his deep, brooding face. Again, she noticed how tired he looked, the grooves around his mouth and eyes taking on a bluish tint.

"I'm going to scramble eggs and fix toast," he said slowly, wondering how they were going to survive in this impossible situation, yet knowing they had no choice. Something had to give. "I'll call you when it's ready," he added, making a small effort to ease the smothering tension.

Danielle stared down at her hands. The thought of

food, of sitting down at the table with him, was intolerable.

She stood up. "You go ahead. I...I couldn't eat a thing."

"For God's sake, Danielle, be reasonable!" Keir cupped the back of his neck with his hands as though it ached. "You need to eat. I'm not telling you, or commanding you, but *asking* you to come and eat breakfast and then let me take a look at that shoulder."

Danielle stood her ground. "No thanks, on both accounts. I'm not hungry and..." Her voice trailed off as she turned aside, unable to bear the penetration of those green eyes, unknowingly revealing to him the vulnerable nape of her neck.

"You have to eat," Keir pressed harshly. Then more huskily, "God, Danielle, you're nothing but skin and bones. How long has it been since you've had a decent meal?"

How could she tell him that she'd never gained her weight back after Ann was born. There had always been so much to do...the responsibility had been so awesome....

"Please...will you just go away and leave me alone. I...I'm tired. All I want to do is go to bed. I want to be left alone."

"Goddammit, you'd try the patience of a saint!" he exploded, his conciliatory gesture forgotten as he stalked out of the room, slamming the door behind him.

The moment she was alone, she immediately began to shed her clothes, gritting her teeth against the pain in her shoulder.

Making her way into the bathroom, she opened the door and stepped inside the shower. Time was of no consequence as she let the water—as hot as she could stand

Everything But Time

it—pound her sore, aching body. But her thoughts were not so easily managed. She couldn't stop thinking.... *No!* she whispered silently, defiantly, as if she were pushing the horror of the last few moments back with both hands.

It did no good. The old weight of despair kept pressing down on her. The rigid anger contorting Keir's face when he had grabbed her swam before her eyes. Did he hate her that much? It was obvious that he did. And he blamed her for everything. But why? she asked herself. Wasn't it obvious that he had come through their affair and parting unscratched? He was doing what he wanted to do: roaming the globe, flirting with danger, dodging responsibilities.

She shuddered in spite of the heat penetrating her limbs. She was still finding it hard to believe that Keir had been an undercover agent for the government before surfacing and becoming a U.S. Marshal. And she hadn't known it. How could she have been so blind?

Would he be willing to change now, especially with a wife in the offing? The muscles in her stomach contracted. She would not think of things like that. But it was excruciatingly difficult not to do so with Keir being so close, touchable and yet untouchable, so distant. What was the woman he was going to marry like? Suitable? Acceptable for him? Was she beautiful? How long had he known her? Did he touch her?...

Suddenly she leaned over and turned off the shower, unable to stand any more of this inner prying. It was over. What she and Keir had shared was over. She made herself say it aloud, "Over."

What she needed now was sleep. She walked out of the bathroom, nothing but a towel wrapped around her, and crossed to the bed. She pulled back the covers and very gingerly lowered her body onto the clean-smelling sheets.

Yesterday and the hellish night that followed began to recede, grew confused, grew dim, as the silence lulled her eyes closed....

She slept.

When Keir stalked out of Danielle's room, he headed straight for the kitchen, determined to carry out his plan. He began opening cabinets, slinging pots and pans everywhere, searching for a skillet in which to cook the eggs. By the time he had prepared himself a full-course meal—two eggs, bacon, toast—it no longer looked the least bit appetizing to him. But he forced himself to eat, knowing he needed the strength. It tasted like sawdust in his mouth. If only Danielle were sitting with him. Danielle. *Dammit man, forget her!* Shoving the food aside, he jumped up and crossed to the window.

He was furious with himself for what he'd done to her; it was a bad sign, a sign that he was not in command of himself. The whole damn thing was crazy, he thought as he began to pace back and forth in front of the window, swearing. He would sure as hell stick to his promise not to touch her again., That was the important thing. He'd keep his distance, distance from her scent and the accidental contact in case it ignited that sexual spark again. As it was, he'd already committed the unpardonable sin, losing control. And he had a woman, a woman who loved him and was waiting to marry him. To keep his sanity, he needed to cling to that and keep clear of all involvements.

Danielle was still upset over what had happened a few days ago. So much so that she had stayed in her room as much as possible. But nothing helped. During the day she could hear Keir moving about in the adjoining bedroom or taking a shower, and then at night the creak of the mattress as he turned. Even when he slept she was aware of him.

They had tried to avoid one another when possible, give the other breathing room. During the times they had eaten together there had been a silence between them which became a strain. And he moved very carefully so as not to touch her, even by accident, when he got up to clear the table. The mounting tension between them coupled with her worry about Ann was driving her crazy.

Now, examining herself in the mirror, the luxurious bedroom reflected behind her, it was not *her* face she saw. Her armor had been penetrated. He still had the power to make her feel weak all over, to make her lose control, dangerous to the sleeping emotions which only he could arouse. That had not changed. For an insane moment an intense longing to go to him, to lean on his strength overcame her, and then she forced herself to be sensible.

"What you need is some fresh air," she said aloud, slipping into a shirt and green wool sweater with a pair of jeans, leaving her throat to rise smoothly from the open neckline. Her hair fell in silky curls to her shoulders and the only makeup she used was a faint eye-shadow and a colorless gloss for her lips. She was glad that she was able to move her shoulder now with only the slightest twinge of discomfort.

When she walked downstairs, he was sitting at the table drinking a cup of coffee.

Danielle hesitated, not expecting him still to be in the house. On previous mornings, by the time she came downstairs he had eaten his breakfast and had gone outside to do odd chores around the place. Splitting firewood took up hours of his time.

"Good morning," Keir said, standing up and reaching for an empty cup.

"Good morning." The words came in a rushed gasp as she sensed immediately that he appeared different this morning, less tense, less apprehensive, and he looked absolutely gorgeous. He was slim-hipped as ever, obvious in a pair of tight-fitting faded jeans. A rough flannel shirt clung to the muscles of his broad chest and shoulders.

"The coffee's strong enough to walk—hope you can drink it," he said, handing her a cup of the steaming liquid. She looked tired, he thought, with shadows under the eyes. But nothing could take away from the smoothness of that incredible complexion. The bright green she wore suited her exactly.

"I'm...I'm sure it's fine." She smiled tentatively as she took the cup from him, feeling a twinge of panic when their fingers touched. Sitting down across from him, she still did not know what to make of his sudden change in attitude. She was uneasy.

"Do you like fish?" he asked suddenly, easing back in his chair. He found himself talking quite naturally. He was determined to do away with the hostility that crackled like an electric current between them. He could afford to be generous now because she hadn't won a victory over him. The victory was his, won in that brief, explosive struggle.

Surprise robbed Danielle of her voice.

He gave her an anxious smile. "Well?"

A warm weakness invaded her body as his eyes fixed on her face for a breathless moment. Was he serious?

"Yes, I'm serious," he said, grinning, taking joy in being able to read her mind.

She flushed. "Well, in that case, the answer is yes."

"What would you say to this deal, then—if I catch them, will you cook them?"

Her eyes widened. "Of course, but where?..."

"In the stream at the back of the house," he said, finishing her sentence for her.

"You mean, that stream has fish big enough to eat?"

"Mmmm." He licked his lips. "You bet. Trout that will melt in your mouth."

"You're putting me on."

Keir's eyes became soft. "You really are a city girl, aren't you?"

"I won't argue that point," she murmured, giving him a tremulous smile that camouflaged her inner turmoil.

"I'll show you. How long will it take you to get ready?"

Danielle stood up. "I'm ready now except for getting my coat and hat." Through the soft fabric of her long-sleeved shirt he could see the outline of her nipples. It was like opening a brown paper bag to find that it contained something one always wanted and hadn't expected to receive, especially not in a brown paper bag.

Keir got up suddenly and walked over to the cabinet and turned his back.

"I'll find the thermos while you get your paraphernalia." He noticed that his hand shook as he reached for the coffeepot; a smothered expletive drowned out her exit.

"I decided the weather was too perfect not to take advantage of it," Keir said. "If the fish feel the same way, everything will indeed be perfect."

They were trudging through the snow, dressed warmly—at least Danielle was. She had on her newly purchased fleece-lined coat, gloves, boots and a crocheted cap, sitting at a jaunty angle atop her head.

Keir, acting as though the twenty-degree temperature did not phase him, wore only a lined jacket over his long-sleeved shirt.

Color was in Danielle's cheeks and she smiled, though it failed to reach her eyes. "I felt the same way when I got up this morning…about the weather, I mean," she said breathlessly, trying to match Keir's long strides.

She could see the mountain stream that was approximately fifty feet from the back of the house. Although it looked like a stream to Danielle, the closer they got to it, the more it sounded like a river as it crashed over the rocks.

Looking around her, she was again reminded of the postcard beauty. The trees dotting the mountainside were still bowed with snow, but the sun, dancing shadows on their white covering, would make any artist eager to grab his brush. Their shimmering loveliness was unsurpassed.

"I'll build a fire so you won't freeze while I'm reeling in our dinner," Keir was saying as they reached their destination, carelessly dumping his fishing gear, a thick blanket and a bucket filled with chips of pine and wood on the white crunchy ground. For a moment he was quiet, his eyes scanning the area around them as though he were looking, watching, for an unknown presence. But when he turned toward Danielle his face was clear.

He was close to her now. She could feel his breath as it warmed her cold skin. She stepped back, ostensibly to stare at the gushing water, but determined to put distance between herself and his overwhelming male magnetism.

"You'd better quit bragging and get to work," she said saucily, feeling safe now that he was no longer within touching distance.

He chuckled. "Bragging, huh! Well, we'll see about that. You just watch an old pro."

In record time, he cleared a place in the snow, built a small but adequate fire and saw her comfortably seated on the blanket. He then grabbed his rod, already rigged, and made his way to the edge of the bank.

The pool lay in deep shadow. Water was swirling here and there on the smooth, dark surface, widening into almost perfect circles . Danielle watched in awe as he made his first cast and came up with a wiggling black speckled fish on the end of the line.

He whirled around and laughed, his eyes sparkling. "What do you think now? Still skeptical?"

For a moment, he reminded her of the Keir of long ago. The Keir she had fallen so desperately in love with. The fierce contraction in her throat made it nearly impossible to speak. "It...it looks easy enough."

"It is," he quipped. "Easy as falling off a log."

She took her cap off and shook her curls away from her face. "Huh, that's what I'm afraid of."

Keir stared at her for a second, thinking that her hair with the sun shining on it looked like a basket of gold filigree. "After I catch our dinner, would you like to try it?" His voice was hoarse and uneven.

Answering nervousness pressed the air from her lungs. "I...I might."

He couldn't draw his eyes away from her, even though he felt as if he were riding in a roller coaster in total blackness, unable to determine what lay before him, unable to prepare himself for the sharp curves, the paralyzing drops, the steep climbs. Suddenly he swung around and for the next twenty minutes concentrated on reeling in the fish.

Danielle watched and said nothing.

Finally the bucket was filled to the brim with fish. He laid down his rod and eased his gangly frame down beside her on the blanket. Neither spoke as he reached for the thermos and, using the lid, poured it full of coffee. A silence hung heavy in the air, an intimate silence that neither was prepared for, but neither could deny.

He watched her with a smoldering gaze that shattered her already-shaken composure.

"Danielle." He did not move, but she felt suddenly as if he had touched her. He seemed terribly close. The way he said her name magnified the tension between them. "I want to know, has there been anyone since…me?" There was an odd timbre to his voice.

Her face was a study of misery as she mulled over his question and how to answer it. *Careful, Danielle.* He was probing again—delicately, but probing nonetheless. Perhaps all he wanted was a simple answer, but things were never that easy. She was afraid of him, afraid of herself. She wanted to go—to escape the disturbing note in his voice, the handsome face so achingly close, the arm that slightly brushed hers. Buying time, she leaned away from him and made a pretense of unbuttoning her coat to expose herself to the warmth of the fire.

"Of course, there've been other men," she whispered at last. *But not the way you mean.* She felt a sudden urge to cry.

His mouth tightened. "I see."

Oh, but you don't see. You don't see that I lied to you, that I couldn't stand the thought of another man's hands on my body, nor the thought of another man being a father to your child. She stared blindly at the ground, fighting for control.

"Danielle," he repeated softly.

She felt like she was suspended in a vacuum as she stared up at him.

Red-hot desire erupted between them with a force that stunned them into complete immobility.

Then with a moan reminiscent of a wounded animal, Keir, clenching his eyes shut, rolled over on his back, his body rigid with tension. "Oh, God, what did we do to deserve such hell?"

Silent agony.

She swallowed, trying to ease the painful constriction in her throat. "Please...don't. What...what good does it do...to keep rehashing old pain?" Tears flooded her eyes, and she could only gulp her words. "You're... you're getting married...."

"God! Danielle, not now."

"It's the truth, isn't it?" Her voice was a tormented whisper.

"Yes," he clipped tersely, unable to hide the irritation in his voice. Dammit, he didn't want to talk about Natalie. He didn't want to think about Natalie. Couldn't think about her, not now, not with Danielle sitting in front of him, her warm body tantalizing his senses, her breasts showing their shape under her sweater. Not when all he wanted to do was squeeze and hug her, bite chunks out of her soft, warm, sweet-smelling flesh....

An awful ache engulfed her as she sat up, searching for the words to ease the brittle tension.

"Maybe we'd better go," he said, slicing into the painful silence, and once again erecting that impregnable wall between them. She had a point; he had no right to demand anything of her, when it could only lead to a dead end road, since he had no intention of breaking it off with Natalie.

His face hardened, and he became the old dangerous Keir.

The smell of fish permeated the entire house.

"Mmmm, that smells divine," Keir said, inhaling deeply. He sauntered into the kitchen from the family room where he had been stoking the fire in the huge rock fireplace. He paused in front of the small television set sitting on the edge of the bar and flicked it on. "Thought you might like to know what's going on in the world," he added.

"Fine with me. Dinner will be ready shortly. Danielle smiled; it almost reached her eyes. "But if you want to help speed things up, you can fix the tea."

"You got it," he said and strode over to the cabinet, getting down the jar of instant tea.

Danielle watched him out of the corner of her eye, relieved that he no longer wore that terse, aloof expression. After they had come in from the stream, she was determined not to ruin the entire day by dwelling on the past and a hopeless future. So by burying her own misery, she had coaxed him back into a civil mood.

After watching him clean the fish, they had passed the remainder of the afternoon in front of the fireplace playing several games of gin rummy, careful not to touch on anything personal.

Now as she lifted the golden brown fillets out of the hot grease, ever mindful of his presence beside her, she thought how this could have been a sweet domestic scene—except for the turmoil brewing underneath the calm surface and the gun resting on the edge of the sink in front of him.

"My part's done. How about yours?" Keir asked.

"Er...set the french fries on the table and we'll be all set."

They had just sat down and were filling their plates when the unexpected and jarring ring of the phone split the silence. For a moment, they were both disoriented.

"Well, I'm certainly glad to have the phone working again," he said. "I'll take it in the office. He shoved his chair back and stood up, looking down into her upturned face. His breath caught sharply as their eyes met and held. She was lovely, he thought, staring at the way her caftan cupped her breasts, emphasizing their alluring fullness.

Danielle couldn't help but follow the movement of his eyes. Seconds ticked by, the phone continuing its insistent ringing. Still they stared, powerless to move. His look sent the blood pulsing through her veins like warm, heady brandy.

Finally, he jerked himself upright. "Don't let your food get cold," he said in a rough unnatural voice, before turning and walking out of the room.

Danielle let her breath out slowly. God, what was happening to her? But she knew. She had wanted to touch him so badly that it made her insides shake.

She began concentrating on her food, desperate to banish the image of his long limbs entwined with hers throughout the long nights, their heartbeats as one....

She closed her eyes, fighting for her sanity. When they fluttered open again, he was standing in the doorway. Her heart jumped.

"You...you scared me," she stammered.

"Who is Ann?"

Chapter 6

Danielle kept the fork from clattering to her plate by sheer force of will. For a moment she was a young girl again, at the orphanage, swinging high in a swing when suddenly she slipped out and watched in horror as the ground rose up to meet her, knocking the breath from her body with a savage brutality. She was experiencing the same feeling now, only much worse.

She could not say a word. Her throat and her stomach hurt as though she had tried to swallow a piece of jagged glass and succeeded.

"Who is Ann?" he repeated, his voice like a razor.

She simply gaped at him, soaking in the steely tension of his rigid jaw, the dark flush of fury staining his face. She held onto the table for dear life while she fought back the panic that threatened to suck her under. *He knows!* she told herself frantically. *He knows. He's placed a noose around your neck; now he's waiting for you to hang yourself.*

When she finally spoke, it was a poor imitation of her own voice. "It's obvious you already know," she said defiantly.

"I want to hear *you* say it." His eyes cut into hers like icepicks."

The tilt of her chin remained firmly upthrust. "She's...she's my daughter."

Keir's sharp intake of breath pierced the air, shattering the moment's silence. "Oh, God, No!"

He felt his heart twist and then collapse like a building in an earthquake. He held his head at an angle. "No," he repeated, not for effect, but as though, perhaps, he had been struck with an immediate and total loss of memory. It was as though he had been able to black out what he didn't want to hear. But it was true. She had a child. *His child?* God! "Danielle..." His hands rose and fell in a terrible gesture of despair.

Danielle opened her mouth to speak, then clamped it shut, held mute against the emotion she saw registered in Keir's green eyes. Her body was trembling unmercifully, and her heart was somewhere around her toes. She closed her eyes and breathed hard trying to relieve the pressure on her heart.

His reaction stunned her. She had expected anger, hatred, cold remoteness, but she had not been prepared for the distress, the pain. It was there, in his voice—that awful, unrelenting agony that twisted one's insides into an aching knot. She had never meant to hurt him, but she had. She had cut him to the core, and there was not one damned thing she could do about it. She could not risk telling him the truth. Ann was her life. She could face the agonies of dying a slow death easier than she could face losing her child—even to its father. Especially to its father.

She turned her back against the burning question in Keir's eyes. Her shock and anger at being caught in this situation had suddenly spent itself, and an intense feeling of guilt was rushing in to fill the vacuum. She dared not stay a moment longer, or she would come apart in front of him.

On legs that were considerably less than steady, she stood up and made a beeline for the door. She had to have time to herself. To think. No matter what the cost, Keir must never know Ann was his.

He reached the door with the agility of an animal springing to its prey. An arm shot out across the threshold. She stopped short of touching him.

"Oh, no you don't," he grated harshly, suppressed fury having taken the place of pain.

Danielle stepped back. "Please...let me go," she whispered.

For a few seconds, he looked away from her, his heart pumping wildly in his chest. She swayed lightly, closing her eyes.

"Whose child is it?"

Her eyes flew open. Keir was staring at her again, his face a cold mask. There was no smile, no alteration in his probing eyes. His unexpected question cut through her like a blade. But then just as quickly, she rallied, throwing her shoulders back, prepared to fight him with any and every weapon she had.

"She's mine," she answered defensively, ignoring the erratic beat of her heart. *Stay cool,* she warned herself. *Don't let him rattle you.*

"I wouldn't advise you to play games with me." His voice had a menacing edge to it.

"When it comes to my daughter, I don't play games."

"Well, we'll sure as hell see about that," he countered sarcastically.

"I don't have to take this from you, Keir McBride, not now, not ever." Although she put up a brave front, her insides were quaking.

"If she's not mine, then whose is she?" His face darkened, taking on a sinister glint.

"Mine!" Danielle repeated in a hissing tone. She turned her back on him and gazed out the window, concentrating on the huge snowflakes falling amidst the shadows of the late evening. She forced herself to gaze at the now familiar sight, the flakes adorning the weeping branches of the pines with a fresh coat of paint. Anything, she told herself, was preferable to Keir's grim countenance and merciless interrogation.

Having decided that his silence proved she had won the battle if not the war, she was totally unprepared for the next attack.

"What did you do, run straight into some other poor unsuspecting bastard's arms and have the baby?" he asked. Then before she could answer, he hammered on, "What happened, you couldn't get him to marry you?"

Every vestige of color deserted her face. "Why... why...you miserable swine!"

"Answer me, damn you!"

Hot fury loosened her tongue as nothing else could have done. She went straight for the jugular vein, just as he had gone for hers.

"But you'll never know the answer to either question, will you?" she goaded, her voice rising with every word she uttered. "Because I'll never tell you! Remember I know how you think; so no matter what I said, you'd still blame me."

His eyes narrowed and cut into her like blades. "You

haven't heard the last of this, by any means. You owe me the truth and I aim to get it. One way or the other.''

Suddenly the fight went out of Danielle. Seeing the fierce determination ground into the lines of his face and the icy warning in his voice, she knew she had pushed him as far as she dared. Besides, she was aware that he could easily carry out his threat once they were back to civilization. Her stomach lurched violently at the thought.

''Please...let me pass.'' Her throat was starting to close, her eyes stung with the need to cry.

He stared into her upturned face, fury lining his features. Then with a muttered oath, he turned around, swinging his tough, rangy body as if it were on ball bearings and walked stiffly into the den.

''Get out of my sight,'' he hissed, ''before I do something that will cause us both to be sorry.''

Danielle lost no time in making good her escape. But when she reached the top of the stairs, she stopped and turned around. Keir had not moved. His back was still to her, his shoulders hunched, seemingly more exhausted than she, as if his enormous strength had failed him.

Her own heart was breaking as she dragged her weary limbs to her cold, empty room and quietly closed the door behind her. She sat down on the bed, wanting to cry, to weep out all the anguish, all the hurt, all the shame. But she couldn't. The tears would not come.

Long after Danielle had gone, Keir stood leaning against the fireplace mantel, feeling sick and stricken inside.

When Cassidy had mentioned to him during the phone call about her child, assuming he already knew, he had nearly gone insane. And then to have gotten no satisfactory answers from her was driving him closer to the edge.

With an explosive curse, he crossed the room to stand by the window. Then he began to walk the length of the room. He had to believe that the child was not his or else he didn't think he could handle it. Yet, the idea that it wasn't kept him pacing the floor, sweating with jealousy. The thought of another man touching her, kissing the mouth he had kissed, loving her, then falling asleep with her in his arms, contented and warm, made him almost violent.

But no amount of pacing could calm his imagination. What the hell had become of his coldness, his indifference? Furthermore, why would anyone in his right mind want to be run over by the same train twice?

He sat down on the couch; he had to get control of himself. Because the reality was that it was over between them. After this assignment was behind him, they would go their separate ways. Somehow he had to banish the desire for her and the sickness of spirit that longed for her so desperately that he felt like a wounded animal. He had to forget what it was like to have her soft, unmarked body molded to his, the fragrance of her body, the way her nipples tasted as he tantalized them into hot points of desire, how she opened like a flower to the sun to admit his seeking, throbbing passion, how it felt to be inside her....

"God!" he groaned to the silent room. *Don't think about her anymore,* he commanded himself. She was not for him. Never had been. *But what about the child?* his conscience whispered. *What if she's yours?*

Unable to sit still another second, he vaulted from the couch, crossed the room to the stairs and trudged up them to his room. He lay down on the bed and stared up at the ceiling. Think about going back to Washington, think about running for the senate, think about Natalie and your future together.

Think about anything, but the woman in the next room....

Two days passed with no change. It was as if a cold war existed between them, each fighting to come to terms with misery. The strain grew more apparent every day. Danielle cooked for him, then disappeared during the day to wile away the long hours. The only bright spot of relief in the solitary hours was the phone calls home. She visited with Jusie by phone at least twice a day and never hung up until she had said a few words to Ann. Every time she heard her daughter's "Mommie, Mommie" she thought her heart would break.

She was finding the situation more intolerable by the day. No matter how hard she tried to avoid Keir, she found it impossible to do so. His hard, closed face followed her wherever she went. But what gnawed at her relentlessly was that she found herself *wanting* to know where he was, what he was doing. In spite of the tension between them she wanted to be near him.

She was just lonely, she kept telling herself. Lonely for a man. *Any man.* What she'd missed was having a man's strong arms around her. No, she argued—not any man. Just Keir. God help her, she wanted Keir. When she relived how it felt to have his talented hands caress every forbidden part of her body....

No! *Don't do this to yourself!* He was getting married, for God's sake, she reminded herself brutally.

With a disgruntled shake of her head, she pulled herself out of her musings and stood up, deciding that she had time to take a shower before going downstairs to fix breakfast.

A short time later, her task complete, she was making her way back into the bedroom when the door of her room opened without warning and Keir stood on the threshold staring at her.

"I...er...knocked," he said, swallowing uncomfortably, "but there was no response, so..." He shrugged, his voice tailing off.

She couldn't control the tremor in her voice as his eyes seemed to burn through her robe to sear her skin. "I...I didn't hear you. I...I was in the shower."

He advanced into the room, not once taking his eyes off her, half closed the door and then opened it again as though having second thoughts.

"What did you want?" she asked huskily, uneasily, holding the sides of her robe together, aware that his painful scrutiny missed little.

Their eyes melted together. His senses stirred. She was so utterly desirable in every way.

He cleared his throat. "Cas...Cassidy wants to talk to you." He breathed in her perfume, staring deliberately at the open neck of her gown. It was made of some soft green stuff, with a long row of velvet buttons. He wasn't concerned about keeping his boss dangling on the phone; he wasn't concerned about anything, not with her breasts showing their shape under the row of little buttons.

He recognized the moment when she became aware of the intensity of his regard. Beneath the fine material of her robe, the hardening nipples sprang to life and were outlined in sensuous detail. His arousal was instant and painful.

Danielle tried to free her eyes from his magic spell. Her palms were damp and there was a film of sweat on her forehead as she tipped her head back and shut her eyes tightly and fought to control the desire churning inside her.

Her eyes sprang open with his next words. "I guess you'd better not keep the man dangling any longer," he said, a strained smile on his lips.

She cursed herself silently as a telltale warmth stained her cheeks. She found her voice. "He wants to talk to me?" Suddenly passion turned to fear. *Ann.* Was something wrong with Ann?

"There's nothing the matter," he said softly, reading her mind. "Cassidy just wants to talk to you."

Reassured, but not completely convinced, Danielle swept past Keir and tore off quickly down the stairs and into the den.

She found that she was shaking when she lifted the phone to her ear. "Hello, Marshal Cassidy." Her voice held a thread of uneasiness.

"How are you, Ms. Davis?" he asked politely.

"Under the circumstances, I'm fine," she lied. She was not fine. Keir was driving her crazy.

"I wish I were calling to inform you that everything had been cleared up, but unfortunately I'm not." An impatient sigh sounded over the line. "So far, the Russians have managed to elude the capable agents of the FBI. But we hope it won't be much longer until this mess is cleared up, once and for all."

Her heart sank. "Is…is that all you called to tell me?" she asked, trying to stifle the depression. Would she ever be able to return home to her family, her job?

"No, actually I called to tell you that we're sending another agent to your home just as a double precautionary measure." Ignoring her sharp intake of breath, he went on, "It's just that, Ms. Davis, a precaution and nothing more. But I knew if I didn't tell you first, before your housekeeper did, you would automatically think the worst.''

''Are...you sure you're telling the truth?'' There was a touch of panic in her voice. She wanted to believe him, was afraid not to believe him.

Cassidy's voice was soft, but guarded. ''You can trust me, Ms. Davis. In spite of what you may think, we're not your enemy. We're trying to make this as easy for you under the circumstances as possible.''

Damn him! What right did he have to make her feel guilty? And she didn't want to feel grateful to him for anything. ''Thank you for telling me,'' she said, hanging onto her control with great difficulty.

''Bear with us, Ms. Davis,'' he said brusquely, before the dial tone replaced his voice.

When she hung up and turned around, Keir was watching her.

''Oh, Keir,'' she wailed, forgetting for a moment the animosity that simmered between them, ''I...can't help but worry about...Ann.''

A flicker of pain darkened his eyes for a split second, but then it quickly disappeared. He took in her white, stricken look and his eyes softened. ''Don't be,'' he said. ''Cassidy briefed me before I came for you. He's on the level. Everything is fine on the homefront.''

Anxiety gripped her heart. ''Are you sure?'' Her voice cracked on the last word.

''I promise.''

The low, husky tone of his voice left her breathless. She looked away, but not before he saw the tiny pulse pounding in her throat.

A hushed silence fell over the room.

''It's another gorgeous day. How would you like to get out of here for a while and go for a hike through the woods?'' Keir asked at last, shattering the unnatural silence.

Her lashes swept up, her eyes wide with shock. ''Do...you mean it?''

''Yes, I mean it,'' he said, his voice warm, a small smile tugging at his harshly etched lips.

His old heart-stopping charisma was working again. Her mind was rational, but her heart was betraying her. She was responding to his kindness like a drowning man finding a rope.

''Run upstairs and get dressed. I'll wait.''

The second Danielle disappeared, the smile deserted Keir's face, leaving him looking once again grim and foreboding. Sudden irritation quickly bloomed into full anger. ''Face it, McBride, you're a god-damned fool, a glutton for punishment!'' he muttered aloud.

But he knew for a fact that they could not keep on going like they had been. The tension between them was like a simmering volcano—it could erupt at any given moment.

Something had to give. It was as simple as that.

''I love this weather,'' Danielle said. ''It's certainly different from East Texas.''

They were walking through the snow at a leisurely pace, following the stream at the rear of the house. Danielle felt like she had been given a special treat by being allowed to roam around outdoors. Keir had warned her never to wander around outside alone. And since he had never offered to invite her to go along with him to cut firewood, she spent her time inside the cabin. The fishing trip was the last time she had tromped through the snow.

The sun felt wonderful shining down on her bare head.

''I agree, it's beautiful here,'' Keir said, his low-pitched voice echoing through the silence. She could smell the fresh, clean fragrance of his cologne as their strides matched perfectly.

Danielle glanced up at him between her lashes. "Do you come here often?" she asked rather shyly. She couldn't remember his having mentioned the cabin to her during their brief time together.

He was quiet for a moment. "No," he said. "I never have the time." He was captivated by the way her sun-kissed hair framed her face in a riot of soft curls.

"That seems such a shame." Her voice was wistful.

"Oh, it gets used quite often. My parents come here when they can get away from Washington. My mother thinks this is the greatest place in the world."

Danielle tipped her head back and looked up at the tall hardwoods. To her they seemed to have a direct communication with the heavens. "I can understand that," she said softly, wishing that she could have been here under different circumstances. But then, determined not to let anything mar this outside adventure, she shied away from any unpleasant thoughts.

Now that they had ventured about a hundred yards from the house, completely opposite from where they had gone fishing, they came upon a huge cleared area. Sitting in the middle of it was a large metal building.

Danielle halted in her tracks. "I...I had no idea this was here."

He peered down into her upturned face. "Does that surprise you?"

She shrugged. "Not that you have it, no. But why here?"

"It's a good thing to have around when there's an emergency, and there've been several since we've owned this place."

A frown wrinkled her forehead. "What happened?"

"My father had a heart attack a couple of years ago, and if the chopper hadn't been here or me to fly it, he wouldn't be alive today."

"Oh, how awful."

"It was at the time," he said grimly, "but he came through with very little damage to his heart." He paused and began walking. "Let's just hope we don't have to use it," he added, his eyes scanning the woods, the mountains around them.

She stopped short again and stared. "What...what do you mean?" she whispered. A shiver ran the length of her slender frame, a shiver that had nothing to do with the sharp, biting cold. For a moment she had forgotten the reason she was here, had forgotten because...oh, God...because of Keir and the power he held over her.

"Hey," he said gently, his gaze wandering over her face, searching eyes that grew dark with an emotion she couldn't name. "Forget what I said. Nothing's going to go wrong, you'll see." A smile deepened the dimples on either side of his cheek. "I'll let you get even by permitting you to clobber me with a snowball." He would do anything to remove that dark, frightened glaze from her eyes. Why hadn't he kept his mouth shut?

Danielle's answering smile flashed like sunlight through a passing storm. "Well, now I just don't see how I can let that opportunity pass," she said impishly.

"And I'll even supply the snowball," he said unevenly, her dazzling smile shortening his breath.

She shook her head. "Nothing doing. When the time is right, I'll make my own snowball and seek my revenge." There was a wicked gleam in her eyes. "When you're least expecting it," she added.

"Then I guess I won't be able to let you out of my

sight, will I?'' His voice was as seductive as a gentle
caress, and a throbbing ache grew within her as their gaze
continued to hold.

How long they stood wrapped in a long, sweet silence
neither one knew or cared. For what seemed like eons,
they were reluctant to move, to speak, to breathe, for fear
of breaking it.

''We'd better keep walking,'' Keir said moments later,
his voice gravelly with suppressed emotion.

Danielle's heart was beating like a frightened deer's as
she fell in step beside him, while trying to smother the
empty feeling of disappointment. For a moment, she had
thought he was going to kiss her.

''Are you cold?'' he asked.

The silence was so long that he didn't think she would
answer. They kept walking. When she spoke, her voice
was just a wisp of sound. ''No…not really…I…'' Her
voice faded away.

''Tell me about your work,'' he said suddenly, unexpectedly.

Relieved to be on safe ground, she responded quickly.
''I own and manage a small bookstore.''

''What kind of books do you sell?''

''All types: paperbacks, new and used, bestsellers in
hardback.''

''Do you like your work?''

''I love it.'' Her eyes sparkled like champagne. ''Especially since it's in my home.''

''You can't beat that for convenience.''

''That's the idea.''

Another silence fell between them as they climbed up
a rather steep incline.

''Who…takes care of your daughter…of Ann?''

Danielle made no response.

"Does she stay with you while you work?" he pressed.

A feeling of impending disaster came to her in a sickening rush. She did not want to discuss Ann. Not with him. Oh, God, not with him. "No," she answered tightly.

"Does her hair shine like silver moonbeams, like yours?"

She caught her breath, only to find that there was no air left in her lungs. "Please..." she whispered desperately, "I don't want to talk about..."

"Why?" he demanded. "What are you afraid of?"

"Nothing," she snapped, clinging to her control with difficulty.

"For God's sake, talk to me."

She stopped and placed her gloved hands over her ears. "I don't have to talk to you. Ever."

"Danielle!"

"No!"

"Yes!"

"I don't owe you anything. You don't care about me, about Ann. How could you...when you're marrying someone else?" she sobbed, giving into the urge to get away from him. She whirled around, and before he could stop her, she went tearing off down the steep incline.

"Come back!" Keir yelled. "You'll hurt yourself."

Danielle paid no heed to his warning; she kept on going, tears blinding her vision.

Keir tore out after her.

She felt him gaining on her, but she could not maneuver any faster through the deep snow.

"Goddammit, will you stop!" Keir yelled harshly.

Danielle kept on going. But it was only a matter of seconds before a hand clamped down on her shoulder.

"No!" she cried, and began twisting and turning in his grasp.

It was at that moment she lost her balance, causing her knees to buckle beneath her. She began to fall. He refused to turn her loose.

"Keir!" Her scream echoed through the silence as they both rolled and tumbled through the hard snow, down the side of the mountain.

Danielle squeezed her eyes shut and clung to Keir for dear life.

They reached the bottom, legs wrapped in a tangled heap, Keir on top.

Gasping for breath, he moved just enough to look down into her pale, stunned features. "Are you hurt?" he rasped, madly running his hands up and down the length of her body making sure that there were no broken bones.

Danielle's heart was pounding against her chest like a sledgehammer as he opened her eyes to stare into Keir's frantic eyes, so close to her own. "I...don't think so," she stammered, fighting for her next breath.

He groaned, his face ashen, his breathing heavy and labored. "Are you sure?"

"I'm sure."

"I'm so sorry, so sorry, he whispered, his warm breath misting her face. "If you'd been hurt, I'd never have forgiven myself."

It was a painful, aching trembling that suddenly choked her breath as their eyes locked and held.

His insides shook as his body fitted to the gentle curves of hers. God, how he wanted her. Needed her.

Lights began to pulse inside her brain. Oh, God, if he touched her now... *Don't let him get to you!* An anguished sob tore from her throat. "Please...let me up," she whimpered.

An answering sob ripped from his throat when he saw the pleading in her eyes, begging him not to take advantage of her. He understood desire; he knew what it could do to a man's nerves. It was working on him now, wasn't it?—ripping his guts to shreds. And he knew how it could distort one's judgment. He knew it because desire was what he felt for her, but resisting the temptation to touch her now was only possible because of other feelings which he refused to give into. Love was not a word his desire would admit. At this moment, he was sure he knew exactly what a man facing a firing squad felt like.

He rolled away from her.

When the knock sounded on Luke Cassidy's door, he was brooding over the latest development in the Davis case.

"Come in," he said shortly, raising his eyes as Tony Welch came striding through the door. "Well?"

Welch came to a halt in front of his desk and eyed his boss carefully. "Couldn't reach McBride. Lines are down again."

"What the hell do you mean—the lines are down again?"

Welch stepped back. "It seems that every time there's a snowstorm in that neck of the woods, the phone lines and sometimes the power lines go down."

"Damn!"

"What...what do you suggest we do, sir?"

Cassidy's eyes narrowed into tiny slits. "What I suggest," he said distinctly, dangerously, "is that you get off your ass and get that message to McBride. Get the god-damned highway patrol to take it if you have to. I don't care. Just see that he gets it the quickest way possible. Understand?'' Although his voice had not risen a single decibel, it sounded as though he was shouting.

Welch paled. ''Yes, sir. I'll take care of it right away.''

''See that you do,'' Cassidy said as Welch turned and walked out of the room.

The moment he was alone, Cassidy lowered his weary body back down into his chair, and cradled his head in his hands. What next? he wondered bleakly.

Danielle remained in her room the rest of the morning and most of the afternoon. She had gone there the minute they had returned to the house, her nerves and heart in a shambles. After she had stripped the clothes from her body and taken a shower, she had done nothing but sit as though in a stupor, staring into space, trying to figure out what terrible thing she had done to warrant such punishment.

It was the loud knock on the front door that finally roused her. The unexpected sound stirred her into instant action. For some unexplainable reason, she was suddenly afraid. Jumping up, she jerked open the door of her room and looked up and down the hall before making her way cautiously down the stairs into the den.

Keir was standing by the fireplace. His hand was locked around the holster lying on the mantel. He tensed when he saw her.

She felt the impending disaster as she watched him draw out the snub-nosed pistol. He raised his fingers to his lips, signaling her to keep quiet, then turned and made his way toward the door.

On legs that were not steady, she followed him, though careful to keep out of his line of vision.

He paused to the left of the door, his weapon raised. "Who's there?"

"I have a message," came the reply.

"Leave it."

"But...but, sir..."

"Leave it," Keir repeated, his tone deadly.

"Where?"

Danielle remained in the shadows, listening, uncertainty curled within her belly.

"Leave it on the doormat and then be on your way," Keir ordered crisply, refusing to take any chances.

He waited, holding his position, the silence reaching a screaming pitch. Then he moved, going to the nearest window and slipping back the curtain to stare into the evening twilight. He looked on as a tall, broad-shouldered man dressed in a Virginia State Trooper's uniform made his way down the path.

He then turned and moved quickly back to the door and cocked his pistol, opening it slowly and cautiously. Seeing and hearing nothing suspicious, he leaned down and scooped up the envelope and slammed the door.

Danielle stepped into the light, fear climbing up her spine with icy fingers. Somehow she managed to push words past her frozen lips. "Please...what does it say?" she whispered.

Hastily, Keir ripped it open. The contents glared at him off the page. The Hawk Is Dead Stop Proceed With Caution. His oath split the silence as he crushed the paper in the palm of his hand.

Numbing terror washed through Danielle's body, threatening to stop her heartbeat. "What...what does it say?"

Keir looked away. "Nothing you need to be concerned with," he lied.

"Tell me, damn you!" she screeched. "Is it Ann?"

"It's John Elsworth; they found him in his cell this morning. He was murdered."

Chapter 7

Danielle instantly went weak with relief that nothing had happened to Ann. Then suddenly she turned cold. The implications of what it could mean to her and to Ann hit her like a vicious blow. If they had gotten to Elsworth in prison, they could surely get to her...or to her child.

"Oh, no," she whimpered, putting her balled fist up to her mouth. Her insides began to shake as the futility of the situation overwhelmed her. Then she breathed deeply, struggling for composure. Now was not the time to fall apart, she scolded herself brutally. Ann would be fine. Cassidy would not let her down. He had promised, hadn't he? Besides, it was her they wanted. She was the only one who could identify Letsukov. Now, however, it was of paramount importance that she keep a cool head.

"It's not as bad as it sounds," Keir said softly, seeing fear pinch her features. He heaved his huge frame to an upright stance. "First thing, they don't know where we are, and the second thing, they have to go through me to get to you.'' His voice and eyes reminded her of cold steel.

She swallowed against the lump in her throat and nodded weakly.

A chill shook his body as he saw the worry and fear remain in her face. ''Why don't you go sit down in the den, and I'll get you a shot of brandy,'' he said with gentle insistence.

''Thank...you,'' she muttered inanely, though she continued to stand still, her face a waxen mask, her body unnaturally stiff. The concern in his voice nearly triggered her tears. Would this nightmare ever end?

Keir stared at her, taking in her pale solemn face. It was all he could do not to pull her into his arms and reassure her again that nothing or no one was going to harm a hair on her head.

She looked so vulnerable, so uncertain, so haunted, yet there was a strength about her that surprised him. He had never felt protective of a woman before, not even Danielle when he'd first met her. And certainly not Natalie; his attitude toward her was like that of an older brother. But there was nothing of that in his feeling for Danielle; there never had been. She was a mixture that had always confused him, constantly arousing new impulses which he had never experienced before. And with each passing moment he was with her, the situation became more explosive, more unbearable...and more dangerous.

Her movement shattered his thoughts. Danielle crossed to a chair in front of the fireplace and sat down, lowering her head in her hands.

He stood a moment longer, watching the firelight play over her. Suddenly every nerve in his body began to twitch. He wanted her; he wanted her in bed. He wanted her so badly it was ripping his insides to shreds. *But*

*you're not going to touch her, goddamn you! Get a hold
of yourself. Do your job. Forget everything else.*

He moved in a jerking motion, striding toward the bar,
angry at himself.

Shortly he returned to the den with glasses in hand.

"Thanks," she murmured, raising the glass to her lips
and downing a small portion of the amber liquid. Although it seemed to explode, creating a burning sensation
in the bottom of her stomach, it did nothing to ease the
dull ache inside her heart.

Keir sat down heavily opposite her, like an old man
whose body had seen the end of the road. He placed the
tumbler, unsampled, on the arm of the chair.

Danielle watched him carefully, her expression grave,
but questioning.

"Why…why do you think Cassidy sent a message instead of calling?" she asked nervously.

Suddenly Keir jumped up as though he'd been shot
and in two agile strides covered the distance to the phone
and snatched up the receiver and placed it against his ear.

"Damnation," he snapped, "just as I thought. The
lines are dead again."

"Oh, no, not again," Danielle cried in disgust, hating
the fact that she was again cut off from communicating
with her home.

"I can't say I'm surprised," Keir said soberly while
chewing on his bottom lip. "We lose power here several
times during the winter months." He sighed. "I only
hope they're working around the clock to get it repaired
by morning."

"Do you think you should've talked to the messenger,
tried to find out a little more?"

"No," Keir answered. "Because I know that he was
a go between and nothing more. Knowing how Luke's

mind works, he got me the message the fastest way possible. Don't worry, he'll be in touch again soon, you can count on that, especially if there's a change in plans."

"You seem to have a lot of confidence in him."

Keir's lips twisted. "He can be a bit trying at times, but he knows what he's doing and I can only respect that in a man."

"It's obvious he feels the same way about you."

"Let's just put it this way. He more or less pulled me up by the bootstraps and took me under his wing at a time when I didn't really care if I lived or died."

The bitterness in his voice stung Danielle's ears. She looked away. *Oh, Keir,* she cried silently. *Why do we keep hurting one another?*

She was aware of him with every fiber of her being, even though she kept her face averted. He was wearing jeans and a tan crew-neck knit shirt, a tan down-filled vest being his only concession to the biting cold. The silver threads running through his dark hair were highlighted slightly by the flickering light.

Out of the corner of her eye, Danielle saw him reach for his glass, gripping it tightly. His long legs, stretched forward in an apparently relaxed attitude, seemed tense too. He was gazing broodingly into the crackling fire. Was he as aware of her as she was him?

Danielle turned her head and stared into his face, and immediately wished she hadn't. He was looking at her speculatingly, not at her face but at her lips.

She felt her cheeks burn as the silence lingered.

"Who...who do you think was responsible for Elsworth's death?" she asked suddenly, desperately.

Keir gave her a guarded look. "Letsukov must have a contact on the inside who was willing to pull this nasty job for him."

Danielle shuddered. "But why would they want to kill him now? The damage has already been done. He's already testified."

"That's the point," he said, a sardonic brow slanting upward. "They were determined to get even, and they apparently succeeded."

She sank her teeth into her lower lip to keep it from trembling. "If…if they were determined to get to John…then it means they'll be that much more determined to get to…to me…."

Her words hung heavy in the air, followed by a frightening silence. Keir finally shattered it, his voice like ice. "If they do, they're as good as dead."

"Oh, God, Keir, how…how did all this get out of hand so quickly?" she asked, the hardening twist of his forbidding jawline and his menacing words frightening her almost as much as the bizarre murder of Elsworth. The thought of Keir actually taking another person's life—well, that didn't bear thinking about. Tears of hopelessness were gathering on her eyelashes.

Upon seeing those tears, something snapped inside Keir, an explosive fury at everyone involved in this escapade, including himself. In spite of the brave front she was putting on, she was terrified, and it shook him to the core. He inwardly railed at Cassidy for having gotten him into this fiasco, himself for having broken the first rule and becoming personally involved. Again. For whether he wanted to admit it or not, he *was* involved—had been since the moment he walked into Cassidy's office and saw her standing there.

And his hands were tied. The frustration of not being able to do anything but wait, possibly becoming sitting ducks while they did so, was placing a heavy strain on his patience. If Letsukov had been able, through connections, to get someone on the inside to murder Elsworth, then Letsukov was capable of getting to Danielle.

But for now all he could do was sit tight and wait to hear from Cassidy. If his superior thought that they were in any immediate danger here, he would have signaled a move. Why then did he continue to feel an uneasiness crawl up and down his spine?

"Are you going to be all right?" Keir asked, thick, sweeping eyelashes partially shielding his expression.

"I'm...I'm fine."

A deep frown etched across his brow. "Are you sure?"

"No, but I'm working on it," she replied faintly.

"Dwelling on it won't do any good, you know."

"I know, but I keep thinking about John...."

"Don't," he demanded in a soft whisper, "don't say it. Don't even think it. In order to get to...Ann...uh—they would have to go through two professionally trained U.S. Marshals. And nothing is going to happen to you." His voice trembled, as a barrage of emotions ricocheted through him. He didn't dare define what he was feeling, but it was there.

"I...I hope you're right," she murmured, her eyes glued to the fire.

"In spite of what you may think, you can trust me, you know," he said softly.

His words, like an arrow, pierced her soul. A ragged breath tore through her as the tension crackled in the air between them. Their eyes, through the shimmering firelight, met and held.

"I think I'll go outside and take a look around." He had to get away from her.

Danielle experienced another twitch of panic at the

thought of him going outside alone. "Is…that necessary?" She couldn't seem to stifle her feeling of paranoia.

His eyes were hooded as he stood up and looked down at her, the firelight emphasizing her drawn, tense features.

Again, he had to fight the urge to haul her into his arms, while damning himself and his weakness.

"Nothing's wrong," he replied, more briskly than he intended. "I just want to take a look around."

"You'll…be careful, won't you?"

Keir's breath caught in his throat. "I…will," he said thickly, unable to pull his eyes away from hers. "I'll be back shortly."

The remainder of her strength suddenly drained from her and a warm, heady longing stirred within her. "I…I think I'll rustle us up a bite to eat while you're gone." The thought of going back upstairs to her empty room upset her worse than sharing an intimate dinner with Keir. Or did it?

"That's not necessary," he said. "You just stay put, and I'll take care of that chore when I get back," he added lightly, then stared at her a moment longer before pivoting on his heels.

His footsteps appeared as heavy as her heart as she rested her head back against the cushion and listened to him walk to the door.

Why had fate suddenly decided to pit her against such overwhelming odds? she wondered despairingly. All she had wanted since losing Keir was to live her life in peace, create a loving home for her daughter and do the work she loved best. Nothing was working out as she had planned. She was holed up in a cabin, hiding from a maniac, only to run headlong into another problem, equally as dangerous—Keir and the rebirth of her love for him.

She saw her neat, tidy world being ripped apart at the seams, and there wasn't one thing she could do about it. She was beginning to depend on, to need, him again. And that was something she had promised herself would never happen. Where would it all end?

"You've barely touched your food," Keir said, eyeing her plate filled with a steak, baked potato and a fresh salad.

After having taken a quick look around the place, his flashlight and his Smith and Wesson as companions, Keir had come back inside to the cozy warmth, finding that Danielle had taken him at his word and remained where she was. He had noticed the empty glass of brandy on the table beside her before discarding his coat and making his way into the kitchen to begin preparing dinner.

Now as he watched her, taking in the dark shadows under her eyes and the weary slant to her mouth, he longed to make her pain disappear. *Sadist!*

"It's delicious, really it is, and I'm grateful to you for fixing such an elaborate meal."

Nervously, she took a tiny bite of the steak, licking her lips with the tip of her tongue as she grew more and more aware of his gaze.

"I'm glad you approve. It's not often I take the time to put together a decent meal." He was becoming mesmerized by the tiny flick of her tongue.

"I'm sorry," she apologized suddenly, pushing her plate away, shattering the tension. "I thought I could eat, honest I did. But…but I feel my stomach beginning to rebel. When I think of John…"

"Hey, take it easy," he pleaded earnestly. "You're only making matters worse. How about another glass of brandy or wine?" A gentle smile touched his lips, driving another kind of pain straight to her soul, a pain filled with an aching, driving need. "It's guaranteed to calm even the worst case of frayed nerves," he added.

"Promise?"

"Scout's honor."

"Go ahead, fill my glass."

"Full?"

"To the brim."

"You'll get drunk."

"I hope so."

"Why?"

"Then maybe I'll forget."

"If it works, will you let me know?"

They were no longer referring to the murder and they both knew it.

Danielle felt herself flush betrayingly. "Yes," she whispered, then looked away to cover herself. Her heart was racing as though she'd just run a mile.

Keir got up suddenly and went to get the bottle of wine out of the bucket that he had left chilling on the bar. Careful not to touch her as she lifted her glass up to him, he poured it full. Then he filled his own and sat down.

A long silence fell between them.

Danielle suddenly turned her head away to hide the tears stinging her eyes. She must stop this now. She had to get a tighter reign on her emotions. Keir was getting married, and besides, hadn't he made it eminently clear how he felt about her? There was no future for them.

"Danielle..."

Her name was whispered in a kind of incredulous despair. But she had to resist. If she gave into the feelings churning inside her, she would be lost.

Keir watched her, could feel her pull back. God! Was

he ever going to get over wanting her? Hadn't this living hell gone on long enough?

He searched for words, but found none. Once again he remembered how they used to be—he saw her naked again, all the angles and curves of her body; he felt her mouth, the surrender in it.

Why her? Why didn't he feel the same burning passion when he looked at Natalie? Why was this woman so special? Had he forgotten all the pain, the disillusionment he had suffered at her hands? Why in heaven's name couldn't he hate her? Yet, he did not. He still wanted her. But how could he justify this feeling to himself, to Natalie? It was wrong for him to betray Natalie, even though she knew he did not love her the way she loved him. He and Danielle still wanted different things out of life. But neither could deny the thread of passion that bound them together, yet kept them apart.

She deserved to be loved carefully. And often. And he still wanted her as much now as he ever had. He would never forget the swell of her breasts, her rib cage, her belly and long thighs as she fitted to him like the missing pieces of an ancient puzzle.

She belonged to him. He would die if he never saw her again.

"Keir?"

He realized then that his thoughts were plainly written across his face for the whole world to see. He quickly turned away. He could not afford to make public his innermost thoughts. He wasn't going to let her make a fool of him again.

"I think I'll go up to my room now, if you don't mind," she said uneasily. "It's been a rather long day."

Keir stood up immediately. "I think that's a good idea." He avoided her eyes. "Good night."

"Good night," she replied. "And thanks for everything," she added softly.

Danielle sat straight up in her bed. Her heart was pounding wildly, and her mouth was so dry that it hurt to swallow. Was it her own cry that had awakened her? Her body began to shake; her teeth began to chatter. Then she remembered; she was dreaming, dreaming about John Elsworth. She had imagined his white, terrified face as she had begged and pleaded with his assailant not to hurt him, only to then have the life strangled from his body.

"Oh, no, please," she cried, burying her face in her hands. Her shoulders shook violently as uncontrollable sobs pounded her body.

She did not hear the bedroom door when it opened. She wasn't even aware that she was no longer alone until she felt the mattress sag beside her. She jerked her head back and stared into Keir's deeply troubled eyes.

"Are you all right?" he whispered, a jagged note to his voice. "God, when I heard you cry out, I didn't know what to think." On the sly, he leaned over and eased his gun down on the carpet.

When he straightened up, he noticed how the moonlight bathed the room in a delicate glow. He could see the warm tears overflowing the shuttered rims of her eyes.

Danielle shivered. "I...was dreaming...a nightmare." She gulped. "It was awful. I...dreamed about John...." She couldn't go on.

"Shhh, don't cry," he soothed, her tears cutting him to pieces. "It was just a dream, nothing more." He couldn't stop himself from touching her. For a moment, his hands closed over her bare shoulders. It was a mistake to touch her, a dangerous indulgence he had promised both of them would never recur. He felt her stiffen and immediately withdrew.

"You don't have to be afraid of me," he said. "I told you that."

"I...I'm not afraid of you," Danielle whispered, the tortured words barely audible. "Only myself."

His groan penetrated the silence. "Oh, God, Danielle, don't say that. As it is, I can't answer for myself much longer." He dug his fingers into the palm of his hands to keep from pulling her into his arms. "I'd better go now. It would be better. Better for you."

Still he did not move as the moonbeams illuminated the entire premises, dancing across the strained, tormented expressions on both their faces.

"Please...don't go." She swayed toward him; he looked down into her eyes. "Don't go away. I don't want you to leave me. I...know what it'll mean if you stay, but I don't care. Do you understand? I don't care." She loved him, had never stopped loving him. It was as simple as one, two, three. And right now she needed him as never before. She thought that she'd surely die if he didn't hold her.

"Are you sure?" he asked. "Once I touch you...it'll be too late."

She put out her hand, and he caught it, turning her palm against his lips. The moist softness of his mouth against her skin set her insides on fire. It had been so long...

"Please," she whispered.

They moved toward one another, and he closed both arms around her. He simply held her for the longest time, the pagan beat of their hearts throbbing in unison as a cloud blocked out the moon, plunging the room into total darkness.

After a while, he pulled back, his hands coming up the sides of her face.

"Can you see me?" she asked.

"I don't have to see you; I can feel you."

"I'm glad."

He leaned down and placed his mouth against her lips, softly, tenderly. She tasted of tears, and her face was cold as he continued to hold it between his hands, stroking the smooth skin. It was a kiss that unlocked her fears.

Her chest ached beneath this gentle assault, matching the ache in his own chest as his hands wandered across her breasts, seeking hungrily.

"Oh, God, how have I stood not touching you?" he asked. The pain of wanting and owning and possessing was no less now than it was that first time he held her. If anything, it was worse, heightened by his having made love to her, having known her passion and tenderness.

The alcohol she had consumed had turned to honey on her breath. "You taste so good, smell so good," he whispered into her mouth. He stifled a moan. He thought that his body would explode for want of her as he felt her softness against him, the softness he had dreamed about for three long years. "Please, I'm not sure I can wait. I'm so hot…it's been so long…I'll try to be gentle…"

"Oh, please love me," she pleaded. "Now."

"Yes, oh, yes."

With quick adept fingers, he removed her gown, feeling her fingers pressing hard into his flesh, her mouth a moist flower opening and closing over his. He wanted to prolong the kiss, to explore her mouth and savor the intimacy, but he could not wait, nor could she.

He pulled away to discard the pair of jeans he had slipped into when he heard her cry. Kicking them aside, he lay down beside her, his body pressing warmly against her.

Suddenly their behavior turned savage. His mouth touched her everywhere. His hands caressed her sweetly, familiarly, following the hungry quest of his lips.

"Sweet, oh, so sweet," he murmured as he grasped her and pulled her on top of him. She melted like hot wax against his aroused body, kissing him deeply, exploring his mouth, building a tremulous stirring heat while she curled her fingers in his hair, over his shoulders, feeling his muscles bunch beneath her hands.

He moaned, shifting to capture a nipple between his hot, moist lips. A slow ache grew deep within her as his tongue began licking wildly. When he entered her it was swift and frantic. She arched her back and began to move slowly, sensuously.

Keir felt the top of his head nearly come off. He could only pray that this would not be the end—surely only the beginning. Yet, she was like a rainbow; at any time, he could open his eyes and find that she had faded to a sweet memory. But what she was doing to him was no memory; it was excruciatingly real.

Quickly he clung to her hips, joining her in her movement, lifting her, kneading her flesh as he accelerated to meet her in this extraordinary incidence of simultaneous timing. He knew in that moment that he had never stopped loving her.

They fell sideways, still joined and lay panting, breathing in the air from each other's lungs.

"Oh, Danielle," he whispered.

She held onto him, unable to speak. He was her fortress where she could hide. His shoulders, chest and arms formed a shelter in which she could rest safe from her fears. She did not want it to end. Ever.

He held her tighter, spreading himself about her like a protective shell.

They slept.

Waking at dawn, Danielle passed her hand over his face to make sure that he was real, not just a figment of her imagination. She did not feel the least bit guilty. Just content, satisfied, replete. And in love. She could no longer deny it. She loved him. She wouldn't think about tomorrow and its painful responsibilities. It would come soon enough. Surely she deserved this tiny sojourn in paradise.

She lay still, eyes closed, stroking the bristly hair at the back of his neck, enjoying the rough tickling sensations on her hands.

His eyes opened in time to catch her smile. He smiled too. She put her arm around his chest and hugged him, mutely and reverently.

"Good morning." His heart swelled with the pressure of ecstasy that was almost like a terrible grief.

He leaned an arm over the side of the bed and fumbled through his jean pocket for a cigarette. After lighting it he fell back on his pillow and looked at her under half-closed lids.

"What are you thinking about when you look at me like that?" he asked huskily, then drew smoke deep into his lungs.

She seemed to give herself a mental shake. She touched his chest. "I'd forgotten how beautiful your body is." And it was. Broad and muscular at the shoulders, narrow at the waist and hips with long, strong legs. "Except for this scar, I might add." She traced her fingers the length of the puffy gash while he ground out his cigarette in the ashtray on the bedside table. "How did you get it?"

Keir trapped her hand against his chest and lifted himself on one elbow and looked down at her body, his hand, straying to a breast, cupping its warmth in his hand, thinking how firm and perfectly shaped it was.

He smiled, feeling for her nipple. "Let's not ruin this beautiful moment," he said hoarsely, "by talking about my beat-up body."

"But I like talking about your body." Still, her resolve was weakening.

He fell to the pillow, carrying her with him, bringing her lips down to his. She had a soft mouth, and he loved running his hands through her curls. It was always the same—like fine silk. *You're a fool.* He had said this to himself a dozen times. A damn fool for living in a fantasy, and what he was doing was insane, for both of them. But he couldn't stop what was happening. It had gone too far. He couldn't stop making love to her, and now he couldn't stop the deadly, insidious joy of loving her.

He smiled at her and she smiled back.

Suddenly she moved.

"What are..." He broke off in midsentence, about to ask her where she was going. But she was sinking beneath the covers. She kissed his flat stomach, licked at his navel.

"Danielle," he muttered thickly.

"I want to please you." Her hands clasped him around his lean, strong thighs and her hair fell forward to dance on his flesh.

"You do please me, baby. You do."

His moans of pleasure exalted her and embraced her. When it was time, he flowed inside her. It was slow, and relaxed, like the rhythm of the sea on the beach. It was beautiful.

They were quiet for a long time.

That explosive night of love set the pattern for the next few days. On the surface they were contented and happy, basking in their rediscovery of one another, making love incessantly.

And if underneath that thin layer of contentment, uncertainty and worry simmered, playing havoc with their souls, they ignored it. And if they were both aware that they were escaping from reality, that nothing had changed between them, that they were both still harboring resentments and bearing scars, they ignored that too. They pushed aside the danger that surrounded them, forgot that time was their number one enemy. In essence they were living for the moment.

For Danielle, those were days filled with magic. She was where she longed to be, and that was locked tightly in Keir's arms, letting him absorb her fears and her anxieties. She knew that she was playing a dangerous game, that she was existing on borrowed time, and it made her much more determined to cram the memories of a lifetime into those days.

She refused to speculate on tomorrow and the pain and heartache it was certain to bring. Instead she seized the moment.

And that was exactly what she was doing when she came downstairs early one morning to a quiet house. Where was Keir? she wondered as she breezed into the kitchen. Then she saw a note in the middle of the breakfast room table. Eggs And Bacon In The Oven. K.

Danielle's heart leapt at his unexpected thoughtfulness. Dropping the note, she quickly rushed to the window and looked out. Just as she thought; Keir was hard at work swinging the axe. Boldly perusing his every movement, Danielle's eyes devoured him hungrily. Absently it struck her that he needed a haircut. Longer, looser now, the frosted curls bounced on top of his head, clinging wetly to his face and neck.

For a moment, she enjoyed the free perusal, taking untold pleasure in watching the hard-toned strength of his muscles as they rippled under his shirt. Her skin tingled at the memory of caressing the taut skin that covered those rippling muscles.

Suddenly an idea formed at the back of her mind. She stood still, nervously twisting her fingers together. Now would be the perfect time, she thought. A grin lit her face. Dare she follow through with her plan? After all, he had promised. Hadn't he?

Chapter 8

With an impish grin warming her face, Danielle dashed back upstairs, struggled into her boots, stuffed her curls into a knit cap, slipped into her coat, grabbed her gloves and bounded back downstairs.

Pausing at the window again, she noticed that Keir was still swinging the axe, his back to her. Cautiously she opened the door and tiptoed across the deck, down the stairs and stepped into the snow. With a grin still plastered across her face, she reached down and scooped up a handful of snow, and began squeezing it tightly in the palm of her hand, forming a ball. From time to time she added to it until she had it molded into a nice-sized ball.

Then she began to sneak closer, stopping ten feet away from him. Was her nerve going to fail her after all?

''Keir,'' she called sweetly.

Just as he raised up with his arms full of wood, the snowball flew from her hand, landing with a thud square on the side of his temple.

A silence followed as Keir shook his head several times, trying to fling the cold liquid out of his eyes.

Danielle stifled a giggle. Then turned and ran like a frightened deer. From where she deemed a safe distance, she paused and swung around.

A leering grin replaced the shock on Keir's face and without taking his eyes off Danielle, he slowly let the heavy wood dribble piece by piece out of his arms to land with a thud in the snow.

"I hope you're prepared to pay for that," he yelled, taking a step toward her.

Danielle backed up. "No...please...Keir!" she pleaded before twirling and running through the snow as fast as she could go, lengthening the distance between them.

Keir followed.

Her laughter sang out in the silence. It was music to his ears as he gained on her.

"You told me I could do it!" she squealed over her shoulder.

He should have heard the sound, recognized it for what it was. But he did not. Not until it was too late.

"Danielle!" he screamed.

At his terrified warning, Danielle froze. Suddenly hearing the loud noise, her eyes followed the sound. She looked up to the top of the mountain peak. She saw it then, a slew of rocks mixed with snow lumbering down the mountainside toward her. She stood stricken, her stomach twisting violently as she saw the dangerous debris sweep and grind everything in its path.

"Move, Danielle!" Keir shouted above the devastating roar, breaking free of the self-paralysis that gripped him, rendering him powerless to move.

She began to run, forcing her feet to break through the

snow, only to realize that she was heading in the wrong direction. She heard Keir's frantic voice calling her back.

Fear gripped her as the adrenaline flowed through her body and her heart pumped viciously against her rib cage. Rooted to the spot, she stared at the terrifying spectacle. There was no dramatic roar, no rushing momentum, only the steady slide of the whole mountain on the move toward her. It was like a wave coming at her in slow motion, a wave of tumbling rock. Her legs buckled beneath her, and before she could stop herself, she plummeted into the wet, white snow. Then desperately she pushed herself up, again trying to make her way to Keir.

She stumbled again, this time sobbing as she tried to stand up. But she could not move. Sharp needles of pain shooting through her ankle and down into her foot rooted her feet to the ground.

His whole body trembled with fear. Suddenly he knew he would not reach her in time and even if he did, the powerful blow of the rocks would hammer them both into the wet earth. Nevertheless, his feet never faltered as he raced desperately against time to get to her, though the ground was shaking so violently at times that he had trouble maintaining his own balance.

Then he saw her fall again. Absolute fright gave him superhuman strength to try to reach her before it was too late. He was panting heavily, realizing that she could not get up. Nothing could protect her from the violent onslaught. The rocks were crushing to pulp everything in their way like matchsticks.

Oh, God. Sweat oozed out of every pore on his body. He had to get to her. He just had to.

Danielle began to crawl through the snow, away from the thunderous roar. She looked over her shoulder and saw the rolling devastation only a few yards away.

"Get up and run!" Keir yelled, closing the gap between them. "Run to me!"

"I can't!" Danielle cried. "My ankle!"

Looking behind her she saw something that made her freeze again. It was too late. The huge rocks bounding down amidst the white dust were almost upon her. A scream froze in her throat, and she knew that she could do nothing to ward off the cascading death.

She crumpled to the ground in a heap, covering her head with her hands, her only way of protecting herself. Then suddenly she felt a blunt numbing sensation on the side of her head, heard Keir's bone chilling cry as he lunged across her, felt the cold snow on her face and then there was nothing....

Hidden from view by a row of trees and several large rocks, a man stood up, instantly bringing relief to his stiff legs. He moved around for a moment, giving a vigorous shake to one leg and then the other. Slowly but surely he felt the blood begin to move through his numb limbs.

A heady sense of excitement built steadily inside him as he watched the scene unfold below him. It seemed as though the two figures in the distance were actors and he was the director, carefully, artistically plotting the heartbreaking demise of the leading lady. A cruel smile thinned his lips as he removed his glasses from the bridge of his large uneven nose. He looked on with suppressed glee as the rocks crashed to the ground, burying their target beneath the rubble.

With anticipation, his grin widened in his sallow face. His superior would be proud of him. He was to be commended; it was a job well done. He couldn't wait to deliver the good news. Yet, something held him back. Caution maybe? Years of disciplined training? It did not matter. His entire political future, his entire life was riding on this assignment. It must be perfect down to the last detail.

But he had to be sure. Nothing must go wrong. He waited and watched....

Danielle awoke to a muted glow hovering around her. Slowly, painfully she opened her eyes, feeling every bone and muscle in her body rebel against even that simple action. Where was she? What happened? Then out of the corner of her eye, she saw movement. She saw Keir. Instantly her confusion receded. Tears of panic shadowed her eyes.

Keir watched silently as she opened her eyes. He moved closer to the bed and peered into her colorless face, blinking back his own tears.

"Hi," he said, bending low and placing his mouth next to her ear, concern and worry contorting his features.

Danielle moistened her dry, cracked lips with the tip of her tongue. "Hi, yourself," she whispered, her eyes fluttering shut for a moment, but when she opened them again, he was still there.

"How do you feel?" Keir asked, his voice a raspy whisper.

"I'm...I'm not sure." Again she tried to lick her parched lips.

"Don't try to talk," he said, reaching for her hand and bringing it up to rest against his bristly cheek.

Danielle squinted her eyes in the subdued light, longing to bring his features clearly into focus. Deep lines creased the corners of his eyes and pulled down the edges of his lips. He looked completely bedraggled, worn out. Even in her fuzzy state of mind, she could see the red streaks in his eyes; they reminded her of a road map.

"How...how long have I been...unconscious?"

He flinched visibly. "Long enough," he whispered, laying her hand down beside her, but not turning it loose.

"What time is it now?"

Keir turned and glanced at the clock on the bedside table. "It's six o'clock," he said wearily.

"What...caused those rocks...?" She couldn't go on, the horror of it all robbing her of speech.

He forced his voice to remain calm, unruffled. "I'm sure it was just an act of nature. Anytime you have snow, ice and rock, it can happen." His eyes softened. "But you don't need to worry about that or anything else right now. All you need to do is concentrate on getting your strength back."

Suddenly he averted his gaze, unable to keep his feelings from showing. His eyes narrowed to tiny slits. Gut instinct told him that the rock slide had been no accident. It smelled like a professional job. But unless he could garner tangible proof, what he thought wasn't worth a damn. As yet, he had not been able to scout the area. He had not left Danielle's side since he had bathed her wounds and put her to bed.

"Oh, Keir," she whispered. "I'm so sore. I feel like every bone in my body is broken." A sob rattled in her throat.

"I know," he said in a torture-ridden voice. "But thank God there are no broken bones. You're suffering from multiple bruises and a mild concussion where a rock struck you on the back of the neck."

"When...is all this going to end?" She lifted round, helpless eyes to his face.

He sighed heavily. "I wish I knew. Oh, God, how I wish I knew."

A painful silence fell between them.

Finally Danielle whispered, "I...remember you threw your body over mine just as the rocks...reached me." She paused. "Were you hurt?"

"Just a few bruises, that's all." His voice was gentle. "But I'm tough; it's nothing this old body can't handle."

"Are you sure?" she asked, concern for him beginning to weigh heavily upon her.

"I'm sure."

A deep relieved sigh escaped through her lips before her eyes fluttered shut. She was so tired....

Thinking that she was falling asleep again, he leaned back in the chair and reached in his pocket for a cigarette.

Suddenly her eyes popped open, wide with fear. "You're...not going to leave me, are you?" She reached for his hand.

Keir felt his heart turn over as their fingers entwined. He leaned toward her. "Not unless you'll let me warm you some soup; it'll make you feel better to put something in your stomach."

She smiled faintly. "Thanks, but not right now. I think I'll sleep a while longer."

"I'll be here when you wake up," he said softly.

"Keir."

"Yes."

"Thank you."

"Shhh. Go to sleep."

He watched her until she was breathing evenly and then very gingerly he got out of his chair and strode to the window to stare outside, his jaw clenched so hard the bones hurt. What now? Pain and frustration gnawed at his insides until they were raw. Pain for Danielle. And frustration because he was unable to do anything about it.

Still he blamed himself. If indeed the rockslide had

been started deliberately, which he was still convinced that it was, then he should have been aware of it. But no, he was too busy letting his heart overrule his head. As a result, Danielle's life was in grave danger. Unless, of course, Letsukov thought she was dead.

But he could not go on that assumption. Those Russian agents were professionals. They would be sure the job was finished before they backed off. Yes, he was certain there would be another attempt on her life. The only thing that had been in his favor was that the phone lines had been repaired, enabling him to talk to Cassidy. Together they had discussed the best course of action to take. He pushed his hands through his hair and then rubbed the back of his sore neck. He just hoped they were right in planning their next move. He knew Danielle would not be able to handle much more.

Oh, God, just thinking about those rocks sliding down the mountain, determined to crush the life from her, made him crazy. If he had been a mere second later...

Reaching up, he wiped the perspiration off his brow with a trembling hand and rested his head against the cool windowpane. Why did this have to happen now? When things were going so well between them? For days there had been no bitterness, no harsh words, as their bodies had become one, night after night. But now it must end.

No! his mind rebelled. He did not want it to end. But he knew that he could not go on like this. Dammit, he'd been trained to think like a professional. Where was his self-discipline and training when he needed it? Why was it failing him now? If he had been doing his job, Danielle would not be lying in that bed, having barely escaped death itself.

But how could he give her up a second time? His fingers curled into a tight ball as his mind replayed the pleasures they had shared: her whimpering moans as her tight warmth surrounded him like a velvet sheath, the way her nipples felt like rough silk against his tongue, the way...

No more! Don't do this. Don't do this to yourself!

Why couldn't he remember that nothing had changed? he asked himself brutally. *Because you love her, that's why,* he cried silently. He loved her! And he couldn't have her.

Suddenly a feeling of such intense desolation overcame him that he wasn't sure he could stand up under the weight of it.

Danielle was scared. ''What do you mean, we may be leaving?'' she asked, with difficulty keeping her voice from rising. She didn't want to take one step out of this lodge unless it was to go home. And she could tell by the tone of his voice that she wasn't going home.

''Cassidy and I talked, and we think it may be time to move you to another location.''

Her eyes narrowed furiously. ''Just like that, without any explanation?''

''Just like that without any explanation,'' he echoed tersely. Then he cursed himself for his rude tone when he saw her wince. But dammit, how could he tell her the truth, that if he'd kept his mind on his business, she would not look like she had just fought the battle of Armageddon and lost. And how could he tell her that the accident was *no* accident, that it had been purposefully planned and meticulously carried out. And that he feared for her life.

Danielle glared at him a moment longer before turning her back and walking with heavy steps to stand in front of the fireplace with the pretense of warming her hands. They had been battling back and forth all morning and still she hadn't gotten a satisfactory explanation as to why they were suddenly going to pack up and leave. In fact she hadn't been able to get a satisfactory explanation about anything from him since the day after the accident.

When she had awakened the following morning, still sore, yet feeling fine otherwise, it was to encounter a distant, cold Keir. Oh, he had been attentive to her every need as far as her physical well-being was concerned, but that was as far as it went. No more of the intimate looks or touches and no more sharing the same bed.

At first she had been hurt, then furious, then bitter, only to come full circle to hate herself for having sacrificed her values, her self-respect for stolen moments in his arms. But even at that, she had swallowed her pride and had tried to reason with him. Had it been only two days ago they had exchanged those bitter words?

She had been sitting outside on the deck, brooding, wallowing in her own misery when she looked up and watched as Keir stalked through the door. He sat down across from her with a frown on his face, a frown that had been there constantly since the accident. She knew that part of his problem was that he blamed himself for what had happened, but she could not understand why....

"Keir," she had said tentatively. "I know you blame yourself for my injury, but..."

A harsh expletive had aborted her sentence. "But what?"

"Why are you being so hard on yourself?"

"Because it was my fault, that's why," he bit out savagely.

She spread her hands. "But you...you said that...any

time you have the combination of ice, snow and rock..."
Her voice trailed off.

Keir stood up and in a jerking motion walked to the
railing bordering the deck and propped his foot on the
top plank. "Spare me. I know what I said."

"We're not talking just about the accident, are we?"
she asked, taking great pains to keep her voice from trembling.

He swung around to face her, his expression suddenly
guarded. "Danielle..." he began, only to stop and jam
his hands into his jeans in total frustration.

Danielle immediately dismissed the notion that she
heard panic in his tone. Anger? Very likely. Panic? Forget it! More like disgust. Guilt.

"Why don't you go ahead and admit the truth?" she
retorted.

"And what is the truth?" His voice was ragged with
an emotion she couldn't identify.

"That...you're sorry...you got involved with me...."
Oh, God, she felt sick.

"I just wish it were that simple," he replied harshly,
lifting his hand to his forehead in a weary gesture.

"Oh, it's simple to me. Simple that you're having second thoughts." She scrambled to her feet and glared at
him. "Well, don't worry, from now on you won't have
to worry about me. I know when I've been had." She
tilted her chin as though to keep it above water. "Was
this your way of getting revenge?"

Before he could answer her question, she turned and
fled with his words, "Dammit, Danielle, come back
here," ringing in her ears.

She did not go back, and from that moment on, they
had existed with a polite wall of silence between them.

Now they were involved in another verbal slinging match from which no doubt he would come out the victor.

Danielle strove hard to hang onto her patience and tried to figure out a way to get across to Keir that she was not leaving here today, tomorrow, or any other day for that matter unless he told her why. She could be just as stubborn as he.

"Would you like to talk to Cassidy?" Keir offered soberly, breaking into the frigid silence.

"Not unless he'll tell me what's going on."

"Well, I can't guarantee what he'll say, but maybe he'll make you feel better, anyway."

Danielle's mind was in turmoil. There was something that he wasn't telling her. She felt it. And because of this feeling, she was becoming more paranoid by the minute. She was conjuring up all sorts of terrible events in her mind. Maybe she was indeed going crazy. If she didn't soon get back home to Ann…

Her shoulders slumped in defeat; she turned away from him. Why did he have to choose now to turn on her? She loved and needed him now more than ever. But pride mingled with fear and anger kept her silent. She would just have to endure on her own. She had made it without him for all those years; she could do it now. Couldn't she? Suddenly a numbness settled over her, and she felt like her soul was withering and dying within her. Damn him!

There was an answering grin set to Keir's jaw as he studied her in the lingering silence. In spite of his resolution not to weaken, he longed to beg her to forgive him, to tell her he was sorry that he had hurt her. But how could he when he was hurting as deeply as she? Dammit, he had to protect her, didn't he? Keep her safe? Of course he did. In order to do that, he had to keep his mind and heart clear, clear of her sweet smell, the feel of her smooth, gentle curves. And though he knew that he could never have her, it didn't stop him from loving her.

"Danielle," he said softly.

She faced him, her face devoid of expression, her eyes dull with that haunted look he knew so well.

He cursed himself silently. "The move isn't set in concrete, you know." His voice had changed, the pitch was deeper. "But remember, if we do have to go, it will be for your own good."

Danielle's conscience pricked her sharply, making her feel guilty for her behavior. She swallowed hard. "I...know," she said, pushing back a wisp of hair that was tickling her cheek. "It's just that..."

"I understand," he cut in.

Their eyes met and held while once again that heady, explosive, magic crackled between them.

Then a sudden boyish grin captured Keir's mouth, easing the sophistication, the cynicism, the hardness. "Would you like to sit with me and soak up some sunshine while I finish cutting and stacking the last of the firewood?" He waited in breathless anticipation of her answer.

Relief flowed in her veins. Would she ever understand the complexities of this man?

Danielle's eyes raked the sky, looking for a cloud, but there were none to be found. It was another of those truly incredible days. The heavens were an incredible blue making it appear solid, the snow-covered mountaintops so sharp and vivid, the craggy outline of each rock and tree so distant. No city haze or fog existed to deaden the color or blur the lines. It reminded her of the fairy tales of her childhood, the enchanted dangerous places and forests. Places she used to dream of escaping to, always yearning for something more than the confining loneliness of the orphanage. The landscape was too enchanted, almost haunted, as though something frightening and hostile lurked in all that beauty.

She shivered suddenly, then scolded herself for letting her imagination run wild. But then, ever since the rockslide and Keir's abrupt change of attitude, she had been on edge, felt a renewed sense of unease. And now that a move was in the offing, it was worse.

"How does it feel to be a lady of leisure?" Keir asked, swinging the axe as though it were made of air instead of steel.

Keir's deep voice jerked her out of her unsettling thoughts. She squinted against the glaring sunlight bouncing off the snow and smiled at him after seeing the teasing glint in his eyes.

"I'd love to help, only I didn't think you'd let me."

"Huh! You think you'd like to help, but once you began working those sore muscles, you'd lose interest in a hurry, believe me."

She frowned and flexed her arms outward and then upward and then around. "Oh, I don't know so much about that," she said. "I only feel a slight twitch when I move."

Keir's eyes were unexpectedly tender. "Well, you don't worry about doing a thing. I just want you to sit right there where I can keep an eye on you, and rest." His voice had grown serious, with an undercurrent of possessiveness that left her weak.

She took a faltering breath, then rushed on to cover her confusion. "If...if you insist.... But how am I ever going to get the soreness out of my muscles if I don't get some exercise? You haven't let me lift so much as a dish towel since...since the accident.''

"That's right." He paused, supporting himself on the handle of his axe and looking at her carefully. "And I don't see any reason to change it now."

She was quiet for a moment as she studied his features: the dark skin leathery, the dark tangled hair that fell across his wide square forehead. With the sun lighting his upturned, relaxed face, his features lost their shadowed, hard look.

"All right, you win," she said at last, making a face. "I won't argue. I'll just sit here, soaking up this wonderful clean air and sunshine and watch while you slave away." A smile teased her lips.

How long she sat there, she didn't know. She lost all track of time. But it must have been hours, she thought. Yet, Keir showed no signs of tiring, nor did she tire of watching him. It was as though his big, brawny body were made of iron, the way he split one log after the other, stopping only long enough to stack them. She was mesmerized by his display of untiring strength. And he was so good to look at.

She never knew, could not remember later what made her suddenly turn and stare off into the distance. But it was that small unconscious action that saved her life.

Stark terror dug at her chest, cutting off her breath. *No!* she screamed silently. Lurking on the mountainside adjacent to them, a man was scurrying around as though looking for a place to hide. Heart thudding, her throat parched, her mouth dry, she watched. The fact that he was there was horrifying in itself, but the rifle he was wagging in his hand made the nightmare shockingly real.

For a moment—stunned—she couldn't react. Then she

raised wild, rounded eyes to Keir, stretched her arm toward him in a silent plea.

As if aware of her panic, Keir whirled around. It was then that he caught his first glimpse of the metal flashing in the bright sunlight.

Then he saw the man crouched down in the snow.

Then he heard the brittle, echoing crack of a shot, heard wood splinter behind him on the tree opposite Danielle.

"Danielle! Get down!" he screamed, slinging the axe aside before ducking and crawling on his hands and knees, dragging his rifle with him, to where she was sitting in a frozen stupor.

"Danielle!"

This time his cry freed her frozen limbs, and she dove head first in the snow, behind the wood, landing on top of Keir just as another bullet passed by their heads.

Out of breath from her fall and shaking as though her bones were coming apart, Danielle clung to Keir, still unable to utter a word.

Above her, Keir's mouth was set in a straight grim line, lips tightly compressed. His face was pale. Fury wound him up as if he were a watch spring; under the strain, the muscles in his neck popped up, taut, impressive, ready to strike.

"Are you all right?" he asked, speaking against her mouth, his body remaining a shield over hers.

"I...think so," she whispered.

Satisfied with her answer, Keir reached for his rifle and cocked it, looking at his target, an evil glint in his eye.

Danielle's heart was pumping crazily, and she felt curiously lightheaded, as though she were a character in one of those old horror movies. But reality returned with a vengeance when she heard a bullet bounce off the front of the wood pile, cracking like a bullwhip.

"Listen to me," Keir demanded savagely. "And do exactly as I tell you. Understand?"

She nodded, biting down on her lower lip, drawing blood.

"When I tell you, I want you to get up and run to the side door of the cabin."

She began twisting and turning beneath him. "No! Not without you!"

"Dammit, you'll do as I say. It's our only chance. I'll cover you by firing in succession. He'll be so busy covering his own hide, he won't be able to get a clear shot at you."

"Oh, God, Keir," she cried as he helped her to her knees.

She clung to his hand, tears streaming down her face.

He looked at her for a brief second, his heart in his eyes. "When I give you the signal, you crouch down and run like hell." He then rolled over on his stomach and began firing. "Now! Run!"

She ran.

Keir did not let up until he saw Danielle reach the side door of the lodge, frantically yank open the door and dart through it.

From the warm interior, Danielle stared panic-stricken as the play of gunfire continued. She was sobbing openly now, beside herself with fright for Keir. *Oh, God, please, don't let anything happen to him. Please not because of me.*

From where she was standing she could see Keir stop to reload and then suddenly try to get up, only to stumble forward while forcing bullets from his own rifle as a cover. He labored toward her, firing the heavy gun.

It seemed to happen in slow motion, yet everything happened in a split second. Was he hallucinating or did he see the assailant fall just as he felt his own head explode with a force that seemed to lift his feet from the earth? He felt his body being hurled and suddenly he was flat on the ground. He was looking up at the sky and trying desperately to breath. He groaned as the world started spinning. Everything dissolved into blackness....

"No!" Danielle screamed.

Chapter 9

Danielle could not stop screaming. Not until she saw Keir move, that is. He was alive! Thank God, he was alive. But her jubilation was short-lived. She had to get to him. Now. Before it was too late. Suddenly without conscious thought of her own safety, she crashed through the door, hit the ground and began frantically crawling toward Keir, tears of relief and terror streaming down her face.

But there were no sounds of gunfire to disturb the uneasy, eerie silence that now filled the air as she thrashed her way through the snow on bowed hands and knees.

"Keir, oh, God, Keir," she cried, reaching out to him. Her fear trembled on the edge of panic as she took in his face, white and stark.

He lunged toward her; she caught him in her arms and bore the brunt of his crushing weight, grinding their bodies deep into the snow.

"Danielle," he rasped. "Go...may...try...again." His words were pushed past his lips, an awesome effort.

She was sobbing. "Don't, don't try to talk. Let me help you."

The afternoon remained silent.

"Can you move enough to get to the house?" A quiver of icy dread tore through Danielle. Keir was right; they were nothing but sitting ducks in these wide open spaces. If the sniper should return again... Or was he dead? Or had Keir only wounded him? If the latter, was he just lying low, waiting for his chance to cut them both down?

Like a demon possessed, Danielle began tugging and pulling on Keir's massive frame. "Please," she pleaded, "you've got to help me."

He tried to get up.

She tugged again, making little headway. She couldn't do it. *Yes, you can! You have no choice.* But he was just too big, too cumbersome, too hard for her to handle.

He groaned.

Cradling his head against her chest, she placed her ear close to his lips. "Are...you trying to tell me something?" she asked desperately.

He nodded, then groaned again, as a piercing pain shot through his head.

Danielle panicked, thinking he'd passed out again. She touched his cheek with her gloved hand.

"Keir..." Her spine prickled.

"Just...a scalp wound...nothing...worry...about."

She went weak with relief that he was somewhat rational, coherent.

"If I stand up, can you get to your feet with my help and lean against me?"

He shook his head in the affirmative, struggling to

stand, using her as his crutch. She gained her footing, Keir's body resting heavily against her.

Danielle felt as though her bones would crumble under his staggering weight, but taking slow laborious steps, they inched forward, terror giving her muscles the lift they needed.

Finally they made it to the door of the lodge.

Managing somehow to wedge her body between the door and Keir, she was able to get him across the threshold.

"Just a little farther," she encouraged, panting, her breath coming in short, uneven spurts, her chest feeling as though it would burst at any moment.

The couch. She had to make it to the couch. One more step, she kept telling herself. If she lost her burden in the middle of the floor, she would never be able to get him up again.

Again he sagged heavily against her. Her heart skipped a beat as she whipped her head around to look at him. Blood was trickling down his face, down onto the collar of his shirt, staining the fabric a dark crimson.

Pushing back her hysteria, she gritted her teeth and took that final step. Sick, weak-kneed, exhausted, she felt at last her leg clunk against the wooden trim on the couch. Sobbing openly now, she held herself at an angle and lowered Keir's body down onto the soft cushions.

She then collapsed against him like a tattered rag doll, sobbing her heart out.

Thank God, Keir was alive. And thank God they were safe....

"How's your head?"

Keir almost smiled. "Other than feeling like I've been

beat with a baseball bat, I'm fine." But his face belied
this; his skin was deathly pale against the dark beard
stubble.

They were huddled in front of the simmering fireplace,
the afternoon sunlight only moments before having suc-
cumbed to the full moon and twinkling stars. It would
soon be time to make their move.

Danielle drew a shallow breath. "Please...don't joke
about it. I..."

"I'm sorry," he interrupted, looking contrite, "but I
had to try to do something to ease that tense, frightened
look pinching your features." He paused, leaning over
and laying his hand on hers, giving it a gentle squeeze
before withdrawing it. "I'm all right, truthfully. You
know how profusely head wounds bleed. They always
seem much worse than they really are. After my head
quits hammering, I'll be as good as new."

"I...I still can't believe the sniper's bullet only grazed
your temple." Her chin wobbled. "When I...I saw you
fall..."

Even now, hours later, she still could not wipe the
scene from her mind. Had it been only a few hours ago
that she had bathed his face to find that he was right, that
the bullet had grazed his temple, giving him nothing
more than a dizzy, pounding headache at the base of his
skull?

A tremor shot through her, and she began rubbing her
hands briskly up and down her arms, trying to generate
some heat to her limbs, which were cold in spite of the
red-hot fire.

"Hey," he pleaded gently, leaning toward her once
again, "don't fall apart on me now. You've come

through like a champ so far; don't ruin your record. What do you say?''

''I'll try,'' she whispered, her eyes fluttering shut for a brief moment as her head fell against the back of the chair. Her face was waxen in the yellowish glow of the lamplight. Fear had left its mark.

Keir felt his chest tighten with longing to hold her. But if he touched her now, it would be fatal to them both. The fight had just begun. They still had the dangerous task of getting to the helicopter undetected and getting away before their tormentor or tormentors returned, whichever the case might be, and tried again. Danielle might not be so lucky next time. He had no way of knowing yet if he had fatally wounded the sniper. More than likely he had not. The only thing he could remember before he blacked out was seeing him fall. How the hell had they tracked them down?

But there was no doubt in his mind that they were no longer safe in the lodge. After Danielle had cleansed his face and doctored his flesh wound, he had gone immediately to the phone to get an emergency coded message to Cassidy. But lifting it off the hook, he hadn't been surprised at what he'd heard: nothing. This time he was certain the lines had been cut. They were on their own.

He felt her eyes on him. He turned and faced her.

''We're not out of danger yet, are we?'' she asked.

''No, we're not,'' he answered bluntly, then expelled his breath heavily, lean features suddenly grimly etched in the subtle lighting of the room. ''If we do make it to the chopper, then we have to assume they might have tampered with it, although when I checked it a while ago and untied the back and front blades, things appeared normal. If anyone had fooled around, I couldn't tell.''

She tugged her fingers through her hair. "You took an awfully big chance scouting around in the dark by yourself."

Keir's eyes glinted dangerously. "Not as long as I'm packing my hardware. If anything had moved other than the trees, I would've blown a hole through it."

Danielle's eyes dipped to the revolver lying on the hearth only a hair's breadth away from his right hand. Close to his heavy booted foot and resting on his thigh, was a long-barreled rifle. Looking at those menacing objects, she was again reminded of the dangerous game they were playing. A game of cat and mouse with high stakes—their lives.

She recoiled, whipping her eyes away from the guns, feeling her insides curl with yet another kind of terror. Death. Oh, God, she wasn't ready to die. But for the first time since the nightmare began, she realized that she might not come out of this alive. And because of her, Keir could lose his life as well.

Hadn't he already taken a bullet that was meant for her? She was finding it all extremely hard to cope with. And the fact that it was his job, what he was trained to do, made not a whit of difference. After all, he *was* the father of her child, the man she loved. Didn't that count for something in this insane world? And now, even though she knew that he did not love her and was planning to marry another, she did not care. All she wanted to do was curl up next to his strong, warm body and beg him to love her. She needed him, his warmth, his strength. Just this one last time. Her vow to rely on no one but herself evaporated in the mist like a phantom horse and rider.

Yet she knew that her deepest yearning was impossible. As she peered at him now, he was again wrapped in a cloak of hostility. As he'd so brutally reminded her before, she was a job, an assignment, nothing more.

She felt the pain within her abate to the dull ache that had become her silent shadow. If only she could stop loving him....

"It's time to go," he said, bringing her sharply back to reality. There was a brittle, controlled edge to his voice.

Getting up, Danielle marshaled every bit of self-discipline she possessed to keep her mind clear. She would not be a burden to him. But the thought of slipping through the inky blackness trying to get to the helicopter made her limbs knock with sheer terror. However, she let none of this show as she faced him.

"I guess I'm as ready as I'll ever be," she answered, somehow managing to keep her voice even.

But Keir was aware of her fear. It was so strong that it was almost tangible. He glanced at her one more time, taking in the lovely picture she made standing straight as an arrow, her shoulders squared stubbornly, her eyes wide and trusting, yet glossed with a touch of uncertainty. She reminded him of a tiny soldier ready to do battle without even the slightest idea of how to go about it. The soldier's only arms, guts and determination. But hadn't some of the mightiest wars of all been won with soldiers such as this? In that moment, he had never loved her more.

"Keir..." She searched his darkening eyes.

He took a deep breath and let it out slowly, wondering what sort of madness held him in its grip.

"Let's go," he muttered brusquely, reaching down and effortlessly lifting the pistol and ramming it down into his shoulder holster. Then he slipped into his jacket and picked up the rifle.

Danielle, already having donned her coat, reached for her cap, gloves and purse.

They were ready.

"I want to go over the plan one last time," Keir said as he switched off the lamp, plunging the room into a muted darkness. They began to make their way slowly, cautiously across the floor to the side door.

"Remember," he went on, "you're to hug my backside like a leech. But if you hear anything that sounds like gunfire or anything out of the ordinary, run for the nearest cover and hit the ground immediately." He paused. "Now you tell me what you're supposed to do if something happens to me."

"If...if I can, I'm to get the rifle and run to the chopper, barricade myself in and..."

'And shoot to kill."

"Oh, Keir," she whispered, moving her head helplessly from side to side, "please, don't..." She broke off as her body jerked violently. "I...don't want to even think about anything happening to you."

"Dammit, Danielle, you have to think about that," he countered tersely. "It's a reality—a god-damned reality. I thought you understood that." He heard her whimper and hated himself for having to use such harsh language and tactics to clear her mind and sharpen her nerves. It was an old intelligence ploy, but it worked. He had to keep her together until they reached the chopper and were airborne.

At present, she was too weary, too heartsick, too scared to argue. She would follow Keir wherever he led. And remembering too her promise not to be an albatross, Danielle said steadily, ''You can count on me.''

''Atta girl,'' he said, his voice having suddenly gone hoarse. Then he touched her hand and she responded by gripping his briefly. His hand was warm as love. Her throat tightly constricted, she followed him wordlessly out the door.

Danielle was positive that she did not breathe the entire time they stole through the dark, cloudy night. She smelled snow in the air. That's all they needed was another storm, she thought. Crouched down, they darted in silence from one massive clump of trees to the other.

Keir dragged her relentlessly, his grip on her arm like a steel trap, never faltering in his determination to outwit his unknown assailant and get her to safety. But with every step they took, she could feel Keir's frustration, hear his muffled curses as the deep snow made their progress slow and difficult. The only thing in their favor was the low, swirling cloud cover.

Yet Keir's sensitive ears were attuned to every sound no matter how slight or insignificant. When he deemed it safe, they pressed on. The moaning wind whipping through the bare treetops was the only sound between them.

When at last the helicopter came into view, she went weak with relief. She knew then the gods were smiling on them. They were going to make it.

She could feel the steel in Keir's body as she leaned heavily against him while stopping one more time before springing to the chopper.

Keir waited, his eyes searching, his rifle raised and

ready. Fear and tension spread between them like a cancer.

Danielle stood in paralyzed silence, still not breathing. Had Keir seen, heard, something she hadn't? Had they come this far only to be fair game now as they made their last bid for freedom? Suddenly their destination seemed a lifetime away.

Then Keir yanked on her hand, giving her the signal to move. Bending low, they began to run.

Sucking in the cold air, Danielle felt her lungs laboring as she lifted her legs high in the deep snow, matching Keir's brutalizing gait step by step.

It wasn't until Danielle slammed the door of the helicopter shut that she breathed.

Wasting no time, Keir began flipping toggle switches on and off, checking needles and dials.

Then he glanced at Danielle, sitting reed straight in her seat, her teeth chattering. Delayed reaction, he thought.

Reaching over behind him, he came up with a blanket and laid it in her lap. "After you put on your headset, bundle up in this," he said. "And stop worrying. Since they haven't made their move by now, they're not going to." He gave her a reassuring smile.

Danielle stopped her teeth from banging together long enough to give him a weak smile before putting on the cumbersome headset and untangling the thick blanket and wrapping herself in it. She felt somewhat better now, content to leave everything in his capable hands.

Keir flipped more toggle switches and the cockpit lit up. A few seconds later the blades overhead began making a whop, whop, whop noise. After that Keir pulled back the stick, and the helicopter rose swiftly in the cold Virginia night.

"Are you going to try and contact Cassidy?" Danielle asked, her heart no longer palpitating.

Keir raked a hand over his hair. "I'm tempted, but I'm afraid to break radio silence. Once they realize we're airborne they'll tune into our radio frequency."

"Is there any chance at all that they won't?"

He hesitated. "A slim to none."

"Do you think we should risk it?"

"Do you?"

"No."

His jaw tensed. "I agree. I don't want to give those bastards another chance to get at us. I'm going to fly us to our training camp where I know you'll be safe."

She tried to ignore the tiny throb behind her temple, but after a while it was hard to do so. It just would not go away no matter how much she kept telling herself that she was no longer afraid.

"Are you warm enough now?" Keir asked.

"Yes...I'm fine, except for my pounding head," she answered honestly.

His eyebrows furrowed as he fumbled in his pocket for a cigarette. "You can relax, you know. The worst is over." *At least for the time being,* he added silently.

"You're sure?"

"I'm sure."

"Why do you think they weren't waiting for us?"

Keir looked grim. "It's my guess they're operating one man short now and have probably gone back to regroup."

"You...you mean you think you actually...killed...?" She broke off, shivering.

"It was either him or us." There was no emotion in

his doubled-edged voice. Just a deadly calm statement of fact.

Danielle shivered again and fell silent.

"Why don't you try and get some sleep," Keir said at length. "Maybe by the time we meet Cassidy, everything will be over. When he gets my message, the FBI will be swarming around the lodge in addition to combing the mountains around it and setting up roadblocks. If they are still in this area, they're good as caught." Was it his imagination or were the controls getting stiff?

"Do you think that it was Letsukov and his partner, Zoya, who shot at us?"

"More than likely. But there's still an outside chance that Letsukov's hired someone to do the dirty work for him. It's awfully risky for Letsukov to get personally involved, but now Zoya, that's a different matter altogether. Again, it's all conjecture on my part."

He paused and drew on his cigarette, watching her tense, pale features reflected in the moonlight. Again he felt that tight squeeze on his heart while suppressed fury gnawed at his belly. How much more could she take? Dammit, it wouldn't do for him to get his hands on those sons of bitches.... It was fast becoming an obsession with him. He tightened his knuckles around the wheel, feeling them almost snap in two under the pressure.

Then forcing a calm to his voice that he was far from feeling, he continued soberly, "Rest now. I'll wake you when we get ready to land." Sweet Jesus! It wasn't his imagination; the controls were jamming.

Reassured by his smooth, confident tone, Danielle threw him a faint smile and eased her head back. For now, they were safe. She refused to think beyond the moment. But she had no more than closed her eyes when Keir's loudly vented curses jerked her upright.

She swung terrified eyes to stare at Keir's rigid profile. "What's...what's wrong?" she asked over her hammering heart, watching him struggle with the controls.

"We're losing god-damned pressure, that's what!"

"What does that mean?" There was a waver in her voice.

"From the way the chopper's behaving, the hydraulic line's sprung a leak," he said roughly.

Danielle's features mirrored her disbelief. "Does... does that mean we're going to crash?"

"No, but it does mean I'm going to have to set her down. Now!"

"But...but how? It's dark...the mountains..."

They didn't want to believe it, but they *knew*.

The terror had begun again.

"Don't panic," Keir pleaded urgently. "Just tighten your seatbelt and hold on."

Feeling as though her insides had been kicked out, Danielle stiffened and tried not to think, tried to blank out what was happening. But she couldn't; it was too horrifyingly real. Oh, God, had they come this far only to end up crashing in the mountains, their bodies mangled and burned beyond recognition? She stared down at her hands, which were clenched, thinking: *This is it. I'll never see my child again. I'm going to die!*

Keir knew that he was gambling, but he had no alternative. It was either land her now in the mountains or die.

It was a curious sensation of helplessness, with not even a button to press, as his only link with reality seemed to be four closing points of orange lights. He could feel the sweat beneath his arms, running down his sides. He knew that under the weight of the grip he was exerting on the lever, his hand was shaking fiercely, his head was pounding, causing his stomach to heave. He prayed...

He threw the lever forward, hoping against hope that he was wrong. No such luck. The gears were jammed. Quickly he adjusted his airspeed, at the same time checking the hydraulic circuit breaker. He was right. The sign flashed: Out—hydraulic failure confirmed.

Losing no time, he switched to manual override, allowing him to steer the chopper manually. Next he reached over and flipped on the bottom landing lights, searching desperately for a place big enough to land.

He dared not look at Danielle, but he didn't have to. He knew that she was going through hell, and there was nothing at this point he could do to relieve the fear. Dammit to hell, he cursed silently. No wonder those Russian bastards weren't waiting for them. Just as he'd feared, they had indeed tampered with the chopper.

"Keir, are we going to make it?" Her voice shook.

His face grew black with determination. "You're damned right," he hissed, though it took all the strength he could muster to manipulate the lever.

Danielle's eyes were glued straight ahead, her hands digging into the seat as Keir continued to fight the lever. It seemed like forever, but in actuality it was only minutes before he guided it onto a flat strip sandwiched between two mountains.

Her heart was in her throat as she felt the helicopter make contact with the hard ground.

Keir sat for a moment, rigid and immobile. Then he wiped the sweat from his brow and faced Danielle.

"Are you all right?"

"I…I think so," she whispered, her eyes slowly filling with tears. "What…what about you?"

"I'm fine," he said, his eyes holding hers.

"Do…do you think they'll be waiting for us?"

He hesitated, his heart still knocking. "Probably," he answered honestly.

She turned away, not wanting him to see her fears, her weakness, and peered out into the grim, silent night. What now? They were stranded in the mountains, cut off from the world, no food, no shelter except the plane, and more than likely still being pursued. She wanted to scream. But she did not; it would be fatal to allow herself that luxury.

Keir saw the tears pooling in her eyes, sensing that she was close to the breaking point. But he couldn't have her falling apart now, any easier than he could have earlier, even though he was worried about that possibility. She had been through hell and not once had she complained or cried. But he did not know how much more she could take.

No doubt, it would be morning before they were rescued, if then. It was definitely going to storm. That meant they were looking at spending the night in the chopper and then tomorrow—well, he wouldn't think about tomorrow. They still had to get through this long, cold night. He glanced through the windshield. Despair hardened his features as he heard the snow mixed with sleet hit the glass.

He sat still for a moment and then reached for Danielle.

* * *

Luke Cassidy was worried.

"Amy," he bellowed into the intercom, "get me Tony Welch in here on the double."

"Sir, are we going to make our move now? Join the FBI?"

Cassidy swung around to face the other occupant of the room. His name was Ray Tanner, a tall, slender man with red hair and freckles who could pass for fourteen instead of forty. But that was as close to a boy as he came. Next to Keir McBride, he was the agency's top man. He was a crackerjack shot and also like McBride had nerves of steel. But he was missing that certain instinct that set McBride apart from other men. However, for this job, he was exactly what Cassidy needed. "We don't have any choice, especially after what we've just learned." Cassidy's features were bleak.

"Do you think they're still alive?"

"If Letsukov and his god-damned muscle men haven't gotten to them first." He pounded his hand on the desk in frustration. "Dammit, how in the hell did they find them?"

"Forgive me if I sound hardhearted, sir, but McBride can take care of himself. He's a mean son of a bitch."

"By himself yes, but not with a woman along."

"Do you think—"

A sharp rap on the door interrupted Tanner's sentence.

"Come in, Welch," Cassidy said sharply.

Tony Welch strode into the room, his forehead creased in a perplexed frown. When his superior sent for him on a moment's notice, he knew something big was going down.

"Sir," Welch said respectively. "Tanner."

"Sit down, Welch," Cassidy said, "and let's cut the polite crap. We've got trouble, big trouble."

Tony Welch flushed and sat down.

"A forest ranger sighted a chopper in the mountains not far from McBride's lodge. We wouldn't have thought much about it except on their radio frequency they picked up a scrambled message from what sounded like two Russians. One was demanding help while referring to their target being in range."

He paused, holding their gaze. "It's just been confirmed that McBride's chopper is definitely gone from the lodge. But due to the snowstorm, the FBI is afraid to risk sending any choppers in there."

"Where do we come in, sir?" Tony asked, finally getting a word in edgewise.

"Storm or no storm, we're leaving at first light of dawn."

Both men stood up and nodded their assent.

Cassidy walked to the door, yanked it open and turned around. "Meeting adjourned, gentlemen."

The shack was securely padlocked. That was obvious from his position on top of the slope that angled down through the pine trees toward the front door. The window next to it was boarded up, as he assumed the others would be. The place looked like no one had been around for a while, but he couldn't be sure. He was taking no chances.

He crawled down from the top of the slope, not standing until he was sure that he could not be seen by anyone from below, and began winding through the trees, stopping from time to time to study the shack from a different direction. It still appeared deserted. His eyes kept dipping to the ground checking ahead of him for any tracks where someone might have gone down to the shack, but there weren't any, although that didn't particularly ease his mind. Anyone after them would know enough to hide their tracks. All the same he couldn't be too cautious.

Keir tromped carefully through the trees, tapering off to one side as he descended. The snow whipped around him. He glanced at the dilapidated structure, glancing around him, continuing to circle. Since he had found the shack, they could have too, and since this was the only one nearby, they could have easily guessed that this was where they might come for food and shelter.

Shelter. Up above where he had first been studying the shack, Danielle was waiting, and if he had to take his time and check out the shack thoroughly, he also had to hurry. Danielle couldn't make it much farther. She was utterly exhausted. From the moment they had awakened in the chopper at dawn, stiff, freezing cold and hungry, they had been on the move. They'd had to take a chance on finding some type of roof over their heads or risk freezing to death. He'd been afraid that any type of rescue was impossible in light of the storm.

Now, all he was concerned about was getting Danielle out of the elements and safe from their pursuers. His gut instinct warned him that the worst was yet to come. Danger stalked them like a tangible evil.

He bolted over to the side of the shack, stopped, pressed himself flush with the building, peered around the corner, gun raised.

No one.

Then he placed his ears next to the shuttered window for any sound from there. Hearing nothing, he made his choice. He spotted and picked up a broken piece of metal, ducked around to the front door of the cabin and worked the metal between the lock and the door. One quick yank and the lock cracked away, wood splintering. Dropping the rusty tool, he angled in through the door, gun ready.

Deserted.

Once his eyes adjusted to the dark, they darted around the room, taking in the old rickety wooden bed frame leaning against the left wall, mattress gone, no springs, just wooden slats, a black potbelly stove to the right with metal ducts going up through the ceiling, a few cans of food stacked on a propped-up shelf. The place smelled clean but damp.

It was a moment before he relaxed enough to move, breathing slowly. Then going to the door, he waved for Danielle to come down.

He met her halfway.

While Keir reached for a weak and trembling Danielle, three men with binoculars watched them from the top of the opposite mountain peak. And when the two weary figures turned and made their way back toward the shack, one man let the glasses fall to his chest and took a sip of cold coffee from a cardboard container while watching the door of the shack close.

He smiled at his companion, oblivious to the pain this brought to his large nose, his thick frozen lips. "We've got them right where we want them now, Comrade Letsukov," he said speaking in Russian. "We won't fail this time."

The second man was as pale as a pallbearer, but nothing could mask the cruel twist of his thin lips. "You had better not, comrade, you had better not." With an evil smile, he took a sip of cold coffee. The third, beefy-looking man kept his silence.

* * *

Once the door creaked shut behind them, Danielle slumped down onto the hard, cold floor, chills wracking her body.

Concern hurried Keir's actions. Although he knew that it would be suicidal to build a fire, he was going to chance it anyway. He had to bring some warmth to Danielle. She had endured a perilously long and hard day. And it wasn't over yet, he thought with a harsh sigh.

"Hang on," he said. "As soon as I bolt the door and put that old bench in front of it, I'll build a fire." He wasn't about to take any chances on being slipped upon unawares.

She nodded weakly.

His eyes searching the room, he saw an old tattered sleeping bag wrapped in plastic on a corner shelf. Quickly, he crossed the room, pulled it down, gave it a hard shake and then threw it on the floor.

"Here, slip into this. It'll help until I get the fire going."

Refusing to think about how filthy it was or who might have used it, Danielle scooted over onto it and numbly let Keir zip it up to her chin, her wide, frightened eyes watching his every move.

"You're doing great," he whispered gruffly, before transferring his concentration to the stove.

"Is there anything I can do to help?" she asked after a moment, struggling to sit up in the sleeping bag.

He was hunkered down, breaking the dry splintered wood into small pieces, making a pile of them on the inside of the stove.

Swinging around to face her, he was struck anew at how fragile she looked. He felt his heart turn over. The creamy skin under her eyes was stained a bluish color, enhancing the vulnerable twist of her mouth. Her features wore a white, stricken look. But again she wasn't complaining. If Natalie had been in similar circumstances... *Damn you, McBride! Stop it.*

"No," he muttered at last, his nostrils tightening, furious with himself for the turn his thoughts had taken. His hands were unsteady as he dug his lighter out of his pocket and lit the kindling.

Misinterpreting his sudden grimace, Danielle caught her lower lip between her teeth and turned away, fighting back the tears. A knife turned in her stomach, knowing that he was wishing hc had never laid eyes on her again. She had brought him nothing but pain.

A silence followed as Keir continued to fiddle with the fire. He looked terrible, she thought. His eyes were sunk deep into their sockets, the bandage had come off his head, exposing the angry scalp wound, lines were deep around his mouth. Her heart ached for him. He was just as cold and weary as she was, but he was putting her needs first. Because of that, and because she loved him, she wanted him to hold her. She wouldn't think beyond that.

"Keir."

"Yes."

"I'm...sorry."

"For what?" he asked tautly.

He was looking at her now, the fire making spitting noises behind him.

"For...getting you in this mess."

"Don't be. I'm not."

He watched her with hungry eyes. He knew that he ought to turn away. But he was aware that she did not want him to and that he did not want to, that now more than ever their desire remained unspoken. It hung in the air, in her half-hidden figure against the weakening light.

And with the closeness of tomorrow, the end of this stolen moment was intolerable....

She too ignored the danger surrounding them, the hunger gnawing at her stomach, the aches in her body, the approaching darkness, the sleet hammering against the crude shed, and lost herself in those eyes. They were gentle, almost tender, and seemed to draw her very soul from her.

His sharp intake of breath shattered the silence.

She held out her arms.

"Are you sure?" His voice was a hoarse whisper.

Watching him in the firelight, she saw the vein in his neck rise, beating, then fall back.

She breathed achingly. "Yes, I'm sure."

Chapter 10

Wordlessly and without taking his eyes off her, Keir removed his boots and then stood up and discarded his jacket.

Still not saying anything he crawled in beside her and folded her into his arms. With a sigh, Danielle melted against him, feeling him absorb her pain and misery.

"Danielle," he whispered, "I…"

She reached up and placed a finger across his lips, silencing him. "Please. I don't want to talk. Not now. I…I just want you to hold me."

With a groan he tightened his hold, and buried his face into her soft, damp curls.

At this moment, the only thing that was real to her was being in his arms, close to his heart. She had been through so much that nothing else seemed to matter. She could no longer separate the bizarre from reality, except when his arms were around her. And he had never held her this way before. Never. Tender and careful and strong. As if his arms under the flesh were made of steel with all the power in the world to crush her or protect her. And that was the way it felt. Safe. *It's the way I hold Ann,* she realized, her heartbeat suddenly staccato.

That was the way it was with Keir. She had come full circle; she had come home.

Time passed and still they clung. They were both aware of the quiet darkness and of the sleet as it continued to fall on the tin roof. But they were reluctant to break the spell that so tenaciously bound them together. After all, she wasn't asking for a lifetime with this man; she knew that was impossible. She just yearned for the moment. Was that asking too much?

Keir was the first to stir, to speak. Easing her back against the tattered fabric, he propped his head on his elbow and peered down at her. "Are you warm now?" he asked huskily.

"Definitely," she whispered, shifting her gaze beyond him to the smoldering embers of the fire. She smiled. "You did good."

"How's that?" he asked, the grooves around his mouth deepening to suggest a smile. Unconsciously he began stroking the side of her face with a finger. Her skin was smooth and soft beneath his touch.

She was finding it difficult to breath, once again blocking out everything except the pressure of his big, warm body against hers.

"You...you built a cozy fire out of nothing," she murmured rather incoherently, his touch doing crazy things to her insides.

"I'm glad you like it," he drawled, giving her a teasing grin, letting her know what he thought of their inane conversation.

There was another disturbing silence as she tried to subdue the butterflies in her stomach.

He smiled at her and she smiled back.

Then suddenly as though their smiles had lighted a torch, the smiles disappeared. A hint of something hung in the air between them, a sense of waiting, a kind of awareness.

She reached up and traced the outline of his lips with her finger, watching his eyes, seeing a deep dark glow that shook her to the very core. She wished he'd kiss her—not just wished—she *ached* for his kiss.

As though reading her mind, he lowered his head and laid his lips against hers without speaking, and her hands touched where his day's growth of beard grew coarse under his chin. She rubbed her fingers into the dark growth, then she traced the formidable structure of his nose.

He kissed her again, hard and fierce, and something inside of him was angry and frustrated at not being able to graft her slender body to his. God, how he wanted her. Here. This minute. In this crude mountain cabin. He wanted her so badly he hurt. Because he knew being inside her was like that, like grafting her body to his, and each time with more and more permanency until they were truly and entirely inseparable.

"Oh, God, Danielle," he muttered, "I want you so much." He moved his lips against her temple, her forehead, caressed her face, causing her eyelids to droop heavily. His touch was tender, too soothing; she couldn't resist it. Her mouth parted. He kissed her eyelids, then paused to stroke her face again before kissing her ears, the sides of her throat, her chin. Her mouth quivered. She began to moan, unable to withhold her response to the gentleness of his touch.

She put her arms around his neck. "Oh, please...yes," she whispered, kissing him softly on the mouth, moving her hands around to bracket the sides of his face.

Unlocking his hands, he turned her toward him, sliding them around under her sweater and up over the wings of her shoulder blades, feeling the tension like flat stones lying beneath her skin.

"Are you sure?" he rasped, kissing the base of her throat.

"Yes." She would treasure these few hours. She would spend each moment like a miser, as if it would be her last.

He had to bend his head to her lips to hear the simple three letter word. Sighing, he pressed her close, breathing in the smell of her hair, aware of the sudden heat rising from her body.

"Oh, God, I care...so much," she whispered thickly, his hands unbuttoning her clothing; unzipping, unsnapping, unfastening. She kept moaning, feeling his lips and fingertips making their way over her face and neck.

She lay naked in the ghostly glow of the firelight, too beautiful to be real.

He stripped off his own clothing, laid down next to her and once again took her in his arms, placing his hands on her hips bringing his body into perfect alignment with hers. She felt him become hard with the eagerness to place himself inside her.

After a while, she could hear his heart pounding—or perhaps it was her own. She sighed deeply and held him.

He explored and worshiped her with kisses. Keeping

hold of her, their mouths avidly joined, he turned with her, his thighs closing around her, so that he was holding her completely.

Yes, yes, she thought. *Hold me, love me!*

His hands stroked her shoulders and down the middle of her back, curving over her buttocks as he rocked gently beneath her, creating a pressure at the apex of her thighs, causing her to moan, to rock with him, heightening the sensations. His tongue in her mouth made her dizzy with desire.

"So lovely," he murmured. "All softness."

He shifted, turning once more, making her gasp as he teased her nipples, luring her just a little closer to the edge. His touch seared her sensitive skin as he moved her down beneath him, his mouth replacing his fingers on her nipples, turning them hard.

Keir ached for her. She was so warm. So fresh. So vibrant. So real. Her flesh trembled as his touch spoke the language of her body, his thumbs gently tracing an invisible circle around the bumpy, dark halo.

She began to groan softly, excitedly. Her breathing grew ragged and fast as he moved to squeeze her breasts in the large gentle cups of his hands as though they were holy and fragile objects. No longer could she think, only feel.

His head moved down. He kissed her taut, concave belly, pressing his face into her, both his hands relishing the smooth, hard curve of her hips. He moved. Lower.

"Oh, Keir!"

His head dipped knowingly. His mouth, his tongue, his fingers all caressing her, so that she groaned, laboring, opening still more, her face, breasts flushed, burning.

She thrashed about. His caress seemed different, new.

Yet deliriously familiar. Unlike anything she'd known. Yet so right, so perfectly right.

Soon he came up and covered her body with his once more, and she took him between her hands, reaching; taking him in, holding her breath.

He looked down into her face, into her eyes, his own glazed.

"Now," she pleaded. "Sweet man. Now…"

He filled her completely. Binding him to her with her arms, she met his mouth greedily like a starving child.

He stirred inside her, then moved back, exciting a response, then forward, her hips lifting to meet him, her thighs parting still more. He drove into her with both power and gentleness, and she felt herself dissolving beneath him.

Magic. Pure magic. Slowly climbing higher, increasing the pace; she was feeling nothing but pleasure; exquisite pleasure, revived in every pore, magnified, all-consuming.

She whimpered and called his name under the onslaught of the engulfing, painful pleasure.

He wanted to hold back, to make this moment last forever, a lifetime, but for once he found it almost impossible to restrain himself. For him, this was more than an act of sex; it was a rejuvenation, a reawakening, a kind of reincarnation.

Danielle cried out, tearing her mouth away from his, withering against him. He moved more quickly. "I love you," he whispered. Knowing she did not hear, he returned his mouth to hers hungrily, wildly, as she arched against him and was hopelessly locked there, trembling as he kept on and on, until she cried out again, sobbing.

He had to stay inside her, feel the fullness of her response. Feeling it, made humble by what they had together achieved, he collapsed gently upon her breast.

She felt his sudden stillness, then the ecstatic flow as he moved again, again...

It was then that she knew. She could never willingly give him up....

That was only the beginning of a night with no end....

Three o'clock in the morning found them hovered around the fire, feasting on the contents of tin cans of food like they were delicious delicacies from a fine restaurant.

"I never knew food straight out of a can could taste so good," Danielle said as she munched on the last of her beef and beans.

Keir smiled, watching her, having already downed his portion in two bites. Although there was not much to eat, only five cans, it was enough to last several more days if they had to remain there, he thought grimly. He shook himself. He wouldn't think about that now. Not with the firelight playing across Danielle's flawless skin, highlighting its silken sheen, shadowing the hidden places he had sought and found with his lips and hands. And the thought of embracing her again made him tremble.

"I...agree," he said, his voice uncontrollably husky.

Still, after hours of lovemaking, he wanted her again and again and again. How was he ever going to give her up?

He smiled at her, his eyes narrowed into a lazy measuring look.

The tip of her tiny tongue suddenly darted between her lips and circled after swallowing the remainder of her food. The center of him swelled and grew hard.

Danielle was not without her own discomforts. Her senses were drugged with the look, the touch and the feel of him. Madness. Sheer madness, that's what it was. But a madness that neither was prepared to ignore or control. They were running for their lives, hiding out in a log cabin in the mountains, with a snowstorm reeking vengeance on the outside. Yet none of this seemed to matter. Nothing mattered except Keir. She would savor these moments in his arms like a rich, heady wine. And because it was forbidden, it was that much more exciting.

Her head was spinning and her mouth was dry as she silently raised a finger to his lips and began to rub across the inside of his plump lower lip. She felt the moistness seep into her fingertips as she continued her gentle assault.

"Yes," he managed to whisper, before he trapped her finger between his teeth and began sucking on it.

A moan escaped from deep within her as he finally let go of her finger and reached for her. "Come here," he whispered again.

As their bodies gracefully eased back onto the bed roll, their lips met in another of those soft, closed-mouth kisses, followed by a hug. He held her, making her eyes close and her skin ripple with excitement as his hand moved up and down over her hair and back.

Then he released her, studying her quietly for a moment, trying to understand what it was about this particular woman that aroused him so fiercely and made him want her so desperately.

Danielle's eyes were closed now, her head resting contentedly in the curve of his arm, the burgeoning fullness of her breasts grazing his chest. He stared into her face, an ache around his heart, seized by love for her.

Her face. He could spend the rest of his life sitting here looking at her face. Lovely woman with her delicate features, fragile eyelids lined with the finest threads of violet, the curve of her cheek, her jaw, her throat....

"Hey," he said suddenly, snapping his mind back to the moment at hand. "Hey, don't go to sleep on me now."

Her eyes opened slowly and she gave him a sleepy smile, pulling his hand up to her breast and holding it there.

Yawning, she whispered, "Why can't I sleep?"

Her breast felt warm against his palm; he cupped it tenderly.

"I want to talk." His voice was deep and raspy.

"What time is it?"

"Does it matter?"

"No."

"Good girl."

"What do you want to talk about?" she asked, disinterested, breathing in the tangy smell of his flesh.

"You."

Her eyes widened. "Me."

He gave her an indulgent smile, then leaned down and kissed her unhurriedly. When their mouths parted, she looked up into his eyes, basking in the pleasure of simply holding him.

"Yes, you," he murmured.

"What could you possibly want to know about me that you don't already know?" *Please don't let him ask me about Ann.*

"Everything." He smiled. "But mostly what it was like being in an orphanage. You never told me."

Relief made her weak. But yet she hesitated, perplexed

that he would ask something like that now. He never failed to amaze her. But he didn't seem to think his question strange at all. He was perfectly serious and he expected an answer.

"I...I don't know," she stammered, trying to remember. How could she describe the long years of an existence so uniform that time itself had no meaning. The routine, the antiseptic smell, the discipline, the crushing lack of privacy. There was only one word to explain it.

"It was lonely," she said at length. "Lonely because you knew you were cut from a different mold, no matter how hard you tried to tell yourself that you weren't. I remember when I finally convinced myself that my mother didn't want me." She grimaced and was quiet for a moment. "Believe me, it was a bitter pill to swallow."

"How could she have done that?" Keir demanded angrily. "How could she have just abandoned you?"

"I used to think that," Danielle said. "I used to sulk about it and call her terrible names—whoever she was. But as I said, I finally understood a little. She must have been poor, frightened. And somehow I got the feeling she was on drugs, and had been seduced and left with no one to turn to. I'm...I'm sure it wasn't easy for her."

"It wasn't easy for you either," he said sadly. "Were you treated well?"

"Oh, yes. But there were so many of us that it was difficult for the sisters to give us special attention. One sister singled me out and gave me extra attention. She asked me to keep in touch after I left and though I call her often, I have not once returned to the orphanage." She paused, as if uncertain how to continue, and then with a deep sigh, went on, "Now you know..."

There was such a bleakness embedded in her voice that

he was beginning to regret having asked her. Yet he felt that he had to know.

"Thanks," he said gently. "I appreciate your telling me."

She turned and buried her face into his chest, remembering the things she wouldn't tell him. The countless foster homes she'd been forced to endure, where more times than not, she had been mistreated. Agony. She was remembering the agony of knowing she would never be adopted, never have a real home, having learned at an early age that couples were afraid to take a chance on adopting a child with no past, especially one whose mother had been on drugs. It had seemed as though she was tainted.

The day she walked out of the orphanage, she had promised herself that she would never look back. And she hadn't. Until now. But somehow, she didn't feel resentment against Keir for making her talk about the past. In a way, it was a link with the danger surrounding them, and it even had a cleansing, healing effect on her heart, knowing that this sometimes dangerous, sometimes gentle, giant of a man had cared enough to ask....

Keir lit a cigarette and smoked it silently, holding her next to his heart, absorbing her pain, making it his own.

Again she ignored the little warning bell in her mind as she raised up and kissed him with renewed passion. Their time together was only fleeting, she knew. But for her it would have to last a lifetime.

"Make love to me again," she whispered.

With a smile they loved through the night, lost in the magic of their own making.

With the dawn came the knowledge they were no longer alone. They were both up and dressed and Keir was preparing to take a look around outside when he heard the noise. He froze.

Keir was never quite sure what followed—Danielle's scream or the small explosion that blew apart the left front window. It could have been Danielle's scream first. Or she could have been screaming from the explosion. He never knew.

His first thought was that someone had thrown something through the window or that the wind had ripped it apart, but then it registered on him that two bullets had whacked close together into the wall beside him, and he dove toward Danielle and the floor.

"Dammit, they're out there. Get down," he hissed before crashing to the floor. As he landed, he covered his face and neck and waited for the debris to settle. When he looked up, his eyes searched the room for Danielle, his breath coming in gasps and his heart pounding a hole in his chest.

After the first stunned moment and hearing Keir's hissing command, Danielle had likewise hit the floor, rolling across to the dark corner of the room, burying her head in her hands, too terrified even to whimper. Then peeping through her fingers, she watched with her heart in her mouth as Keir tried to make his way toward her.

The wind was shrieking outside; snow gusting in through the shattered window, bullets splitting the air.

Keir raised and pointed, he inched his way on his belly toward Danielle.

Although paralyzed with terror, she managed to reach out and latch onto the front of his shirt, drawing him toward her. He made a terrible sound, one that cut through her as he flung his arms around her, seizing her with all his might, holding her crushed against his chest.

Her lips shook violently as she tried to speak. "What...God...what are we going to do?" she whispered, clinging to him, shaking as another round of bullets riddled the cabin.

Keir reached for his rifle behind Danielle, while slamming the pistol in Danielle's hand. Then he aimed the rifle toward the window and the door.

"It's just a matter of seconds before they'll be on us like a swarm of bees, making sure we're dead." He paused, searching for breath and feeling Danielle's bones as they seemed to rattle in her slender frame. His eyes found and locked on the back door that was in reaching distance of his foot. Deliverance. Maybe. Better than nothing.

Cupping her cold face between his hands, he forced her shocked eyes to meet his. "When I shove open the door, I want you to start firing and take off running. I'll be covering you from both the back and the front. Whatever you do, don't stop shooting as you run toward the woods."

She clung to his hand, her eyes wild. "But...they'll kill...you," she cried, thinking that this was a replay of the day before.

He shook his head roughly. "No, they won't. Don't argue. Remember I won't be far behind you." Dammit to hell, where was Cassidy and the FBI when he needed them?

Positioning her hands on the trigger, still crouched, he slammed his boot against the door, shoving it open.

"Go!"

With her mind completely divorced from her body,

Danielle darted through the door, struggling to fire the pistol, both hands gripping it tightly. She battled the snow, spotting a clump of trees to her right. Sobbing, her chest heaving, bullets dancing through the air, she pushed on, sometimes stumbling, sometimes not. How long she ran, she didn't know.

She was freezing. Her heartbeat exploded and her breathing grew rapid. She felt as though every muscle in her body had been pummeled with a club.

Reflexes took over. One more step and she would have it made.

Then suddenly she stopped dead in her tracks.

Her heart slammed into her throat.

A man's booted feet blocked her path.

Fear rendered her motionless. *Oh, God, I'm going to die after all.*

She forced down the scream and slowly, defeated, she raised her eyes.

"Thank God, you're alive."

She fell in a dead faint into Luke Cassidy's arms.

Keir saw the man follow Danielle, cutting across the snow. Keir halted, spun around, dropped to the ground, rifle aimed and shouted, "Zoya, take another step and you're dead!"

There was not a flicker of emotion in Keir's eyes as he kept them pinned on the Russian.

Then suddenly from another angle, a bullet whizzed by his head. Lunging to the side, Keir leveled his rifle and fired. Zoya dodged. His bullet only grazed him. Stumbling, Zoya continued to follow Danielle's path.

An expletive flew from Keir's lips simultaneously with another bullet whining past his ear, driving him to seek cover. Dammit, he cursed again silently. If only he could see where the shots were coming from or how many there were to contend with.

He brushed the snow out of his eyes and licked it off his lips as he tried in vain to find his culprit. If it was only Letsukov, then he was in good shape, he thought. He could outlast him or waste him. One on one. But it wasn't himself he was worried about. It was Danielle. His only hope was that the bullet he had put in Zoya had slowed him down, keeping him from getting to her. Danielle. He had to have all his wits about him to get out of this and help her. With him dead, she did not have a chance.

"Come out, McBride. You're covered," a heavily accented voice shouted. He saw him then. It was Letsukov all right. He, too, looked exactly like his picture. Good. It was between the two of them. He liked it that way.

"I'm going to get you!" Letsukov shouted again in broken English.

Keir didn't bother answering. He edged sideways, through the thick falling snow, the scattering clumps of tree and rocks providing him with cover. He slipped, slid and scrambled in the snow, hoping to circle to the rear and come up behind Letsukov. He thought of Danielle in Zoya's clutches and did not pause to catch his breath. With luck, he'd get one clean shot.

As soon as Keir spotted Letsukov, his luck ran out. There wasn't one man to face, there were two.

Suddenly a beefy arm circled Keir's throat and lifted him high off the ground. He felt the tightening of that forearm on his windpipe. He was losing consciousness. Fast. He had to escape. Kicking back, Keir smashed his heel hard into a kneecap.

"Damn!" the man grunted in pain, but the hold didn't slacken. Desperate now, Keir raised his leg, sending his heel into his groin.

The goon fell with a thud as he released Keir. It took both of them the same length of time to recover, the man from the intense pain Keir had dealt him and for Keir to get precious air back into his straining lungs.

Both of them rose to hands and knees, then dropped to a crouch. Like wary animals, they circled. He was big and strong, a head taller than Keir, with the physique of a wrestler, a street brawler. But he didn't have an edge on Keir in that department. Keir was like a bull moose. And he knew every alley-fighting technique in the book.

Suddenly Keir feinted. When the goon straightened slightly to catch his blow, Keir again went for his knee-cap. Keir felt the kneecap yield.

"Ahhh!" the man howled in pain, bending over to clutch his injury.

Taking advantage, Keir spun and aimed his foot for the point of jaw.

Crunch!

That one blow was all it took. The man lay sprawled face down in the snow, out cold.

Letsukov. The only one now between him and Danielle. Just as Keir hurled his body toward the Russian agent, a sharp sting in his side doubled him over.

The Russian's laugh filled the air. Using the beefy man's inert body as a shield, Keir rolled over behind him, clutching his side.

Keir peered over the man, but Letsukov wasn't anywhere to be seen. Keir, oblivious to the pain, scrambled for his gun. Reaching it, he slipped it between his stomach and the snow laden ground.

He waited, gritting his teeth, growing weaker by the moment.

He saw the feet, before he saw the face.

"Surely you didn't think you could outsmart us, McBride." Letsukov's voice held an icy sneer. Raising his gun, he pointed it at Keir's head and laughed. "Too bad you won't be around to watch Ms. Davis suffer the same fate."

Reacting instinctively, a strangled cry erupting from his lips, pain blinding him, Keir came up and rammed against the man.

He heard it then. The sharp crack of a rifle. *Oh, God, please, not Danielle!*

Letsukov slouched on top of him just as he seemed to hear a voice, distant and high, and feel a hand on his shoulder, pulling at him....

He knew no more as a sweet darkness sucked him under.

Chapter 11

It was one of those rare winter mornings in East Texas when both the sun and the temperature are in complete accord. By mid-afternoon, the weather forecasters were promising the temperature gauge would rise to the upper fifties. If the weather did indeed hold, maybe she would leave the store in the hands of her assistant and take Ann to the zoo, Danielle told herself. Maybe an outing would help.

The last month's weather had been horrendous. The constant dampness, combined with the low mercury readings, had taken their toll on everyone's temperament.

Dangling her feet off the edge of the bed, shaking in spite of the blaring central heat, Danielle stared at the cream-paneled walls just as she had the day before and the day before that. An unbearable loneliness consumed her as she rose and tightened the quilted robe around her waist and walked into the bathroom.

She tried to ignore the weariness dragging at her spirit as she stepped into the shower, letting the water cascade down her skin. Why couldn't she get a hold of herself? Why couldn't she be thankful that she was back home with Ann and Jusie? Why couldn't she be thankful that her life had been spared? Why couldn't she be thankful that the nightmare was over, that she was out of danger?

But she *was* thankful, she argued. Thankful for everything, but— It was the "but" that was her problem, that was filling her days and nights with mental anguish and despair. She had not heard from Keir.

Since she had boarded the plane for home in the company of Tony Welch, she had lived in silent agony. Thoughts of Keir filled her heart and mind every single moment of every single day. Oh, she knew that physically he was going to be all right. He was recovering from his wound satisfactorily. Cassidy had assured her of that each time she had spoken with him by phone. And he had also assured her that both Letsukov and Zoya would never bother her again, nor would their sidekick. And that once she came to Washington and gave her deposition, she would never hear from the U.S. Marshal's office again.

Yet his confident words did nothing to stifle her concern or her fear. Keir had nearly lost his life twice because of her. That was a burden she was finding hard to bear. The nights were horrible. She would wake up sobbing, her gown drenched with perspiration.

Each time this happened, she would get up and stumble into Ann's room and sit by her bed and stare at her. Other times she would just sit and hold Ann and cuddle her. She was her lifeline.

Still nothing relieved the pain of not hearing from Keir.

Was she wrong? Had she just imagined that he still loved her? Had he gone home, married his fiancée? No. She would not, could not, believe that. She had seen the look in his eyes; she had seen love.

And when she did hear from him, what then? Would he forgive her when he learned about Ann? And if so, would they be able to overcome their other differences? Would he be willing to change? To give up his dangerous job?

With tears gathering in her eyes, she slipped back into her robe after completing her shower and walked with purpose out of her room and into the kitchen. It was early yet, not even seven o'clock, she noticed, her eyes glancing at the wall clock, her hands busy with the routine of putting the coffee on to brew. Once that chore was done, she opened the refrigerator and poured herself a glass of fresh orange juice.

With a deep sigh, she sat down at the table and sipped on her glass of juice, disinterestedly watching the coffee as it dripped into the glass pot. When the wall phone jangled, she jumped; then her heart began racing. She stared at it a moment longer before gathering the courage to answer it. She had been disappointed so often....

"Hello," she said tentatively, lifting the ivory receiver.

"Good morning," a chirpy voice countered on the other end of the line.

Her caller was Marge Beckman, a close neighbor and bookstore customer.

"Hello, Marge," Danielle said, trying to keep the disappointment out of her voice. *You're a glutton for punishment, Danielle Davis!*

"Did you hear what I was saying to you?" Marge was asking in her hyper little voice.

Danielle shook herself, feeling all chewed up on the inside. "Sorry. Would you mind repeating it."

Marge hesitated, before rushing on, "Oh, it was nothing really. I was just apologizing for calling you so early. But I saw the light on in your bedroom...." Her voice faded out.

"That's all right. I was up," Danielle said, rolling her eyes upward, preparing herself for another of Marge's long-winded conversations.

She could picture her friend, sitting in her den, her feet propped up on a footstool, smoking incessantly, her bright brown eyes a perfect combination for her red hair and freckled face.

"How's Ann?"

This brought a smile to Danielle's lips, as did any mention of her daughter. "Oh, she's fine. Her usual contented self."

"Huh," Marge said, "you should've seen her while you were gone. She wouldn't stop crying. Jusie had her hands full, but she managed just beautifully, as she usually does. Have I ever told you how much I envy you, Jusie?"

"Many times," Danielle answered wearily.

For a brief moment, a short silence fell between them. Danielle feared what was coming next, and she was prepared for it.

"When are you going to tell me where you were those days you so mysteriously disappeared?"

Danielle prayed for patience while calming her racing heart. "I'm not," she said bluntly. And rudely. But she had no intention of going through a replay of a conversation of two days ago. Ever since she had returned from her ordeal, Marge had tried every way she could, using every ploy she could think of, as had several of her other friends, to find out where she'd been only to return looking as though she had been to hell and back.

Well, she hadn't explained then, and she had no intention of doing so now. She hadn't even told Jusie the whole bizarre story, only the parts she deemed necessary. And even that had been somewhat of a trauma. But she'd had no choice; she'd owed it to Jusie. She owed Marge Beckman nothing.

"Well…er, what I really called for was to invite you to a party," she said hurriedly, rebounding from Danielle's bluntness. "At my house. Friday night."

"I don't…"

"Please, don't say no, Danielle," Marge cut in before she had a chance to do exactly that. "It'll do you good to get out."

"Marge, you know…"

"Promise me you'll at least think about it," Marge interrupted again before she could answer. "Relax and enjoy yourself for a change. I know the pace you've been keeping at work since you've been back home. When I left the store the other day, you looked like you'd had it."

Perhaps being around people bent on having a good time would do her good, she told herself.

"All right, all right. I'll think about it."

"Good. Now for the best part," Marge said. "Hal has a new assistant. Mmmm, he's a hunk: tall, six feet plus, unattached, and he invited him to the party…"

Danielle's skin went cold. "No. Absolutely not."

"But, Danielle…" The frustration was plain in her voice.

"No, Marge," she stressed again, panic-stricken. "You...know how I feel about that."

"Oh, Danielle, your attitude just proves you're in some kind of trouble," Marge whined. "Why won't you tell me, let me help you?"

"Good-bye, Marge," Danielle said without emotion and dropped the receiver on its cradle, oblivious to Marge's continued frantic prattle.

Trouble. Is that what one called it when a person's heart ached and her soul was plunged into the very depths of despair? When one kept hearing the bullets, seeing the blood, Keir's blood. Trouble. Such a small word to hold so much devastation.

Getting up, she strode jerkily to the cabinet and poured herself a cup of coffee only to have it slosh all over the counter top. "Damn," she muttered, mopping up the spill. Forcing her hands to stop their trembling, she poured herself another cup of the hot liquid. Then holding the cup carefully, she walked to the table and sank into a chair.

A shudder shook the entire length of her body.

For the first time she allowed herself to remember the last time she had seen him, every detail as vivid as if it had happened yesterday. Closing her eyes, Danielle could hear Cassidy's voice....

"Thank God, you're alive," he'd said.

But when she had come around a short time later, a stranger was hovering over her, anxious to make sure she was all right.

Blinking several times, she'd tried to sit up. Gentle hands were holding her down, a blanket thrown haphazardly over her shoulders.

She looked around wildly. "Keir!" she cried, struggling to stand.

"Shhh, calm down," the strange voice ordered. "You're not to worry about him; he's being taken care of."

Danielle struggled that much harder against his restraining hand. "No...no...needs help...must get to him!" Her heart was in her mouth and her lips were dry as she remembered the harsh sounds of bullets, Keir bounding out of the cabin, covering for her as she ran for safety. "Must go to him," she said again, frantically scrambling to her feet, pushing the stranger's hands aside with determination.

"Please, Ms. Davis," he begged, "my orders are to get you to the helicopter, keep you out of danger."

Danielle began to back away from his pleading eyes, shaking her head. "No. Not...not until I see Keir!" Turning suddenly, she began to stumble in the direction of the sounds. The sounds of gunfire. Oh, no, Keir! Was she too late? No!

Hurry! Hurry! Hurry! A voice taunted her as she plowed through the snow, praying.

"Ms. Davis, come back," her protector yelled, though following close behind.

Another voice came out of nowhere. "Dammit, Mason, you were supposed to get her to the chopper. Cassidy'll have your ass for this!"

Danielle never paused. She kept on running.

She saw Luke Cassidy the same time he saw her. He was bent over, staring at a body. Keir's body! She gasped in horror, slamming her hand to her mouth to keep from screaming. Cassidy's eyes were on her as he rose. God, no, please. She couldn't stand it.

Cassidy reached for her as a team of men carrying a stretcher hovered over Keir, lifting him gently. But Danielle couldn't move, couldn't speak, couldn't cry. She was locked in a web of pain so intense, so powerful that it was crushing the very life from her.

"What the hell are you doing here?" Cassidy demanded. "They were told to keep you…" Then he broke off, seeing the look of dazed shock on Danielle's face.

For a moment he just stared at her tragic, lonely figure standing as straight as a reed, the snow curling about her face.

She looked up at him.

Cassidy swallowed against the lump in his throat. "He's not dead," he said softly, "seriously wounded, but not dead."

Her chin trembled. "I…want to go with him," she whispered, her eyes glazed with pain.

Although Cassidy's eyes held sympathy, he spoke with soft authority. "I'm afraid that's impossible. He's on his way to the hospital. But don't worry, McBride's a tough old dog." He cleared his throat. "But then, you ought to know that. He saved your life." He paused again, a bright light flickering in his eyes. "He'll survive. He doesn't have much choice. He's got a wedding date to keep. Remember?"

She reeled as though he had physically struck her *No, No!* she screamed silently. *You're wrong. He loves me!*

He was staring at her strangely, though his voice was gentle. "How would you like to go home, Ms. Davis, home to your child? At last, you're a free woman."

Free? Oh, God, if he only knew.…

"Mommie, Mommie!"

A shudder raked Danielle's slender frame. How long

had she been sitting there tormenting herself? She couldn't seem to stop. But when those men had lifted Keir's still body onto the stretcher and had taken him away, she had wanted to die.

"Mommie!" Ann called again.

Brushing the tears from her cheeks and breathing deeply, she stood up, calling softly, "I'm coming darling. Mommie's coming."

Something disturbed him. A noise? What was going on? He couldn't seem to focus his eyes. He felt a heaviness in his left arm.

"Mr. McBride?" He heard a strange feminine voice. "I think he's finally coming around, Doctor. His eyelids were flickering a minute ago, and I just saw him move his arm."

Keir felt fingers probing around his side. He gasped painfully as they touched the area around his chest.

"Mr. McBride!" came a firm voice. "Mr. McBride, can you hear me?"

Keir tried to force his eyes open. Yet it was proving impossible. He wanted to tell them that, but all he could manage were inarticulate grunts.

"Just relax, Mr. McBride. Relax your body and try to open your eyes," he heard the man say.

He breathed deeply and let his body go limp as he exhaled. Now with practically no trouble at all, he opened his eyes. Two faces were peering down at him. They broke into smiles.

"What's happened?" Keir whispered as best he could. He felt the heaviness in his arm again. It felt like a red hot poker was pressed to it. He turned his head and tried to focus his eyes to see what it was.

"No, please, take it easy," clucked the nurse. 'You've got a hole in your side and you're bandaged tighter than Dick's hatband. You've been drifting in and out since surgery three days ago now. You're at Walter Reed Hospital."

Surgery? What was she talking about? What hole in his side? "What happened?" he moaned weakly. His speech was clearer now. The doctor began examining him. He heard the door open and recognized Dr. Samuel Calcutt, the organization's physician, as he breezed into the room.

"Well, Keir, you're back with us," he said, crossing to the foot of the bed. "You had a close call. How are you feeling?"

"Head hurts, side bloody aches," Keir mumbled.

Dr. Calcutt smiled. He stepped to the side and pulled back the sheet. "In addition to the hole in your side, you have a few fractured ribs. Do you remember anything of what happened?"

Keir wrinkled his forehead, trying to think back. He let out a groan as the pieces began coming back to him. He looked back at Calcutt wildly, frantically. *"Danielle!"*

"Calm down, Keir." He patted his arm. "She's all right. She's at home. You're at Walter Reed."

Keir's head was raging, his tongue dry, heavy.

"We had to perform surgery. You'll be out of commission for quite a while."

Keir tried to look down at his side, but quickly turned his head back as the pounding worsened.

"It's going to be all right, Keir." Calcutt smiled.

"It hurts," Keir breathed, closing his eyes. "I hurt all over."

"You're going to do that for several more days. But you're out of danger now."

Keir was still somewhat confused. "My head is pounding."

"You need more rest," Calcutt said.

Keir stared as the nurse stuck a needle in the IV tube. The room began swimming. Keir didn't like the feeling. Suddenly he was back in the cabin in Virginia...with Danielle....

"Keir, Keir, my boy," he heard from a distance. He opened his eyes. As the blur sharpened in focus, he recognized Cassidy. His head wasn't pounding as badly as before, but his side was throbbing. He saw Sam Calcutt beside Cassidy.

"Is he going to be all right now?" he heard Cassidy ask the doctor.

"Let's give him time to wake up. He's doing well. Vital signs are good. I would say he'll be able to talk, yes. He's out of danger now and he remembers pretty well."

"Cassidy," Keir whispered.

"Oh, good, you know me," Cassidy said.

"What...what happened?" Keir asked, still groggy.

"I was hoping you could tell me." Cassidy laughed.

Keir moved. He felt awfully uncomfortable. He looked over and saw the tube, then the needle in his right arm. "Who put that crap in my arm?" he moaned.

"Ha!" Calcutt laughed again. "Anytime he's conscious enough to remember his dread of needles, then he's going to be just fine.'' Still smiling, he turned and left the room.

Cassidy watched the doctor leave and turned back to Keir.

''Well, my boy, you've done it again.'' He smiled, shaking his head. ''An excellent job.'' He bent over the bed. ''We've finally got those two Russians where we want them, flat on their back in the hospital and then off to the clinker.''

Keir looked at Cassidy. ''You mean neither are in the morgue?''

Cassidy laughed outright. ''Not yet, but close. Zoya's in critical condition from the wound you gave him. And the same goes for the beefy goon they hired. You did a number on him. He was on the operating table for several hours.''

''What...what about Letsukov?''

''He's in intensive care.''

''Why the hell didn't you let me do the honors?''

''I can certainly understand why you feel cheated, but when we arrived on the scene, it looked to be fairly even. Then just as I pulled the clip and aimed, deciding to shoot, you got the drop on him, and had him right where you wanted him. But then again I was afraid to gamble even for a second with your life. I knew you were badly hurt, so I pulled the trigger. End of story.''

Keir shook his head as he thought back to the incident. He had never been so scared in his life, scared for Danielle, himself. ''I didn't...even know you were there. All I could think of was killing that bastard and the pain in my side.''

''No wonder, your side had a hole in it as big as the Grand Canyon.''

"Calcutt told me..." Keir groaned.

"But you're going to be fine—just fine."

"Sounds like it," Keir said sarcastically.

"Now, calm down, don't get excited. I know you hate being flat on your back, but we'll compensate you handsomely, you know that. Anyway, you're in no condition to argue with the doctor. And Calcutt is insisting on a rest period."

"How long?"

"Oh, I'd say a month, maybe six weeks at the most."

"Dammit, Cassidy," Keir said, struggling to sit up. "I can't stay here for that long. Sweet Jesus, I'll go out of my friggin' mind."

"Hey. Take it easy." Cassidy patted his arm, gently pushing him back down in the bed. "Don't you know it won't do you any good to argue with Calcutt? Anyway, you don't have to stay in the hospital all the time."

Keir felt relieved, though his head was banging again. He grimaced and closed his eyes.

Cassidy looked down at Keir, a worried frown on his face. "Don't worry, we'll have you back on your feet and one hundred percent fit in no time. After all, we can't keep the bride waiting forever, now can we?"

Keir's eyes flew open as his heart skipped a beat. Natalie! Oh, God, he hadn't even thought about Natalie. *Only Danielle.* "No, I guess I can't," he said quietly, knowing, though, that he could never marry Natalie. He turned his head to the side.

Following a long moment of silence, Cassidy asked, "Are you up to talking?"

Keir twisted his head around and grimaced, the sudden action sending a sharp pain through him.

Before he had a chance to speak, Cassidy went on, "It's not over yet, Keir."

Keir's facial expression didn't change. Cassidy might as well have said it was raining outside.

"Although we did put Letsukov and Zoya out of business, they're just the tip of the iceberg. There are others just like them here in Washington, operating right under our nose. Only these are much bigger fish. Computer high technology."

"What the hell does that have to do with us, with me? That's the FBI's problem. Not ours."

Cassidy fingered the railings on the bed. "They want to make it our problem, your problem."

Keir eyed him carefully. "Luke, what do you say you quit beating around the god-damned bush and tell what's going on?"

Cassidy prowled around the room, stopped, looked at Keir. "What I'm trying to tell you is that Lofton, assistant bureau chief, has been hounding me day and night to let him talk to you."

"So."

Cassidy sighed heavily. "So, they want to use you on a special assignment."

Keir suddenly felt the weight of the world on his shoulders. "Dammit, Luke, why me? They've got more competent men now than they can say grace over. Why the hell do they want an aging beat-up body like mine?"

"Huh!" Cassidy snorted. "Who are you trying to kid, McBride? You know why they want you. You're the best and they damn well know it."

Keir remained silent. The last thing he wanted to think about now was another assignment. God forbid, he had barely survived this last time with his life. Since regaining consciousness, all he wanted to do, ached to do, was see Danielle, hold her, touch her....

"Well?"

Keir closed his eyes wearily. "Maybe later, Luke, I'll consider it. But not right now. I don't want to even think about it now." His voice was bleak.

"Well, you have an advantage in your favor, if you can call it that. You have to recuperate for a while yet. Then we'll take it from there. But for now all you have to worry about is getting well and keeping Natalie happy." His sober eyes now held a twinkle.

Keir was quiet.

"What's the matter?" Cassidy smiled. "You getting cold feet now about tying the knot?"

Keir sighed. "If...if you don't mind, I'd rather not discuss it."

"That's your choice, my boy. Don't mean to pry." Cassidy began buttoning his coat. "All you've got to do is lie here and get well; then go home and think about the big fat check you'll be getting every week for lying on your ass."

"The money's not important and you know it," Keir said tersely.

"Sorry, I forget you're not one of us struggling American citizens." He shrugged. "Somehow, you don't look like a millionaire."

"Luke!" Then he saw the impish grin that spread across his face. The man had the weirdest sense of humor.

Cassidy held up his hand. "I'm going. You get some rest and I'll see you tomorrow."

Keir nodded and watched as Cassidy made his way to the door.

Placing his hand on the doorknob, Cassidy swung around. "One more thing before I go. What's Danielle Davis to you?"

The surge that went through Keir made the hair on his neck stand on end.

"Why do you ask that?" he snapped, suddenly on the defensive. His head was beginning to throb again.

"Cool down, Keir, my boy, your bandages are beginning to smoke."

"Dammit, Luke!" he said, his eyes flashing with rage.

Cassidy laughed. "See you later, Keir." He shut the door softly behind him.

For a while Keir lay with his eyes closed, feeling exhausted. And thinking of Danielle. Suddenly he felt an ache for her so intense that it almost overwhelmed him. But he was helpless with nothing left of her but memories, memories that were slowly ripping him to pieces.

He couldn't stop his mind from churning, thinking...the way she looked as she lay naked on the tattered bedroll in the firelight, her hair shining, gracing her shoulders the way he liked it...the way he kissed her sweet mouth, her fresh-smelling skin...the way her eyes had changed as she awakened him with a half-strangled cry and lowered her face, opening her mouth over him. Oh, God, the pain of remembering.

He groaned and turned, careful not to disturb the needle in his arm. But still he couldn't halt the flow of restless thoughts. She hadn't even called to check on him. Gut instinct told him that. But why should she? he chided himself unmercifully. She was out of danger now, back in her nice, secure little world. Fear had caused her to turn to him, nothing more.

Whatever was happening to her now, whatever she was

doing, he knew that he was the last person she wanted to see.

Keir walked slowly across the grounds. He'd been at his parents' estate outside of D.C. for a few days now. His stay in the hospital had turned into almost a month due to an unexpected bout with pneumonia. But he was stronger now, much stronger.

Cassidy was still clucking over him like a mother hen, as were his parents and...Natalie, until yesterday, that is. Had it been just yesterday that he had told her he couldn't marry her? He winced against the pain. He had been walking as he was now when he heard someone calling his name....

He had looked back and saw Natalie running toward him. Why couldn't he love her? She was pretty. She had a thick crop of neatly kept dark brown hair, nice full breasts and long shapely legs that accentuated her tiny waistline.

She swung her arms around his neck and kissed him warmly.

"Aren't you going to eat dinner with us?" she asked.

"I'm not very hungry right now," Natalie," he declined wearily.

Natalie looked away.

She didn't understand, he knew. And he despised himself for what he was doing to her. To himself.

Natalie fell in step beside him, her eyes shadowed. "What's the matter, Keir? You're different." She lifted her shoulders. "I know you've been seriously ill, but..." She paused, as though groping for the right words. "It's all right if you want out," she said softly.

He told her then. Told her that he couldn't marry her

now. Not ever. The words simply spilled from his lips, and with them a heavy burden fell from his heart. Oddly enough they had parted friends.

Yet his misery was immense. Even now, his aimless wanderings did nothing to help him. He thought distance would help. Distance, he expected, would make him free. But it hadn't. The merest thought of Danielle made his pulse race. She was inside him, in his head and in his heart. Finally, he gave up and let the pain, the loneliness and fatigue drive him back to the house.

Raymond McBride saw the change in his son. Breaking his engagement to Natalie was the first indication that something was wrong. What had this last assignment done to Keir, made him a blasted eunuch? He noticed his son's tenseness increase as each day passed. Something was definitely on Keir's mind, and Raymond McBride was going to get to the bottom of it.

He looked up as Keir came into the house.

"Come here, son," he said.

Keir looked surprised at the tone of his father's voice. He entered the den.

"Please, sit down." Raymond indicated one of the plush velvet seats.

Keir sat down with a sigh, wondering what this was all about. Although he and his father weren't close, he admired him greatly. And he had seen the anxiety on Raymond's face and knew he was concerned, as was his mother. He was sorry to have put this strain on their lives.

"What's wrong, son?" Raymond asked. "What's gotten you down like this? Your work? What?"

Keir smiled, thinking that his father had lost none of his sharpness. When it came to sniffing out a problem, he had the instincts of a bloodhound. That was why he was a born politician.

"It's a combination of things—nothing special," he lied.

"Who is she?"

Keir leapt to his feet, stunned. "How...how did you know?"

"I may be old, son, but I'm not senile."

Keir laughed outright for the first time in a month. "I agree. You're not senile." Then he suddenly became serious again. "It's something very special. But...oh, what the hell, there's no point in discussing it. It's hopeless."

"Do you love her?" Raymond frowned.

"Yes."

"Have you told her?"

Once a long time ago. "No," he said.

"Then how do you know it's hopeless?"

Keir stared at his father as though he was seeing him for the first time, and remained silent.

"I know you don't believe this, but all your mother and I want is your happiness. I...you're all we have." He paused. "Oh, I'll admit we're disappointed about you and Natalie. But if it takes another woman to put the life back into you, then I'm all for it."

"Oh, Dad, there's so much you don't know...." Dare he hope? Take a chance? Once in the cabin she had looked at him with love And there was still the unsettled question of Ann.

"I've never known you to give up so easily," Raymond said.

"I haven't ever before."

Suddenly Raymond picked up the newspaper and

headed for the door. Before walking out, he turned around.

"What are you waiting for, son? Go to her." With a determined step and the slam of the door he was gone.

A smile softened his lips. The old man had a point. What *was* he waiting for?

As it turned out, Danielle did not go to the party. Ann was sick. Thursday morning she began running a temperature. She lost her breakfast, conked out immediately after that, then got sick when she woke up. Danielle called the doctor for an afternoon appointment and spent the rest of the day imagining that Ann had all kinds of rare, terrible diseases and telling herself she was being ridiculous, overimaginative.

Ann behaved well through the examination, but Danielle couldn't stop herself from fearing the worst.

"It's just a virus," the doctor said. "I'll give you a couple of prescriptions. If she isn't better by Friday, call Lucy and make another appointment."

Friday dawned clear and crisp, finding Ann much better.

"Are you going to Marge's party?" Jusie asked over coffee that morning. It was early and Ann was still asleep.

Danielle shook her head, noticing how her shoulders ached. From too much bending and stooping in the store, she thought fleetingly. "I don't think it would be a good idea, do you?"

Jusie pursed her lips. "Sure do."

"Well, I don't," Danielle said stubbornly.

Jusie's brown eyes wandered over Danielle's wan, pale features. "You can't keep this pace up much longer.

You're working too hard, not eating—why you're practically a skeleton. The only time you relax is when you're with Ann. And even that doesn't seem to help much.''

"Oh, Jusie," Danielle wailed, fighting back the tears, "don't you start too."

"What do you mean, too?"

Danielle curled her fingers tightly around the coffee mug. "Marge. She raked me over the coals the other day, asking questions, telling me how awful I look."

Jusie snorted unbecomingly. "She's nothing but a nosy busy body. But at that, she has enough sense to know you're flirting with a nervous breakdown. Even Ann senses it."

That was the crowning blow. Danielle withered like a flower on a broken stem. Tears began trickling down her face. Dear Lord, Jusie was right. She was grieving. Grieving for Keir and for what might have been. How much longer could she endure being torn between love and fear?

"Oh, honey," Jusie said softly, seeing the spasms of agony cross Danielle's face. She got up and put her arms around Danielle's heaving shoulders, pulling her against her bosom, rocking her like she did. Ann. "Don't cry. Maybe if you talk about it, it'll help."

"I'm...I'm so mixed up, Jusie, so unhappy," she sobbed. "I...I love him, yet..."

"Shhh, don't cry," cajoled Jusie. "You'll make yourself sick." She smoothed Danielle's curls away from her face. "I think the time has come for you to get it all out of your system."

Danielle pulled away, struggling to get a hold of herself. But she couldn't stop trembling. "I...I don't know if I can."

"Of course you can," Jusie encouraged softly.

Danielle forced the words through stiff, dry lips. "You remember...I told you about the marshal that was with me in Virginia." She paused. "Well, I...uh...had known him before...a long time ago. I...I didn't think I'd ever see him again."

"You loved him." It was more of a statement than a question.

"Yes," Danielle whispered.

"What's so terrible about that?"

Danielle swiped at the tears drenching her face. "It's...you don't understand...."

"Go on."

She fought for her next breath. "Ann is his daughter," she said dully, "and he doesn't even know it."

For a moment there was nothing but a profound silence in the room. Then Jusie stood up, her expression never changing. "I'd better make more coffee. I feel like we're going to be here a spell."

Danielle was late opening the bookstore. But it didn't matter. She felt much better, her heart lighter, having unburdened it to Jusie. She had told her everything, except of course those intimate moments she had shared with Keir. They were too private, too sacred to share, even with her beloved friend. Some things were better left unsaid.

After that, she had dragged her weary body to her room and gotten dressed and then checked on Ann to make sure there was no recurring fever. Ann had been cool as a cucumber. Still Danielle wasn't about to leave her and go to Marge's party.

Now as she turned the sign around, indicating that she

was open, she felt hope for the first time in weeks. Maybe it wasn't hopeless after all, she thought. Maybe when he came, they could work things out. But why hadn't she heard from him? It had been over a month. Could she have been wrong in thinking he still cared? No! She would not think about that. Now now.

Hazel Standley rescued her. "Good morning, Danielle," she said, breezing through the door, leaving the chimes tinkling behind her.

Danielle could have hugged her. "Good morning. How are you?"

Hazel smiled. "Just fine, that is if you have something new to read."

Danielle's eyes brightened. "You're in luck. Your favorite romances came in yesterday."

"Great," Hazel chirped. "Those *are* my favorites. Now how about novels?"

"Mmmm, let's see," Danielle said, weaving between the racks to stand in front of the displays filled with historical romances. "How about this one?" She reached out and plucked it off the shelf. "It's wonderful."

And so it went. Although the day was long and tiring, it was fulfilling. With the fireplace blazing she visited with customers, worked up orders, crawled around on her hands and knees unboxing books and straightened the romantic fiction section.

By the time she turned the sign around to read "Closed" at six o'clock, she was bone weary. It was all she could do to make it up the stairs. Uppermost on her mind was a hot bath and crawling into bed.

It was a while however before she got her wish. Ann wanted to play. After thirty minutes in the water, she laughingly told her daughter, ''Darling, if we don't hurry and get out, we're going to look like prunes.''

Ann giggled as she splashed water. ''What's prunes, Mommie?'' Mixing tears with water, Danielle grabbed her daughter and hugged her fiercely, thinking she had never seen her look more like her father.

''How did you sleep?'' Jusie asked, watching Danielle like a hawk as she walked into the room, dressed in a plum-colored suede jumpsuit. She was stunning, except for her eyes, Jusie thought.

''Fine,'' Danielle lied, smiling her thanks as Jusie handed her a cup of coffee She hadn't slept at all. Restless dreams of Keir had kept her awake.

''Well, you sure don't look like it to me,'' Jusie quipped. ''If your eyes sink much further in your head, you'll lose them.''

Danielle laughed, although it never reached her eyes. ''Hope not. Couldn't read then.''

But she hadn't fooled Jusie, not for a minute. ''Why don't you let Judy mind the store today. It's Saturday; you won't be very busy. Go shopping, eat out. It'll do you good.''

Danielle chewed on her lower lip. ''Oh, Jusie, I don't know.'' But she was tempted. It was a beautiful day and she did need a break.

Jusie saw her weakening. ''If the weather holds, I'll take Ann to the zoo. She had such a good time with you the other day, I thought I'd take her back.''

Danielle smiled, this time transforming her face. ''Oh, Jusie, I love you,'' she whispered.

Determined not to brood, Danielle made a day of it. Finally, too weary to take another step, she piled her packages into her car and headed for home. North Street was practically deserted as she drove down it, the majority of the college students having gone home for the weekend.

Feeling better than she'd felt in a long time, she parked the car in the driveway and scooped up her packages in her arms. Then carefully she made her way to the door, opened it and began climbing the stairs. "Jusie, Annie, I'm home," she called.

Silence.

Frowning, she crossed the threshold into the family room, only to freeze suddenly in her tracks.

"Oh, God!" she mouthed as the packages fell from her arms and scattered across the floor.

"Why didn't you tell me?"

Chapter 12

If Danielle lived to be a hundred, she would never forget the scene that greeted her eyes. She blinked several times. Nothing changed.

Keir, his massive body filling the rocking chair to capacity, was sitting by the fireplace rocking a sleeping Ann. The child's dark curls were tumbling across his muscled arm, and one rosy cheek was nestled against his chest. A tiny hand was wrapped possessively around his thumb.

Keir looked up at her, tears clinging to his thick lashes. "Why didn't you tell me?" he repeated brokenly.

Danielle felt the bottom drop out of her stomach as she stood motionless. Was he furious with her? Would he follow through with his threat to take Ann away from her? No! She would find some way to stop him. Even if she had to change her identity again, flee the country. She couldn't bear being separated from her child.

Fear held her mute as she tasted the bile that rose in the back of her throat, threatening to strangle her.

Their eyes locked and time stood still.

Dread filled Danielle's heart as the standoff continued. She felt panic seep into every part of her body. *Oh, Keir, is that hate I see in your eyes? Please don't hate me. At the time, I had no choice. Please understand…I love you. But I can't give up my child, not even for you.*

The atmosphere sizzled with suppressed emotion and expectation.

She wet her lips and tried to speak, to plead with him, to grovel if necessary, if he would just understand how very sorry she was. It was obvious that he was hurting—this big, proud man, who faced danger every day of his life without flinching, was torn apart by the sight of his daughter. And seeing father and daughter together for the first time, the likeness uncanny, it hit her squarely between the eyes what he must be feeling at this moment, knowing that he had been deprived of the first years of their child's life. But again, she cried inwardly, what choice had she had?

Neither spoke.

Suddenly, a whimper escaped from Danielle's lips, and she jerked her head around and the room began swaying. She struggled for breath, fighting off the waves of nausea that were washing over her like a tide.

''It's going to be all right, you know,'' he whispered, smiling through his tears, though his heart was breaking.

Stunned, positive that her ears were playing tricks on her, she swung her head back around, tears glistening in her eyes, streaming down her cheeks. He was still smiling.

''Oh, Keir,'' she groaned, feeling herself yield to the

pressure on her heart. Broken sobs began pelting her body, robbing her of speech.

His own eyes still filled with tears, Keir rose slowly, and clutched his precious burden against him. ''Please don't...I can't stand to see you cry.''

Danielle fought to get hold of herself, knowing that if she did not, she would never be able to stop crying. Seeing Keir like this after a month of uncertainty was almost more than she could handle.

''Show me her room, and I'll put her down,'' he said. His voice trembled fiercely.

Wordlessly, Danielle glided on legs that were made of air instead of bones and preceded Keir out of the family room, down the hall to Ann's room. *Everything is going to be all right. I just know it is.* She crossed the threshold and then paused just inside the door, switching on the Alice-in-Wonderland lamp. Suddenly the room was bathed in a warm, cozy glow.

She stood by helplessly as Keir strode across the room to stand in front of both a baby bed and a twin-sized bed. He turned toward her and raised his eyes in question.

''Please,'' Danielle whispered, ''put her in the baby bed. She's been sick and...and restless. I don't want to take a chance on her falling out of the bed,'' she finished lamely.

''Aren't you going to undress her?'' he asked.

''Later,'' Danielle moved to stand beside him as he gently laid Ann's relaxed body on the bed. ''She'll probably wake up and howl, then I'll give her a bath and put her back down for the night.''

'Why wait? Let's make her comfortable at once.'' He laid the child down and with gentle, awkward fingers began to unlace her shoes.

"Please, Keir, I'll do it," Danielle said with a some-what strained smile. What if she was wrong about his motives? What if...

"You're afraid to let me touch her, aren't you?" His mortified tone, his hurt eyes, sent a stab of pain through Danielle's heart.

"I only mean—well, if you want to, then do stay and help me," she finished in a warm, sweet, rushing fashion. "Can you slide her sock off? That's right." She watched as he managed to draw off the socks without disturbing the child. "Now for the clothes." But Ann awakened as her mother attempted to unbutton her top. She did not cry, however; she gazed at them both drowsily and said, "Keir," in a satisfied voice.

Danielle shouldn't have been surprised that Keir had managed to worm his way into her daughter's heart and charm her, she thought as she crossed to a chest of drawers and drew out a tiny fresh nightgown. Ann lay holding tight to Keir's thumb as he leaned over the rails for her greater convenience.

"She's perfect," he murmured.

"Yes." Danielle's voice held an odd, hurried note. "At...least I think she is." To busy her hands, she latched onto Ann's teddy bear at the foot of the bed and placed it against her stomach.

"She reminds me," he went on, "so much of myself."

One of Danielle's hands went to her breast. *Oh, please just let him be proud and not greedy. Don't let him want more than I'm prepared to give.*

"Let me put the nightie on, Keir."

"Oh, of course." But he did not move, still studying the exquisite little figure, the flushed baby face and tum-bled black curls. "I have it! That painting of me when I was about three. I had forgotten it, except for her eyes. The shape of her face, her mouth—even her hands. Look at that.'' He measured a long, sensitive hand against the baby one, which was a miniature of his own.

Danielle uttered a faint, choked sound as if she had attempted to speak and found her voice gone.

Keir swung around abruptly and saw her standing there, white as paper, clutching her breast.

His face was filled with awe. ''My God,'' he breathed, ''she's really and truly mine.'' It was as though he still did not, could not, believe it.

Ann, neglected, gave a protesting whimper. As if released from bondage, Danielle bent over her, put on the nightgown, covered the child and kissed her.

For a brief second, green eyes fluttered open again. ''Mommie,'' Ann murmured softly.

''It's all right, love, Mommie's here. Go to sleep,'' Danielle cooed. Then she turned to Keir. ''If you'll go on,'' she added in a whisper, ''I'll turn off the light.''

He left the room and she followed him.

In the den he stopped and faced her. ''What possessed you not to tell me?'' He struggled to keep his tone even.

Her stomach revolted. She wasn't out of danger yet. ''Tell you? How could I? And even if it had been possible, I'd rather have gone to the stake,'' Danielle cried passionately, ''than have told you in that way. Remember you weren't ready for a home with a white picket fence around it and a family.''

''Oh, God, Danielle, we could have worked something out.''

She remained silent.

''Was this your revenge?''

''There...there was no revenge about it. It was over

between us. You weren't interested in...in settling down.''

''But I didn't know. I never dreamed—do you suppose, for one instant, that if I'd known, I wouldn't have turned over heaven and hell to have found you.''

''I tell you, Keir,'' Danielle's eyes were lit with anger, ''nothing would have induced me to make such a plea.''

''Don't be a fool,'' he cried roughly. ''You had no right to conceal this. The child was mine as much as yours.''

Her shoulders slumped in defeat. ''How...how was I to know you'd still want me? Anyway, it was too late. After I became involved with the government...nothing was the same.'' She spread her hands.

''Oh, God,'' he groaned, ''if only I'd known. The agony of all those years without you, without seeing my child is almost more than I can stand.''

Danielle's face changed, her mouth trembled and her eyes, a moment before brilliant with rage, darkened pitifully.

A muttered curse split Keir's lips, followed by a harsh sigh. ''God, I'm sorry. I've no right to turn on you now, reproach you—I'm making a blasted idiot of myself. I was just as pigheaded and stubborn as you were, and I got exactly what I deserved and ought to be kicked for raking you over the coals.''

''I didn't do this to hurt you. I just...''

''God in heaven, if only one could turn back the pages,'' he whispered, his voice raspy, broken.

''It's too late; one can never do that,'' she said gently, keeping her own tears at bay by the greatest of effort.

They looked at each other; Danielle's heart began to

throb, Keir's hands closed until the knuckles were white and the fingernails bit into his palms.

He smiled through his tears. "No, my darling, it's not too late. Not for us."

"Keir. I..." Her voice failed as she watched him brush a tear off his cheek with a clumsy finger and felt the renewed sting of tears behind her eyes as the lump in her throat grew too big to swallow. She could stand most anything, except his tears.

Unconsciously her head began to weave from side to side. "I'm sorry, so sorry," she whispered.

He turned toward her then and folded her within his arms.

She nestled into his warmth, letting it surround her like a soft veil.

He held her as though he'd never let her go, but still he did not say what she so desperately craved to hear, that he loved her and wanted to marry her, that he wanted to make a home for her and Ann.

After a moment, she lifted her eyes, searching for his, unable to hold any longer what was in her heart, her soul. "I...I love you," she said sweetly, then was as startled by her own boldness as Keir appeared to be, but she couldn't stop herself. She could only plunge ahead recklessly, speaking too fast, in too much of a rush to express what could no longer be left unsaid. "I love you, Keir McBride. And if you want me to, I'll stand here the rest of the evening and night saying it over and over until my voice wears out."

He stared down at her, his beautiful green eyes a darker and more intense green than she had ever seen them before. Yet he remained silent and just looked at her.

She tried to read those eyes, but she couldn't tell a thing about the thoughts behind them.

As she waited for him to respond to her declaration, Danielle wondered with a sinking heart if she had misunderstood his words of a while ago, misinterpreted the message in his eyes. Yet how could she be mistaken about the way his arms were folded around her now and the hammering of his heart as it answered the hammering of her own?

When his silence reached a screaming pitch, she almost wished that she could call back the words she had spoken, roll back the clock just one minute. But no, she could not take back a word of it. She loved him, had always loved him, and after what he'd done for her she owed him that and much, much more.

Then he kissed her.

His lips pressed against hers, tenderly, yet forcefully, both giving and taking, seeking and demanding. She responded to him instantly, with a heat that made her dizzy, made her lose touch with reality.

The kiss involved not only lips, teeth and tongues, but passion, hunger and need. He cupped her face, holding her gently but firmly, as if he were afraid that she would reconsider her commitment and would pull away from him.

"Oh, Danielle, Danielle," he whispered against her lips, "there are thousands of things I want to hear, to ask, about Ann—us, but right now all I want to do is to hold you and never let you out of my sight again. But even more than that, I want to make love to you, to show you how much I love you, how much I've missed you, how my life these past weeks has been hell without you."

"Me too," she echoed softly.

It was a healing, cleansing time for both as they remained locked steadfastly in one another's arms, oblivious to the sounds around them, aware of nothing but their own happiness.

The revelation concerning Ann had shaken him to the core; still, he could not resolve his emotions, could not get his swirling brain into any sort of order. *Ann.* That precious baby, that exquisite little figure with her silky black mop and dark-lashed green eyes and rose-colored face. Ann was his—his own child, his and Danielle's. Oh, God! he groaned silently. Fool that he had been, mad, blind fool to have given up so easily, to have thrown away the gift God had given him.

But now, miraculously, he was being given another chance. And this time he would not blow it. He would love her and Ann, take care of them, cherish them for the rest of his life.

His arms around her were like bands of steel as he tightened them around her slender frame. "Where's your bedroom?" he asked, his warm breath bathing the inside of her ear.

She shivered. "Mmmm, down the hall."

"What are we waiting for?"

"I haven't the foggiest."

He laughed and gave her another of those breathtaking hugs.

When he let her go, she looked up, then frowned. "Jusie! Where is Jusie? We...can't...I mean..."

He leaned over and kissed the tip of her pert nose, drinking in the fresh fragrance of her skin, her hair. "Don't worry about Jusie. She's gone to visit friends. For the night, I might add."

Danielle's eyes widened in surprise, and her mouth fell open.

"Shut your mouth," Keir ordered, grinning. "She wanted to make sure we had plenty of time alone to do our thing. At first she was reluctant to let me in, but when I told her who I was, a complete change came over her." He grinned. "We had quite a conversation."

"You're crazy, you know," she said breathlessly.

"Crazy about you." He couldn't get enough of her. His need was raging. He craved the taste of her lips, was starved for the feel of her skin and the soft tension of her flesh. He wanted to undress her slowly and kiss her breasts and slip deep inside her.

Her lips touched his throat. She did not kiss him. Not exactly. She prolonged the feeling of passion in the artery that stood up and thumped in his neck.

He turned to her, moved into her, and they pressed harder together, belly to belly. Her breasts were squashed pleasantly against his chest. He kissed her forehead, her eyes.

She felt slightly intoxicated as she slipped her fingers into his hair, feeling, touching, loving…. For this moment was the culmination of all her hopes, her dreams for the future. The sins of the past were forgiven, the hope for tomorrow was bright and shining as a beacon. Perfect. Everything was perfect. He would ask her to marry him; they would settle down, no more running, no more hiding, no more danger, and no more being parted. What more could she ask for?

"Ah, my darling, you cause such a storm in me," he whispered as he bent down and scooped her up in his arms. She seemed weightless, and he felt as if he could lift the earth.

She clung to him. In her clear eyes there was a vulnerability that touched his heart.

"I want you," she whispered.

They went into her bedroom. "I love you," he said. "I nearly went crazy without you," he added before kissing her deeply, sweetly, reaching for her soul. When he drew away, she brought him back. His kisses sent darting spasms of response through her. He was so strong, so solid and positive and whole. And he was hers.

When they separated, she found herself taking in air in small gasping gulps, taut with expectation as his hands unzipped her jumpsuit and the cool air touched her skin.

Her hands sweetly touched him before moving down to unfasten the snap at his waist and sliding the zipper down. Then she put her mouth on his collarbone, the side of his neck, the base of his throat. His skin was smooth and warm and fresh. It felt good against her lips, even the scar where the bullet had pierced his side had healed nicely.

They took their time undressing one another, stopping to kiss and touch, finally lying down on the bed together.

He circled her nipples with his tongue, bathing them in the dew of his mouth, causing her to suck in her breath with exquisite pain. Her hand fell lightly on the back of his head to keep him there.

"Oh, Keir, I can't believe you're here, touching me like this," she whispered, opening under him, drawing him down to her.

"I love you so much." He traced a finger down her thigh.

"And I love you. Oh!" She quivered as his fingers dipped into her. "Keir!"

She placed her hands between them, guiding him forward. But she no longer needed to direct him. He was there, parting her, entering, his hands caressing her breasts as he knelt between her thighs and immersed himself fully into her, then stopped, resting there. She raised her arms and brought him up to her breasts, anxious to please, to love him.

His hips shifted, beginning a counterpoint, playing a melody that was perfectly timed to his slow-thrusting theme. He held her, filled her more completely, more perfectly than ever before.

"God, you're perfect," he whispered.

She closed her eyes as he moved inside of her, stirring something deep, something profound, something so wonderful that a soft dying cry came from his mouth. She shuddered and clung to him moaning softly, her eyes still tightly shut as she rose, then fell, gasping. A minute later, as the last of the spasms were passing, she felt him come inside her.

He was aware of her rising even closer to him in great love and gladness, his own hopes and love reaffirmed.

Her thoughts and fears suddenly seemed unimportant because whatever happened, he really was going to be there. She simply knew it all at once, believed it absolutely; he was going to be there always.

"I'm so happy," she said, a long time later.

"All I want," he said as he caressed her arm, "is for you to be happy."

"And that makes you happy?"

"Need you ask?" He pulled her on top of him. "For the first time in years—well, since you all but threw me out—I feel alive."

"It's just that all this seems like a dream come true."

He smiled. "Well, if it's a dream, I never want to wake up."

Snuggling close to his warm body, she said, "Me neither."

"Speaking of waking up, hadn't we better go check on our daughter?"

She smiled up at him thinking the word "our" was suddenly the most beautiful word in the English language. "Oh, you don't know Ann," she said. "The minute she wakes up, she starts calling, and if I'm not around, she calls for her Jusie."

"Then you think we're safe?"

"Trust me, we're safe. In fact, she may not, probably won't, wake up until the morning. I'm sure Jusie fed her before she left, so she won't be hungry."

"She did," he said and grinned. "Jusie was just beginning to feed Ann dinner when I got here, and by the time Jusie was finished, we were fast friends."

Danielle felt a glow around her heart. "You had both Ann and Jusie eating out of your hand, is that what you're saying?"

He chuckled. "That's right."

"Did Jusie feed you too?"

"No."

"Are you hungry?"

"Terribly."

"Want to sneak in the kitchen for a midnight snack?"

"Thought you'd never ask."

Keir got up and slipped into his pants as she scooped up his shirt and put it on, holding her arm up to her nose, sniffing at his sleeve.

He laughed. "What are you doing?"

"Inhaling you. It's like putting a part of you on, wearing you around."

"Crazy!" He took her arm and steered her toward the kitchen.

Together they prepared an omelette, bacon and toast, and by the time they consumed the food, checked on a peacefully sleeping Ann, Danielle's eyes had begun to droop.

"It's back to bed with you, my sweet."

"But I'm not sleepy." She smiled. "Really, I'm not, just relaxed, satisfied."

He gave her a leering grin. "Let's go back to bed anyway."

She laughed and grabbed his hand and led him toward the bedroom. Immediately they rid themselves of their scanty clothing and, straightening the covers, crawled back into the bed.

He put his arm around her and held her warmly in the crook of his arm. After a moment of contented silence, he confessed softly, "You know, you've never been off my mind. I kept finding you in every revolving door."

"I've never been without you," she answered, turning toward him with her heart in her eyes.

Thus began a play in separate acts with intermissions of kissing, talking and touching.

He told her about Natalie, how she was a substitute for her, that she was a wonderful person but he had never loved her. He also told her about taking dangerous assignments, one after the other, in order to keep his mind and body active so he would not think about her. The more dangerous the job, he said, the better he liked it.

His hands were warm against her flesh by the time she spoke of the loneliness she had endured after they parted.

He wanted to know the details of Ann's birth, and she told him. She told him how in the hospital she had longed for him to share in that miracle but had known that no matter how much she ached for it, it was impossible.

After they had emptied their souls to one another, they lay quietly on their backs, close together, her head on his arm, exhaustion apparent in the drooping flutter of her eyelids and tired slant of her mouth.

"I love you," she whispered, burrowing closer.

"Go to sleep, my love." He brushed his lips across her forehead.

"You too?"

"Me too. We'll talk in the morning."

Long hours into the new day, arms wrapped tightly around one another, they fell into a deep sleep.

Sensing that she was alone, Danielle awakened in a blissful state of happiness. Keir. Their coming together had all been everything she had hoped for and more. At last they were to be a real family, she thought. Stretching contentedly, her eyes strayed to the numbers on the clock. Suddenly she jerked upright. Good Lord, it was nine o'clock. Ann. Surely she wasn't still asleep? And Jusie. Where was Jusie? She didn't hear her banging around in the kitchen.

After bounding out of bed and making a quick detour by the bathroom, Danielle paraded into the kitchen, tightening the sash on her robe as she went.

"Mommie, me full," her daughter greeted her the minute she crossed the threshold.

Danielle lovingly glanced at a happy Ann, who straddled Keir's knee, egg mixed with grape jelly staining her cherub face. Then she raised her eyes and collided with Keir's brilliant green ones.

For a heady moment, they were alone in the room.

"Good morning." Keir spoke softly, but his eyes spoke another message. *You're wonderful,* they said.

"Good morning." Could that weak, wispy voice be hers? Clearing her throat, she moved closer to Ann and leaned down and kissed her on the cheek. And for the first time, her daughter didn't hold out her chubby arms to her. It was apparent that Keir was still an unqualified hit.

"Your daughter's a little pig, no doubt about it," Keir said, running his big hand through Ann's curls affectionately.

Danielle merely stood there, her heart swelled with love and pride at the picture father and daughter created together. With Jusie nowhere in sight, it was obvious that Keir had opted to feed and bathe Ann while she slept. Then a sudden sting fanned her cheeks as she remembered how little sleep they had actually gotten.

As though reading her mind, Keir grinned, darkening her blush even more. "Hungry?" he drawled, helping a squirming Ann down from his lap.

"A little."

"Good. Sit down, and I'll prepare you a McBride special."

Danielle laughed, scooping her daughter up in her lap and giving her a squeeze. Then, unconsciously, she reached for a napkin and began wiping the goop from her daughter's face. "Hold still, little wiggle worm," she demanded when Ann began turning her face from side to side. "All right, get down, but first give Mommie a kiss, then go get your coloring book and colors and show Dad...Keir...how well you can color.''

"When are we going to tell her?'' Keir asked a moment later as they watched their happily occupied daughter in the corner of the den.

"I'm...ready when you are.''

Suddenly his eyes narrowed as he leaned toward her. "Aren't you forgetting something?'' he asked thickly.

She looked momentarily puzzled. "I am?''

"This,'' he said and dipped his head and gave her a searing kiss.

Once again, Danielle found herself drowning in the sight, smell and touch of him. She never wanted this high to end.

Pulling back, he whispered, "Let's get married. Today. This morning. Doesn't that sound like heaven?''

"Like heaven,'' she echoed into his mouth. Now, she thought, now he would tell her what she longed to hear, that he would give up his dangerous job, find work here in Texas, never leave her and Ann alone again.

"But we won't be able to leave right away. There's so much we have to take care of before we can go back to D.C.''

The sudden businesslike tone of his voice sent a cold chill of foreboding through her. She raised her head to look at him. "Leave?''

"Of course. He rushed on. "We'll stay here until we can find a suitable buyer for the store, and Jusie—well, if she wants to go with us, I...''

Pushing him away, she lunged to her feet. "What?'' Then before he could answer her she went on, shaking her head in bewilderment. "Leave? But why? I...I thought...I mean,'' she stammered, suddenly feeling as though she were foundering alone in the middle of the ocean in a life raft that had sprung a leak. Then abruptly she turned to go to Ann, needing to get away from him, to think. But before she could take a few steps, Keir had closed the distance between them, his hard fingers circling her waist.

"Danielle, honey, what's wrong?" he asked, taking in her pale features. "I don't understand."

"Well, apparently neither do I," she whispered. "It's...it's just that I thought now that you wouldn't be working for the government any longer, we wouldn't have to leave." Her voice had dwindled almost to nothing.

"Where did you get that idea?" His fingers tightened on her wrist; she could feel the heightened tension in his body.

The silence that fell over the room was formidable.

Danielle's stomach was churning, and the tears were dangerously close as her gaze dropped pointedly to his clenched fingers. "Let me go," she said dully.

"Answer me," he demanded, trying to ignore the rising heat at the base of his throat, the sense of panic festering in his gut.

"I...I just assumed this time...you would give up working for the government...knowing that I'm still against it," she said, swinging back around to look at him, catching the tail end of the expression that passed briefly over his face. Distracted by her own heightened emotions, she did not want to name the ones flickering across his face. Pain? Disappointment? Frustration?

"I'm sorry if I gave you that impression," he said coldly, "but I have no plans to give up my work."

Danielle could not believe that she had heard him correctly. But she had. His hard features were a testimony to his words. She should have known that it was too good to be true, she lamented. His work still came first. They were from two different worlds, with different values. Love, it seemed, was still not enough. She stood silent, her heart breaking.

The silence stretched endlessly.

"Danielle," Keir said at last, "nothing's going to happen to me. Do you think that I'd take any unnecessary chances knowing that I have you to come home to?"

She ignored that odd, almost desperate sound in his voice, hardening her heart. "No," she uttered on a strangled whisper, "but..."

Keir's narrowing lids failed to conceal the anger flaring in his eyes at her persistent stubbornness. "But what?"

"I...I haven't changed, Keir," she said, unchecked tears beginning to trickle down her hollow cheeks. "I still want...a real home, white picket fence and all for me...for Ann. And a husband who will always be there, not one who's constantly chasing danger."

"Correct me if I'm wrong, but this conversation sounds awfully familiar to me." Keir's tone showed evidence of the strain on his control.

"I won't deny that," she lashed out at him. "But my God, Keir, after what we've just been through, what do you expect?" A shudder tore through her body as she walked to the cabinet. With trembling fingers, she poured herself a cup of coffee before turning back around to face him. "I thought once you found out about...Ann you'd be eager to give up your dangerous globe-trotting to settle down. I...I thought we'd be a real family." She choked back a sob.

He cursed, raising his arm to tunnel his fingers through

his thick, tousled hair. Watching his movement, her eyes were drawn to the muscles tightening on his exposed chest, before dipping lower, taking delight in the shadowed dent in his stomach, to the bold outline of his masculinity heightened by his close-fitting jeans. She averted her gaze, hot coffee sloshing on her hand. She winced.

"Danielle, honey, turn around," he ordered gently. Like a puppet on a string, she responded to his command. "Don't you understand that we *will* be a family. All of us together. Me. You. Ann. For the rest of our lives."

Danielle couldn't stop her lower lip from trembling. "But if you're gone all the time, that's not being a family," she wailed.

He wanted to touch her so badly he could taste it, but something held him back. Something he couldn't name. Suddenly she seemed untouchable. His heart skipped a fearful beat.

"In the first place I won't be gone all the time," he reasoned. "And in the second place nothing is going to happen to me. You've got to believe that." His tone was pleading now. "Anyway, I have responsibilities, obligations to people other than myself. They depend on me. Right now, they're waiting on me to head an undercover operation that, if successful, could keep the Russians from walking off with any more of our technological secrets. I can't just back away from that."

"No. I guess you can't," she said bitterly. *But you can sure as hell walk away from your responsibilities toward me.* "And I'd never have a minute's peace of mind. I'd worry about you night and day, wondering if you'd come home shot up, maimed or dead."

"Dammit, that's a cop-out and you know it. As far as that goes, I could walk out the door and get run over by a truck. I love you and want to marry you. Isn't that enough?''

"How can you say that," she cried, "after what you just went through protecting me?" She was choking on the hot throbbing ache that was growing within her. "I love you, but I can't...I won't live with the shadow of fear. Not...not anymore. I've told you what I want." She paused. "I refuse to...to settle for less."

He felt sick on the inside, sick that he was losing her. *Oh, God, not again,* he cried silently.

"Danielle," he reasoned patiently. "I know you've been through a living hell the last three years as well as the past few weeks, but that's all over now, behind you. We have a wonderful future in front of us. Don't throw it away. Let go of the fear, once and for all. Lean on me—trust me.''

No. Her mouth formed the word, but it never got past her lips. Was she being unreasonable? Was she afraid? Afraid to venture beyond the world she had made for herself, for Ann? No, of course she wasn't. She loved him. Oh, how she loved him. Hadn't she paid her dues? Hadn't she earned the right to live in peace?

Yet, perhaps there was some truth in what he said. Maybe his work was not the real problem. Maybe it was something inside her that she could not change. She just knew that she had to have security and roots. For her it was synonymous with love.

"Keir...please..."

"You're going to do it again, aren't you? Just like before. You're going to walk out on me?" Keir asked, rage etching the lines of his face. "Because you're still afraid to get involved, to take a chance, right?" He was towering over her now. "I want to know now if you're coming with me."

She answered him with silence, turning her back.

"All right, Danielle, you win. I won't fight you anymore. If living in a vacuum will make you happy, then so be it. But don't expect my daughter to do the same thing, because I won't allow it."

If he had physically slapped her, she couldn't have been more stunned. She was trying to recover from the verbal blow and find her voice as he crossed the room to the door. There he paused.

"My lawyer will be in touch. See you in court."

The door slammed shut behind him, shattering her heart into tiny pieces. She crumpled to the floor, too numb to cry.

Chapter 13

The days crept slowly by, and with each one that passed, Danielle's despair deepened. She was at a loss as to how to deal with the fear and pain that haunted her relentlessly. Fear that she would lose her child and the pain of having lost Keir again.

Yet she was determined to pick up the pieces of her life and go on as though Keir had never become a part of it again. But that was easier said than done.

Since he had walked away without a backward glance over three weeks ago, she had tried to exorcise him from both her heart and mind, but thoughts of their parting and his bitter words continued to torment her soul. She had worked like a Trojan in the bookstore, cleaning, rearranging, moving books and shelving until she was exhausted.

But it was those hours after she closed the store that were the hardest to endure. She tried to fill her evenings with Ann, reading to her, coloring with her, or simply holding her, but oftentimes Ann would fall asleep in her arms and have to be put to bed early, leaving her to face the remainder of the evening alone, staring at the four walls.

Although Jusie tried repeatedly to cheer her up, Danielle could not be consoled. She refused to contact any of her friends, choosing instead to be with her daughter and work, her panacea for making it through the days.

The only word she'd had concerning Keir was from Luke Cassidy. He had called her shortly after Keir left. Both the call and the conversation had further upset her. She remembered every word that had passed between them. The phone had rung just before closing time....

"Hello," she'd said softly.

"Ms. Davis, is that you?" a deep voice had asked.

"Yes," she said with a sinking feeling, recognizing Luke Cassidy's voice immediately.

"How are you?"

"I'm fine," she answered politely.

"Well, I won't keep you long. I'm calling to let you know both Letsukov and Zoya survived their wounds and that as soon as it's convenient for you, we'd like to make arrangements for you to fly to Washington to give your deposition and make a final identification of Letsukov. Then, we hope you'll never hear from us again."

"It doesn't matter, Marshal Cassidy. I'll come whenever you want me to." She hated the thought of going back to Washington, but she had given her word.

"Fine. I'll have my office contact you with the final arrangements."

Danielle hesitated a moment. "Before you hang up," she said, "I'd like to thank you again for taking care of me all this time. I...I don't think I've ever stopped long enough to let you know that in spite of all that's transpired, I am grateful to you and your office for saving my life.''

''It's our job, Ms. Davis, but it's nice to be thanked anyway,'' he said brusquely.

A short silence fell between them.

''Was that all you wanted, Mr. Cassidy?'' Danielle asked at last.

This time he hesitated. ''Well, actually it's not. Have you by any chance seen or talked to Keir McBride lately?''

Danielle's breath caught in her throat. Had something happened to Keir? ''Why...why do you want to know?''

''Well, uh,'' he paused and coughed, ''he's sort of disappeared. What I mean is, no one's seen him for about a week now, and we need to get in touch with him, and the last thing I heard him say was that he was going to Texas to see you.''

Another silence.

''I...don't know where he is.'' She paused and wet her dry lips. ''He...came, but he's gone now, and I don't know where he is.''

''I see. Well, thanks, anyway. We'll be in touch. Goodbye, Ms. Davis.''

Now as she stood peering out the window of the bookstore waiting until closing time, looking out at the slow winter drizzle, she was consumed with pain. She kept asking herself what would happen if Keir would burst into the store and present a solution to all their problems.

Absurd! Telling herself that merely plunged her deeper into despair. But her mind betrayed her with images of him; his face, his smile, his gentle arms.

Fate had sent him to her, and she had sent him away. But what choices had she been given? She simply could not live with the fear of waiting for him to come home only to be told he never would.

Even knowing that he was not willing to give up his work, to make a sacrifice for her or their child, that she would never come first in his life, she still loved him and ached for his touch. Madness.

With a deep sigh, Danielle turned and focused her eyes on the clock, noticing that it was now after six o'clock. It was closing time, with nothing to look forward to but another long, empty evening in front of her. She cringed at the thought. Even Ann seemed to be impatient with herself the last few days. Nothing seemed to please her either. Maybe she was getting sick again, Danielle thought, mechanically reaching behind the counter and grabbing the key. After dragging her weary body to the front door and inserting the key, she flipped the sign to ''Closed.''

Leaving a portion of the inside lights on, she began making her way toward the back and the stairs leading up to her apartment. Suddenly she stopped and gasped aloud. Catching her reflection in the antique mirror that dominated the wall above a slew of racks, she was horrified. She looked ghastly. Pausing a moment longer, she looked down at the slenderness of her limbs; the bones were revealed through her thin wool pants and cowl neck sweater.

But she had known and had only been fooling herself. She had climbed on the scales in the bathroom yesterday morning. Until now, however, she was able to convince herself that the loss of weight was a figment of her imagination, but now she knew this was not so. The reason her clothes, even tight-fitting jeans, were hanging on her was because she had lost over five pounds, five pounds she could not afford to lose.

Nevertheless, while the mind was capable of absorbing a certain amount of pain, the body was less resilient.

Dammit, if she didn't know better, she would say she was pining away. But how could she be such a fool to pine over a man who threatened to take her child away from her?

With an exclamation of self-disgust, Danielle made her way out of the store, and up the stairs into the apartment. After dropping her black order book on the nearest table she went into the kitchen. She heard her daughter chattering nonstop to Jusie.

"Mommie!" Ann clamored the second Danielle stepped into the brightly lighted room.

"Hello, darling," Danielle said, stooping down to lift her daughter into her arms, giving her a quick hug. "How's my best girl been today?"

Ann's tiny mouth spread into a grin as she fingered the gold chain around her mother's neck. "Me good. Played with Lisa."

"Oh, that's right. Mommie forgot Jusie was taking you to play with Melissa today."

After giving Ann a kiss on the cheek, Danielle lowered her to the floor and turned her attention to Jusie. However, before she could say anything, her daughter yanked on her hand.

"Yes, moppet," Danielle inquired absently, her eyes following her housekeeper as she added tomatoes to a bowl of fresh green lettuce. For the first time in days, Danielle felt her stomach rumble with hunger pains.

Suddenly the yank became harder. Danielle looked down.

"Mommie, why don't I have a daddy like Lisa?" Ann asked. "I want that man, Keir, to be my daddy. Can he?"

For a moment—or was it eons?—the room began to spin. Danielle blindly reached for the back of the nearest chair and clamped her hand down onto it to keep from falling.

"Danielle, are you all right?" It was Jusie's voice, but it seemed to be coming from far away, although Jusie's hands as they touched her arm were real and secure. Without protesting Danielle let Jusie gently push her trembling body down into the chair.

"Mommie, what's wrong? You sick?" Ann's face was puckered in a frown, her eyes wide with fright as she stared at her mother.

Danielle took several deep breaths, struggling for control. Shortly the room and her daughter's face once again became a stationary object. And Jusie's face swam back into focus. But nothing, nothing short of a miracle could help the pain around her heart. Ann's words had hit their mark. Oh, God, was she wrong in depriving her child of her father? She had tried so hard to be both mother and father to Ann, but it seemed as though her best hadn't been good enough.

Keir's sudden reappearance had obviously changed all that. He had disturbed once again her well-ordered life, and nothing had been the same since.

Danielle forced a smile to her stiff lips and gazed down into Ann's trusting, upturned face. "Don't…don't worry, moppet," she said in a reassuring tone, "Mommie's all right. Just a little dizzy, that's all. Why don't you go play with your toys for a minute, then we'll eat."

"Me go play." Satisfied, Ann took off eagerly toward the den and the small toybox that occupied one corner.

The second Ann was out of hearing distance, Jusie sat down in front of Danielle, her kind face lined with both concern and disapproval. "You can't keep on like this much longer, you know."

"I...know," Danielle responded softly, tears glistening in her eyes.

"Do you love him?"

That softly phrased question caused Danielle to jerk up her head. "Yes," she whispered, sounding as if that three letter word was torn from the depths of her soul.

"Well, then, why are you punishing yourself like this?"

For a long moment Danielle sat silent, her forehead knitted, her fingers lacing and interlacing. "It's just not that simple," she wailed, wanting desperately for Jusie to understand. "I want roots, stability for Ann, for myself, and he...he can't, won't, guarantee that."

Jusie did not understand. Her next words proved it. "Oh, Danielle, Danielle, how can you be so blind? If only you could see that love and being loved is the most important thing in the world. Look at me, for heaven's sake, a woman who was never lucky enough to find a man to love her. She paused and took Danielle's soft hands between her warm, rough ones and squeezed gently. "Please, I beg you, don't throw the love of your life away because you're afraid to take a chance. Haven't you learned by now, my precious, that life offers no guarantees to any of us? Don't do this to yourself, to Ann."

Danielle sat staring mutely at Jusie, oblivious to the tears that flowed down her cheeks in a steady stream.

Was Jusie right? And Keir? He had accused her of the same thing. Yes, of course, they were right.

Suddenly it dawned upon her that a home, family, roots were meaningless without Keir. He was her roots. Without him life had no meaning. To be completely fulfilled she needed Keir. Even though she dearly loved Ann, she could not replace Keir in her life. Nor could she deprive Keir from being a father to her child. She knew that now. Sharing Ann would be her ultimate sacrifice.

She realized, too, that it no longer mattered what he did for a living. He could be a government agent for the rest of his life if that would make him happy. It was no longer important. But accepting him and loving him for what he was, was the important thing. She had made a grave error in trying to change him; she could see that now. That was what Keir had been trying to tell her, but she had been blinded by her own selfish needs.

Did he still love her? Or was it Ann he wanted now and not her? Was it too late to salvage the mess she had made of her life? Would Keir, would life, give her another chance? Dare she try?

Jumping up, a brilliant smile changing her features, Danielle scooted around the table and flung her arms around Jusie, holding her in a tight clench for a long thankful moment.

Then she cried jubilantly, "Washington, D.C., here I come!"

The phone was ringing off the wall when Keir walked into the den of his plush Washington townhouse.

"Dammit!" he swore aloud, reaching for it; then he changed his mind. He decided to ignore it. He knew that it was Cassidy trying to track him down, but he was the last person Keir wanted to talk to right now. He still wanted to be left alone, alone with his punishing, torturous thoughts.

The moment he had returned to Washington from Danielle's, he went to work, or went through the routine of his work, he should say. He wanted to contact her. He invented explanations inside his head. He silently recited the speech to her dozens of times while he worked. Yet he was continuously distracted; nothing was holding together for him.

His conduct was apparent to everyone, and his colleagues were alarmed, especially Cassidy. But Cassidy dared not say a word. Keir would not welcome his interference, and the office knew it.

Was it possible to die from a broken heart? he wondered as he strode impatiently over to the desk that dominated the corner of the large room. Looking down, he suddenly recoiled as though having been struck by a snake. He felt the blood drain from his face. Occupying the middle of his desk was a bulging envelope bearing the name of a well-known group of attorneys who specialized in child custody cases. His stomach rebelled. With a muttered oath he turned away.

Could he go through with it? Could he take his child away from her mother? No. He could die easier than he could do that. His threat had been just that—a threat and nothing more. But he hadn't known that when he'd contacted the lawyers three weeks ago, before he'd decided to go to the house in Virginia to be alone, to think, hoping to sort out the mess he'd made of his life.

He had been miserable at the cabin. It was haunted with the memories of Danielle, her presence, her laughter,

her soft spoken voice. But at least there he had come to
the soul-searching conclusion that he could not take Ann
away from her. Brokenhearted, he had returned home.

But now he must come to terms with the fact that it
was over. Finished. She would never come to him again.
But oh, God, how was he going to survive without her?

Then he knew. He wasn't going to survive without her.
He was not going to let her go. Not this time. He knew
what he had to do. But first he had to see Cassidy. Now.

Danielle was nervous. So nervous that she was not sure
she could get out of the taxi now that it had pulled up
alongside the curb in front of Keir's Washington townhouse.

Had she taken leave of her senses coming here unan-
nounced like this? She chewed nervously at her lower
lip. What if he wasn't home? Hadn't Cassidy said he'd
disappeared without telling anyone where he was going?
On the other hand what if he was home, but refused to
see her or talk to her? Well, all those were possibilities,
but she had known that when she had thrown a few necessary articles in an overnight bag and caught the first
available flight out of Houston that morning.

Now, having come this far, she was not about to back
off. Realizing how much she loved Keir was all the in-
centive she needed.

"Lady, you going to get out or what?"

Shaking herself, Danielle took a deep breath and began
rummaging through her purse for money. Dry-mouthed
and visibly shaken, she handed the driver the money
as she got out of the car and managed to stammer,
"Thank...thank you."

"You're welcome, lady, and good luck."

Was it that obvious she was upset? Drawing on strength she did not know she possessed, she made her way up the walk to the front door, fighting back the memories of the wonderful, loving times they had shared here.

Somehow she reached the door and pushed the bell.

Nothing.

Please, oh, please, be home, she cried silently.

The door opened, but it wasn't Keir who stood on the threshold, but a strange woman with a coat and purse draped over her arm.

"May I help you?" the woman asked formally.

Danielle circled her lips with her tongue. "Yes... Uh...is Keir...Mr. McBride here?"

The woman—housekeeper more than likely, Danielle thought—raised her hand to push back a stray silver curl. "No, he isn't, not at the moment."

"When...when do you expect him back?"

"Not sure, ma'am."

"Would it be all right if I came in and waited for him? You see, I'm from out of town and I came especially to see him."

The woman looked both skeptical and uneasy. "I don't know, ma'am, I'm just leaving and I don't..."

"Oh, please," Danielle rushed on, a desperate note in her voice. "I'm a...friend. The name's Danielle Davis, and I've traveled a long way. I...I must see him."

The woman's kindly wrinkled face was showing signs of weakening.

"Please," Danielle pressed, stopping short of begging.

The woman shrugged and stepped back, opening the door wider, obviously deciding that Danielle appeared sincere and harmless. "Oh, all right," she acquiesced, "come in. Mr. McBride has mentioned you. I guess you're involved in some legal dealings. But be sure you tell Mr. McBride that you talked me into this.'' She smiled, taking in Danielle's pale, drawn features. "By the way my name is Hannah, Hannah Robbins.''

Danielle held out her hand. "Hi, good to know you.''

"Nice meeting you.'' She paused and looked at her watch. "I have to go now. Have to pick up my grandbaby at the nursery. There's a bar in the den if you want something to drink and there's a cozy fire in the fireplace. Make yourself comfortable.''

Danielle forced herself to smile again. "I'll be fine, Hannah. Don't worry and thank you.''

"You're welcome.''

Finally alone, Danielle, familiar with her surroundings made her way into the den. After shedding her leather coat, she went to stand by the fire. But she didn't tarry there long. Jumpy as a cat on a hot tin roof, she began pacing the floor.

What made her pause at the desk, she guessed she would never know for sure. Maybe it was the way the papers were strewn across the top that caught her attention. Or maybe it was the lawyers' names on one of the pages. Then before she realized what she was doing, her hand reached out and latched onto the top sheet. Her eyes began scanning the page, more for something to keep her mind occupied than anything else.

Suddenly, her face whitened as though she'd seen a ghost. "Oh, no!'' she cried aloud, stunned, sinking trembling limbs into the nearest chair, still clutching the paper in her hand. *No, it can't be,* she told herself. Hannah Robbins had mentioned some legal dealings, but surely not this. Yet it was. It was there in black and white. Keir was going to try and take Ann away from her, after all.

She had waited too long. Her stubbornness had killed his love. Surely, if he still loved her, he would not be doing this to her, to Ann.

Fool! You should have known. Life doesn't give third chances.

Frantically, she tried to stand. She had to leave, to get out of there before he came home. But her legs refused to cooperate. They were threatening to buckle beneath her. Trying again, she finally made it to her feet.

Then just as she took a tentative step forward, she heard the front door open and close She stood helpless, unable to move, unable to speak.

"Danielle!"

He stepped closer as though he, too, had seen a ghost.

"Are you real?" he whispered. If possible, his eyes deepened in their sockets as his eyes dipped to the paper in her hand and the panicked expression on her face. "No," he groaned as though in agony, "it's not what you think. I'll admit I went so far as to contact a lawyer, but I never meant to go through with it," he added thickly. "I was planning to leave tonight for Texas to tell you that and to tell you..." He paused on a ragged note. "And to tell you that I can't live without you, no matter what."

Still Danielle could not say a word, but her mind was reeling. Had she really held this haggard-looking man in her arms? Had she really felt the walls of her heart ready to burst with the flood of love for him? She had tried to negotiate with the person in charge of the universe— plead if necessary—to get Keir back. And now she was hearing the words she had longed to hear. For a moment, she was afraid her heart would burst with happiness.

Looking at him now, with darkened eyes, she understood completely and forgave. Keir, she wanted to say, but her throat would not utter the sound. It was clogged with unshed tears.

Keir stared back at her, his face tormented. Then he put his arms around her, tightly, as though he would never let her go.

"Don't, my darling, don't," he whispered gently, lowering his cheek to her tumbled curls. "I'm...I'm so sorry," he moaned, kissing her neck.

She did not want to reason anymore. He was in her arms, and she was content to stand and hold him and hear his heart beating in her ears. No other emotion could equal her love.

"Love me," she whispered, meeting his eyes, touching the gaunt shadows in his face as if to prove to herself that he wasn't a mirage.

"I would never have tried to take Ann from you. Please...please believe me," he said brokenly, his mouth hovering above hers.

"I'm sorry, too, for so much," she whispered.

He closed his eyes, his mouth shaking. "Oh, God, Danielle, darling, I love you so much and want you so much. For a while there I didn't trust my ability to stay sane."

"Oh, Keir," she said, "I felt the same way. Nothing seemed to matter if I couldn't have you."

His hold tightened. "I know we need to talk, but I don't think I can." He groaned. "Right now, all I can think about is loving you, body and soul."

"Me too," she sighed, her lips probing his ear. "It's been too long."

She moved and he released her, watching her covetously.

With shaking hands, he began unzipping her dress.

When she was standing in front of him in naked splendor, Keir did not move. His eyes roamed over her.

Then he began discarding his clothing. When he was naked at last, Danielle went sweetly into his arms and began kissing his face, his shoulders, his throat, moaning at the feel of his cool scented skin under her mouth.

Her soft hair spilled over the carpet as he lowered her gently onto it, his hands wooing a breast, meeting her mouth wildly, her arms wrapped around his neck, pulling him toward her.

"You are," he whispered into her mouth, "perfectly beautiful." Then his lips seared hers before moving lower to close over a nipple. Her fingers clutched at his hair while his bold lips and tongue paid homage to her swollen breasts.

Slipping away from him, she urged him onto his back and murmured, "Let me...love you." Her hand dipped down over his stomach to close around him.

"Oh, yes, yes," he said hoarsely, shutting his eyes, feeling the breath rush from his lungs in one sharp exhalation as she continued the gentle assault, her hands skimming down the length of his inner thigh. Hands pressed into her shoulder blades, but she was scarcely aware of his fingers dipping into her flesh while her mouth, a moist flower, opened over him.

Because she was making him happy, she felt happy, incredibly happy. This was one time when there was no outside interference; there was only the two of them, heart to heart, skin against skin. And it was pure magic.

Keir could stand no more. He reached for her, cupping her chin, and kissed her mouth slowly, warmly. He gazed at her for a long moment, adoring the sight of her face, stretching to the limit the sweet pain churning inside him.

"Oh, God, Danielle, this is so right, so good," he whispered, effortlessly lifting and easing her gently onto him. "The feel of you when I'm inside you, the way you respond—it's perfect."

"My darling," she said incoherently, dying to know all of him, urging him in one desperate drive as far into her as it was possible for him to be.

Suddenly everything inside her was melting, drowning, giving way. She answered his throaty cry, racing headlong through glass walls that shattered one after the other as she reached that final, awesome, breathtaking splendor, drawing him with her into that perfect center.

"I love you. I love you." Her voice was a dazed whisper emerging from the depths of tranquility.

"...I love you," she heard him say as she closed her eyes and with him still joined to her, fell into pure white silence.

"Wake up, sleepyhead," a voice murmured in the delicate folds of her ear. "Are you going to sleep all day?"

Languorously, Danielle stretched, then her eyes flew open. She looked around the room, realizing that she was in a bed, Keir's bed. Then, instantly, she remembered being carried to bed in his strong arms. She relaxed against him, snuggling against his body.

Keir moved heavily, stretching, then his eyes stared down into her flushed face. "My darling, my love," he said deeply.

As she watched his beloved face, a silence fell between them, while Danielle sought the words to tell him what was weighing heavily on her heart. "I...I just want you to know that it no longer matters to me what you do for a living," she said. "I'll support you one hundred percent, even if you're gone five days out of seven, or even if it means becoming a senator's wife,'' she added with a smile.

''Oh, my darling, you're priceless,'' he said, peering down at her, worshiping her with his eyes. ''And you don't know how much your saying that means to me. But I too have a confession to make. I had just come back from Cassidy's office, having told him I wanted a desk job, effective immediately.''

Danielle gasped, causing him to pause with a sweet smile.

''That's right, my darling, I'm through trotting the globe, as you so aptly put it. I'm a changed man. Can you ever forgive me for being such a headstrong and selfish bastard, demanding you give up everything, but not willing to make any sacrifices myself? Life wasn't worth living without you.''

''We're so lucky,'' she whispered, ''to have been given a third chance.''

''Marry me.''

''Whatever you say.''

Suddenly his face clouded again. ''Would you mind very much living in D.C. part of the year, since my office is here? Maybe you could open up a bookstore here. I know how much your work means to you.''

''We'll see, my love,'' she said. ''But right now all I want is to be with you, no matter where it is.''

Before he could say another word, Danielle locked her arms around his neck and kissed him, her lips filled with love and promise.

A long silence followed.

Giddy and drunk on love, they pulled apart. Danielle

was the first to speak, wanting to be rid of any and all ghosts that lurked in their past.

"You have your daughter to thank for my being here, you know."

"Oh, really. Well, I can tell you that I was never so shocked in my life as when I walked into the room and there you were. But I didn't care why or how, only that you were and that I'd get another chance."

"Ann wanted to know why you couldn't be her daddy," Danielle said soberly. "It was then that I realized what I was doing to Ann, to you, and to myself."

For a moment, Keir was speechless as tears gathered on his thick lashes. "Remind me..."—he paused and cleared his throat—"to thank my daughter properly when we get home."

"Home," Danielle murmured, her lips against his neck, his arms around her. "That's the most beautiful word in the English language."

"Home, my darling, is where the heart is," he pledged softly, "and my heart is yours forever."

*   *   *   *   *

MARY LYNN BAXTER

Just keeps getting hotter!

*Here's a teasing, tantalizing sneak peek
at her next mainstream title for MIRA.*

SULTRY

*will be in stores in June 2000—
just in time for your own
long, hot, summer....*

Be tempted!

"Okay, how badly is he really hurt?"

Lindsay Newman tried to keep the tremor out of her voice, but she couldn't. Her father, a retired heart surgeon, had been injured in an automobile accident. She was afraid the truth concerning his condition had been kept from her.

"Like Tim told you on the phone, it's not serious." Peter Ballinger frowned, knitting his thick, dark brows together. "Cooper's not serious. He's going to be all right."

The instant Lindsay entered the master suite, her brother rose to his feet, met her halfway and gave her a brief hug, which she returned. Then her eyes sought the man who was in the bed, propped against massive pillows.

"Oh, Daddy—" Her voice broke as she crossed to his bedside, grasped his hand, then bent and kissed him lightly on the cheek.

"Ah, hell, I'm fine. Don't fuss so." Cooper cut his eyes over at Tim. "If I had my way, I'd be on the golf course right now."

"Dream on," Lindsay muttered, gazing toward her brother, then back to Cooper. "I have to say, you don't look like you've been run over by a truck."

"I don't feel like it, either."

Lindsay scrutinized him. If it hadn't been for the brutal-looking circles under his eyes, circles that heretofore hadn't been there, and the purplish spot on his right cheekbone, no one would have known he'd just experienced a life- threatening trauma. Dr. Cooper Newman was still a striking figure.

Blessed with deep-set, piercing green eyes, a thick head of silver hair, and a tall, lean frame, he was downright good- looking. When he was dressed for success, no one would guess he was in his middle sixties.

"Well, he has a concussion to prove it," Tim said in a firm tone.

Lindsay's gaze shifted back to her brother, who did not have anywhere near the commanding presence Cooper had. Yet in all fairness, Tim had no trouble holding his own, looking like their mother, Emily.

Perhaps if he didn't wear glasses and have a mustache, there might be more of a resemblance between father and son, Lindsay had always thought. At thirty, four years her senior, Tim was tall and fine-looking in his own right, with light brown hair and dark brown eyes, the same as hers, eyes they had inherited from their mother.

"What about his heart?" she asked into the silence, her voice anxious.

"My ticker's ticking right along," Cooper snapped before Tim could answer.

Lindsay raised her eyebrows toward her brother. "Is it?"

"So far so good. Other than what's visible, and the fact that his muscles have to feel like he's been in a war zone, he came out of the fiasco relatively unscathed."

"Thank God for that."

Cooper made a strange noise. "Would you two stop talking about me as if I'm not here?"

Lindsay cut her gaze back on Cooper and smiled. "You haven't even said you were glad to see me."

"There was no need for you to come home," he muttered deeply.

"I disagree. That's precisely what I should've done."

"Dad's right, you know," Tim said. "You could've remained in London. I had everything under control."

"I know you did, but I had to see for myself. Anyhow, I was ready to jump ship, so to speak."

"Bored, huh?" Tim asked.

Lindsay ignored the mocking smile that seemed itching to break across his thin lips. "A little." She shrugged, unsure of what else to say. She hadn't sorted through all the emotions that were warring inside her as yet, so she couldn't share them with anyone.

"Now that's a problem I could love."

Cooper snorted, then glared at his firstborn. "That is your problem. You don't want to work."

"That's not true," Tim countered mildly.

So mildly that Lindsay picked up on the insincerity behind his tone. It was obvious Cooper had, too, for he snorted again, this time with more disgust.

Tim's face flooded with color, but he didn't say anything.

In order to fill the growing and uncomfortable silence, Lindsay asked, "How long do you have to stay in bed?"

"Through today only," Cooper said fiercely.

Tim merely looked at him. "We'll see."

"No, you're the one who will see—"

"Hey, time out!" Lindsay exclaimed. Then, turning back to Tim, she added, "Now that I'm home, I'll see that he behaves."

Cooper's eyes shone with disapproval. "I'm not all that happy you cut your trip short and deserted your friends."

Tim held up his hands. "Hey, I'll let you two duke that out. I'm gone."

"Don't go, not yet anyway," Lindsay said quickly. "Dolly's making some tea cakes."

Tim halted with a smile. "In that case, I'll meet you on the porch."

Once her brother had left, another silence descended over the room. Finally Cooper broke it. "You're a good daughter, Lindsay."

"I try," she said, not sure where this conversation was leading. His out-of-the-blue statement had taken her aback. Rarely did her father compliment her on anything.

By and large he made demands that were to be carried out. Within the confines of the house and grounds, one soon learned that Cooper ruled and didn't like to be crossed.

"Sometimes you try too hard."

Lindsay almost shivered, thinking how difficult he was to love and how much he tried to make both Tim and her bend to his strong will.

"How's that?" she asked, though she already knew the answer.

"You know. It's time you married and had children. You're certainly not getting any younger."

How well she knew. At twenty-six, she had never married, and she'd never lived away from home. Circumstances had been such that she had remained here, occupying her own suite. When she wasn't busy raising money and heading her favorite charity, she acted as Cooper's hostess when he entertained, which was often.

To the outside world looking in, she had everything money could buy.

"I want you to stop dallying and set a wedding date."

Lindsay rubbed her forehead. "You know I don't want to marry Peter."

"Why the hell not?"

"You know that, too. I don't love him."

"So what?"

"Daddy!"

"You'll learn to love him. It's that simple."

Lindsay felt like she was beating her head against a rock. He was one stubborn and opinionated man. "Simple? I don't think so."

Cooper's features turned cold. "I'm counting on this marriage. Please don't disappoint me."